"I'M JUST A GUY WHO'S GOING TO KILL SOME PEOPLE, AND I'D LIKE TO TALK ABOUT IT..."

GUEST SHOT

IT'S NOT ALL TALK.

"I think you'll agree it could make great television."

His quiet appeal won him a reprieve. "Okay. I'm listening."

"Well," he said, and paused as if to deliberately dramatize his revelation, "I'm going to kill some people. But before I start, I thought I'd love to come on the show and tell people about it. The how, the why, even the who—oh, not the exact names, maybe, but hints. That's it, that's my idea. Don't you think it could make a dynamite show?"

Lori sat speechless, rigid. It was as if the thing in her hand had turned into something vile and alive, not a phone receiver, but the head of a venomous creature. Maybe because his voice was so pleasant even as he spouted his sickness, it made her blood run cold.

"Well, Lori," he prompted, "what do you think?"

GUEST SHOT

DAVID LOCKE

JOVE BOOKS, NEW YORK

This is a work of fiction. Names, characters, places, and incidents either are the product of the author's imagination or are used fictitiously, and any resemblance to actual persons, living or dead, business establishments, events, or locales is entirely coincidental.

GUEST SHOT

A Jove Book / published by arrangement with
the author

PRINTING HISTORY
Jove edition / December 2001

Visit our website at
www.penguinputnam.com

ISBN: 0-515-13203-9

A JOVE BOOK®
Jove Books are published by The Berkley Publishing Group,
a division of Penguin Putnam Inc.,
375 Hudson Street, New York, New York 10014.
JOVE and the "J" design
are trademarks belonging to Penguin Putnam Inc.

PRINTED IN THE UNITED STATES OF AMERICA

10 9 8 7 6 5 4 3 2 1

For my dear Uncle, and good pal, Marvin

A pretty good talker himself. . . .

CHAPTER
1

LORI SWANN LEANED back in her chair and pushed away from her desk. She had been on the phone almost seven hours straight since arriving for work this morning. Through the window of her office on the fifty-fifth floor of the General Broadcasting tower, she could see it was a sunny day, one of those perfect April days when it was easy to ignore all the hassles of living in New York for the sake of the excitement, the energy, and a good career opportunity. On a day like this, Lori would have enjoyed a walk over to Fifth Avenue on her lunch hour, to shop for a new dress.

But today she needed every minute at her desk. Yesterday, in a suburb of Memphis, Tennessee, there had been another one of those horrendous high school shootings: a girl who'd been rejected from the cheerleading squad had taken an assault rifle from her father's gun cabinet and opened fire at a basketball game, killing two cheerleaders, a player, and wounding many more. Frequent as such happenings had become, this was one of the rare times the young shooter was a girl, and that made it special. New.

In her job as the guest coordinator for Barry Stoner's

talk show, Lori was charged with securing the people who would appear on camera. A lithe twenty-seven-year-old with silver-gray eyes and hair of the pale white-blond color most often seen on toddlers, she had been hired five years ago straight out of a midwestern college's school of communications as a production assistant, and had worked her way up within two years to her present position. This required her to make phone contacts with the best of the prospects, do the office interviews, and draw up the short list of those who were most interesting and seemed least likely to be so nervous that they would get "cottonmouth" and be unable to speak on the air. Today it was left to Lori to try making the initial contacts with as many of the people close to the Memphis case as possible—parents and friends of the shooter and the victims, local law enforcement, teachers at the school—and see which, if any, she could persuade to come to New York and appear on the show. Not right away, perhaps, but in the next week or two before the story had lost all its sizzle. And of course, in special cases like this, only the first contact would be hers. If the people she spoke to showed any willingness, as opposed to rigid insult at the invasion of privacy, then the show's star, Barry Stoner himself, would make a follow-up call to close the deal. It often amazed Lori that even in times of extreme emotional distress and family tragedy many people would be willing to appear, lured by the free plane fare to New York, a night or two in a nice mid-rank hotel, a ride to the studio in a stretch limo—not to mention the ten minutes of fame they'd get from their appearance. Even so, it remained a mystery to Lori, what drove ordinary people to freely expose before millions of strangers the sort of dark, family secrets that were once only whispered rumors, or were shared—if ever—only behind the closed door of a psychiatrist's office or priest's confessional?

To refresh herself for another round of calls, Lori left her office and went along a hallway to the small staff kitchenette, where she made herself a tall glass of iced coffee. The large suite of production offices was quiet, with only a few secretaries working; during this hour between four and five in the afternoon most of the staff were usually down in the studio attending the show's live broadcast.

Carrying her glass of iced coffee, Lori was heading back along the hallway when she heard the phone ring in her office. She ran to catch the call, grabbing up the phone from the wrong side of her desk on the third ring. "Stoner—booking."

"Lori . . . ?"

A man's voice, but not one she recognized. "Yes," she said, "this is Lori Swann."

"You sound a little out of breath. Everything okay?"

"Yes, I was out of the office a second and ran to pick this up." His slightly familiar tone puzzled her; it didn't sound like anyone she knew. "Who is this?"

He ignored the question. "Do you want to take a second to relax? I want you to be able to appreciate what I'm calling to offer."

Offer? Maybe it was an agent or a lawyer for one of the people connected to the Memphis story. Sometimes it didn't take long for those at the center of such a sensation to realize their value to the media and take measures to get the most out of it. "What sort of offer, Mr.—?

"To appear on your show of course. You're the one who arranges that, aren't you?

Evidently he'd been professional enough to do some research; that inspired Lori to probe a bit further. She eased around into her chair "What sort of show do you think you'd fit into, Mr. . . . ?"

Again her try for a name was passed over. "I don't know that I'd *fit* into anything. My guest shot—isn't that what you call it?—would be a solo."

Obviously not a celebrity or at the center of some current news sensation—those people always had their representatives call first; so the man's assumption that a show could revolve around him alone smacked of egomania. Ordinarily that would have been enough for Lori to ease quickly out of the conversation. Yet the caller was well-spoken, and the few things he'd said were delivered with an appealing brightness. "What story can you tell that would deserve a show all by itself?" she asked.

"It's not exactly a story. I'd just talk about my hopes and dreams."

"Your hopes and dreams . . ." Lori repeated, her judgment firming now that he was abnormally grandiose.

"Yes. About things I'm planning to do. I'll talk about them before I carry them out, about why I want to do them, how they'll be done."

No doubt about it. As bright as he sounded, the man was out of touch with reality. "Look, Mr.—whoever-you-are," she began impatiently. "Unless you—"

He cut right in. "I know, Lori. You're going to give me a brush-off, you think I'm not worth your time. But if you'll just give me another minute and hear exactly what I've got to offer, I think you'll agree it could make great television."

His quiet, pleasant appeal won him a reprieve. "Okay. I'm listening."

"Well," he said, and paused as if to deliberately dramatize his revelation, "I'm going to kill some people. But before I start, I thought I'd come on the show and tell people about it. The how, the why, even the who—oh, not the exact names, maybe, but hints. That's it, that's my idea. Don't you think it could make a dynamite show?"

Lori sat rigid, speechless. It was as if the thing in her hand had turned into something vile and alive; not a phone receiver, but the head of a venomous creature. It was far from the first time a sicko of one kind or another had gotten through; with the volume of calls that came to the show, Lori had learned to expect them. There was the woman who'd threatened to plant a bomb if Stoner didn't use the program to help locate a heart transplant for her cat. A man who'd insisted Stoner should join him on a spacecraft with extraterrestrials, and had sworn to abduct the talk show host if he didn't go willingly. Hell, more cranks than Lori could remember. But *this*! Maybe because his voice was so pleasant even as he spouted the sickness, it made her blood run cold.

"Well, Lori," he prompted, "what do you think?"

And he knew her name! She still couldn't answer.

He filled the gap himself. "Got to be a crowd pleaser. Your audience will hear me talk about it, then I'll go out and do it. But that's not the best part. After the first one, I'll come back, talk about what it was like. And again after the second. See? Everyone will follow along with the case as it develops."

Lori's mind raced. Her task now was clear: get some useful information to trace this maniac before he really did any harm. She struggled to establish a conversational tone to keep him talking, to reveal himself, maybe lure him into the open. "It certainly is . . . unusual," she said at last. "Barry ought to hear more about this himself. So can we maybe . . . um . . . pick a date and you'll come to the office to be interviewed? We do that with all our guests, you know, meet them first. . . ."

He laughed lightly, the sound so eerily *good-natured.* "I really don't think that would work. But let's mull over what happens next. All I wanted for now was to touch base, make sure your people are open to the idea. I think I've covered enough for today. You can pass along what I've told you to your boss, and get his feelings about it. I'll get back to you for an answer after the reactions are in."

"Yes . . . fine," Lori said, stalling. "But . . . can't you tell me anything about yourself? We . . . uh . . . we like to get a sense of, you know, how you'll come across. . . ."

Christ, she was blathering stupidly, Lori thought, so all-fired desperate to keep him talking, lure out some clue to identity.

"What's to tell? I'm just a guy who's going to kill some

people, and I'd like to talk about it on your show—to be . . . your mystery guest." He gave his eerily pleasant laugh. "If you think your audience would be interested, then we can do business. That's it for now, Lori. I'll be in touch."

"No. Wait—!"

But the line had gone dead. She stood holding the phone, momentarily immobilized by amazement and revulsion. Then, glancing at a wall clock, Lori saw the show still had another eight minutes before it was off the air. She dropped the receiver without hanging up and ran for the elevator.

THE SHOW WAS NEARING THE END OF THE HOUR AS SHE slipped into the control booth of Studio 12-A on the twenty-first floor. Several men sat at a long console, staring out through the soundproof window at the stage below them. Lori moved up behind Joe Candelli, the show's producer, sitting at one end with the show's director to his left, and leaned over his shoulder.

"Need to talk, Joe," Lori whispered urgently.

"Break's coming up," he muttered. Tall and lean with a narrow, angular face under bristly, iron gray hair, Candelli resembled Abe Lincoln, albeit a Lincoln airbrushed into handsomeness.

"Joe," Lori insisted, "this is hot!"

"And we've got eighty-five fucking seconds to run to commercial," he hissed back. "Think it can keep that long?"

Lori moved back against the booth's rear wall and tried to distract herself from that sick voice replaying in her mind by watching the show unfold. The guests today consisted of a several young women who were either currently working as high-paid call girls, or had done so in the past. In the first segment the women had exposed some lurid details of "the life," and during the second half husbands of

the retired veterans had agreed to come on and talk about
the pros and cons of being married to an ex-hooker. Having just taken a question from someone at the rear of the
raked section of audience seating, Barry Stoner was now
sprinting down the aisle to hold the microphone up to one
of the women on the stage so she could answer. For most
of his one hour program, Stoner was usually on the move,
pacing the stage as he talked to guests, or racing around the
studio to take questions from the audience. Although in his
mid-forties, this constant movement combined with his
plain midwestern good looks (the mop of full, dark hair
and his bright green eyes) combined to lend an aura of
youth and vitality and enthusiasm. To see his innocent
farmboy quality surviving even as he confronted so much
human dysfunction, perversion, and misery was reassuring
to viewers. No matter how much sickness you may see
here, it testified, I have remained uncorrupted by it—and
so you, too, can watch without fear or shame.

Arriving at the stage, he held the microphone up to one
of the younger women in a row of chairs, a busty blond
with a hundred-dollar haircut and thigh-high patent-leather
boots.

"Well, how about it?" Stoner said, prompting her to
reply to the question that had come from the audience.
"Did one of your customers ever beat you up?"

"Not really beat me. But a guy slashed me once, over
here." She touched her thigh. "A lawyer—they're the
worst."

"How about that?" Stoner declared. "One of her johns
cuts her, and she's still up here telling us it's a great way to
make a living! Can't one of you talk some sense into her?"
He thrust his microphone at of one of the retired call girls,
a fortyish brunette named Margo.

"A whore has to lie to herself, Barry," she said. "That's
how we get through the day. We pretend it's no big deal,
tell ourselves it's a way to take care of ourselves that pays
better than waiting tables."

"Well," Stoner said, "I *have* heard the money can be darn good at the high end—so to speak." He often played both sides of the argument to keep it stoked up. "Tell me, Stan,"—he turned to a husky man seated beside Margo, her husband—"did your wife bring a good dowry with her? You've told us some of the perks of marrying a . . . a woman experienced in the bedroom. What about financial benefits? Did she come with a tidy little nest egg tucked away in her panties?"

This kind of snide prying could get a man killed in everyday circumstances, but everyone knew they could expect stuff like this from Barry Stoner. The husband answered straight-facedly, "I didn't marry her for her money, Barry, if that's what you're suggesting."

"I know. But just for curiosity's sake, Margo, did you save any of what you earned? Do any of you manage to build some security out of all your hard work?"

Before Margo could answer, one of the still-active girls piped up, "I've got a thousand shares of Disney."

As the audience laughed, Stoner spotted the floor manager signaling for a commercial break. "And that's America folks," he proclaimed jauntily. "Where a girl can trade on her private assets to end up owning a piece of Mickey Mouse. We'll be right back after *this*."

Straight into a commercial for adult diapers.

During commercial breaks, it was Stoner's custom not to discontinue the conversation in the studio, but keep going so the momentum would be there when the cameras came on again. He stayed with the money angle, asking all the other women how much they made and what percentage they'd kept.

In the booth, Candelli swiveled his chair from the console. "Okay, Swannee," he said, using his personal pet name for Lori, "what's the big goddamn emergency."

"Can we talk outside?"

Candelli gave an assenting shrug and followed her out

to a corridor where they were alone. "Why so cloak and dagger?"

"I think we should keep this quiet," Lori explained. "We've got a murderer who wants to appear on the show."

Candelli responded passively. "Yeah. And . . . ?" Over the years there had been dozens of murderers on the show —convicted, acquitted, condemned, young, old, sane, crazy, men, women, even kids. Nothing new about murderers.

"No, Joe," she said. "This is different. This one hasn't killed anybody yet."

Candelli's brow furrowed. "Then what makes him a murderer?"

"He's *planning* it," Lori explained. "Says he's going to kill some people—more than one, Joe—but first he's offering to talk about it. On our show. Then he'll go out and do it." She swallowed, her own throat going dry. "But that's not all. He says, he'll come back each time and talk more, how he did it, how it felt, all that. . . ."

The light flared in Candelli's eyes. "Holy shit." He glanced at his wristwatch. "We'll be off air in a couple of minutes. Let's catch Barry backstage. He's gonna *love* this."

Lori stared after Candelli as he disappeared back into the control room, wondering whether or not he was just being sarcastic.

CHAPTER
2

STONER, IN SHIRTSLEEVES, stood looking out the window of his huge corner office in the GBS tower as he listened to Lori recount the strange call. Ever efficient, she had taken a couple of minutes before coming into the meeting to jot down as much as she could remember of the exact words.

When she and Joe had grabbed Barry in the studio right after the show, he'd only had to hear the bare bones of the incident before deciding they'd better talk upstairs, in private. Now, as Lori read off her notes from the yellow pad in her lap, Stoner gazed down thoughtfully at the river of cars and people flowing at rush hour through the concrete canyon far below. God, what an incredible species they were, these humans; no end to their bizarre behavior—fortunately for him.

Lori ended her account. "He said if we thought our audience would be interested, we could do business. Then he said he'd be in touch, and hung up."

Stoner turned to look at Lori, who was seated in a club chair facing the slab of black marble that served as his desk. " 'Do business,' " Stoner repeated. "Those were his words?"

"Yes. Is that significant?"

"Maybe next time he'll ask to be paid." Stoner broke into a soft chuckle.

Lori and Candelli exchanged a puzzled glance.

"Don't you get it?" Stoner exclaimed. "It's a setup! One of those guys who writes a column on the media testing us, wanting to see how far we'll go. Or it might even be those pricks at *Sixty Minutes,* trolling for some dirt on talk shows. Wouldn't they like to see if we'd even *pay* someone like this to come on the show?" He shook his head. "Boy . . . all we'd have to do is start a real conversation with this guy, they'd be down on us like a ton of bricks, preaching how Barry Stoner and his ilk don't know where to draw the line."

"I don't know, Barry," Lori said cautiously. "It could be real. This man sounded smart . . . determined."

"Sure, real. So we've got a guy who'll *confess* on TV to a murder he has yet to commit, then after he's done it, he'll come *back,* admit it again, then—what?—he thinks he'll walk away to kill more? You tell me how's he going to manage *that*?"

Lori was silent. She had no answer.

Candelli spoke. "What worries me, Barry, is that *you* might be in danger. Maybe we should at least hire a couple of bodyguards."

"C'mon, Joe!" Stoner scoffed. "Remember the guy who called on the air and said he was coming to shoot me full of holes because he didn't like my position in favor of gun control? How long did we have the bodyguards that time? Six months? And did the guy ever show?" Stoner got up and came around the desk, signaling an end to the meeting. "Don't worry, I'll be fine."

The others stood. But Lori remained uneasy. "He said he'd get back in touch—for your answer about doing the show. If he does call, what should I say?"

Stoner still couldn't believe it was anything but a scam. "Let's jump off that bridge when we come to it."

Lori regarded him with concern for a moment, then nodded and left. Candelli stayed behind.

"What?" Stoner asked, seeing his producer's face still etched with worry.

"You're acting as if this is nothing. But don't you get the feeling that with all the crazies around somebody like this *had* to turn up sooner or later? I'm not saying he can do what he says, but if he just thinks he can, he's not harmless."

"Let's wait and see if we ever hear from him again." Laying a friendly hand on his producer's shoulder, Stoner steered him to the door. "Go home, Joe. See you bright and early."

Alone, Stoner drifted back to the window. True, there was no end to the crazies out there, but the way Lori had described him, this caller wasn't simply a nut. He had some sort of . . . agenda. The only logical assumption Stoner could make was that it was a plan to discredit him, and the way to stay out of trouble was simply not to fall for it.

Still, as he gazed down at the streets, the river of humanity, he couldn't resist playing with the fantastical notion of the kind of shows he could do if the opportunity were real. What would it be like to see the transformation occur right on camera, from a man still innocent to a murderer? Jesus, that could be one hell of an interview, all right—series of interviews, the way the caller spoke of it.

And no one would know better than he, Stoner thought, how to get the most out of it—or could want as badly as he did to know what made such a man tick. Running a talk show might seem like it took no talent at all, nothing more than a photogenic presence and a modest amount of charm. But Stoner knew in his marrow he had a special ability to

make the talk add up to more, to get people to reveal themselves down to their core.

A little smile formed on his lips as he gazed out at the
deepening dark. Yes, he assured himself, no one alive
could take such a situation and turn it into better talk. It
seemed almost a shame it couldn't be real.

CHAPTER
3

THE INTELLIGENCE DIVISION of the New York City Police Department occupied five floors in a monolithic sixty-year-old building in lower Manhattan. The division consisted of a number of details assigned to duties that fell outside standard procedure. Protection of the mayor was one. Surveillance and collection of data on organized crime was another. On one floor, occupying one large, open room of several hundred square feet furnished with eight desks (only six of which were in regular use), and a couple of smaller rooms, was the Sensitive Case Detail. The S.C.D. dealt with matters distinguished by some unusual factor from those handled by regular street detectives, as when a celebrity or VIP was centrally involved in a serious case. The supervising lieutenant of the Sensitive Case Detail was a thirty-six-year-old woman named DZ Hayes.

At a little past five-thirty on this Thursday afternoon, DZ was still at her desk. It had been the kind of quiet day when she would normally have kept standard office hours, but she was working on the personal essay to go with an application to Columbia Law, and wanted to use the office copier to make duplicates.

The ring of the phone broke her concentration, but there was no second ring and she realized one of the other detectives must have picked up the call in the duty room. She kept working on the essay until there was a soft knock on the open door of her office. She looked up to see Detective Gable. DZ had been fairly certain the other late worker would be Gable; he generally worked as her partner, and almost never left until she did.

A large man, he filled the doorway. "Are we still on duty? Got a call, but it doesn't sound like an emergency."

"Why'd it get thrown to us?"

"Celeb put a call into the commissioner, but he's away at that law enforcement conference in Sweden, so the first dep bucked it over here. That was him just now; said it'd be okay to follow up in the morning."

DZ pondered a moment, then rose and pulled her suit jacket off the back of the chair. "You know how the commissioner sucks up to the stars. He wouldn't like us putting it off overnight." She hoisted her shoulder bag and swept the application papers into it. Gable went back to his desk to pick up the address given to him by the first dep.

They met at the elevator. "So who's the name?" asked DZ.

"That Stoner guy—y'know, with the talk show. . . ."

"THERE'S A DETECTIVE HAYES OUT HERE TO SEE YOU."

"Send him in, Carol," Stoner said, "then you can go home." That would empty out the offices, Stoner thought, except for Candelli and Lori, who were here with him. As soon as a second call had come this afternoon from a man offering to talk about some murders he planned to commit, Stoner realized they could no longer put off bringing in the police. But it was agreed between the three people here now that as few as possible should know the situation had escalated, to keep the office rumor mill from churning up a panic.

The door opened and DZ strode in.

As he came out from behind his desk to greet her, Stoner managed to curtail his surprise to a mere lift of the eyebrows. It wasn't only because the detective was a woman, but because she was possessed of a degree of style he wouldn't have expected of a woman who did the famously wretched work of a cop. She was lanky—willowy might have been the word if she were walking a designer's runway instead of working a beat—and her face had a feline quality; narrow, with large wide-set eyes over high cheekbones that made her naturally sexy. However, her coloring worked against any impression of softness, a severe palette of blacks and whites. Onyx eyes, impenetrably dark, though maybe with a hint of blue at the center like the flame at the heart of a coal fire; long, very thick, jet-black hair, pulled back with a barette to fall between her shoulder blades; and the sort of blue-white skin that seems almost translucent. Playing off her natural coloring, she wore a black suit with a plain, white blouse. The skirt was short enough to reveal excellent legs, Stoner also noticed, and the jacket was cut loose—not for fashion, he assumed, so much as to drape innocently over a gun in a shoulder holster. A black leather shoulder bag completed the outfit.

From his long experience of reading people quickly, Stoner sensed an inner weariness about her that subtly enhanced her appeal, perhaps because without the faint hint of vulnerability, she would have seemed too thoroughly hard and inaccessible.

"How do you do, Mr. Stoner?" she said. "I'm Detective Lieutenant Hayes, NYPD Intelligence Division. This is Detective Gable." She flipped a thumb over her shoulder.

Only when she referred to him, did the man who had trailed her into the room seem to become visible. As much as Hayes was sharply limned in black and white, Gable was enveloped in a haze of gray—a middle-aged veteran

with thinning gray hair, a rumpled gray suit, a face gray
with fatigue, and eyes that had been bluer once but had lost
most of their hue.

"Thanks for coming." Stoner said. "This is my producer,
and one of our production executives." He introduced Joe
and Lori by name and went on quickly. "Tell me, Ms.
Hayes—"

"Detective Hayes," she corrected sharply.

"Sorry," Stoner said smoothly. "You mentioned you're
with the Intelligence Division. Would you tell me why—"

DZ didn't need to hear the end of his question. "This is
what we call 'a sensitive case,' Mr. Stoner—one where a
public figure is involved. Sensitives are generally handled
by Intelligence."

Gable moved up to stand beside DZ. "We were told
you'd received a death threat. . . ."

"Not exactly that," Stoner said. "Not in the usual sense,
anyway. I haven't been threatened."

"Who has?"

"Nobody yet."

The detectives exchanged a questioning glance.

"Mind if we sit?" DZ asked with a slight edge, as if to
point up an oversight in Stoner's manners.

He swept his hand toward the sitting area. "Please."

Candelli gestured to a place beside him on the sofa.

Gable took a chair near the desk. "So explain this
threat." He pulled a palm-size spiral notebook from a
jacket pocket; it had a gray cover.

Lori described the first call she had fielded two days earlier. She had saved the notes from her yellow pad and used
them now to give a concise summary. She repeated verba-
tim any key phrases the man had used that she could remember. *An ordinary guy who wants to kill some
people. . . .*

The detectives let her read through her transcription un-
interrupted while jotting notes of their own. DZ had taken

from her shoulder bag the small leather-bound sketchbook she used for this purpose.

"I tried to keep him talking," Lori concluded, "extract anything that might help identify him. But when I asked him to tell me about himself, he cut it short. His last words were that he'd be in touch."

"And that was two days ago," DZ noted. "Why did you wait to call the police?"

"My fault," Stoner answered. "I didn't take it seriously until he called Lori again today." He explained the suspicions he'd had about critics and muckrakers. "What he's threatening still doesn't add up, but I realized we couldn't do nothing."

"Called you both times," Gable said to Lori Swann. The young woman was very attractive he saw—the kind who might easily inspire the unwanted attention of a stalker. "Any chance you might know this guy?"

Candelli broke in. "Lori's our guest coordinator," the producer explained. "She'd be the natural person to call for someone offering to be a guest."

"Or a 'mystery guest,'" DZ observed, remembering the phrase from Lori's retelling of the first call. "That's the way he referred to himself. . . ."

Lori nodded.

"Now let's hear about today's call," DZ said.

"It was much shorter. He seemed to assume we'd want him; just said we should be preparing for his appearance. I tried to stall again—told him he should speak directly to Mr. Stoner—and he said he'd only do that on the air, but he was sure Barry would be glad to have him; that he was perfect for our show."

Stoner chimed in, "It's understandable he'd choose mine over the others. My show is gritty, up-to-the-minute, in the same ballpark in which he sees himself."

DZ turned to study the talk show host. He sounded curiously proud that his program was the one chosen for even this brand of lunacy. "Of course," she observed, "it's possible yours isn't the only show he contacted. We'll check with the others."

"Wouldn't they have let you know," Candelli said, "like we did?"

"They might have gone to the FBI," Gable said.

"Should we have done that?" Stoner asked quickly.

"I'm not sure this is a federal matter," DZ replied. "In legal terms, it's not even certain that what your caller has done so far is a crime. This might qualify as nothing more than a couple of nuisance calls."

"Imagine that," Stoner said tartly. "A nuisance. So what has to happen before this 'nuisance' has broken the law?"

"If he actually *names* a person he intends to murder," Gable said, "that would do it."

"What else?" Stoner asked.

"If he demands money *not* to do it," said DZ, "that would be extortion. Or . . ."

Stoner and Candelli prompted in unison: "Or?"

Quietly, DZ said, "He starts the killing."

There was a sober silence. Then Candelli was reminded of something. "Hey," he said to Lori, "you didn't tell the other thing yet—about the eyes."

The detectives focused on her.

"Oh, yes—this was really off the wall. Right before hanging up today, he said if I wanted proof he meant to do what he said, then I should take a good look in Stoner's eyes. Those were his exact words."

"In *my* eyes," Stoner said. "What do you make of that?"

"It could mean he won't proceed with this idea," DZ replied, "unless you're willing to have him on your show."

Candelli bolted up from the couch. "Sonofabitch!" he proclaimed hotly. "Does this maniac think in a million years we'd ever put him on camera to gab all he wants about people he wants to murder?"

"Wait a second, Joe," Stoner said calmly. "Think about it: Right now all we know about this guy is he may be very dangerous. So the goal is to get him off the streets. You see a better way than to go along with him?"

Candelli stared incredulously at Stoner.

"*Pretend*, I mean!" Stoner said quickly. "We'll go through the motions of putting him on the show just to bring him in."

"You're right about one thing, Mr. Stoner," DZ said. "We're dealing with someone who may be very dangerous. I don't think we want to be encouraging his plans in *any* way."

"So what's *your* idea for catching him?" Stoner challenged.

DZ ran down a list of steps the police would take. The caller was probably smart enough to use public phones, but there was always a chance of getting a lead from pinning down at least a locality where he was based, so department technicians would install devices on phone lines in the office and studio to trace the caller if he made contact again.

Also, a computer check would be run on a list of the people employed by Stoner's production company to see if any names came up with prior police records.

"You really think it could be someone who works with us every day?" Candelli asked anxiously.

"Why not?" Gable countered. "You got—what?—forty, fifty people involved with getting this show on. Who's to say one of them's not carrying a grudge, or crazier than they look?"

"We'll need a list of your personnel and their addresses," DZ said.

"I'll do a computer printout right now," Candelli said.

"Good. Detective Gable will go along to get it from you." Gable dutifully dragged himself up out of his chair and followed the producer from the office.

DZ dropped her notebook into her bag and pulled out her business cards, embossed with the NYPD logo, and printed with her direct phone line and cell number. She stood up and held out a card to Lori. "That covers it for tonight, Ms. Swann. If you hear from this man again, call me right away—any time." As Lori took the card, DZ added, "I'd like to be able to review those notes you made. I get the sense that a lot of what this man says has hidden meanings."

"Of course, Lieutenant." Lori held out the pages.

"No, keep those to look over, think about whether you want to add anything. Just make me a copy before you go home."

Lori nodded and left.

DZ held out two more cards to Stoner. "For you and Mr. Candelli."

Stoner came from behind his desk to take them. "I'll need your permission for our technicians to hook into your phone lines." DZ said.

"Sure, whatever you need. Do you think he *will* keep calling?"

DZ shrugged. "This one's a real wild card. He might just show up for an audition."

He gave her a nervous smile. "If he calls, we can't simply keep stalling. He'll see through it. And then we might . . . lose him."

DZ gave him a sharp glance. "You worried about losing him in the crowd? Or to a rival show?"

"I just want to see him caught before anybody gets hurt."

"That's what we need," DZ said. "More good citizens like you."

He heard the edge and took it with a smile. "So what's your bet: will he or won't he?"

"He'd have to be nuts to try it," she replied. "Except the way Ms. Swann made him sound, he's anything but. Which means it's either a hoax . . . or he has the potential to do what he says. Because if he were sane, we never would've heard from him unless he already knew how to get away with it."

Stoner mulled it. How was it possible for someone to

confess to a murder before millions of witnesses not once, as he had threatened, but showing himself again and again . . . yet still think the smallest chance existed of getting away with it.

In the silence, DZ examined him. What had the caller said? If there was any doubt he meant to do what he said, *then take a good look in Stoner's eyes.* Now she saw the sparkle of fascination was there. Not much doubt about it, DZ realized: given the opportunity, Barry Stoner wouldn't hesitate to put this mystery guest on the air—indeed, already regarded him as not so different from any in the broad range of human perversions and sicknesses and brutalities that his program showcased for an hour every weekday afternoon.

CHAPTER
4

*G*ABLE DROVE DZ home. They had worked late, locating a judge to write a court order for the tap on Stoner's phones, then meeting a couple of technicians at the production offices to get the phones rigged when the offices were deserted.

For most of the ride downtown to the Tribeca neighborhood where DZ lived, they were wearily silent. Crossing Canal Street, Gable said abruptly, "Where do these freaks come from? What makes 'em think up this crazy shit?"

"We do," DZ said. "Everybody's so goddamn ready to watch the next sensation. Murder trials on TV. Massacres and hostage standoffs broadcast live. Somebody was bound to come along and take it up a peg—murder as a spectator sport. Move over *Monday Night Football*."

"Gee, kid, you sound a little pessimistic about the human race."

"Nothing that won't be fixed by a good night's sleep." Though how long had it been since she'd had one?

"So you think this is for real?" Gable asked.

"A guy who takes the trouble to dream up an idea this

wild may not see that much extra effort in going all the way."

"But no one'll let him on TV!"

"Didn't OJ do pay-per-view? You missed seeing the gleam in Stoner's eyes: he wouldn't mind if this played out. And the caller seems to know it, told us where to look if we had any doubt."

The silence returned.

"Oh, hey," Gable said with a sudden change of tone, "I got tickets for the hockey play-offs this weekend. Great seats, pair on the floor in the B row. How about coming with me?"

DZ could tell how hard he'd worked to make the idea sound spontaneous. "I don't think so. That sport's a little too violent for my taste."

His mouth twitched, a little smile of disappointment. "Figured it might be."

Long ago DZ had realized the reason Gable stretched out his departure from work was to be available to her; give her the rides home. Until tonight he'd never proposed a kind of date, but she wasn't blind to the fact that he carried a slow-burning torch. She had wondered if it didn't merit a change in partners; their work could be compromised, their service endangered by this emotional element, and it was within her area of responsibility to have him transferred. But so far DZ had opted to spare Gable the hurt. What harm in the status quo? Until the time his feelings spilled over in some way that affected performance, she preferred to maintain the pretense that there was nothing more complicated to their bond than the one shared by any other partnership. If it was nothing more, though, she would have gone to the hockey game.

Gable turned the car onto Franklin Street, and stopped at the converted coffee warehouse that housed DZ's loft.

On the sidewalk, she leaned back into the car to give him a smile. "Sorry about the hockey. But thanks for the thought."

"That's okay, kid. G'night."

"Good night, Clark."

As Gable had once explained it, he'd been born a month after his mother had seen *Gone with the Wind,* and like millions of women of the day, his mother was in love with its suave male star. Since the family already owned the back half of the name, what else should she call her baby? It explained why Gable was so colorless, DZ thought. Knowing he could never hold a candle to his screen namesake, he'd simply tossed in the towel and bleached himself out.

Not that she'd fared any better in the christening sweepstakes. Dorothea Zenobia Hayes—her Oklahoma-born father's tribute to his pioneering great-grandmother who had fought the Cherokee to establish a homestead before she ended up taking one of the enemy for a husband. The Cherokee blood accounted for DZ's hair and "those Indian eyes," according to her mother, who credited her own Irish blood for the pale complexion. As a child, DZ had hated every variation family and friends could wring from either name—Dorrie, Dot, Thea, Nobi. When she was old enough to make it stick, she'd announced she would answer only to the initials.

DZ rode up to her loft in the old freight elevator, big enough for a truck. Reaching the top floor, she pulled the rope that parted the elevator's doors horizontally, and was home. The loft's twenty-six-hundred square feet was mostly open, with high windows running along the front and one side. One corner was walled off for a bedroom and bath, the rest was carved into areas for sitting, dining, and a galley kitchen. She'd renovated it all herself—drywall, electric, plumbing, the works. A capable woman; the legacy of growing up fatherless.

The only time she'd ever used her official position to personal advantage was to get the loft. Five years ago, when she was with Sex Crimes, the young hat designer who'd rented the place had been found there murdered.

During the investigation of the crime (never solved), DZ had met the building's landlord, and when he'd asked if she knew anyone to rent the empty loft, she couldn't resist the opportunity. She felt ghoulish, but hey, all that *space*!

Upon entering, DZ dropped her shoulder bag on a table in the entranceway and kicked off her heels. She crossed the living area to the galley kitchen and took a bottle of New Amsterdam Amber from the refrigerator. As she downed the first swigs, she replayed that sad moment when she'd had to refuse Gable's request for a date. The first time he'd dared to cross that line in all these years. It bothered hell out of her. More than it should have, maybe. Just a shy plea for a little more of her time, one night away from the job.

Yet why choose tonight of all nights to cross a boundary that was so important to maintain? She could only wonder if it hadn't been sparked by the case. The possibilities of what was being threatened were so strange it could blur anyone's perception of established limits. What indeed might be this nut's influence on an unbalanced society if he ever succeeded in getting wider exposure?

DZ got the copy of Lori Swann's notes from her shoulder bag, then moved to the couch and started reading through them. Even second hand, the mild unemotional tone of the caller came through. As in his self-description that Lori had set down: *Just an ordinary guy who wants to kill some people.* And his amiable pitch: *I'd love to talk about it on your show—to be . . . your mystery guest.*

Something about that phrase itself rang a bell. *Your mystery guest.* She looked up, trying to dredge the connection from her memory. Something from long ago . . . Hunger began to gnaw at her, and while she kept trying to pin down the elusive relevance, she went to the galley kitchen and threw together some greens with a can of water-packed tuna hashed in. Standing by a counter, she ate half the crude salad, and all the time it nagged at her. *Mystery guest.* Some kind of game . . . something children played?

Desperate to stop her mind from churning with the grim concerns of work, DZ went to her bedroom, stripped, and gave herself the pleasure of a long, hot shower. As the water sluiced down onto her skin, she was able to put the case out of her head. But her agitation wasn't completely washed away. Her predicament with Gable moved back in. Through the drumming of the shower spray, she heard the echo of his poignant plea. *Great seats . . . pair in the B row. . . .*

The more it stayed with her, the more she felt it was dogging her not because she was annoyed with Clark, but because this, too, as with the words in the notes, left her groping for a meaning she couldn't quite grasp. As she dried off, it kept hovering at the edges of comprehension, a vague irritation like a single grain of sand in a shoe. Then, looking into the bathroom mirror while she rubbed her face with some thirty-dollar-a-jar grease that promised to keep her looking twenty forever, her mind shifted gears again. She found herself staring into her own eyes, searching them, thinking back to the promise of the mystery guest that the proof of his intentions could be found by looking into Stoner's—

Damn! All these riddles tangled up in her brain—they were driving her a little nuts, too. She needed to get the case out of her head. What she really needed, in fact, was another life. From a hook on the back of the bathroom door, she took a kimono and slipped into it. She wrapped her hair in a towel and went to fish the law school applications out of her shoulder bag. Plopping down on the long, soft-leather sofa, she spread the papers on the old printer's rack she used as a coffee table. But she only had to stare at them a few seconds to know she didn't have the concentration to deal with them now. Grabbing up the remote control from the sofa arm, she turned on the TV, which sat on an old drinks trolley.

Jay Leno appeared, talking with the bubbly actress who had won an Oscar for best supporting role a few weeks ago. DZ changed channels. Letterman was teasing a crusty codger from the Ozarks who had recently won the title of World's Fastest Whistle Whittler. She surfed across a few more channels. Charlie Rose was with a journalist plugging a book about two wealthy teenagers who had gone to jail for murdering the baby they'd conceived out of wedlock. A tabloid show had an item on a man who had murdered and mutilated three strippers in Florida.

No more murder, please. Restlessly she went back around the dial and hit Letterman again just as a rock band on the show finished their number and he announced a commercial break. For a few seconds the camera panned across his cheering audience, row after row of people seated in the same theater that had once been the home of Ed Sullivan's famous Sunday night variety show. Sullivan had gone off the air when DZ was a child, but she'd seen him on retrospectives of the Golden Age of Television and knew Sullivan had given America its first look at Elvis, the Beatles. She remembered now that one feature of the show was to have celebrities and newsmakers rise for a bow from their seats in the audience. In those days, it was enough for people just to see them, they didn't have to talk—and, DZ mused, back then the man-in-the-street wasn't dreaming up all kinds of crazy shit so he could grab his own moment in the spotlight; wouldn't be just a nonentity like those shown cheering in Letterman's audience, row after row of—

DZ bolted up. *Row after row,* that was it—the thing that had been nagging at her subconscious since Gable had mentioned the tickets: ". . . a pair in the B row." Every row was marked with a letter of the alphabet. . . .

She ran to her bag and got out the personnel list Candelli had given her. She found the producer's phone number, went to the kitchen. The clock showed it was past midnight, but she hesitated only a moment before picking up the phone.

. . . look in Stoner's eyes. DZ smiled grimly as she dialed the number. Oh, he was a cute one all right, their mystery guest. So fucking *cute*!

CHAPTER
5

AT EIGHT A.M. the next morning, DZ and Gable were outside the doors of studio 12-A to meet Candelli and a uniformed security man, who unlocked the doors into the main seating area. With seventeen rows of raked seats running from row A through row Q, studio 12-A accommodated an audience of 544 people. The seats were divided by two aisles into three sections, with two more aisles against the walls.

DZ headed straight to the ninth row from the front, in the center section, and started searching the seats, working from one end to the other. She was just beginning to doubt her brilliant guesswork as she approached the aisle seat on the end opposite where she'd started, and then bingo—in row I of the studio, where the talk show was broadcast: *Stoner's I's*. Secured with black electrical tape to the underside of the seat was a black vinyl pouch about the size of a book. DZ crouched to study the package. The plastic base of the seat's underside was also shiny black, so cleaners could have easily missed it day after day.

"So the sonofabitch was right here," Candelli said in a low mutter.

DZ stood. "We'll need Forensics, Clark, and the studio has to be sealed until they've gone over everything."

Gable took a cell phone from his jacket to call in the request for a forensic unit and a couple of uniforms to guard the studio.

"You can't seal this off," Candelli protested. "We've got a show to do."

"We need an hour or two to check if our visitor left any traces," DZ explained. "You'll have it for the broadcast."

She crouched again to run her fingers gingerly around the tape securing the package. Then she took a handkerchief from her bag, draped it over her hand, and wedged a finger under an edge of the plastic pouch to slowly pry it loose. Gripping it with her handkerchief, she hefted the package to check the weight, then sniffed it and pinched the edges to see if she could feel any wires.

Candelli guessed from her routine that DZ was wondering if the pouch masked a bomb. "You going to open that?" he asked nervously.

She didn't answer, but lifted the pouch to her ear and gave it a delicate shake. It made a faint rattling noise. "I think it's a videotape," she said finally.

She passed it to Gable along with the handkerchief for his opinion. He went through the same routine and nodded. "Seems safe to me." He took a key ring from his pants pocket, which had a penknife attached, and opened a blade. He was on the verge of slitting one end of the pouch when Stoner charged into the studio through the rear doors; Candelli had made his own early morning call.

"Found something?" he shouted, hurrying down a side aisle. Instead of his usual show-time clothes, he was in jeans and a worn, leather, bombardier-style windbreaker. His thick brown hair was tousled and uncombed, and showing a few streaks of gray because it hadn't been touched up by his makeup artist.

"A video," DZ answered.

He reached them. "You sure it's not a bomb?" He

glanced to Candelli. "Remember, Joe, we did that show about the dangers of being a judge; had this guy on whose arm was blown off by a letter bomb smaller than that."

"We're trained in what to look for," DZ said calmly. "This seems fine."

"Shouldn't a dog sniff it or something?" Stoner persisted.

DZ smiled, nodded to Gable, and he slit open the pouch. "Yup," Gable said, peering inside. He handed it back to DZ along with a ballpoint from his breast pocket. She stuck the pen into a sprocket-hole of the video cartridge and extracted it from the pouch. Now the black plastic cartridge was seen to have silvery lettering on top, as if written with party-girl nail polish: LESSON ONE.

Stoner shook his head and chuckled softly.

"You think this is funny?" DZ said sharply.

"Not funny, exactly. But I can't help being amused. The guy certainly shows some imagination in the way he's putting this production together." The group eyed him coldly. "Well, hell, that's what it is—a production. This is *his* show, and I admit it: he's got me hooked. I can't wait to see what's on that tape."

None of them could.

They went up to the control booth where there were a couple of tape players. The first thing that appeared on the monitor was a shadowy moving shape, indistinct for a second, then identifiable as a figure moving across a dim room. The figure extended an arm, reaching for something, and suddenly a glowing rectangle appeared in the center of the taped image; a television set had been switched on. The murky figure retreated to the edges of the screen, leaving just a shoulder visible at one corner, as if the figure had sat down in front of the video camera aimed at the television set.

The picture on the TV wasn't color, DZ noted, but black-and-white. The sound that came from the television set was low, unclear—voices, laughter. The image on the monitor jumped to a closer view of the television screen. The sound and picture became clearer. A man in a tuxedo sat at a small lectern facing a long counter, where two other men in tuxedoes and two women in evening gowns sat at microphones.

"And now we come to that regular feature of our game," said the man at the podium, "where we ask our panel to put on blindfolds and identify a mystery guest."

"I'll be—!" Stoner exclaimed, *"What's My Line?* Old game show, one of the first, very popular thirty or forty years ago."

"That's John Daly," Candelli said, indicating the MC. "Same name as the golfer. Classy guy."

"My folks loved this," Gable said. "Never missed it. Every Sunday night, nine o'clock, they'd be—"

"I think it was ten o'clock," Candelli said.

"Whatever," Gable said, "we never missed it."

The tape showed the panel of four people putting on satin blindfolds, black for the men, white decorated with cartoon eyelashes for the ladies.

Gable pointed to one of the women. "That chinless dame, that's Dorothy Kilgallen. Sob sister for the *Daily Mirror*—remember the *Mirror* . . . ?"

"Blindfolds all in place, panel?" asked the MC.

The four people at the counter spouted assurances.

Gable rambled on, "Found her dead in bed one morning; the official line was a bad reaction to sleeping pills and booze. But a buddy of mine was on the investigation. Told me she was hit because she was digging up too much about the Kennedy assassination—the John one—and she was going to—"

"Quiet," DZ cut in.

On the monitor, the MC was saying, "Will the Mystery Guest sign in, please?"

The image changed to a close-up of a hand picking up a piece of chalk and scrawling a signature on a blackboard. At the same time there was applause and appreciative mur-

murs from an audience as a small, elfin-faced man with close-cropped black hair was shown taking a seat alongside the man at the podium.

Candelli and Gable spoke nearly in unison: "Peter Lorre."

DZ remembered seeing the actor in some great old movies on TV. *The Maltese Falcon* and *Casablanca*.

"Strange guy," Stoner said. "Always played creeps in the movies."

"Came over from Germany," Candelli said.

On the monitor the MC said, "We'll start the questioning with Dorothy."

Then the monitor went black. But the group in the control booth kept watching the screen, waiting for another image. Five seconds went by, ten more.

"That's it," DZ said. But she told Candelli to forward the tape and check if there was anything else.

The rest was blank.

"So what's lesson one?" Candelli asked.

"The way he sees this whole thing." Stoner said. "A kind of television game show."

"We're the guys in blindfolds," Gable said, "trying to figure out who he is."

"Or maybe what his 'line' is," Candelli suggested, "aside from killer."

"I get all that," DZ said impatiently. "But *What's My Line?* was on the air every Sunday for—what—fifteen years?"

"Much more," Candelli said.

"Okay, so there were hundreds of broadcasts. Why show us that program in particular?" And how did it tie in to the Mystery Guest they'd been shown? she wondered. Was their own Mystery Guest named Peter? German? An actor?

"Maybe it's the only one he could find," Candelli said. "Programs went out live in those days, and only some were documented with a process called Kinescope—that's what we were watching, a tape of the kine. But they're not very easy to come by."

Which underlined for DZ that such material would be more easily obtained by someone who worked in broadcasting.

Through the control booth window, Gable spotted a couple of uniformed cops entering the studio with other men in plainclothes carrying large black satchels. "Forensics," he alerted DZ.

Looking down into the studio, the rows of seats, DZ thought of the Mystery Guest planting the tape. She turned abruptly to Candelli. "This morning a guard unlocked the studio for us. Is it kept locked most of the time?"

"Those are—the ones to the seating. We open them an hour before airtime to let in the audience."

"So chances are that's when he planted the tape." DZ looked at Stoner. "You go into the audience a lot, don't you? The cameras pan around and show all the people. . . ."

"That's right," Stoner answered excitedly. "So you think the Mystery Guest has already been on the show. . . ."

Looking back at Stoner, hearing that he sounded anything but worried or disappointed by the turn things were taking, DZ was struck again by the cleverness of their quarry. He could've picked any row, after all, to leave the tape. "Yeah," she said. "In your I's."

Without a doubt, she knew as she looked at Stoner, their Mystery Guest had meant the hint to be taken both ways.

THEY GOT CANDELLI TO MAKE COPIES OF TAPES FROM THE last two weeks of Stoner's shows and took them back downtown to watch on the detail's ancient VCR. DZ wanted to look through parts where the audience had been on camera, maybe use them to lift photos of all the people who had been in or near seat I-24.

The tapes supplied a good across-the-board sampling of

a typical week's fare on *Stoner*. Like the show titled
"Aphrodisiacs—Are They Real and Do They Work?"
which included a segment of Stoner in New York's Chinatown buying such contraband substances as powdered
rhino horn and tiger musk. In a studio segment, a woman
who called herself "The Love Chef" prepared aphrodisiac
recipes, which were fed to volunteer couples from the audience, who were then steered into risque confessions
about their love lives.

"So that's where she got it," said Ray Culver, one of the
detail's other detectives who stood by kibbitzing as DZ
and Gable reviewed the tapes. "My wife made a dinner last
week with fried oysters, and sprinkled this brown powder
on them. I didn't have the heart to tell her, but the whole
thing tasted like dirt."

"What happened after dinner?" said Gable.

The detective thought a second. "You know," he said, "I
might ask her to make that dish again." He wandered away.

There was a show on incest, with a woman who was
pregnant by her *younger* brother. Another where obese
children talked about the cruelties they endured. DZ
stopped paying attention to the topics and speeded through
the tapes, simply studying the people who had sat in or
around the suspect seat location. The Mystery Guest had
probably been in disguise, but DZ and Gable studied the
faces closely to discern any hint of fakery. She hoped their
man might even have stared brazenly into the camera at
some point; the nature of his scheme suggested that part of
his thrill was in daring them to catch him.

They saw nothing particularly helpful, though.

"Maybe we'll get something off the mailing list," Gable
said after they'd spent two hours in front of the VCR. DZ
had asked Candelli how show tickets were allotted, and
he'd explained that people wrote in and were sent any
number they requested for a particular date. Since the
names and addresses were kept in a computer, DZ had
been able to obtain a printout of all those who'd been sent

tickets for the same two-week period in which the tape had probably been planted. Unfortunately, seating was on a random basis so there was no way to match a name to a particular seat. Still, it was possible that one of the 5,440 people who had been in the audience on those ten week-days had left the tape.

But DZ doubted it would be that easy. Candelli had mentioned, too, that seventy or eighty tickets for each show were given out on the street daily by staff members, who offered them to tourists and passers-by. "Barry likes people in the audience who didn't plan to be there. It adds to the spontaneity."

The Mystery Guest could have known about the wrinkle, and used it to enter the studio without giving his identity. Still, the names on the ticket-mailing list would have to be checked.

Ray Culver reappeared at the doorway. "The first dep is on the phone for you," he said.

Having given her the case, DZ realized the deputy commissioner must now want a status report.

"So what about this Stoner thing?" he growled when she picked up. He was a graceless man in general, and DZ's chemistry with him had never been good.

She told him about the two phone calls, and the tape found in the studio.

"Peter Lorre? *What's My Line?* Shit," he said, "watched that when I was a kid. But what the fuck's it supposed to mean?"

"It ties in with what he likes to call himself," DZ explained. "The Mystery Guest."

"Oh yeah, I remember—there was always somebody famous the panel would try to identify with their blindfolds on. So what's your take on this, Lieutenant? Is it a crank or do we really have something to worry about?"

DZ weighed her answer. It was going out on a limb to say a man who spoke of committing murder and finding a way to boast about it repeatedly on television without being stopped should be believed. But that was her gut instinct, and she wanted to ask for the investigation to be geared up a few notches. That would cost the department money, though, and if it ended being money unnecessarily spent, there would be a scapegoat for the decision. Guess who?

"Sir," she said at last, "this M.G. seems very clever. I do think—"

"M.G.?" he interrupted. "What's that—like M.O.?"

"Mystery Guest," DZ explained. She paused, reflecting on the fact that she'd abbreviated it without thinking—as if turning the moniker into initials might put him more on her own wavelength, make him easier to know. She went on: "I think he's clever enough that his threat could be real."

A grunt came from other end of the line. "So what are you doing about it?"

She told him about the traps already in place on the phones in Stoner's office and studio. About the forensics sweep, which had turned up thousands of fingerprints in the studio (though probably none were the perp's). Finally, she mentioned the ticket mailing list and requested more manpower to check the thousands of names. She also asked for additional detectives to trace where the planted videotape had been purchased.

There was a long silence before the first dep answered. "I dunno, Hayes. Sounds like you need to pull a lot more men—maybe for squat. I'm gonna leave it to Number One to decide. I'll fax him in Stockholm to fill him in. Tomorrow's Saturday; he's set to be back in the afternoon. You can take it up with him direct."

THE DETAIL SPENT THE REST OF THE DAY CHECKING STONER'S personnel to see if any had police records, and starting on the mailing list—calling people who'd been in the studio on suspect days, asking whether they'd seen anything suspicious, gauging whether they sounded suspicious themselves. Nothing turned up.

When DZ left the office, she brought along the tapes she had of Stoner's show, and M.G.'s "Lesson One." On the way home, she stopped at a video rental and took out *Casablanca*. She wanted to see more of Peter Lorre than she'd gotten in those few seconds on an old TV game show. If that tape found in the studio was called "Lesson One," then it was meant to teach. Something more specific, she thought, than merely that his threat was serious. But what? That figure dimly glimpsed watching the old game show, did he look like the once-famous movie actor on the tape? Did his own creepy plan relate to some role Lorre had played in a film?

At her loft, DZ opened a New Amsterdam, microwaved a Healthy Choice fish dinner, and settled in front of the TV with the meal to watch everything again.

She finished her viewing three hours later with the movie, watching it straight through, except to pop up now and then for another beer. By the time Bogie had walked off with Claude Rains agreeing it was the start of a beautiful friendship, she was groggy from the alcohol and wrung out from the old-fashioned schmaltz—more than ready for bed.

And she'd learned only two things: that *Casablanca* was a great flick no matter how many times you saw it, and there was nobody, absolutely nobody, like Bogie.

CHAPTER
6

ARMS FOLDED ACROSS his custom-made monogrammed shirt, Hermes tie pulled loose, feet up on the desk with his black Gucci loafers crossed at the ankles, Police Commissioner Brendan K. Leacock sat tipped back in the swivel chair behind his desk, eyes trained on the TV monitor showing "Lesson One." DZ and Gable were in two hardback chairs in front of the desk, the first dep on a sofa by the wall behind them. The tape hit the blank section.

"Once more," Leacock said, and the first dep depressed the Rewind button on the VCR remote in his hand.

This time DZ watched Leacock, not the tape, wondering how he'd decide the case should be handled. Trim, shrewd, self-confident, Commissioner Brendan Leacock was born to the cop life, his diaper probably pinned with a badge. His father had been a foot patrolman in Fall River, Massachusetts, and one of his three brothers had died as a Boston rookie in a shoot-out with a bank robber. After climbing through the ranks to be chief in Fall River, Leacock had been hired to reorganize the police in Cleveland. Succeeding famously, he had been summoned to New York to straighten out a department demoralized by a shrinking budget and festering corruption. Within a year he'd cleaned up a few rotten precincts, put in place a new foundation of rank-and-file loyalty, and reduced the crime rate enough to make him the mayor's biggest rival for the public's affection. Leacock was ideal for the public-relations part of the job, too; steely blue eyes set in a narrow attractive face, always ready for inspection with a recent haircut and well-cut dark suits (top of the line at the insider discount).

DZ thought Leacock had gotten a little too swept up in his own image lately, his perception of the line between public servant and indispensable kingpin becoming blurred. For the first fifteen minutes of today's meeting, he had talked about his Stockholm trip, commenting on all that was wrong about the way the Swedes ran their police operations. But when Brendan Leacock first came to the department, DZ recalled, he wouldn't have wasted fifteen seconds before demanding to be briefed on news from his own battleground.

At last, though, she'd been asked to run down the M.G. case. She'd saved the videotape for last and before showing it, had underlined the general no-clue situation by reporting no prints had been found on the cassette, nor had any useful latents turned up on the studio seat where the tape had been left.

The *What's My Line?* video finished a second showing. "Interesting," Leacock said. "Add music and they'd show it on MTV." He pulled his feet off the desk and sat forward, blue eyes targeted on DZ. "From what you say, Lieutenant Hayes, we're nowhere on this. Everything you've got so far on the perp could fit into a flea's asshole with room left over for the mayor's heart."

Behind her, DZ heard the first dep chuckle, but neither she nor Gable cracked a smile. No joke if friction between Leacock and the mayor was getting worse. Politics would always interfere with the department's work.

"Given that," Leacock added, "we should be damn

happy this whole deal is probably nothing more than a scam."

"I don't see it that way, sir," DZ said.

"You've made that clear, Hayes. The fax I got from my deputy said you want two dozen more men to work the case."

"There are five thousand names on the ticket mailing list, sir. That alone—"

"Is useless. You mentioned that fifty tickets for the show are handed out on the street every day. If your 'mystery man' knows enough to wipe his prints off that cassette, he's not going to let his name and address drop into our laps."

"But we caught Son of Sam," DZ observed, "because he left his car where it got a parking ticket while he was a block away killing one of his victims. My understanding of detective work, Commissioner, is that as long as there's anything that might be a lead, you follow it."

She was out on a limb being so snotty, but if they weren't going to trust her to handle the case, apply her instincts, then she was ready to dump the whole thing and put stamps on those application envelopes.

Leacock gave her a hard look, then stood and turned to the window behind his desk to contemplate the panoramic view of boats gliding across the sunlit harbor. His own opinion was that the case didn't merit a major effort, yet it was hard to dismiss because it involved a celebrity—one who had a platform on television that could be used to embarrass the authorities if they performed badly.

"What's our status with the FBI?" Leacock asked.

DZ and Gable traded a glance. The question was a measure of the commissioner's anxiety about being involved in a fiasco. He was never keen to let federal come in and call the shots, but this would be a way of saving face and money—and there were grounds to use it.

"Routine so far," DZ said. "All prints went to their index for reference, but we didn't explain why."

"You didn't ask anyone on their Psych squad to give us a profile, an opinion on whether the guy's for real?"

"Once they know it involves network TV, they might claim jurisdiction."

"And you wouldn't like that, Hayes," the commissioner said, still facing the view. "You think you've caught a real big one, and you want it for yourself. . . ."

He was making it perfectly clear: the blame would be dumped on her if it blew up and she couldn't handle it. But yes, damn right, she wanted it. She was hooked—as Stoner had put it.

"Yes, sir," she said, "as long as jurisdiction allows, I want to keep it. And right now it's on our turf."

Leacock resumed his chair. "Okay. I'll give you more men—until we see if this is going away. Make 'em work, though. You need to cover more than the names on that mailing list."

She nodded. "We'll check out all people with connections to Stoner, and look into other talk shows; maybe competitors want to destabilize his operation."

"How about the *What's My Line?* angle?" Leacock said. "The program seems to have some meaning for this guy. You might look into how he could get hold of that film clip."

The first dep spoke up. "See if anyone who once worked on that show works for Stoner."

Facing away from the first dep, Gable gave his eyes a half-roll. Leacock caught it and scowled at him.

"Commissioner," DZ said quickly, "that show hasn't been on the air for thirty years. Of course, we'll cover the angle. But the link between *What's My Line?* and our guy seems to be in the nature of the game itself. He's challenging us to guess who he is, what he looks like, what he does."

"While we're in blindfolds," Gable added.

"Then let's change the rules," Leacock said. "He says he wants to do Stoner's show, so if he does call again—"

DZ understood where he was headed and cut in. "Sir, the man we're dealing with . . . he's a bomb waiting to go off. Before he can, there's a detonator that has to be activated. He's indicated he wants to go on Stoner's show *before* he kills anyone. Once he does, the detonator is armed. I'd urge in the strongest terms that, if this man does make contact, we do *not* agree to let him on television."

"I don't understand, Lieutenant. There's no quick way to collar this guy unless we get near him. If he offers the opportunity, why not take it?"

"I'm sure it won't be that simple—he won't stroll in so we can grab him"

"Why not?" said the first dep "The guy's obviously a wacko. He could be screwy enough to keep the date and let us strap him right into a straitjacket."

For the first time DZ turned to look at him, a bearish man with greasy gunmetal hair, black mustache, and a weak mouth. The sort, she felt, who regarded every halfway attractive woman as an enemy because he knew they could never love him. "Or maybe," she said, "wacko enough to turn up at Stoner's studio with twenty pounds of dynamite strapped on his body. If we don't let him cruise out again, everything blows—right there on national TV."

"Is that what he said?" Leacock asked with alarm.

DZ faced him again. "No! He hasn't said word one about *how* he plans to appear in front of millions, admit intent to murder, then walk away, do it, come back, and walk away again. But Gable and I have run a few scenarios. That's one."

"Tell me another," the commissioner said.

"Come in handcuffed to a hostage," Gable said.

"Commissioner, it's like any hostage situation. Keep the dialogue going, but stand firm. Play his way, we may just put more people in jeopardy."

Leacock studied her. DZ could see the balance shifting back and forth. At last he said, "All right, Hayes, you want the case for yourself, shut federal out, fine. But I won't let you bank on million-to-one shots. Not when an opening exists to get near this guy."

"Sir, it's like pulling the pin on a grenade—"

He cut her off. Jabbing his finger at her, he made his wishes clear. "When we hear from him again—if he wants an answer about the guest shot—the answer will be 'yes.' Understand? Bring him close. We'll figure out a way to guard against getting sandbagged."

DZ flashed Gable an exasperated glance.

Leacock stayed on her. "Your choice, Hayes: do what it takes to haul him in fast, or sign off."

Gable tried once more. "Sir, if we agree to let this guy on TV, we won't be able to keep the deal undercover anymore. Even before he goes on it's got to leak—from Stoner if nowhere else. And once it goes public, there'll be a media firestorm. And you'll take most of the heat."

"True, Sergeant. But I'm up to the job—long as I know I've got people like you and Hayes backing me up." Translation: human shields to take the arrows while the commissioner made his getaway.

Still, she couldn't walk away from a chance to head up what might become a huge homicide investigation, one of the biggest ever. "Okay, sir," she said quietly. "We'll tell him yes."

"Good. I'll call chief of detectives and tell him to give you twenty-five more men." Leacock came out from behind the desk. DZ and Gable took the cue to rise. "I assume Stoner won't mind cooperating," the commissioner added as he herded them to the door.

"Mind?" DZ said. "He'd send a limo for this guest— even *after* the killing starts."

CHAPTER
7

*H*ER FATHER WAS an Oklahoma oil wildcatter whose ventures in search of a gusher had become longer and farther until one day he'd left their small apartment over a paint store in Tulsa and simply never returned. DZ had been nine.

Destitute after being abandoned, her mother contacted a sister who'd gone to New York and married a Greek who owned a bar in Queens. DZ went with her mother to live in two rooms over the bar, and each in their turn had paid their way by waiting tables and tapping beers.

A majority of the bar's steady customers were cops from the precinct house two blocks away, so at an early age DZ was drawn into the fringes of their society. At seventeen, her virginity was lost to a rookie patrolman who spoke of marriage "someday," but she never heard from him after he was transferred to a precinct in the Bronx. No matter. A husband, she had learned, was someone who left you flat whenever it suited him.

While paying her way through Queens College, DZ was often advised by cops at the bar to think about joining the department after graduation. She had bigger plans, though.

Law school. Family law, maybe, helping hold families together—or at least getting a fair shake for the women who were used and thrown away.

Then, in the early part of her junior year, her mother had gone to the doctor with digestive problems and by winter she was dead from pancreatic cancer. The cops had all been so nice to her—the collection for the funeral taken up in the bar's back room, another at the precinct to help with her school expenses—she began to regard them as family; a slew of caring uncles and brothers. She stopped laughing off their talk about becoming a cop, listened as they told her the job's good points, the benefits, the excitement, the camaraderie, and—if you cared about such things—the chance to serve the community.

The department was becoming more open to women at the time she applied—though an unwritten code still ruled. She was hazed in the training, given extra burdens—until a man of rank she knew from the bar heard, and the trouble stopped.

A few years on patrol, a couple of citations. She was seen by her superiors as a good candidate for promotion. Urged by friends at the bar, she took the exam for detective. She was assigned first to Burglary. Good place for a woman: interviewing tourists who'd gotten plucked at the hotels, East Side matrons mugged for a necklace. From Burglary she went to Vice, from Vice to Sex Crimes. More good places for a woman, applying those feminine insights to reeling in the hookers, comforting raped coeds, playing surrogate mom to molested kids.

But like most detectives, DZ had ambitions to do the work that really got your juices flowing—Homicide. She talked to her mentors at the bar. Patience, she was told. But the years passed. She invested her impatience in solving the worst of the sex crimes—if she could.

At last one of the honchos on Homicide called her in. He sat her down in his office for a whole afternoon, checking her on procedure, running her through a thousand what-ifs.

Her answers were solid, and the interview seemed to be winding up on a positive note when he rolled his desk chair out from behind the desk until he was almost knee-to-knee with her, and started talking about the importance of "close cooperation" on the squad, and the difficulties of being a woman breaking into a "fraternity."

"You come to Homicide, Detective Hayes," he'd said, "there's guys here who'll make it tough in all kinds of ways, and the way you handle it will decide whether you can be the kind of team player we need. And that'll pave the way for any of your sisters who come after. So, DZ, think you can handle it?"

It was at some point during that spiel he'd laid his hand on her leg, well above the knee.

She'd let him leave the hand there while she did the inventory. Not bad looking, pretty good dresser—for some reason, the guys on Homicide usually went to more trouble with their clothes—and the wedding band on his finger. Then she factored in the odds on coming out ahead if she blew the whistle, or even used her friends to come back at him. She saw only one way to handle it and still have a chance.

"So," she'd said, looking him square in the eye, "you want me get down on my knees and suck your cock here and now? Or do I get to go dancing first?"

After a second he'd taken the hand away and rolled the chair back. "Not bad," he drawled, his smile taking on a razor edge. "Not bad at all."

Had it been merely a test of whether she was tough enough to deal with the shit she might get from other men? Or had he seen that she was going to be too much trouble by the way she blunted his threat with the two choices most likely to confuse and immobilize any rapist (as you learned at Sex Crimes): either perform on cue for a passive partner . . . or turn it into a real romance?

She never knew for sure. In any event, he'd seen what he needed to see. The interview ended with his assurance that she would have the department's determination within a month.

It came even before the time was up—her transfer from Sex Crimes . . . to Intelligence. In the department, the prevailing view was that Intelligence was a backwater depot for the burnt out, the troublemakers, and—what else?—the slow-witted. DZ didn't complain, though. It was a chance to do different work, some of it interesting. She waited a while before putting in another request for Homicide. Then, and a few times since, the answer had come back that the time wasn't quite right. A year ago, she'd been made lieutenant over the detail.

Now choosing the department over law school had begun to seem a bad choice. She'd hit the shady side of her thirties, and would like to have been married by now—but cops married cops, it was part of the dogma, and it didn't work for her. She'd dated them now and then, because they asked, and it passed the time. But with the exception of the rookie who'd been her first, and a one-night stand on a particularly depressing New Year's Eve when she was about to turn thirty, she had never again let one get her into bed. She was as leery of committing herself to a cop as all the nonblue men who'd shied away from her. For the same reasons, perhaps—because it brought the danger home, brought in all the reminders of corruption and impermanence and craziness and death. And she longed for a man who could help her forget all that.

There had been lovers she'd lived with for months at a time—like the painter she'd met downtown who'd been struggling then but had since become a hot commodity. It was a rare man, though, who didn't feel the whole natural biological order threatened by bonding with a woman who depended on her gun for protection more than on him. Yet it wasn't just womanly needs that had made it harder lately to accept her work.

DZ felt the job was finally turning her into a person who didn't believe in the future, whose innocence and hope—

her ability to believe in the basic goodness of human nature—was being eroded by the hard, daily grind of working in a society where a growing tide of inhumanity could
no longer be stemmed. A world where eleven-year-olds
were gunned down by their schoolmates, and pregnant
women were murdered by other women who would cut the
baby out of the womb. She ached to belong again in the
sweeter domestic world of women. To wear an apron instead of a holster. To give a child a bath, dry the kid off
with a towel stamped with a Disney cartoon from the latest Blockbuster family movie, then put her feet up and wait
for a kind and familiar man to come home. A man who
hadn't been hardened by his own daily contact with the
worst experience of human nature.

Why wait for it? She'd been asking herself every day for
the past few months.

But today, in her confrontation with the commissioner,
she realized why she hadn't quit—couldn't—why the applications were still hanging around only half filled out. It
was because she refused to buckle, to leave a loser, to be
beaten down by the job . . . and by the men. Because, goddammit, she wouldn't ever let it matter that one of them
had left her and her mother to survive on their own without even so much as a fucking good-bye note. If she quit,
it had to be on a high.

And now she had a chance—if this creep was for real.
This was *her* case, and she could see it getting big, real big.
See it providing the proof she craved that all these years of
her life hadn't been a pathetic waste.

CHAPTER 8

"**H**ELLO, JOE. WHADDAYA know?"
Just got in from Kokomo.

Joe Candelli was asleep in bed at his weekend house in East Hampton when the phone's ring pulled him from sleep. Hearing the voice on the receiver, Candelli's subconscious dredged up the rhyme from an old vaudeville routine.

But a moment later he was on full alert, staring wide-eyed into the darkness. "Who is this?" he whispered so as not to wake his wife beside him.

"Your best nightmare, Joe, that's who."

The reply sent Candelli's heart into double time. It had to be this freak who was stirring things up at the office. Now he was reaching into their homes!

"Let me move to another phone," Candelli said softly. "I don't want to disturb my wife." And moving, he thought, would also give him a chance to look out the window. If this bastard knew where he lived, then the guy could be nearby, even calling from a cell phone right outside.

"No, Joe, don't move. Just stay right there and listen. Your wife can sleep—I'll do all the talking. The thing is,

Joe, I've gotten tired of waiting to be booked as a guest. I know you want me, and I've got a schedule of my own to keep. So I'm coming on the show this week. Expect me on Thursday."

The objection, the angry cursing refusal to accept any demand from this maniac began to rise in Candelli's throat. But he controlled himself. Bring him in, that was the order of the day. "Why Thursday?" Candelli asked. Hadn't the last phone call also come on a Thursday?

"Let's say . . . because I'm Thursday's child. Tell Stoner to be ready, because you'll see me there in time for the show."

"At the studio, you mean? You're really coming—"

"Four o'clock," he said. "I'll be there with bells on."

The connection was cut.

Candelli cradled the phone and turned on a bedside lamp. Drained by an odd combination of terror and exhilaration, he took a couple of deep breaths, then grabbed a pad and pencil from a night-table drawer and jotted some notes on the conversation, things that struck him as possibly helpful to the cops.

"What's going on, honey?" his wife asked drowsily without opening her eyes.

"Technical problems," he said. Occasionally he got late calls from broadcast engineers.

Satisfied, she burrowed back into the bed.

Candelli turned off the light and left the room. He needed a stiff drink. Then he'd dig out that card he'd been given by Lieutenant Hayes and spoil her sleep, too.

CHAPTER
9

DZ STARTED TRYING to reach Stoner as soon as she came out of the meeting with Leacock; it was important to let him know the police strategy she'd been ordered to implement. All day and into the evening she had tried the unlisted home phone numbers she'd been given on her first visit to the production office—for his duplex on upper Fifth Avenue and the horse farm in Millbrook where he bred prize Arabians. On one call to the duplex, a maid had answered and said Stoner was at his farm for the weekend, but there had been no answer there.

After receiving Joe Candelli's frantic call at 4 A.M., it became even more important to inform Stoner. In the predawn hours, she tried all his numbers again. Still no answer. She called back to Candelli to ask where Stoner might be. The producer observed that Stoner was single and popular with women; he might have spent the night anywhere. DZ still hadn't connected with him when she went to the office.

This Sunday morning began with giving out assignments and briefing the new detectives who'd joined the investigation. One group she put on the mailing list, a process that entailed converting addresses to phone numbers, calling and determining if there was any reason to put that person on a suspect list. Suspects were then cross-checked to obtain dates of birth via motor vehicle departments of their home states, and DOBs used for computer checks with the Bureau of Criminal Investigation for any prior arrests. Another detective team was assigned to run a similar check on Stoner's personnel.

The mission she gave Gable was to gather background material on Stoner. "He's at the center of this thing," she told him. "I'd like to know more about him."

"Got him down for a suspect?" Gable asked. "This could be good for him, after all. It's what these talk show guys live for—the more sensational the better."

"I don't know," DZ said. "But dig deep. I doubt he's behind this—but we can't rule it out, either."

DZ herself followed up on the M.G.'s call to Candelli. The phone company was able to tell her only that the call had come in over long distance lines; further details had somehow been lost in the computerized switching system, probably because the caller was able to scramble the electronic data.

The only other information of any value DZ got was in the details Candelli supplied about his call from the M.G. DZ believed now that hidden meanings were always salted in and a couple of things seemed to carry special significance.

Thursday's child, he'd called himself. A phrase from an old nursery rhyme, DZ remembered—or was it merely a poem about children? How did it go . . . ? *Wednesday's child is full of woe, Thursday's child has far to go.* So what was the meaning there?

And there was the prideful little phrase he had flipped off right at the end, when boasting he would appear for Thursday's show: *I'll be there with bells on.*

Candelli also felt it was significant. "It's what people say when they're really looking forward to being someplace," he said. "Like if they're going to a celebration. I guess that's what this is for him—he's so goddamn happy about manipulating us."

But DZ thought it meant more. *I'll be there with bells on.* Turning it over in her mind, she remembered reading somewhere that in ancient times lepers were made to wear bells so that people in their path would be warned lepers were near. Was the Mystery Guest equating himself with those pariahs, cast out from society because of sickness . . . ?

I'll be there with bells on.

As with "Stoner's I's," it was his code for something. But she doubted it could be deciphered until he was ready to drop another hint. That was part of his game—tossing out clues while keeping them in blindfolds.

Finally, in the middle of the afternoon, her constant efforts to find Stoner met with success. He answered the phone at his country house. "Have you heard from Candelli?" she began.

"No. I just got here. Why?"

DZ told him about the M.G.'s call, then about Leacock's strategy.

"So it's really going to happen," he said quietly when she finished.

DZ couldn't tell from his tone if he was simply subdued or pleased. "Or the hoax is being pushed to the limit," she said. "We'll try to nail him before Thursday, of course, but if we don't we have to be prepared. I'd like to meet with you, Mr. Stoner, talk about your end of things."

"I'll be back in the city this evening. We can meet then."

"All right. The Intelligence Division is located at—"

"No," he interrupted. "My apartment."

It was the first time she'd heard him use that tone, the one that came with being a star—who expected things done his way.

She had an impulse to slap him down: he was a citizen and she was the *police*. But she was curious to see how he lived. "What time?"

"Eight o'clock. And don't bring that partner of yours. He depresses me."

She thought that over, too. The rule was to go in pairs, both for protection and validation. But for getting information from Stoner, being one-on-one would be better.

She said she'd see him at eight and hung up.

AT THE END OF THE DAY, GABLE BROUGHT HER A PACKET of material on Stoner—old newspaper files and magazine pieces, and publicity and press handouts prepared by the network. He'd also worked the phone to see if anything questionable turned up in records from places Stoner had lived in the past, but so far nothing.

DZ thanked him and told him he could leave for the day. Since it was Sunday, she'd already told other members of her "task force" they could leave as long as they came in early tomorrow.

Gable gestured to the pile he'd just left on her desk. "I'll stay and help you go through that stuff, then give you a ride home."

"Thanks, but I won't be going home."

"Well. I can drop you wherever—"

"Clark . . ." It was all she had to say.

"See you tomorrow," he murmured, and left.

She started her reading with a reprint from a special 1993 issue of *TV Guide* that had marked the 5,000th *Stoner* show and traced the host's career from its beginnings.

One of five children of a dairy farmer, his full name was Beryl Isaac Stoner. His father was a breakaway from the sternly puritan sect of Pennsylvania Amish who accepted a draft into the Second World War rather than ask deferment as a conscientious objector. After the war his father had settled in Iowa and started dairy farming. After a bovine disease had destroyed his father's herd and the family needed extra money, fifteen-year-old Beryl Stoner had gotten a job sweeping floors at a local TV station. Eventually he'd begun pestering the station's news director for a chance to go on the air, and he was rewarded finally when he started bringing in anecdotes about local people that made feel-good tags for the news—like the woman who had finished fourth in the Pillsbury national bake-off with a casserole recipe that included chicken feed. Young Beryl's interviews with these quirky folks were always humorous, and were soon a regular feature. By the age of twenty, now using the name "Berry," he had a daily half-hour of his own called *Sticks and Stoner* interspersing a selection of performances by local talent with taped interviews of the most peculiar people he could find. Three years later, the popularity of the show was noted by a network affiliate in Des Moines and Stoner was invited to move it there, cut the amateur talent, and just do interviews with unusual Iowans, plus any celebrities passing through town. Renamed *Stoner!* it became a popular late-morning fixture. A station exec had also persuaded him to change Berry to Barry: "You don't want to be called a fruit, do you?"

He began including more serious interviews, and then a sensational crime occurred in Des Moines. A wealthy older man was murdered and his much younger wife was presumed guilty. The woman claimed she'd been framed by her own teenage daughter from an earlier marriage, who was having an affair with the stepfather. Stoner persuaded the mother and daughter to come on his program and confront each other. Television sets throughout Iowa were tuned to the show—and viewers were electrified as the daughter broke down on camera under Stoner's questioning and admitted she had stabbed "the horny old bastard" after telling him he'd made her pregnant, and he'd tried forcing her to have an abortion.

The rest was history. Stoner couldn't present something so dramatic every time, but with the format he conceived the potential would always be there. Real people, telling the truth about themselves, no matter what it was. Over the years, the format had been refined. In the beginning, only the people he interviewed were in the studio with him. Then Stoner realized it was more dramatic if an audience was present to offer live comments. At first, he'd interacted with this audience from a stage, but soon he discovered the atmosphere was livelier when he went among them. The formula became what it remained to this day: he moved around, dashing up and down aisles to take questions and comments from every corner of the studio—the very picture of a man on a breathless pursuit of the truth.

Twenty years ago, the format was something new, and Stoner's rapidly growing audience was noted at network headquarters. The show was moved to a larger market: Detroit. Nine years there with more and more affiliates signing on all the time to carry the program in the afternoon. Finally Stoner had yielded to the network's desire to move his base to New York for a broader range of program material, a larger base of screwed-up people, as well as access to more celebrities.

So here he was, carried all the way from a corn crib in Iowa to a duplex penthouse on Fifth Avenue; from eighteen bucks a week for odd jobs in a shoebox radio station to a gross of sixty-two million dollars a year for his production company, lifted up and carried all that way on a great surging wave of *talk*.

ON THE DRIVE UP TO STONER'S APARTMENT, DZ DROVE PAST an open book chain superstore and remembered a small piece of research she wanted to do. In a section filled with books on cinema, she searched for anything relating to Peter Lorre. There was nothing devoted solely to the actor, but in a paperback *Guide to Films on TV* there were capsule bios of the stars of the '40s and '50s. One devoted to Lorre gave dates of birth and death, a few sentences about the genesis of his career in Germany, and listed all his films. She bought the book.

For the remainder of the drive uptown, DZ mulled over what she'd learned about Stoner. It would be going too far to say he'd actually *invented* the talk show; the interview/call-in format has existed since the days of radio. But Stoner had been one of the first to see the potential of tapping into the nature of ordinary people for television. Fifteen years ago, if you wanted to see people exposing the most intimate details of their sex lives, or kids in ghost-white makeup boasting about the pleasures of belonging to a satanic cult, you tuned to *Stoner,* nowhere else. Now the format had become such a staple of television that there wasn't an hour around the clock when you couldn't find a show just like his on one channel or another. They ran simultaneously on every network and cable channel. So many that they were not only competing for the audience, but beginning to exhaust it. Just lately the ratings for all were sliding. To revive the genre, and his own place at the top of the heap, it had to be tempting for Stoner to be presented with an opportunity to push the boundaries further, a way of capturing more of an audience with something unique—a once-in-a-lifetime "get"—that could never be seen anywhere else.

So wasn't it conceivable he might even *create* the opportunity?

CHAPTER
10

*T*HE DOOR OF the apartment swung open and Stoner stood there dressed in a green-and-black checked lumberjack shirt hanging out over faded jeans and oxford loafers, without socks, on his feet. His dark brown hair, always carefully combed on television, was rumpled, accentuating his farmboy quality. In one hand he held a large kitchen spoon.

"Come in, Detective," he said hastily. "I've got something on the stove that needs watching." He hurried away.

DZ stepped over the threshold into a long oval gallery with a white marble floor, a domed ceiling of sky blue, and an encircling mural of fields of wildflowers, painted in realistic perspective. A curving staircase led to the upper recesses of the duplex. Beyond an open portal along the perimeter of the gallery was a living room that faced Central Park, furnished in the English style with lamps glowing in corners and leather wing chairs scattered among highly polished antique tables. Other open doors revealed a paneled library and a spare, modern dining room. All around, recessed lighting cast gentle beams on a tasteful but eclectic mix of paintings and sculpture. *Architectural*

Digest must have published the place at some point, DZ mused: "At Home with Barry Stoner."

But where had he gone? Standing amid the painted fields of wildflowers she felt like Dorothy tossed from Oz to Kansas after the tornado. "Hello?" she called.

"Over here." He reappeared at a doorway then dodged out of sight again. She caught up with him in a connecting hallway that ended at an immense kitchen with a gleaming, black-granite floor fitted out with restaurant-quality equipment. One corner was carved out for a dining area, French brasserie tables and chairs surrounded by crockery planters overflowing with live indoor blooms. The table had been set for two with dishes glazed in a colorful naif floral pattern. Charming.

She hovered on the fringe watching him stir one of two pots on the stove. He glanced over and smiled.

In this casual setting, DZ realized it was the first time she'd had a really good look at him. Until now, his face had been essentially an image imprinted on her mind—not from TV, since she couldn't catch his weekday broadcasts, but from those huge ads plastered on the sides of city buses. She had looked at him as not wholly real. Now he was flesh and blood, a guy spending an evening at home. To her surprise, she found him appealing, not simply because he was attractive, but because he came across here as far more complex and intriguing than he did on his show. On television, he seemed to be a man who had no secrets, no dark corners; but of course that was the role he had to fill—a counterpart to all the devious and abnormal people arrayed before him. Now it struck DZ that he had his secrets, too.

He looked back to the pot. "Just spaghetti and tomato sauce."

"I don't recall anything being said about dinner."

"I figured maybe you didn't have a chance to eat after work. . . ."

No point in *not* eating. So—his way again. She moved

to the stove for a closer look. The pot he was stirring held a thick red sauce. Its garlicy aroma made her mouth water.

He gave her a little smile. "Do you cook?"

"I microwave. When I get home I'm too wrecked from the job to cook for one."

He put down the spoon and went to a cabinet containing several glass containers filled with different pastas. He seized one filled with spaghetti. "For two?" he said.

She yielded a nod.

Stoner set up the spaghetti in boiling water, then crossed to open another cabinet, reveal a wine cooler stocked with racked bottles. "This okay—or can't you drink on duty?"

"Dinner can be off-duty. We still need to talk, though."

"I suppose you want to prepare me for what's to come. . . ." He selected a bottle, opened it, and went to the dining area to pour a little into a glass. She watched him do the connoisseur bit—inhale it deeply, then sip at it with the brisk intensity that indicated a refined palate. "Needs to breathe awhile," he said, and went back to stirring the sauce.

He'd come a long way from the farm, DZ reflected. "What I wanted to talk about," she said, "is the kind of co-operation I need from you."

He tossed her a glance. The body language said he wasn't used to being told what to do. Not even about being asked to cooperate.

"My commissioner thinks you should keep playing along with this thing," she continued. "So I can't openly disobey. Personally, though, I don't approve of saying 'yes' to this guy at any time. Not ever."

"Not even as a tactic to catch him?"

" 'Yes' is a mind-set. You start by saying 'yes' and sometimes you find you can't turn it into a 'no' when you want. You can't *un*melt a snowflake, you know what I mean?"

Stoner fished a strand of spaghetti out of the boiling water with a fork, and nibbled the tip. "Another minute," he said.

"So if it were up to me," DZ went on, "you'd be doing everything possible to make sure this guy got the message that no matter what he does he won't ever be heard or seen on the public airwaves." She took a breath. "But that hasn't happened. A dialogue's already begun. This creep got his foot in the door, and I think he already senses he's got a chance of doing his whole pitch, and maybe even making the sale."

"To sell what?" Stoner said. "What's he doing this for?"

As if he didn't know, she thought. "C'mon, Mr. Stoner—"

"Please," he put in, "Barry."

She skipped past it. "You know why they *all* come on your show. They want to sing 'me me me,' and the rest of the words don't matter. This guy just wants to top all the rest, and what he's selling along with himself is . . . the lure of murder."

He gazed at her thoughtfully a moment. "So what kind of cooperation do you want from me? I mean you, not Leacock."

"The M.G. says he'll come Thursday. You have three shows before then. Starting tomorrow spend some time on each show to send a message that you won't talk to him under any—"

She was distracted by a musical chime from a timer noting that the spaghetti was done. Stoner tested another strand from the pot, gave a satisfied nod, and moved the pot to a sink to drain it into a colander. "Go on," he said.

"You see, Mr. Stoner, this man—"

"Barry," he reminded her.

"Barry," she allowed. "What you should understand is that this man is . . . a kind of terrorist. We ought to take the same position as when dealing with any terrorists—not to negotiate under any circumstances."

" 'Terrorist' is a pretty strong term, isn't it? This man hasn't done anything so terrible yet. He's just . . . well, 'nuisance' was *your* word."

"It doesn't matter what you call him—as long as you don't let him on TV and talk to him."

Stoner put the spaghetti in a serving dish, took garlic bread from the oven, and brought out the plates.

She let the silence last rather than nag him.

"Come to the table," he said finally.

He dished out the spaghetti and poured sauce on it with the air of ceremony that comes naturally to cooks who care. Surveying the nicely prepared table, DZ wondered if it was meant to be Step One in a seduction. Who were Stoner's women? Where had he been when he wasn't at either of his homes?

Before eating, he raised his wineglass to her. "To making the world a safer place," he toasted. She matched the gesture, and they sipped. "Like it?" he asked.

"Nice," she replied. Playing dumb. She'd expected the wine to be magnificent from the moment she'd seen the label on the bottle, a Gaja Barbaresco, '67. Growing up in a bar had given DZ's schooling in wines a good start. This one, she knew, cost enough to put it in bribe territory: the last time she'd seen a '67 Gaja on a restaurant menu the price was over six hundred dollars a bottle.

She set her glass down. "You're not going to let it go, are you? You want to play it for all it's worth."

Stoner waggled his head, the kind of amiable half-yes Ronald Reagan had made famous. "DZ, you're the cop here. I don't understand why you're against anything that puts this guy in reach."

"But you *do* understand the power a program like yours has to influence people. If this man threatens to kill someone, and does . . . and all the while you're talking to him, it gives him a kind of legitimacy. It's like . . . legalizing murder."

At last DZ tried the spaghetti. Grudgingly, she found it superb.

"Be logical," Stoner said. "This guy can't get beyond step one. As for letting him on once : . . . well, I won't deny

I want to display the whole range of human behavior."
Stoner took a quick sip of his wine, eager to continue.
"That's why my audience looks to me—to see how diverse
human nature can be, the best and the worst."

"So as long as it's entertaining, anything goes," she said
acidly.

"Entertaining isn't the standard I apply."

"What is?"

"Fascinating. I'm fascinated by the strange things people do, and I share my fascination with the world."

Their eyes held, and she wondered what had brought
him to his curious vocation, formed a fascination in which
he seemed to regard humankind the way an entomologist
might regard an ant colony.

He motioned to her plate. "You've hardly touched your
pasta."

He looked so guileless. DZ was conscious of the attraction again—and she slammed her will against it. "Listen,
Mr. Stoner—"

"I thought we settled the name thing, DZ?"

"No. We haven't settled anything, and I won't be side-
tracked by wine tastings and trading recipes for spaghetti
sauce. So I'm back on duty." She pushed her chair away
from the table. "I'd like you to use your next three programs to take a moment to say something that might talk
this man into giving himself up—and affirming that he'll
never be given airtime."

Stoner washed a mouthful of spaghetti down with wine.
"I'll consider it."

"It's about time the police also spoke to the executives
at your network," she said. "They may have something to
say about this."

"What happens on my program is entirely up to me."

"So you haven't spoken to them?"

"No, but I don't mind if you do. I know how Skip will
react."

"Skip . . . ?"

"Edward Corcoran, top man at GBC. He's known as Skip—short for Skipper—from his hobby, sailboat racing."

"I will talk to him," DZ said.

He gave her another amiable Reagan head waggle.

DZ looked at her wine glass. She longed for another taste of the Gaja, but wouldn't back down from her business-only stand. "That covers it," she said, laying her napkin onto the table. "I'll count on you not to do anything that makes the situation worse."

He sipped from his wine. "I wish I could persuade you to stay," he said. "I opened such an incredible bottle."

"Yeah, I know. But it's been a long day." She stood. He started to rise with her. "Don't bother," she said. "I remember the way out."

He eased back into his chair. "Good night, DZ," he called as she left.

"Good night, Mr. Stoner."

Crossing the foyer again, she happened to notice that painted into the *trompe l'oeil* mural, there was a farmhouse, very small, giving it the perspective of being on the distant edge of the field of wildflowers.

He must like being reminded, she thought, of how very far he had come.

CHAPTER
11

*I*N THE DAYS leading up to Thursday, DZ worked the task force hard, keeping everyone on double shifts and sending them out to pursue every strand of the pitifully spare leads they had.

Among her own tasks was to follow through on interviewing Edward Corcoran, the man with ultimate responsibility for determining the broadcast policy of GBS. But DZ found herself stonewalled by Corcoran's secretary. "I'm sorry, Mr. Corcoran is out of the country at the moment," the secretary said.

"Where is he?"

"I'm not at liberty to say. He's involved with confidential negotiations."

"The next time you talk to him, tell him to call the NYPD Intelligence Division," DZ commanded.

But her calls were never returned.

Finally, she called the commissioner's office. Everyone knew Leacock was tight with a number of Wall Street biggies; it was widely assumed he was trolling for a high-paying job in the corporate sector for whenever he gave up being a policeman. If she couldn't get through to Corcoran, the commissioner surely could. The first dep intercepted her call, however. He promised DZ that the commissioner would speak to Mr. Corcoran and explain the importance of his getting in touch directly with her about the investigation.

She had taken the precaution of assigning several detectives to maintain live surveillance at Stoner's offices and studio. Her sense of the M.G., from everything he'd said and done so far, was that he'd hew exactly to the schedule he'd set; take pride in doing it. But she didn't want to be caught off guard if he decided to apply the element of surprise.

On Monday, she joined the other detectives to watch from backstage as Stoner presented a show called "Romeo and Juliet in our Town," a gathering of parents, educators, and clergy to discuss two teenagers who had killed themselves in a suicide pact after being forbidden to pursue a puppy-love relationship. Stoner gave not even a fraction of the show to making the kind of statement DZ had requested.

She didn't go to the studio on Tuesday, but took an hour to watch the show in her office along with Gable. This time, the talk show host set aside a minute right before the program ended for a special message. The camera moved in on a close-up of Stoner, his face set in an expression of earnest concern.

"I'd like to take just a moment to address someone who's been offering to appear on this program for a purpose that . . . well, let me say only that it's a matter that indicates this individual is very disturbed. At the request of the police, I'm making this announcement so this man will know that everyone here is cooperating fully with the authorities to see that he's apprehended. But my hope is that he'll come forward voluntarily and allow us to arrange for him to have the kind of help he obviously needs." The camera pulled back as Stoner signed off with a quiet, "See you tomorrow, everyone," and the show's usual closing music played.

DZ realized at once that the way he'd contrived to do it

worked against what she'd intended. There was no firm
avowal that the appearance would never be tolerated. Instead, Stoner was building it up, introducing it into the
awareness of his audience, creating curiosity.

Infuriated, DZ increased efforts to reach Corcoran and
protest. She knew now that no appeal to Stoner would
make a difference.

On Wednesday when she watched the show, her fury only
increased. At the very beginning of the show, he made reference to an increased volume of viewer inquiries about the
Mystery Guest—introducing the name for the first time—as
a result of his mention the previous day, and then used a
minute to blatantly hype audience expectations for Thursday,
albeit in the guise of merely reporting facts and asking for
public assistance to identify and apprehend the man.

"He's been in contact with us to say he'll appear tomorrow to talk more about his plans and his motives. Of
course, that seems unlikely to say the least. But if any of
you out there have information about who this man might
be, please call me. Or call the Intelligence Division of the
New York City Police and speak to Lieutenant DZ Hayes.
You may also want to tune in tomorrow, to see how this
turns out."

At the very end of the hour, he reminded the audience
that the next day's show had at least the potential to give
them a viewing experience that was "completely unique to
my show . . . or, in fact, any other."

Meanwhile, there wasn't a shred of progress in the investigation. The only new development was a sudden
flood of tips from people who'd heard Stoner's appeal for
help, and knew or suspected someone of having offered to
appear on his show for nefarious purposes. They'd have to
be sorted through for anything remotely useful, but as for
how long that would take . . . God only knew.

And then it was Thursday.

CHAPTER
12

*I*N THE SATELLITE monitor center on the 45th floor of the GBS tower, three engineers sat at long control consoles facing a wall of eighty-six screens, most small, arranged in squares around a few larger ones. The men's faces were softly lit by the bluish glow of digital readouts displaying the status of the several communications satellites comprising GBS's Skyseeker system. At any time in a twenty-four-hour cycle, at least one of these satellites was accessible to signals sent up from the surface of the earth to be bounced back down and gathered in to parabolic antennae. On the roof of the GBS tower, twelve of these computer-guided parabolic dishes tracked the satellites as they whizzed through space 9,000 to 12,000 miles above the earth's surface at a speed of 17,000 miles per hour.

At present, many of the small monitor screens were blank but for white numbers and letters against a plain, black background—noting each satellite's current location over the earth's landmass in precise coordinates, the time it had last passed over the sky above New York, and the time it would reappear. But several screens were alive with images coming from every corner of the globe.

In Moscow's Red Square, a GBS correspondent transmitted a report on riots over recent food shortages to be taped and used on the evening news three hours from now. In Jerusalem, a camera crew collected shots of a supermarket where a mother and her two children had been blown to bits by a suicide bomber.

Other screens displayed a mosaic of images—a golf tournament in Hawaii, a flood in Pakistan, a forty-car pileup on a foggy Belgian highway. The large central screens displayed the program currently going out on the network, or live, remote feeds waiting to be patched on. To one side, a separate bank of monitors was showing images of streets around the GBS tower, cops talking by barricades, angles on different building entrances—sent from cameras set up solely to cover the Mystery Guest story.

At their control bank, the three engineers switched tape machines on and off as various reports began or ended, and adjusted controls to keep satellite reception free of "hash"—the visual interference caused by storms in the high atmosphere. A soft litany filled the room as they spoke into headsets, confirming contact with a transmitting reporter, or giving instructions to improve the signal.

"Take that last paragraph over, Charlie. You got lost in the hash for a second."

"Okay, Johnny, ready for your golf bit."

"Two more minutes on the riot before we lose signal."

Every satellite transmission was prebooked, the time and channels used by the networks reserved on a regular basis. Engineers prepared for incoming downlinks against a computerized log, so when anything unexpected lit up one of the monitors it was noticed no less quickly than an air-traffic controller spotting a UFO in heavily used airspace.

"Maury, look there," a rangy, laconic engineer named Dan said to another. "What's that on twenty-six? We got nothing booked."

An older, heavyset man tilted his head back to examine

the top tier of monitors. A screen running black until a minute ago showed the corner of a small room with white walls and a gray carpet, unfurnished except for a single chair at the center. As two engineers watched, the camera eye panned the room slowly.

"Sid, looka' this," Maury said, alerting the third engineer. They watched, and each referred to his log of planned transmissions. "That bird's not supposed to be in range for another five, six minutes," Maury proclaimed.

Sid, busy keeping tabs on a news transmission, went back to watching a different monitor. But Maury and Dan, still eyeing the white-walled room, saw a figure move into view from behind the camera, a stout man in dark blue trousers and blouse with lines of white piping and a white cap on his head—a sailor in traditional navy issue, his face masked by dark glasses and an ample, dark beard. He walked to the chair and sat down. Looking straight into the camera with as much presence as any regular anchorman, he then spoke a rather jocular, "Ahoy there," after which he added only four more words.

"Holy shit!" Maury shouted.

"Get Pettick here," said Dan. *"Fast."*

The third man had already grabbed the phone.

NED PETTICK, CHIEF OF GBS'S NEWS DIVISON, BURST INTO the Sat-Center minutes later. A heavyset man with thinning sandy hair, he arrived puffing and red-faced after a brief ride in the tower's superfast elevators and a dash along the corridors. "Where?" he panted.

"Twenty-six," said Maury. "Bugger hasn't moved."

Pettick looked at the picture of the seated sailor, calm and erect in his chair.

"Jesus," Pettick muttered. "You sure that's him?"

"Told us," Dan replied. "Said 'I'm your Mystery Guest.' "

Pettick stared at the screen another second. "Throw

video down to something lower, will ya? I'm getting a crick in my neck."

Maury flipped a couple of toggles, and the picture lit several previously dark screens on the lowest bank.

"You rolling tape?" Pettick asked.

"Shit, no," Maury said, and threw a switch to start. "We were so spooked."

"What's it coming in on?" Pettick asked.

"Skyseeker 4," Dan said.

Pettick clawed a hand through his thinning hair. "Any idea where he's got the uplink?"

"A bounce off that bird?" Dan said. "Gotta be southwest quad con-U." Short for continental United States.

"Well," Pettick said tartly, "that only covers a few million square miles." He snatched up a phone from the control bank and barked at a switchboard operator. "Get me security."

"We ought to be able to take coordinates for that transmission off the satellite computer."

"So get busy!" Pettick snapped. His connection came through on the phone. "The Mystery Guest is here. . . . No, not *right* here—on the SAT. Get hold of that cop Hayes and hustle her up here asap."

DZ HAD BEEN WITH STONER IN THE STUDIO. SHE ARRIVED with Gable in two minutes, trailed by a pair of network security men, an NYPD squad commander, and his deputy. The commander was in charge of the police who were scattered around the GBS building. No one had anticipated the satellite trick—though now it seemed so obvious: all the man had said was that he'd "appear" on the show.

Pettick pointed DZ to the row of five, small screens now showing the identical picture of the bearded sailor seated in the bare, monochromatic chamber. "He told us who he was—that's all. Not a peep since. I've tried to make contact over the same link, but we're not sure he hears us."

DZ stared at it. "How are you getting this transmission?"

"Satellite uplink."

"From where."

"Hard to say. Could be mobile equipment—like our news vans. Or maybe from a navy ship cruising somewhere—they all have satellite transmitters aboard."

DZ discounted that idea. The sailor suit was surely a disguise, along with the navy-type beard. The possibility of a news van she took more seriously. One could be stolen, or hijacked. "Can't you pinpoint where he's sending from?"

Pettick looked to Maury, who had moved to a computer keyboard to try getting more exact coordinates off the satellite. He had been punching at the keys with increasing frustration since before DZ had arrived.

"Computer doesn't have it," the engineer said. "Your boy up there must know enough about the system to make contact without giving away his position."

The security men standing behind DZ were murmuring among themselves. "You guys aren't needed here," she snapped. The GBS men left slowly, reluctant to abandon a front-row seat. She turned to Pettick. "Any chance he's near?"

"I don't know. Maury—?" he referred to the engineer.

"Not likely. The bird bouncing this is now above latitude degree three-nine, longitude one-oh-two. It would get the clearest bounce up from the land mass directly below."

"Which is?" DZ asked.

"Western United States," Gable put in. He often surprised DZ with what he happened to know.

"Southwest," Dan amended. "California over to Colorado, Mexican border up to mid-Wyoming."

"So there's no chance he's nearby?" DZ persisted.

"Not unless he routed a signal from here out to there," Pettick said, "and then sent it up."

DZ whirled to the squad commander. "Put out a call for our cars in the area to sweep the streets, twenty blocks in every direction. Look for a van with one of those dishes on the top. Any one you spot, seize and enter."

"Lieutenant Hayes," Pettick objected. "There's apt to be a dozen news vans from all the networks cruising in that area."

"Right. And our guy just might be in one of them. Get on it, Commander." He left, taking his deputy. DZ frowned as she watched him go. As firmly as she had to speak to quell opposition, she doubted the sweep would lead anywhere. Still, every base had to be covered. She looked back to the engineers. "I assume whatever comes in here can be fed to what goes out on the network."

They nodded in unison.

Glancing at a clock above the engineers' station, she saw it was 3:54—six minutes until Stoner went on. She looked at the sailor again, here as promised to do his live give-and-take. "Give me your headset," she said to Pettick. He handed it over, and she spoke into the mike without wearing it. "Hey, sailor. Do you hear me?" There was a movement of his beard around the mouth—a smile. He didn't answer, but she knew that he'd heard. "What would it take to get you to bag this whole thing—call it off without hurting anyone?"

A voice came back clearly. "Am I speaking to the lovely police Lieutenant Hayes?"

So he knew her name. Probably from the time Stoner had mentioned it on the air. "Yeah, this is Hayes," she barked.

"Your question will be answered when I talk to Stoner," he replied. "I'll say nothing more until then."

Glancing again at the clock, she saw it had advanced another minute. "Clark, get down to the studio and make sure Stoner knows his guest is here."

"Then we're really putting him on?"

"Commissioner's orders," she reminded him. Gable hurried out.

DZ spoke into the headset again. "C'mon, sailor, just a little preview? Tell me why."

There was a tiny movement of the beard again, but it didn't surprise her that no answer came: he did everything exactly as he said he would. Even his costume was testament to the ability of this strangely warped sociopath to turn a seemingly idle remark into a pledge: a sailor's trousers were traditionally "bell-bottoms." She gave the headset back to Pettick. "I'm going to watch from the studio."

"You realize what you're up against?" Pettick said. "I mean, this guy must be some kinda fuckin' wonderboy to pull this off—manage the uplink, fudge the computer, hide his location. . . ."

"Yeah—not to mention he showed up just the way he promised," DZ observed as she went out the door. "With bells on."

CHAPTER
13

TODAY THE PROGRAM didn't start with Stoner's usual opening yellow-on-blue logo and the perky theme music. Just the talk show host standing alone, nervously fingering a handheld mike, followed by a close-up of him looking straight into the camera. Candelli had suggested the no-frills approach to underline the grim reality. Another difference was that there was no studio audience. Stoner spoke solely for the cameras: "Ladies and gentlemen . . ." he took a deep breath and closed his eyes a moment, well-practiced tics his habitual viewers associated with a need to compose himself. He opened his eyes and resumed. "As many of you may know, I've always been open to viewers who call with ideas for shows, or who offer to be my guests to talk about their problems. Well, recently we heard from a man—" Stoner paused again, and gave a puzzled bemused shake of his head—"a man who calls himself the Mystery Guest. He told us he wants to appear with me and have a give and take about his desire to—" dead stop, and a moment to exhibit a frown of distaste—"to commit murder."

In the control booth, the director called for a shot from a different camera: Stoner pacing across the stage.

"Until minutes ago, I couldn't imagine he'd really find a way to be on the show even once without getting hauled off to the booby hatch." Stoner faced the camera again, and the director called for a close-up. "But he has. He's beamed himself into our studios by satellite. So today, in a program unlike anything ever done before, you're going to meet a man who'll confess to you that he intends to kill one or more of his fellow human beings. And then, he says, he'll come back again to . . . to share the experience with all of us. Who this man is—who he plans to kill—when and why? We don't know any of the answers."

New angle, and a more matter-of-fact tone. "But it's because we're hoping to get them that he's being allowed this appearance today. Hoping for answers, I should add, in the interest of saving lives." With a practiced look of regret—that momentary bite of his lip, another familiar tic—he said, "I guess that's all the introduction we need." He cast his eyes up to the control booth and nodded.

The sat-link went to network. On TV screens all across the country, viewers saw the bearded, dark-spectacled sailor suit sitting in a monochromatic, cell-like room, hands folded, eyes down. It seemed he was unaware of being observed.

"You're on with me now, sir," Stoner's voice was heard.

The sailor lifted his head, dark glasses aimed squarely at the camera. "Good day to you, Barry," he said cheerfully. "Glad you could make it."

The picture changed to show Stoner on stage, but now beside him was a large television monitor with the satellite picture shown life-sized. " 'Glad I could make it.' " Stoner mimicked sardonically, as if *he* were the guest and this intruder the *host*. "Listen, is there something I can call you aside from Mystery Guest? You took that from an old TV game show, and I don't like trivializing this to that."

A split-screen format came on, the two men side by side.

"But that's what it is," said the Mystery Guest. "Call it . . . let's see, how about 'Catch the Killer'—the game all America loves to play. If it helps, though, for today you can just call me 'Sailor' "

"What's that about? You don't really have anything to do with the navy . . . ?"

"I needed a disguise. This one's as good as any."

Stoner paced the stage, taking a moment to choose his next question. The Guest's reactions were all so eerily natural that he felt himself relaxing into the mode that had carried him through thousands of other shows, confident his natural curiosity would form questions any average viewer would ask.

"You've said your purpose in appearing here is to talk about committing murder. It's a hell of a scheme, as fascinating as it is demented. What can you tell us about yourself to explain this violent wish, and going about it this way."

Glancing down, the Guest ran pinched fingers very slowly along his navy blue trousers to sharpen the crease. He seemed to be working to keep his emotions under control. "Make no mistake, Barry," he said at last, looking up, "I'm not some guilt-ridden screwball with a subconscious desire to aid in my own downfall. Don't expect me to reveal anything that helps you identify me. I'll only talk about what I intend to do."

"So why *this* way?" Stoner insisted, agitated. "Bringing me into it!" He waved at the camera. "Everyone!"

"Oh c'mon," the Guest said with a belittling tone. "There's nothing new about that. The media jumps on a story, the public gobbles it up. Usually it's only after killers or bombers or whatever claim their victims. I just thought I'd play along from the very inception, let you know exactly what you're dealing with."

"Okay then," Stoner said hotly. "Let's hear it!" He snatched a clipboard from beneath his arm and his eyes grazed the top sheet—Lori's notes of the M.G.'s first call.

"In contacting us, you proposed to come on and tell us about these murders—how you'd do it, who your victims would be—not the exact names, perhaps, but the sort of person—and explain why they should die. All right, Sailor . . . deliver!"

The harsher interrogatory style seemed designed to dramatize Stoner's moral distance from the murderous stranger.

The Guest wasn't shaken. "The why is simple," he said mildly. "The people I'm going to kill deserve to die." He looked squarely into the camera. "When the victims are known, I'm sure most of you out there will agree I did a good deed."

Stoner paced wider circles around the stage, easing off the adversarial tone while probing for insight. "If you really believe my audience might approve, test it. Give us a name or two, tell us why they deserve—"

"Sorry, Barry, no advance warnings."

Stoner took a new tack. "You said you'd also tell us how it would be done."

"I'm a hunter," the Guest said. "And we're in the land of the gun."

"Shootings, then?"

"That's right, Barry. I'm going to—what's that phrase the police use?—shoot to kill."

"And when?"

"Let's see," the sailor said, as if simply calculating the time of a low tide, "today's Thursday . . . perhaps I could come back and see you again on Monday."

"That soon?"

"Or a week from Monday. . . ."

"Monday," Stoner repeated. "I thought you were Thursday's child."

"Oh," he said, "I'm Monday's child, too."

• • •

DZ WATCHED FROM THE CONTROL BOOTH, GABLE STANDING beside her. But they weren't the only visitors. Behind the console for the director and engineers, the booth was crammed with GBS executives. From their perspective, a piece of broadcasting history was being made. Conspicuous among the spectators, standing at the shoulder of the show's director, was the man who had introduced himself to DZ before the show as Edward Corcoran, President of GBS. Periodically, DZ saw his tall frame lean over as he murmured to the director.

While most of the booth's spectators watched silently, the engineers and the director kept up a muted patter "Go to camera two . . . Ernie, clean up sound . . . head shot on four." A litany as eerily mundane as the Mystery Guest's own matter-of-fact tone.

The Mystery Guest's reference to himself as a hunter was now being pursued by Stoner. "You talk about hunting as if the people you're going after are nothing more than animals."

"These are. They made the choice not to be human."

"So now you're playing God—deciding where everyone fits into your animal kingdom."

The sailor weighed his reply quietly. In the lull, DZ tried to see past the disguise. The contours of his face could have been altered with makeup, his nose transformed by a blob of putty, the hair a wig. The man was so at ease in front of the cameras, he might indeed be an actor, skilled at makeup.

"I wouldn't presume to play God, Barry," he answered at last. "But if He exists, we can be sure of one thing: I'm one of His creatures, too. So whatever happens must be His will."

Stoner looked suddenly like a lawyer outsmarted by a witness in the box. He'd raised the subject of God, but the answer he'd gotten made pursuing it a dangerous proposition. He spun toward a camera, a move the show's director understood called for giving Stoner a tight, full close-up.

"Ladies and gentlemen, due to the nature of this program, many of our sponsors have waived their time. But not all . . . so we'll pause for those messages."

It took DZ a moment to absorb it. She gazed dumbly at a monitor as a commercial for hand cream came on. Then she exploded. Charging through the pack of spectators, she shouted furiously. "Corcoran, goddammit! Get that shit off the air! This bastard won't sit still for that crap! We're going to lose him!"

"Hell we will," Corcoran replied coolly. "He knows what he bargained for coming on a show like this."

DZ glanced around at the clustered executives. "I don't believe you people! We're trying to catch a homicidal maniac—and it's still business as usual!"

"And don't you think *he* knows it?" Corcoran shot back, flinging a hand toward a monitor screening the satellite image of the sailor. "Look at him!"

As earlier, the sailor was sitting in a quiet pose, waiting for contact with him to resume.

Corcoran went on, "This isn't your bleeding-heart public broadcasting; this show *always* runs by different rules. Barry's had every kind of criminal on—devil worshippers, cannibals, guys who chopped up their wives and stuffed 'em in the garbage disposal. And every ten minutes it's still 'time out for these messages.' We gave sponsors today an option to use their time or not. Some opted out." He shrugged. "Some didn't."

"Which means they'll *all* come back rather than lose a competitive edge."

Corcoran smirked. "That's showbiz."

DZ stared at him in mute frustration. Showbiz? This was life and death!

Corcoran moved away as one of the lesser execs called to him, "Skip, can I have a word . . . ?"

Skip. The name did it for DZ, suddenly made the connection. Short for *skipper,* she remembered, a legacy of his hobby. DZ thought of what the Mystery Guest had said about his disguise: this one seemed as good as any. So he was a sailor . . . and Corcoran was captain of the ship. She understood it now, another of the M.G.'s hidden messages revealed: the skipper was responsible for this situation, not a mere yeoman.

DZ was aware suddenly of the broadcast monitor showing Stoner in front of a large screen projecting the sailor in his anonymous room.

"We're back live now," Stoner announced to the camera, "continuing this unprecedented conversation with a man who's planning a murder spree, and wants to tell us about it." He turned to the large monitor. "You've told us about why you picked your victims. What about . . . why you picked yourself to do this. How were you brought up? What goes into making someone like you?"

"I told you earlier, I won't talk about anything that would help the authorities."

Stoner paused. Aware he'd lost a subject that would have held the audience, he was uncertain where to go next. "Okay, you've got the floor. What do *you* want to talk about?"

The sailor was ready and waiting. "Let me state this first: if you want me back on this program, Barry, don't ever make me sit through another two minutes of those shit commercials. There are lives at stake here. It disgusts me to see how little that seems to matter to you."

DZ was astonished to find herself inwardly cheering for her criminal prey. She shot a look at Corcoran, standing nearby with his arms folded. He tipped her a glance and a conciliatory smile.

"Now," the sailor said, "maybe I can throw a little light on my first—what shall I call him?—my catch of the day. This person won't be a stranger to you, Barry."

Stoner blanched. "Wait a second, you wouldn't—"

"Oh, I *would.* I'll do *any damn thing* I want."

Stoner's tone became faintly pleading. "Look, I don't want anyone hurt—no one—but none of the people close to me fits your criteria at all, would deserve—"

The Guest cut him off. "We'll see."

"Listen, this—"

"No, you listen!" For the first time, the eerie amiability of the Guest vanished and an underlying rage was bared to the camera. Cords of muscle in his neck stood out as he snarled: "This isn't a negotiation. I'll set the terms, and any time you get tired of hearing them, fine . . . tune me out, switch me off. But it won't change what's going to happen." He sat back, and the tension in his face and body eased a little. "For now, we've reached the point where actions will speak louder than talk. So that's it for today, Barry—my part of it. Here's looking at you, kid. Till next time . . ." He raised a hand, palm outward, in a gesture equally reminiscent of a farewell wave and a witness taking an oath. Then the other hand moved to the underside of his chair and in the next second the transmission ended.

"The bastard switched off!" The director cried. "What the hell happens now?"

"Wait to see who he shoots," said one of the anonymous executives.

"That's later," the director bellowed. "I mean *now*, for chrissakes. We've still got forty fuckin' minutes of airtime to kill!"

CHAPTER
14

*O*VERNIGHT THE INVESTIGATION mushroomed into an all-out manhunt. Now that the Mystery Guest had shown himself, new leads were expected to develop fast. Leacock authorized DZ to pull another forty detectives from other precincts and take over any facilities needed to house expanded operations. To facilitate liaison with Stoner and GBS, DZ arranged to lodge the whole "M.G. Task Force" in a building farther uptown also used by the Intelligence Division—called "The Triple Nickel" because the building number was 555.

Since the M.G. had warned that the victim would be known to Stoner, his production offices were put under police guard. Stoner, Candelli, and Lori Swann were given additional armed bodyguards paid for by the network. The threat prompted DZ to feel the genesis could be rooted somewhere in Stoner's past. She needed to dig into it, she thought, go deeper than the biographical material she'd already seen that was obviously shaped by people with an interest in guarding Stoner's image. DZ assigned a young police administrative assistant at Intelligence named Julie

Nelson to check databases for information about Stoner
other than stuff put out by network publicity.

The investigation was also joined by the FBI. Within an
hour of the end of Thursday's broadcast, the police commissioner was contacted by Kenneth Chafee, chief of the
Bureau's New York field office, to request a full briefing
on the status of the case. Leacock told him to contact the
commanding officer of the Task Force.

Chafee's call to DZ came that evening while she was
setting up her new command post at the Triple Nickel. The
improper use of nationwide communications facilities,
Chafee explained, had brought the case within FBI jurisdiction.

"So you're taking it over. . . ." DZ said, dispirited.

"No. We'll work in tandem with you. There's plenty of
cause for you to be fully involved. Tell me what you've
done so far."

Relieved, DZ gladly filled him in, and admitted that
hardly any concrete progress had been made.

"No reason to feel bad," Chafee said. "Took us seventeen years to get the Unabomber."

DZ liked the sound of the FBI agent, and quickly agreed
to supply him with copies of all relevant evidence, such as
the tape found in Stoner's studio. She agreed, too, that the
Bureau, with agents in field offices throughout the western
U.S. was far better equipped to take the lead in pinpointing
the location from which the satellite transmission had been
made.

"I'll have the Psych Unit at our serial killer squad in Virginia do an analysis," the agent said, "and share the results
with you soon as I have them."

After speaking with Chafee, DZ felt foolish that she
hadn't availed herself of these facilities right at the start.
Chafee seemed reasonably sensitive to the issues of jurisdiction and willing to recognize the contribution she could
make.

Though if a psychological analysis was going to be done, DZ decided, why leave it entirely to the Bureau?

THE TAPE FINISHED REWINDING. DZ PUSHED THE PLAY BUTton and the now-familiar voice and image reappeared:

Good afternoon, Barry. Glad you could make it.

This was the sixth time she was rerunning yesterday's program. Seated across a conference table from DZ and Gable, listening through the playbacks, was Dr. Marilyn DeJesus, one of several psychologists attached to the NYPD. As she listened, DeJesus scribbled constantly on a steno pad in her lap.

A tall, slim Hispanic woman in her mid-forties, elegantly groomed in a dark tailored suit, the psychologist's regular duty was to provide therapy for policemen suffering job-related stress. In the eighteen years she had worked for the department, Marilyn DeJesus had also built up a successful outside practice, and launched a happy marriage to a radiologist. By now what the police paid her was a minor part of her earnings, but she had once told DZ that this was the work she cared about most—her way of "giving something back." DZ had met and formed a high regard for Marilyn DeJesus at the time she was at Sex Crimes. There had been a particularly horrendous rape, a lovely young woman, not only sexually violated in the most perverse and vicious ways but bludgeoned so that she was left with the mental capacity of a nine-year-old. DZ had become so totally wrapped up in the case she had broken down on the stand when called to testify against the apprehended rapist. It was suggested she seek counseling, and DeJesus had been a wise and helpful adviser.

So that's it for today, Barry—my part of it. Here's looking at you, kid. Till next time. . . . The sailor raised his hand, palm outward, the farewell gesture, and the screen on the monitor went black.

"That's enough, DZ," DeJesus said. "I think I've gotten all I can."

"Okay, Doc, run it down."

DeJesus flipped her pages of notes back and forth, absorbing what she had written. "The overall picture takes no great insight." She spoke quietly, the faintest trace of a Spanish accent giving her inflection a pleasant musical lilt. "He speaks well, and takes pains to be polite. Coming from a man whose ultimate purpose is to terrify and harm, this exaggerated friendliness is passive-aggressive behavior in its most extreme form. A personality capable of this would be the same that might thank someone whose throat he was about to cut for being good enough to sit still."

"Or someone he's about to shoot," Gable put in.

"An iceman," DZ said.

"Yes, a sociopath of chilling dimensions. Yet it would be characteristic of such a personality to be absolutely aware of the normal distinctions between right and wrong—with one gray area. He reserves the privilege of defining for himself the outer limits of those two opposites." She rested her glittering, dark eyes on DZ, then Gable, making sure they had followed this much.

It was DZ who put it into capsule form. "What you're saying, Marilyn, is that—by the customary legal definition—this guy isn't crazy."

"I'm not just splitting hairs, DZ. In my opinion, he's fully functional, self-aware, and—from what we can hear—probably strikes people he meets in the course of his daily life as very likable, even charming. Not at all the common profile of those who commit crimes like this to attract attention—usually assumed to be an introverted loner, a repressed social misfit."

"Isn't it possible," Gable asked, "the M.G. *is* a misfit who just talks smooth when he's safely hidden behind a phone or a phony beard."

DeJesus shook her head. "What I hear on that tape is a

level of self-confidence that never falters. What you hear is what you'll get."

"If we get him," Gable said.

"Okay," DZ chimed in, "we know we're not looking for a bug who lives in a hole and never takes a bath. Keep going, Marilyn."

DeJesus consulted her pad. "In the notes I saw of his earliest call, he said that if Mr. Stoner liked his offer they could 'do business.' Taken along with the confidence, other hints about the kind of figure he cuts, it's possible he thinks literally in these terms—that he could be an executive, even quite successful."

"The figure he cuts," DZ echoed "What do you mean, Marilyn?"

"As careful as he was to hold back information about himself and disguise his appearance, he quite willingly— indeed, purposely—did provide one item of physical self-description."

DZ thought she knew what the psychologist was referring to. "Monday's child," she said.

DeJesus nodded. "Exactly. The familiar child's rhyme says 'Monday's child is fair of face.' Suppose for him, it was . . . a kind of boasting while drunk with the achievement of bringing the first part of his plan to fruition, appearing before millions of people. Then perhaps the description can be given greater weight."

"How?" DZ posed. "Fair of face means nice-looking. Hardly enough for a wanted poster."

"As a boast it suggests more. Handsome. Perhaps even extraordinarily good-looking, charismatic."

"A movie star," Gable said, and DZ saw him wince.

"You may indeed be seeking someone whose looks stand out in a crowd," DeJesus said. "Not impossible— though I'm less sure about this—is that 'fair of face' could even relate to coloring. A pale complexion, or blond hair. This man takes great pleasure in the game element, and would be amused to give one clue several meanings."

That tallied with DZ's intuitions, though narrowing the population down to look-alikes for Redford or Brad Pitt didn't move them a hell of lot closer to nabbing the Mystery Guest before he claimed a life.

DeJesus went on. "Now, put it all together: an outgoing, charming man, who may be outstandingly attractive and talks as if he's got the world on a string. It suggests he would be a success at whatever he attempted. If we grant him a little time to climb the ladder, I'd speculate his age is in the range of late-thirties to mid-forties. In locating him, DZ, consider such a profile goes with a behavior pattern that might yield a pool of informants, people intimate enough with him to notice a pattern of suspicious behavior."

Gable was first to understand. "I get it! The guy would have ladies in and out of his life all the time. Maybe one gets close enough to know his secrets. . . ."

"It's something to hope for down the line." DZ said. "But how do we use it now? Make a public appeal to women everywhere? 'If your boyfriend's a stud who watches talk shows and had a rotten childhood . . . ' " She broke off.

"Significant is that he may be a womanizer." DeJesus said. "A man who likes to exercise his ability to seduce."

"Okay, so he stands out in a crowd and fucks who he pleases. What else?" DZ couldn't hide her impatience. They were starting to produce the likeness of a figure, but it was still so vague, carved out of mist.

DeJesus glanced at her notes. "There's the way he talks about games, calling this 'Catch the Killer.' It has almost a childish element, as if he's merely playing tag. Add that to the use of a nursery rhyme to describe himself, I assume his associations with childhood are not random, that they're close to the surface—could indeed be mixed up in his motive for doing this."

"He got no love 'cause Mommy spent all her time watching talk shows," Gable offered.

DeJesus paused to regard him seriously, as if while being facetious Gable had hit on a useful interpretation.

In the silence, DZ stood and walked around the edges of her new office, larger than the one downtown. It was unfair, she knew, to expect a miraculous breakthrough to come from this kind of speculation. In fact, DeJesus had pulled some possibly useful threads of identity out of very sparse material. Yet it was depressing to confront the gulf that yawned between what they could theorize and what could produce quick results.

The psychologist reviewed her final page. "Ah, this is important. The Mystery Guest obviously has a sharp sense of irony—well, it's right there in the name he chose for himself. But this is where it registered most strongly. After his show of temper about the commercials, he says, 'There are lives at stake here. It disgusts me to see how little that seems to matter to you.' You see? He's the killer, but it's others who don't care about life. He also says that whoever he kills will deserve to die. . . ."

"So what're you telling us?" Gable demanded. "That this is some kind of Boy Scout with a code of honor?"

DeJesus closed her pad. "Let me sum it up. As I see him, the Mystery Guest is an achiever, a man who'll do exactly whatever he says he's going to do, and take pride in doing it well."

"But then what the hell's his motive?" Gable cried out. "He's got the looks, the babes, maybe earning big bucks. With all that success, why the hell go into the threat business and risk losing it all?"

DZ needed an answer, too. "What about it, Marilyn? If everything else you've said *were* true, what could possibly impel him to do this?"

DeJesus hesitated, staring at her notepad. At last she said, "To want to kill—more than that, to want to *announce* to the world his desire to kill—and to have that supersede any other accomplishments, he must be driven by a colossal rage that blinds him to the value of everything else in his life."

"Rage against what?" DZ persisted. "Not just the people he wants to kill. If that were all, he'd go straight after them without all this rigmarole."

DeJesus nodded, agreeing with DZ's logic. "The way he's contrived to use a particular medium, using it in a way that criminalizes and debases it—I'd say the focus of his rage is pretty clear." She glanced to the monitor, the darkened screen that still seemed haunted by the images of the Mystery Guest on Stoner's show that had replayed so many times. "It's beyond me to know why," she concluded. "But certainly one element of what this man hates with a consuming homicidal passion is the very medium itself." She paused and added the defining word:

"Television."

CHAPTER
15

*O*N A SECOND pass around the table in Skip Corcoran's private corporate dining room, one uniformed waiter offered a platter of smoked Scotch salmon and Finnish sturgeon while the other refilled coffee cups. One after another, Candelli, Stoner, and Pettick waved off the food and accepted the coffee.

A silence lasted until the waiters disappeared. It was understood the floor was now to be Corcoran's.

"Skip" Corcoran had been brought to the top job at GBS after successfully piloting several businesses to vastly increased earnings—among them a company that filled the frozen food chests of America with TV dinners, and a chain of auto supply stores that had diversified into video rentals. Corcoran was basically a financial mechanic who'd never worked a day in broadcasting until he'd taken the reins at the network, a "bottom-line" man whose guiding principle was that whatever people would buy should be pumped out in volume at the lowest cost. Back in the '70s he'd come close to being named skipper for the U. S entry in the America's Cup, hence his nickname. At age fifty-seven, he still looked able to take the helm going around Cape Horn in a force nine blow—big and strong across the shoulders with thick, iron-gray hair, and shrewd, hazel eyes that always seemed to be searching the horizon for a rogue wave. His business style, too, owed much to nautical custom, issuing orders in the manner of an admiral commanding his battle fleet. The message he'd wired last night to Stoner, Candelli, and Pettick read simply: "Breakfast tomorrow, 0900 hours. Be there."

Since the Mystery Guest's appearance yesterday on live television, the storm to be weathered under Corcoran's command had continued to gather force. The evening news on all networks had led with the story of a man promising a murder spree on the popular talk show, and the eleven p.m. follow-ups had included the revelations that the man had first contacted Stoner two weeks ago, and background reports on the woeful status of the police investigation since. These had prompted Corcoran—freshly back from London after negotiating for Olympic coverage in 2004— to send out orders for today's breakfast. What particularly stuck in his craw was that his own employees hadn't informed him of the case; in fact, he'd first heard of it not from anyone in the company, but from the police commissioner. Corcoran had spent the earlier part of the breakfast berating Stoner and Candelli for what he regarded as their disloyalty. Then he'd moved on to quizzing them about any other information they'd held back, at which point the fish had been passed again, second cups of coffee poured.

With the waiters gone, Corcoran resumed. "So, who do you think phoned *me* at six this morning?"

"No!" Candelli exclaimed, taking the easy guess.

"No, not your maniac," Corcoran said emphatically. "Senator Francis Tauresco. Since I tossed a check into his last campaign, the senator and I are on very good terms, and my pal Francis wanted to ask me if this whole situation is really as out of control as it seems from studying the news. Tauresco has as much morbid curiosity as any average couch potato; he wanted inside stuff. Well, I wasn't about to tell the senator that I'd been locked out of my own kitchen while this particular shitcake was being baked. The best I could do was feed him some bull about how I was under strict orders from the police not to discuss the thing. Then my buddy Francis moved on to other questions—the kind that are more up the alley of a U.S. senator. Like do I remember that federal broadcasting licenses are subject to congressional oversight, and can be *revoked*?" Cocoran hardened. "And did I recall that Francis himself is chairman of the Internal Affairs committee, which has a subcommittee on communications, and he sits as well on the Senate Banking Committee, which also holds the fate of large corporations in its hands—corporations that have an obligation not to create public panic?" Corcoran took a breath and resumed in a quieter but more acid tone. "You see the problem, gentlemen? Depending on how this thing goes we just might be playing for all the marbles." His eyes bored in on Stoner. "What do you expect to do now that you've made this guy a star if the next thing he does is go butcher someone? Tell me, Barry!" he roared now. "What the fuck do you do for an encore?"

"Easy, Skip," Stoner said. "This isn't the *Bounty* and we're not jumping ship to sail for Pitcairn Island."

Corcoran rewarded the Bligh joke with a thin smile. "Forgive me," he said with exaggerated grace, "but we are up to our necks in an ocean of shit. I am sincerely interested in knowing how you propose to swim through it."

"The script I'm following isn't mine," Stoner pointed out. "The police commissioner thought letting the guy connect with us was the best hope for a good, fast end."

Corcoran gave Stoner an opaque stare, then looked around the table. "You all go along with that? Can we answer for what we do with the good old Nazi excuse that we were only following orders?"

No one said anything.

Corcoran's smoldering eyes made another circuit of the table. "No! People die, we'll be tied to it. Every newspaper is already running editorials about the responsibility of broadcasters." He swung toward Pettick. "You're quiet this morning, Ned. But I presume you know why I included you at this meeting. . . ."

"Well . . . because it's news," Pettick answered.

"And . . . ?"

"You want to know how we're going to cover it."

Corcoran kept the test going. "And . . . ?"

Pettick hesitated. The past few years had taught him the way his boss's mind worked. Corcoran's strategy for making the network cost-effective had been to cut coverage of hard news to the bone—politics, economics, education— while taking what couldn't be cut and transforming it into some form of entertainment. Categorizing a show as "news" shielded it from being judged by the strict standards of public interest watchdog groups. On top of which, if you could make it *entertaining* you could put more of it in prime time, and it was cheaper to produce than sitcoms and cop shows; fake blood cost money, the real stuff was free. So Corcoran put more and more news magazine shows into prime time. News, especially the sensational stories, had become the vein of purest gold in network schedules, and they were always looking to mine more of it.

With that as the rule, Pettick understood what Corcoran was driving at now. "You want my assessment," he said, "of how far we can go with this story, and still be protected."

Corcoran rewarded his news chief with the sort of smile third-graders got from the geography teacher when they named the capitol city of Nebraska.

"It's a First Amendment issue straight down the line." Pettick continued. "Putting this guy on the air is no different from printing a threat letter from a terrorist. You balance the potential for panic against the public's right to have fair warning. Letting people know this live bomb is out there could fairly be defended as a public service."

Corcoran waved to Stoner. "Does 'freedom of the press' cover Barry, too?"

"At this point," Pettick replied, "he's not reporting the story, he's part of making it. And he's passed the essential litmus test of whether what he does qualifies as news: we're not the only ones putting this story up in lights."

Corcoran stood abruptly and went to a sideboard. He picked up a stack of papers and passed them out. "I called our research department last night and had them run projections on how Barry's viewers will feel if there's a killing. . . ."

Corcoran circled the table silently, letting the men scan the reports for a couple of minutes. "The projections were done overnight," he said then, "so there's an error margin of plus or minus eight percent. Even so, the prospect is for the Monday—when this guy said he'd come back—to be the most watched daylight show since Princess Di rode horizontal through the streets of London."

Candelli tossed his research analysis onto the table. "Then you don't mind . . . ?"

"Naturally, I hope and pray nobody gets hurt." Corcoran spoke as if reading the words off a TelePrompTer. "But we have a duty to report the news."

Pettick interrupted. "Reporting is one thing. But exploitation on this level—"

Corcoran rode over him. "Comes once in a lifetime. There never *has,* never *will* be anything else like this. You understand that, don't you, Barry?"

Stoner's eyes stayed on the ratings projection, though a thin smile acknowledged that he'd heard the question. He said nothing, though.

Corcoran turned back to Pettick. "You're worried about how we define news?" His eyes swept the table. "Look, boys, once upon a time news was reporting what had already happened. But TV made that as outmoded as Ubangis beating jungle drums. Real news isn't what happened yesterday, it's stuff that happens *as we see it*. Missiles falling in Baghdad, bodies being pulled out of the rubble in Oklahoma City, those kids running out of Columbine. As long as it's happening in front of us, it doesn't even have to be real *history*." He resumed his pacing around the table. "So here's the play on this story: full throttle. Lead on all news shows. Late night updates, break-ins for any development. And fill our news mags with special features once—" The momentum paused as he pasted on a look of fatalistic regret. "I mean, *if* he does what he's threatening. Stay in front on this one. Stoner already has the big 'get,' the rest should be ours, too. Barbara, Diane, those fuckers at *Sixty Minutes* go for the gets, chop 'em off at the knees. I want everything nailed down *first*!" His firey glare darted from one man to the next. No one pointed out the impossibility of making *every* get.

But Corcoran took their silence for a pledge. Returning to his place at the table, he sat down. "All this sound okay to you, Barry? You know, if you think you're in any personal danger with this thing, that would change the picture."

"Worried because you like me, Skip? Or because my ratings are up?"

"That's a hell of thing to say. You know I consider you a friend."

Stoner grinned at him, then addressed the question. "I doubt I'm in danger personally, but now that we see how he can come back risk-free, I'm sure he will. And, to be honest, I've got butterflies." He paused as if to let them settle. "But two things still make it viable. We're only cooperating with law enforcement to bring him in. And like you said, Skip, it's a shot at the grabbiest stuff that's ever played our medium—pure television, and one hundred percent *made* for me."

"Then we're all aboard?" Corcoran double-checked Candelli and Pettick with a glance. Candelli nodded. Pettick took a deep breath, and nodded, too.

The discussion turned to plans for Stoner's upcoming

shows. They'd keep the focus on the Mystery Guest. Have a panel of FBI profiling experts. On the chance the M.G. was caught in the next few days, Johnnie Cochran and other legal stars were being lined up to talk about how such a client might be defended.

"And give Tauresco time," Corcoran suggested. "Slot him into some survey on . . . how the federal government is guarding us against . . . " He took a moment to come up with a catchphrase "TV Terrorists. The senator will forgive us anything for ten minutes of free network airtime."

The official position resolved, orders given, the skipper stood and his crew understood they were dismissed.

As they filed out of the dining room, Corcoran had a sudden afterthought. "What about this lady cop, the one in charge of the case? She looks hot. Can we get her for something more personal than the usual ten-mike press conference?"

"She's a line detective," Pettick observed. "Can't do anything but play by the rules, equal access to all."

"Let me deal with that one," Stoner put in.

The others paused to check him with a glance. Something in his tone hinted he might already have an inside track.

CHAPTER
16

*I*N MID-AFTERNOON DZ was summoned down to Police Plaza to front a press conference ordered by the commissioner. Leacock wanted the six o'clock local news and the nationals half an hour later to include the standard police assurances that "everything that can be done is being done." DZ found herself facing a horde of reporters and camera crews that included a large contingent of international press. The vision of a man masquerading as a sailor, promising before millions to commit a number of murders and, as he did, keep returning to a talk show, provided the kind of grabby feature that attracted interest around the world.

Sensational as the case was itself, DZ realized that her own role added extra sizzle. NYPD had never had a woman as the lead detective on a case this big. After facing the barrage of demands for information, and having to admit there was yet to be a single break in determining who M.G. was or what his motives were or why he might have chosen to appear on *Stoner*, DZ was wrung out. She also felt resentful: by forcing her to appear so soon and admit so far her investigation had accomplished nothing, the commissioner could already be laying a foundation to relieve her of command, so a man—one of his protégés—could be moved into the spotlight on this high-profile case. Paranoia? You couldn't be a woman in the department without such thoughts crossing your mind.

She arrived back at the Triple Nickel to find a file folder left on her desk by Julie Nelson, the PAA she'd assigned to look for fresh material on Barry Stoner. She was about to delve into it when Gable sauntered into her office.

"How'd it go?"

"Don't make me tell you, just watch it on the news."

"That bad, eh? Speaking of news, you read your *Times* today?"

"At the moment, I have an aversion to *all* media."

"So you missed this." He tossed down an article clipped from the newspaper. "I happened to catch it during a coffee break—first page of the Business Section."

DZ scanned the clipping. It was headlined GBS ON THE BLOCK? and reported that recently the network had been in quiet talks with Wall Street investment banks about brokering a buyout. Cable and home video had eroded the profitability of "stand-alone" television networks, and GBS's board of directors was looking to sell to a communications conglomerate at a probable sale price, according to the report, "of somewhere between four and five billion dollars."

"Think there could be a connection?" DZ asked Gable.

He shrugged. "Network gets hot, I'd guess the 'somewhere' goes higher."

Estimates on the price already had a billion-dollar spread, DZ reflected. A spike in GBS's popularity might indeed add even a few hundred million. "There's plenty of contract men who'd do a hit for fifty grand," she remarked. "Should be easy to buy murder with all the trimmings for a few million."

Gable said he'd started some checking while she was away, made calls to various brokerages. The attention the network was receiving had already made a difference; after hovering around seventy dollars for a few months, its stock price had risen over the past week to ninety-eight.

DZ raised her eyebrows. "Run with it. Take a group down to Wall Street for a closer look at trading in—"

It was Friday, he reminded her, the market was already closed until Monday.

"Soon as you can let's get the names of the biggest holders and most active buyers of GBS stock. I'd like to know how much Corcoran stands to gain."

"And Stoner," Gable added. He said he'd put together a group of Wall Street commandos for a Monday foray and left.

DZ turned again to the folder on her desk. A note clipped to the cover by the PAA explained that most of what she'd found were magazine pieces similar to what DZ had already seen. However, the information in the file predated all of that.

Inside DZ found photocopies of press cuttings expressed to the Task Force from *The Dalton Falls Journal*—the newspaper in the town where Stoner had been raised. The first bunch of news items concerned the death of Laurel Stoner, twelve, suffocated when she fell into the grain silo on the family farm. From the listing of survivors in a short obituary placed by the local church, DZ determined that the girl had been third in line of the five Stoner children. The death was initially termed "an accident," but a subsequent newspaper article reported that the county attorney had convened an inquest because the previous year another young girl had died in an identical manner on a regional farm. This raised concerns that both girls might be victims of a killer. However, the inquest finally declared the fatal tumble into the silo to be an accidental death, any similarity to the earlier one sheer coincidence.

Another clipping from the hometown paper reported the death of Stoner's mother in the county hospital at the age of forty-six; no exact cause was given, though the item added that "Sarah Stoner had been in poor health for the past three years." Noting that the dates on the stories of the two family tragedies were separated by just three years, DZ perceived that Mrs. Stoner's decline muct have begun with her young daughter's death and guessed that "poor health" could be a small community's euphemism for problems with alcohol.

It puzzled DZ that Stoner had kept these details from being mentioned in any of his official biographies. It surely wouldn't hurt his standing to share a direct experience of the kind of personal tragedy he regularly purveyed on his program.

She was staring toward the doorway, mulling the puzzle over, when she found herself looking at the man. The confluence with her thoughts made her wonder for a few seconds if he was a mirage.

"Aren't you going to invite me in?" Stoner said at last.

He was wearing pearl gray slacks under a dark blazer, with a darker gray patterned shirt, tieless and open at the neck. Casual but stylish.

"To what do I owe the pleasure?"

"You did ask me to come see you at the office. . . ."

"But we had that meeting elsewhere."

"Aren't there new things to talk about?" He advanced across the threshold to the chair in front of her desk. "Mind if I sit?"

She nodded and he sat. "It strikes me as a little odd," she said, "that this late in the day you didn't call ahead to be sure you'd find me here."

"Big investigation, I assumed you're on the job around the clock."

It occurred to her, too, that if she wasn't here, he might have used his starpower to get someone to give him a look at the whole file.

He glanced around the office. Since DZ had only moved in days ago, it was bare of any personal touches. The furniture was all of the institutional gray metal variety, a desk, two wooden chairs, scratched file cabinets atop which piles of paperwork were already accumulating. He brought his eyes back to her. "I suppose it would only make you more suspicious if I suggested we might do our talking someplace more pleasant. Like over dinner—unless you've got other plans. . . ."

Was this what he'd really come for? Step two in a seduction? All right, there was still plenty about Stoner she wanted to learn. "Okay, but nothing fancy."

Outside he had a car and driver waiting, but she stuck to her demand for something basic and suggested they walk a block to Ninth Avenue, where there were several restaurants. He sent the car away.

The April evening was pleasant for walking, yet as soon as they set out DZ regretted accepting his invitation. For a start, Gable had seen her leave with Stoner, and his hangdog look stayed with her. She also felt grubby in the pale green shirtwaist she'd been wearing all day.

As they walked he asked what progress had been made, if any. One new element she didn't mind revealing—though she had withheld it from the press—was the psychological profiling she'd done. She related the conclusions DeJesus had made from things the Mystery Guest had said to Stoner.

Stoner mulled over the analysis. "An executive-type, successful . . . nice looking . . . not crazy. Could be anyone."

"Not quite. None of it's on an average level. The picture is of someone of high achievement, exceptionally good-looking, and probably extremely smart." DZ watched Stoner as she spoke, aware his own image fit reasonably well into the frame.

Soon after turning onto Ninth, they came to a small, popular, French bistro. The man greeting customers recognized Stoner and tried to juice up the place by seating them near the door, but they asked for a table out of the way. A noticeable hush descended as they were led to a rear corner.

A waiter took their drink orders and left—a vodka on ice for Stoner, for DZ a neat Glenfiddich.

"I saw Corcoran this morning," Stoner said then. "He got me wondering if I'm in danger myself. What do you think . . . ?"

Perhaps this was what had brought him to her, a need to be reassured. "The M.G. couldn't see this through without you. You're the last person he'd hurt."

"That's the way I read it." He fiddled with a fork on the table. "Seeing this through—where do you think that will lead?"

"In *his* terms? Killing the people he wants to kill. As for who they are, how many, it's still a blank. But we could start to get the first answers pretty soon."

"Monday," Stoner said quietly.

The drinks came and they sipped thoughtfully.

"If something bad happens," Stoner said, "I suppose you'll blame me, too."

"You gave him the platform."

"If it wasn't me it would've been one of the others."

"No," DZ said strongly. "He picked you because he guessed you'd be the one who'd give him his turn, but the others would back off."

Stoner took another swig of vodka. "Think you've got me down pretty well, don't you, DZ?"

"No, all I've got is a small part, the part I've seen on the box. I've seen that you really do want to get inside the people you talk to you on your show. That's why they open up, because you have a true desire to understand, even a need. Oh, I can see you use them, too; you know how to make it a performance. But something deeper happens, you're always trying to figure out how people can do what they do, the strangest ones especially." She sat back. "That's what he sees, too, and why he gave you the gig. Because nothing would turn you off. In a way, you're a matched pair."

The waitress returned for their food orders, but neither had yet picked up a menu. They sent her away and spent a quiet minute reading over the choices.

With her eyes still on the menu, DZ said evenly, "There's talk GBS is up for sale. As the ratings climb, so would the price . . . ." Out of nowhere, a wild pitch to see if he jumped.

He stopped reading and looked at her. "So you think this whole thing could be a caper to boost the stock?"

"If it is, the take could be in the hundreds of millions."

He shrugged. "Well, a lot of stuff people confess to on my program is no crazier than that. You should check out the idea."

"Oh, I will. For a start: how much stock in GBS do *you* own?"

He smiled thinly. "Is that part of your theory? That *I'm* the one who dreamed this up to improve my net worth?"

"Like you said, there's no limit to how far-fetched reality can be."

His eyes went back to scanning the menu. After a moment, he said, "At the current price, I've got roughly thirty-two million dollars of GBS. Gone up about ten mil since this began. But if the network's sold, I'm not the one who'll make the big killing—so to speak."

They kept the menus up between them. But DZ wasn't thinking about food, and supposed he couldn't be, either.

"Right or wrong, DZ," he said across his menu, "I'll give you credit for interesting ideas. This one, and before—that the Mystery Guest and me are a good match— they put quite a spin on the whole scheme. If you feel strongly about those opinions, you shouldn't keep them to yourself. . . ."

She looked up sharply and he lowered his menu to confront her gaze. "In fact, I'd be pleased to give you a platform. Come on the show. You can talk about the case, make an appeal to the guy right there to give himself up—"

DZ slapped her menu down onto the table. "Shit!" she hissed with disgust. "*This* is the reason, isn't it?—why you came to me. To sign me on. Another 'get' for that sick circus of yours!"

He replied evenly. "You want to catch the guy? Then you should use every—"

"Not this one! You know, Stoner, that's where this kind of sickness begins—with the stupid confusion created by seeing it all through that little window you make for us. News and soap opera, all mixed up in some big sloppy stew of screwed-up feelings. The dividing line between real and unreal is so blurred it's . . . it's not even there anymore. Rapists, pederasts, wife-beaters, victims, murderers, you've got 'em all up there, every day, nothing more than another branch of showbiz so we have no pity left for anyone. This bastard may just be desperate to see if anything can make us feel again. Creep that he is, he might be just the one you made in your laboratory, Stoner—your own personal Frankenstein monster."

"Bravo, DZ. Great speech. Let everybody hear it, I don't mind. I repeat my invitation to—" His words caught for a second as she reached down to pick up her bag and stood. "Oh, c'mon," he brayed. "You're not going to walk out on me again!"

But she was already on the move. And he knew there was no point at all in chasing after her.

Marching along the avenue, ready to hike the whole goddamn way downtown while the steam kept leaking out of her, she wondered what made her keep bolting from him. Couldn't she laugh off his pitch to put her on his show instead of getting up on her high horse? For the sake of getting inside *him,* if nothing else. Was she truly so offended by what he represented?

Or was she merely hurt that he didn't see her as anything

more than the way he saw everyone else? Just one more
guest, one more talker, one more troubled soul to amuse
his viewers for forty minutes on a weekday—an hour,
minus the commercials.

CHAPTER
17

ON THE FRINGE of the farming town of Goshen in northern Indiana, a man named Stanley Portreck had lived alone for two years in a ramshackle house rented from the daughter of a deceased farmer. Portreck's previous home had been the Ohio Penitentiary at Marion, where he had served five years after being found guilty of publishing and selling a magazine called *Innocent Youth* that featured photographs of naked children between the ages of five and twelve, shown singly and in groups of as many as six, engaged in all kinds of sex acts. The "magazine" was actually no more than a stapled assemblage of poorly reproduced photos—though the quality tended to enhance their forbidden nature, making them all the more titillating to subscribers.

At the time of his arrest, Portreck shared a house in Columbus, Ohio, with a man named Giles Fulton. Fulton was assumed to be the source of the photographs. Though the police never established how Fulton acquired the images, it was believed he traveled in the rural South, paying indigent families to let their children be photographed in lewd poses.

Fulton could not be made to admit, either, that there was anything suspicious about the small bones discovered in a pit of lime when police searched the basement of his house at the time he and Portreck were arrested. He insisted the bones were the remains of a beloved dog. But in a plea bargain, Portreck swore to police that Fulton had told him of murdering two children years before the men were companions. Confronted with the statement, Fulton countercharged that he and his friend had acted together to murdering two boys, five and eight years old. It was Fulton's last word on the matter since an hour after this confession, he had been found hanging in his cell with strips of a torn mattress cover. With the failure of police to connect the bones to any missing child, Portreck, sentence-reduction deal in hand, was given a prison sentence of five-to-nine years. A model prisoner, at his first appearance before a parole board, he was granted release. Eventually he had been able to leave Ohio and move to Indiana. No attention was paid to the man who lived alone in an isolated farmhouse on the edge of a small town.

Until a little past ten o'clock this Monday morning, when the mailman on his usual rural route noticed that the farmhouse door was wide open and decided he ought to stop in and make sure everything was all right.

Having gone no farther than the threshold of the front parlor, the mailman could see that everything was decidedly not all right. Backing out the front door, he ran straight up the road to use the phone at the next house.

CHAPTER
18

STONER HAD BEEN on three *TV Guide* covers, and count-less covers of various Sunday newspaper supplements, but the cover of *TIME* planned for next week would be a first. To take the picture, the magazine had commissioned Susie Myrowitz, the hot young photographer whose work was considered the coolest.

Keeping with the theme of "cool," her studio was in a converted cold storage in the wholesale meat district, by the river below 14th Street. As soon as DZ and Gable arrived and showed their shields, they were conducted by one of Myrowitz's assistants to the studio atop the building, a cavernous, white-walled space topped by a skylight. A corner farthest from the door was being used for the portrait shoot, and a forest of lighting tripods kept DZ and Gable from being noticed when they entered. The assistant started forward to inform her boss of the police presence, but DZ held her back, preferring to observe for a while.

His face set in a deadly earnest expression, Stoner was perched on the same sort of high draftsman stool that he used during those rare moments on the air when he sat down. Behind him, stacked in several tiers, were forty large-screen TV sets, all displaying head shots of other talk show hosts past and present—some had already disappeared from the air. In the background hung a floor-to-ceiling screen of silvery material.

"Turn a little more this way," the photographer shouted as her motorized camera rapidly clicked off shots. "Look grimmer . . . angry . . . 'the whole thing stinks'. . . that's it . . . good . . . let me see some fire in the eyes. Great!" A diminutive woman with short brown hair, wearing overalls, Myrowitz circled Stoner as she exhorted him. "Now, try it with a glance toward the back, toward him. . . ."

At the mention of "him," the assistant leaned over and whispered to DZ and Gable, "We'll process a big image of the Mystery Guest over that rear cyc."

"I wondered how you could leave him out," Gable said.

Unhooking the camera from around her neck, Myrowitz shouted: "Empty! Dara, bring me the Leica with a thirty-eight mil!" Another assistant took a camera from several on a side table and scurried to her boss.

"Now," DZ said, giving a nudge to the girl beside her.

"Susie . . . !" the assistant called out. The photographer whirled, irritated. But Stoner had spotted DZ, and he interceded to make introductions.

"Sorry to barge in, Ms. Myrowitz," DZ said, "but I need to talk privately with Mr. Stoner."

"Not for long, I hope," said the photographer. She started to drift away, then turned. "This *TIME* story is about your case. Could I get you in a few shots?"

"Sorry. Requests like that have to go through the department."

The photographer walked away. Stoner gave DZ an inquiring look.

"It's happened," she said. "His first."

Stoner stared at her for a couple of seconds. "Someone I know . . . ?"

"You tell us," Gable said.

They moved to a long table against a side wall where the

cameras were arrayed. DZ removed a manila envelope from her shoulder bag, and pulled out three photographs and spread them onto the table. "These were faxed to us from the police in a little town in Indiana—a place called Goshen."

Though darkened by fax transmission, the essential subject matter was clear enough. DZ heard Stoner's sharp intake of breath as he saw the most gruesome of the pictures. "That bloody lump in the chair is—was—a man," DZ explained. "He was found two hours ago by the mailman."

"Jesus," Stoner muttred. "Looks like he stuck his head in a cannon."

"Not so different," Gable said. "The weapon was very heavy gauge—a shotgun, we assume—fired point-blank."

Stoner took another breath, quelling nausea. DZ lifted the other two photographs from the table, both close-ups. The first she handed Stoner showed a piece of foolscap resting in the victim's lap—the dead man's two hands gripping the edges. Printed large and neat on the paper, evidently by computer, were the words

KINDEST PERSONAL REGARDS FROM YOUR MYSTERY GUEST.

She exchanged the first picture for the second. Framed within the photo was a rectangular black card the size of a book cover propped atop a vintage television set, resting against a rabbit ears antenna. The numeral 5 stood out in white at the center of the card's black field.

Stoner tossed the picture down onto the table. "I don't get it."

"Nor do we. Could mean anything. Maybe this is actually his fifth victim."

"You sure our guy did it?" Stoner asked.

"Let's see if you know the victim," DZ broke in. She reached again into the manila envelope and extracted another sheet showing the standard front and profile views taken of prison convicts at check-in time. "This is what the victim looked like when he had a face." She passed the mug shots to Stoner. "If he's not a stranger to you, I think we can assume the killing wasn't done by a copycat."

Stoner studied the mug shots. "Tell me his name," he said with a tinge of urgency.

"Stanley Portreck."

"Yeah. Sure! Had him on—must be eight, nine years ago." Stoner had an encyclopedic recall of the people who had been on the program going back to the days of interviewing the guy who'd grown the largest turnip in Iowa. "We did a show on pornography. Had on people from all points of view. Civil rights advocates, anticensorship people—and some of the scum who print the garbage. This guy was one of the latter, belonged to a group called, if I remember, the Man-Boy Adoration Society—men who say it's okay to treat children as sex objects as long as there's mutual consent. As if there *could* be. I knew when I put him on he'd be a lightning rod. Hitler wouldn't have brought in worse hate mail."

For a moment they mused without sympathy over the pictures of the corpse with only the vestiges of a shattered skull attached to the stump of a neck.

Then Gable brought Stoner up to date on the victim—the plea bargain that had saved him from a possible capital sentence in connection with the torture-murder of two young boys.

"Guess it won't be a crowded funeral," Stoner said.

"Which doesn't change the fact," DZ said, "that it's murder, against the law, and we've got to stop the killer." She put the pictures back into the envelope.

"There's dozens of people who might have wanted to kill Portreck," Stoner said. "Even if he wasn't a stranger to me, it's no sure thing our guy was his killer."

"It's a lot more than fifty-fifty," Gable said. "He's also the type of victim the killer said he'd be gunning for, someone who deserved to die."

From across the studio, the photographer called, "You guys done? Barry's supposed to be out of here by three."

Yes, there was still his show to do, like any other week-day. "Just going," DZ called back, before saying to Stoner, "What's today's program?"

"Staying with the case. Candelli has Tauresco lined up . . . and they're still trying for the attorney general."

"Listen, Barry, this stuff came through just half an hour ago. The press doesn't know about the killing yet. We can't keep the lid on too long, but let's try to hold down the hysteria level. You understand?"

"Sure. You don't want me to break the news on my pro-gram. And I won't bring it up—unless our news depart-ment already has it. Corcoran ordered all stops out, so you can bet if it comes over the wire they'll break into my hour for a bulletin."

DZ nodded acceptance and moved toward the door with Gable.

The photographer took up her position again to shoot. "Okay, Barry, chop-chop if you want to make airtime. We'll try some with you seated on that pile of TV sets." She pointed to a stepladder placed beside the stack of big-screen TV sets.

"DZ," Stoner called. "Are you free later? I'd like to hear more about—"

She called back from near the door. "I'm flying out to Indiana."

As she left, DZ glanced back at Stoner, already seated atop the stacked televisions. "Chin in your hand, elbow on your knee!" Susie Myrowitz was saying.

Stoner as "The Thinker," DZ realized. Why not? He had a hell of a lot to think about. They all did.

Emerging from the warehouse building, it suddenly struck her—information filed away without realizing its significance until this moment. DZ clapped a hand to her forehead as she cried out: "That's it! *Peter Lorre!*"

Gable gave her a puzzled look.

From her shoulder bag, DZ took out the guide to films on television she had purchased a few days earlier. Since then, she'd read over the brief capsule on Peter Lorre's career several times. Now at last it made sense. She opened to a dog-eared page and read aloud to Gable the lines that mattered: " 'Lorre began his film career in Germany, and was brought to Hollywood after the international success of his 1931 film *M*. Based on a true case, the film cast Lorre as a psychopath who randomly murders young children, and from then on he was cast—' " The rest didn't matter, she put the book into her bag. "Get it? The M.G. told us right up front *exactly* who his victim would be—a child killer."

"We never could have figured that out in advance," Gable said.

"We weren't meant to. But it's one more proof."

"Of what?"

"That every single choice this guy makes, every goddamn thing he says or does, is sending a message."

CHAPTER
19

*T*HE MURDER IN Indiana, linked to a threat made over a national network, with further evidence of the killer's activity on the East Coast and the Southwest, left no doubt that federal enforcement had to take the lead. The FBI took over the case.

Because the case had originated in New York, Ken Chafee was designated to run the Bureau's end, and he contacted DZ personally, asking her to come to the murder scene. Her daily involvement with the case from the beginning made her the closest thing to an expert on the M.G. that existed. He didn't want any other Department people, though. Gable could stay home.

On her rush to the boarding gate at JFK, DZ passed a food kiosk where a television on a work counter was tuned to Stoner's program. With merely a passing glance she recognized the face being shown in close-up as Senator Francis Tauresco—sharp and rodentine (albeit along the lines of one of Disney's more cuddly rats) and spruced up by the ever-present bow tie. Checking her watch, DZ saw the program had already been on for twenty-five minutes. Her watch also told her she had just two minutes to be at the gate to make the flight.

But she halted in front of the kiosk. "Mind turning up the volume?" she asked a girl behind the counter who was ogling the TV.

The girl obliged and Tauresco's raspy, nasal voice rose in the middle of what sounded like a denunciation.

The countergirl moved between her and the screen. "What can I get you?"

"Nothing, thanks. I just want to watch that program."

Peeved, the countergirl moved aside slowly. The picture had changed to a split image of Tauresco with Stoner.

". . . waste no time in formulating a policy that covers vile incidents of this kind," Tauresco was saying.

"What would be the elements of such a policy, Senator?"

"Determining that is the purpose of the hearings my committee will hold—to give us an idea of the sort of controls we can fairly and realistically impose."

"Controls? On the media? You mean censorship?"

Tauresco gave his cuddly rat smile. "I'm aware that freedom of the press is one of the most hallowed tenets of our—"

DZ glanced at the clock again and reached down for her bag. From the debate's general tone and substance, it seemed safe to assume news of the murder hadn't yet broken.

But as she turned toward the departure gates, she heard Stoner's voice saying, "Then maybe it will help you formulate policy, Senator, to take some calls from our listeners."

She whirled back to the kiosk as Tauresco replied, "Fine. Let's hear what America has to say about this."

Moving back to the counter, DZ watched the TV screen with the same horrified helplessness anyone in the terminal would feel if they saw an airliner suddenly starting to plunge out of control. *Jesus*, surely Stoner realized what he could be inviting! It was Monday, for chrissake!

Stoner picked up a phone, and a woman asked Tauresco if his position against tightening gun controls had been changed by knowing the Mystery Guest meant to shoot people. The senator launched into the reply of a practiced politician—"couldn't agree more with the need"—side-stepping the real question.

They went to a second call, a man suggesting a federal death penalty for using public communications to sow panic.

"If it actually leads to murder," Tauresco said, "it's an option we definitely ought to look at. . . ."

The second phone call ended, and Stoner was saying they'd be joined by the attorney general from Washington right after the commercial break when DZ heard the terminal P.A. calling "Passenger Hayes" for the flight to Chicago.

At the same time, she heard a hitch in Stoner's smooth delivery, and saw his eyes dart sideways and upward— looking toward the control booth, DZ realized. His eyes widened with shock, and next she heard him say there would be no break, after all: there was another caller for the senator.

Tauresco plucked up the phone. *Oh no!* DZ thought. Had Stoner given the senator any warning of what to expect . . . ?

"Hello, this is Senator Tauresco."

DZ could hear it at once: Tauresco's voice was too steady and friendly. He had no idea. Stoner and his producer wanted the full shock affect.

Now the other voice—cheerful, assured. "Good afternoon, Senator. May I compliment you first on the way you've taken up this issue. It needs to be handled with a firm hand, and a fine ethical mind like your own."

"Thank you," Tauresco said.

The same wit, too, DZ mused. *Ethical mind?* Powerful as Tauresco was in the senate, there had been so many questions about his fund-raising and nepotism in assigning

his staff jobs that he'd escaped an investigation only because the probers themselves had just as many indiscre-
tions to hide.

"My question is this, Senator. Whatever laws you pass
to prevent this kind of public outrage in the future, what do
you intend to do now to stop *me*?"

Tauresco opened his mouth as though to reply—then the
full sense of the question sank in. He froze, gaping, his
eyes searchingly aimed at the camera as if trying reverse
its purpose and see into the world.

"Senator . . . ?" The voice coaxed.

Tauresco's mouth snapped shut into a grim line. He
looked sharply to one side, eyes blazing, his feral features
devoid of cuteness now, looking for prey. *Is this some kind
of joke?* the expression read, *and who's responsible?*

Again: "Senator . . . I've asked you a question."

DZ heard the P.A. paging her once more. "Passenger
Hayes, last call for Flight 610—" But her eyes stayed riveted on the screen, where Tauresco stared into the unfor-
giving cyclops. America was out there, and he knew he had
to make himself look effective and powerful. His cerebral
computer was calling up decades of TV debates, reviewing
all the great one-liners that had won it for others. *There you
go again.*

"Well, Senator, what are you going to do about me?
Maybe you don't know yet, but I've already gone to work.
Got my first. Yes indeedy, one little piggy crying 'wee,
wee, wee all the way home.' So you really can't sit back
and take time for hearings, and think that could possibly
make me—"

Tauresco blew, tossing away any script experience
might have written for him. "You sick murdering bastard!"
he screamed, spittle flying off his lips. "Don't think—
don't imagine for one goddamn *minute*—you'll get away
with this, because we're gonna get you, you sonofabitch.
Just wait, you just wait. I'm gonna see to it!" Used up by

the outburst, Tauresco paused. He looked ill, pasty and sweating.

"You're gonna get me?" The voice mocked. "Oh, I don't think so, Senator. Not you or the snake you rode in on."

Tauresco's mouth worked, but he held back words as he realized it was a no-win situation. He could only look more ridiculous, dripping sweat while he held on to the phone with a killer at the other end, far out of reach. All at once the senator bolted from his chair, and reached high for a hovering boom microphone. Hauling it down in a white-knuckled fist, he stared into the camera and made his vow to the electorate: "We'll get him. We'll get this . . . this beast and punish him to the full extent of the law. For now, he's all yours, Stoner." Tauresco stormed off.

The caller could be heard laughing lightly. Then: "Man's got a hell of a mean temper, doesn't he?"

The shot went to Stoner, alone, looking at his call-in phone on its customary pedestal. As he moved to pick it up, the caller added, "By the way, Barry, I hope you're saving time for me next week. There's a lot more talking we have to do."

"What about?" Stoner demanded. Silence played back at him. "For god's sake, you can't go on with this. Give yourself—"

The sound of the dial tone cut in. Stoner stared blankly into the camera. For only a second. Then he was obliterated by the eye-catching graphic that flashed onto the screen with the words

SPECIAL GBS NEWSBRIEF

CHAPTER
20

*T*HE BURNISHED GOLDEN light of a spring evening was
casting long shadows by the time DZ arrived at the
scene in a cruiser from the Goshen PD. FBI Agent Kenneth
Chafee was sitting on the steps of the farmhouse porch,
jacket off, talking with an older man seated beside him.
Chafee was lean, with a tawny, weathered face under light
brown crew-cut hair. He and his companion could have
passed for two rural cronies enjoying the air—if yellow
crime-scene tape wasn't strung everywhere like a Day-Glo
spiderweb, and Chafee wasn't wearing a Walther semi in a
shoulder holster. Cars from the FBI field office were all
over the scrubby yard, and four dozen agents and state police were scouring everywhere around the property. On her
way here DZ had seen roadblocks half a mile away, blocking access to battalions of TV trucks and other press.
Though they weren't able to prevent the news choppers
from doing almost constant flyovers.

As she went to the porch, DZ noted the black satchel on
a step beside Chafee's companion; the local coroner, she
guessed.

Chafee stood to greet her. "You were in no rush to get here. . . ."

"Took time out to watch my favorite TV show." After missing her original flight to Chicago, she caught another and from there, a small charter took her to an airfield in Elkhart, Indiana, eight miles from Goshen, where she'd been met by the local police.

"The body couldn't wait for you," Chafee said.

"He'd been here since last night." The other man stood, too, and picked up his satchel. "Had to get him on ice."

Chafee introduced the older man as Dr. Merton, the county coroner. "A Bureau pathologist will do the autopsy," he explained, "but the Doc was first to the body, and stayed around in case you had questions."

Not just cooperative spirit, DZ thought. This was probably the first murder around here in decades, the biggest in the whole country no less, and the Doc liked being in on the action. It struck DZ as odd, in fact, that there weren't a lot of other local mucky-mucks hungry hanging around. "Where's the police chief?" she asked.

"Went to town to do a little crowd control," Chafee said. "The media's been pouring in."

They went inside. It was the classic farmhouse layout. A hall with a ratty linoleum floor led back to the kitchen, stairs along the hall went up to bedrooms; at the front, doors either side entered rooms facing the porch. Chafee went to the left. What had been a dining room had been turned into a cluttered den-office. Four FBI techs were minutely examining everything from the dust-caked carpet to light bulbs in a ceiling fixture (on the chance warm air currents had caused any incriminating filaments to settle up there). Near a front window was an easy chair of frayed, brown velour, the ugly fabric made even more repulsive by huge blotches of dried blood and clinging bits of bone and flesh. The faded floral wallpaper behind the chair was marked by a broad arc of spattered blood like the fanned tail of a peacock. At a level above the chair back, a hole the size of a grapefruit was gouged right through the wallpaper and plaster to the lath.

"What made that?" DZ gestured to the hole.

"Same thing that blew away the dead guy."

The hole was so large DZ assumed an FBI agent had dug out the bullet for evidence. "Can I see what you took out of there?"

Chafee called to one of the other FBI men. "Swain, bring me what we got from the wall?"

A young man wearing latex gloves went to an open metal case on the floor, then brought over a transparent polythene pouch. Chafee took it and dangled it in front of DZ's face. Through the clear polythene, she saw fragments of bone with clinging shreds of pink matter, and clumps of blood-caked hair.

"Brain matter mostly," said Swain. "The hair is probably horsehair from the wall. It was often used for insulation in these old farmhouses."

"What about the bullet?"

"Wasn't in there," Chafee said, returning the baggie to Swain who carried it away.

"You mean, *he* dug it out?" DZ stared at the hole.

"Yeah. But from the damage to the body we can still tell something. Had to be a big charge, probably pushing a lead slug."

A slug, DZ mused. An uncommon method—except in mob executions. Fitted to a shotgun shell in lieu of buckshot and fired at short range, a slug did indeed have the destructive power of a small cannonball.

"So we're thinking it might not be your guy after all," Chafee said. "Shotgun and a lead ball, old Sicilian method. The mob's in the porn racket, they could've hit this perv for cutting in on their territory."

"So Portreck was still in the business?"

Chafee gestured to the office area. "Mail-order videos of grown-ups doing all kinds of nasty things to little kids. Sold to subscribers at a hundred bucks a pop."

DZ moved pensively across the plastic sheeting that had been put down to guard the carpet from contamination. So maybe it was coincidence that he'd been on Stoner's show. A contract killer would've thought it was real cute to leave a note giving credit to America's "most wanted" of the moment.

Yet a mob guy wouldn't have dug out the bullet, he'd simply have tossed the gun in a river. And there was the Lorre tape, the *M* connection. She told Chafee about it now.

"Not a clincher," he said. "Peter Lorre only played weird guys—and the M.G. is also a weird guy. So that could be why he chose the actor, nothing to do with hinting at this case." He waved to the death chair.

DZ didn't try to convince him. She moved farther into the room, scanning. Now she noticed that the gore-stained chair was positioned to face a vintage television console, right of the doorway where the local medical examiner stood, waiting to be useful. She looked at the card propped atop the old TV console against a rabbit ears indoor antenna. Eight-by-ten inches, a white numeral 5 on a black background. "Dusted this?" she asked.

"Sure. Like everything else, no prints. The only sets anywhere are the victim's, and a few from the mailman who found the body."

"Tire tracks?" DZ asked, eyes still on the card. "Killer had to have a car to get way out here."

"Only impressions we've got are from the lawn, a couple places where the grass is thin—the soles of a pair of Nike running shoes."

" 'Just do it,' " DZ quoted the Nike slogan.

Chafee half smiled. "The guy must've left his car down the road, then walked the asphalt. We're looking for tread-marks half a mile either way—but everything's so clean I'd lay odds the guy brushed 'em out. Another bet? The Nikes were bought new for cash, worn once, and went straight to an incinerator."

All the time she listened the number stared back at DZ.

5

"What do you make of that?"

"Something Portreck put there, maybe."

"No," DZ asserted. "It's the signal from our guy that this was his work. *He* left it on top of the TV." And like everything this killer did or said, the 5 had meaning, too. Turning from the taunting number, she saw the coroner in the doorway. *All right, let him feel important.* "Dr. Merton, what can you tell me about the body?"

"What's to tell? Head blown off, cause of death. From lividity and rigor when I got here—about 2 P.M.—I put time of death around twelve hours earlier."

"Two in the morning. . . ."

"Give or take."

"Any sign of a struggle?"

"Not-a-one. Victim wasn't even tied up. Sat in that chair calm as you please and let it happen."

DZ paused. The nice old gentleman had waited around for nearly five hours just to be available, but she couldn't think of anything else she needed to ask.

She was about to let him go, when Chafee said: "Don't forget the toe."

"Oh, yeah. For sure that must've been done after the shooting. If he'd been alive, he'd couldn't have sat still for it without being tied—"

"Hold on!" DZ cut in excitedly. "What toe?"

"Little toe was cut off. Right foot."

"That's *it*, one hundred percent proof it's our guy!" This was one of the things she'd noodled over during her time on the plane. "When he spoke to Tauresco, he said this really strange thing. 'Got my first . . . got me one little piggy, crying wee wee wee all the way home.' Like the nursery rhyme you say when you play with a baby's toes? 'This little piggy went to market.' His line goes with the little toe. He did it here maybe, 'cause Portreck was a man who turned children's bedtimes into nightmares. Made him squeal like a pig. . . ."

"Heavens to Betsy," the coroner muttered in disgust.

"Now I'm sure the other stuff figures in," DZ went on quickly. This, too, from the notes she'd puzzled over on the plane: "Why does he start here—in a town called Goshen? You know what the name comes from?"

The coroner replied, "The Bible. Goshen was the land of plenty. There's towns in lotsa places given that name by pioneers, thinkin' it'd bring luck."

"But Goshen was also described as 'a place of light,' " DZ said, "where good prospered because it was immune from evil." She scanned the squalid room where an ugly business had been run. "So our killer comes to this Goshen to tell us that's bullshit—in the real world evil dwells even where it's banned in the Bible."

"If you're right about the Bible stuff," Chafee said, "we could be dealing with a religious fanatic—even a group of some kind, a cult."

DZ shook her head vigorously. "One guy, alone. The Bible reference is just his kind of ironic humor."

Chafee paced in a circle. "One guy, huh? Drops a video in New York, makes calls from out of state, pipes himself by satellite from the Southwest, cuts off piggy toes in Indiana. I never knew any one killer to move around so much so quick."

"You never knew any killer to do what this one does," DZ said quietly.

Old Doc Merton cast his vote. "Sure sounds like a bunch of fellers to me."

Chafee and DZ turned to him together. "Thanks, Doc," Chafee said. "You can go now."

The old man heard the edge. He reminded them he was available anytime to answer questions, and left. Through a front window, DZ could see him go down the porch steps.

"He'll make a good one," she said.

"Good what?" Chafee said.

"Guest on *Stoner*—or *Geraldo,* any one of the other gab shows. They'll go after these guys now, every last cook and bottlewasher, anyone who's been near the action."

They were quiet a moment, imagining the fallout.

"Look around on your own, if you want," Chafee said then. "I want to see if they've found anything else outside."

Alone, DZ went for a closer look at the bloody easy chair. She let her mind play through the murder, building a scenario around the few things she'd been told. Time of death between one and three A.M. So Portreck was roused from bed ... or maybe sitting up, watching television. That triggered a couple of questions, and DZ fished her notebook from her bag. TV, 1–3 A.M., she wrote, then went back to studying the scene. The victim hadn't been bound, hadn't resisted, but he'd been shot point-blank from the front. Which fit with the analysis of the M.G.'s personality —quiet, self-possessed, with that eerie amiability. An iceman who might thank his victim for sitting still while he cut his throat.

She continued her tour of the room, pausing in front of the TV console.

5

She spun to look back at the chair where the body had been found, then back to the TV. She took a closer look at the tuning dial, and made a note on her pad of the channel number to which it was set. Then she went outside to find Chafee.

In the gathering twilight, he stood talking with a few men near the steps. She called him over. "Ken, when you got here was the TV on or off?"

"Off."

"The mailman who found the body, did he turn it off?"

"Never thought to ask. Does it matter?"

"This whole thing's about TV, one way or another. It

was late at night. The killer marched his victim from bed to sit in front of the TV. So maybe he made him watch a particular show before shooting him. Might carry a clue."

"A late night rerun of *I Love Lucy* is going to mean something?"

"I'm telling you, Ken: everything this guy does has a meaning. Everything."

Chafee sighed. "Okay. We'll check it. "

A police car wheeled into the drive and screeched up in front of the house, headlights cutting through the gathering twilight.

"Chief's back," Chafee said.

He unloaded himself slowly, a large man with a round, ill-shaven face who looked like he'd put on quite a few pounds since the department had paid for his last pair of dark blue pants and powder blue shirt. He spoke to Chafee, as though DZ was invisible:

"One hell of a ten-ring circus we got back in town. Every motel and leaky cabin colony within twenty miles is booked solid. Even got crews out from Chicago workin' for Jap TV."

"Chief LaBorret," Chafee said, "meet Detective Hayes from New York. She was the first one on this case."

He sized her up. "Well now, little lady," he said, his voice dropping to a syrupy register, "my pleasure I'm sure." He tipped his cap. "Chief Alonzo LaBorret at your service."

DZ held back the scalding retorts she usually had for men who patronized her. Way out here maybe condescending to women still passed for charm. Though she didn't want him forgetting she was on the job, shipped in from a place where murder was a common police concern. "Give me your opinion here, Chief," she said. "You think the scumbag who got his shit blown away here was offed by some prick on a mob contract, or just whacked by a fucked-up psycho?"

The chief gazed at her, his eyebrows rising and falling

like waves on a bad sea. Behind him, Chafee smiled thinly, well aware of why DZ was laying it on so thick.

At last the Chief said, "Well now, Missy, I don't really—"

"You can call me detective," DZ cut in sharply. "Or lieutenant."

The chief looked at Chafee, as if needing assurance he wasn't on *Candid Camera.* Chafee gave him a nod.

"'Scuse me," he replied gruffly. "Detective. I was going to say I don't have an opinion on that. Which is why I'm so glad to have the FBI here helping out. Along with a gen-you-wine big-city police . . . person." He gave her a flicker of a smile. "Anything else?"

She was sorry now. "After the body was found, were you one of the first to get here?"

"Yes, ma'am. Soon as Bud Hollins—our mailman—called in, I had all my cars out here pronto. Not 'cause I knew it was a world-famous deal. This kind of thing just doesn't ever happen around here."

"Remember if the television was on when you entered the house?"

"Matter of fact, it *was.* I switched it off." Quickly, he added. "Didn't touch nothin' else, but just—hell, a dead man sittin' in front of *The Price Is Right,* didn't seem respectful, you know?"

Ordinarily DZ would have been concerned that prints on the knob had been ruined. But this killer wouldn't have left any.

"Why'd you want to know about the TV?" the chief asked.

"It helps me get into the mind of the man who did this."

LaBorret regarded her and his expression softened to something markedly paternal. "Missy—'scuse me, Detective, the last place on earth I'd ever want to be is in the mind of that man."

She had no more questions, but he said pleasantly he'd keep himself available and went around to talk to the members of his own force who were helping the FBI.

DZ went back inside for one more look at the murder scene. She scanned it slowly and ended on the "postcard."

Chafee had followed her in. "Maybe it's a countdown. 5-4-3-2-1. Then he'll stop."

This monster would never stop himself, she knew. He was out of the cage now, would be stopped only when he was caught.

Outside, the light had faded to a thin, glowing lavender line along the flat horizon across from the house. As she came onto the porch, DZ felt suddenly weary, as much from thinking about what lay ahead as her efforts to date. She wished she'd had the foresight to book a hotel room for the night.

She asked Chafee his plans, and he told her he'd be spending the next day in Goshen; the postmortem would be done at the local hospital by an FBI pathologist on his way from Virginia headquarters. The FBI contingent had taken half the rooms in the four-story hotel.

"I'll fly back," DZ said. "Maybe a good idea to stay close to Stoner. The killer's going to make contact again. Fax me your reports as soon as you can."

Chafee agreed just as the chief appeared around a corner.

"Could one of your men drive me to Elkhart?" DZ asked

"Flyin' away so soon?" the Chief questioned.

"I forgot to reserve a place to stay, and you said it's—"

"No problem, litt—I mean, Lieutenant. I'd be pleased to put you up for the night." She hesitated and he read her expression. "I mean Mrs. LaBorret and I would be pleased to have you as our guest. You could have my daughter's room. She's up at the medical school in Chicago."

Something clicked for DZ. A realization that here, in the heartland, there were insights still to be gained. "All right, I'll take you up on that if you're serious."

"Get your suitcase. I'll drive you myself."

She fetched her overnight bag from the other car and got in with the chief. "This is really kind of you," she said.

"Think nothin' of it, Lieutenant. Delighted to help out a lovely lady like you."

She turned to him. "Call me DZ. Everybody does."

"Right-ee-o." He started the motor, then sat still a moment. "Just one thing I'll have to insist on, DZ," he said earnestly, turning to her. "Not for me, y'understand, but for Mrs. LaBorret. When we're in the house, you'll have to be a mite more careful what you say." He put the car in gear. "Some of the things that come from that mouth of yours'd just about peel the paint off the walls."

Then he gunned the cruiser and they zoomed out onto the road, siren screaming to let the roadblocks know he was coming straight through.

CHAPTER
21

I T WAS A modest two-story house on a street of similar houses behind neat yards with picket fences. They were barely through the door—the Chief hollering "Jane! Company!"—before his wife rushed forth from the rear like a genie released from a bottle. A trim woman wearing a flowered apron over a plain blue shirtwaist, she had short silver hair and a plain face that radiated sweetness. Jane gently scolded Lonnie for not giving her more notice of a guest, but barely listened to his explanation of who the guest was before warmly welcoming DZ and leading her upstairs to a bedroom, where she was urged to settle in. The room was bedecked with the prizes and pictures of the happy youth enjoyed by the youngest of the three daughters the chief had boasted about on the ride over.

DZ had time to shower and rest, then dinner was called. The chief had cleaned up, too, and looked much more appealing in casual clothes, which fit better than his uniform. They ate in the kitchen at a table that Lonnie boasted he had crafted himself in his basement workshop. The meal was roast chicken, mashed potatoes, green beans, and a delicious home-baked lemon sponge cake the chief's wife pulled from the freezer to serve with cinnamon tea.

Right at the start, the chief stated firmly that shoptalk was forbidden at dinner, a rule dating from "when my girls were little." He steered the conversation to general questions about life in the big city, and encouraged his wife to tell about her recipe column for the tri-county, biweekly newspaper.

But over dessert Jane LaBorret could no longer resist expressing surprise to DZ that such a "pretty thing" should be working for the police. "I'd have died if one of my girls ever wanted to be a policeman," Jane LaBorret said.

"Couldn't have been a police*man*, dear," the chief said with a wink at DZ. "Nowadays it would be policeperson."

"Call it what you will, Lonnie, it's bad enough to think of *you* anywhere near what you're involved with now, let alone the girls. A thing like that here in Goshen—makes you think the world's coming to an end."

"The world's gonna be just fine," Lonnie said, "and that bad business won't involve me much more. It's up to the FBI now . . . and DZ here." He rolled his napkin into the wooden napkin ring he'd turned on his own lathe, thanked Jane for the delicious meal, and rose from the table. DZ started to help clear the dishes, but was shooed off by Jane: "I'm sure you and the chief have business to discuss."

She joined him in the front parlor, where he had turned on the television and planted himself in a recliner. She sat down at one end of a sofa. The chief pointed to a cabinet. "Got cream-dee-mint in there. Help yourself if you're so inclined."

"Thanks, I'm fine."

For a few minutes they watched a show he'd switched on—*Cops in New York*, of all things. At the commercial, LaBorret muted the sound with a remote and sat up, leveling the recliner. "What's this fella want, DZ—the one who blew the head off that weasel other side of town? I mean, stirrin' things up so much, gettin' the whole world to watch . . . then he shoots that piece of human garbage. What's it add up to?"

"I don't know, Lonnie. Where I'm from, sometimes it seems people killing people is just another side of what they say about the reason men climb mountains."

He nodded. "'Cause they're there. Well, not like that here. Oh, the killin' happened here . . . but it wasn't one of our own that got killed or done it. Never could be. Life's still worth more than that in these parts."

DZ glanced around the pleasant, comfortable room. From the kitchen came the sound of running water and radio music, the dishes being hand washed as Jane LaBorret sang along with Crystal Gayle's "Don't It Make My Brown Eyes Blue." "Yes, I can see it is, Chief," she said. *So far.*

The commercials ended, the chief unmuted the volume and the TV cops said smart things on their infallible way to solving another case.

"I should go up," DZ said. "I have to get an early start. But thanks, chief—this hospitality is the nicest thing that's happened to me in quite awhile."

"Think nothin' of it. I'd want folks to do the same for my girls."

She was heading for the kitchen to thank the chief's wife when he muted the TV again. "This thing he's bein' called, DZ—the Mystery Guest—is that just 'cause he's doin' the talk show but we don't know who he is?"

"No, there's also another twist. Long time ago, there was a TV game show—"

"What's My Line?" The chief exclaimed. "Loved that show. That's what hit *me* when I heard 'Mystery Guest.' So I was thinkin' that might explain the five."

"The five?" DZ realized then he meant the placard at the victim's house.

"On the show, when the panel tried to guess the identity of the Mystery Guest, each time they asked a question and got a 'no,' they'd lose some money. The emcee, he'd flip a card over in front of the guest to tally it up. If I recall, fifty bucks was the total prize if the panel got ten guesses wrong. Five bucks each, see? So after the first stumper the card showed a five. Like the one out there today. . . ."

As soon as he had explained it, DZ knew it was dead-on. Just the kind of joke the M.G. enjoyed to underline that he'd stumped them the first time out.

"So whattaya think?" the chief said.

"What I think, Chief, is you'd make a hell of a detective."

He smiled. "Not for me, thanks. But anytime you need some advice, little lady, you know where to come."

She said good night and went to thank the chief's wife. Jane LaBorret gave DZ a hug, then held her at arm's length for a motherly word: "You take care, dear."

In her room, DZ found the bedcovers turned down. Laid out on the pillow was a pink flannel nightgown that smelled of soap and drying in the sun. Her habit was to sleep nude, but she put on the nightgown, possessed by a desire to step into whatever costume, whatever skin went with living in this house, this good and simple life. Raised in a room over a bar, her mother serving beers while she dozed off to the din of a brutal city, DZ felt a yearning for the lost chance to be a girl who could fall sleep all the nights of her youth in *this* room. When she turned out the light and lay back, she heard no sirens wailing through the open window as you did every night in the inner city; only the rustle of trees stirred by the night breeze and the barking of a dog, faint but clear, half a mile away.

The invasion of this innocent place by the killer seemed meant to inform not only his pursuers, but his whole audience, that evil could exist anywhere. The Mystery Guest was a stalker, DZ reflected, one who was stalking a whole country, looking at them and targeting them through that glass window they all sat in front of an average of five hours a day.

Mind churning again with the case, she switched on the

bedside lamp, fetched the notebook from her tote bag, and made a list for herself. As Chafee had observed, the killer was moving around a lot, and quickly. All the airlines that flew in and out of the larger terminal cities within driving distance of here, in the Southwest, and in New York had to be checked. Tickets issued on days that coincided with areas of the M.G.'s activity might yield a name of someone traveling the same pattern. Car rental agencies within a four-hundred-mile radius of Goshen should be contacted. The M.G. could have used aliases—but then he'd probably have to use cash for tickets and cars rather than credit card or bank check; paying cash might also make him memorable.

Surveying all possibilities was a Herculean amount of work, but the FBI had the resources; Chafee might have already thought of it all, but in case he hadn't, DZ jotted a reminder to call Gable in the morning.

At last she lay back again in the quiet darkness of a place that seemed so uncommonly safe even after one instance of random violence. Then an image rose to her consciousness of that distant farmhouse she had seen painted on a wall in Stoner's apartment—a reminder that he had grown up in a place not so different from this one. Did that relate to the reason he had been chosen as the conduit to carry the message?

A question worth answering, maybe.

Before falling asleep, DZ had decided: she wasn't going home tomorrow. She was going deeper into the heartland.

CHAPTER
22

*T*HE FIELDS AROUND the house on the crest of a low rise were not—as in the idealized mural—a colorful blanket of wildflowers, just stretches of rye grass being grown for hay. And there were outlying farm buildings, too: a silo, animal pens, a vintage metal-fan windmill that might still be used to pump water. Standing in the road beside her rented car, DZ wasn't sure exactly what had drawn her here. From inquiries at the nearby town of Dalton Falls, she had learned that the property was several times removed from ownership by the Stoner family. An area realtor, his memory refreshed by calling a crony who worked in the county records hall, had told her that after Mrs. Stoner's death the property was sold by bank executors on behalf of the surviving five children, and since then had changed hands several times. DZ's research in Dalton Falls had also revealed that knowledge of Stoner's connection to the place didn't come automatically to its two thousand-odd residents. The gas station attendant who'd filled her tank after the drive from Cedar Rapids knew of Stoner, but not his connection to the town, and he hadn't been able to direct her to the farm. She had only found "the old Stoner place" after stopping in at a local diner called The Blue Ribbon. There an old man named Chet Volmer had been pointed out to her as someone who'd once had close contact with the Stoners.

With the drive to Dalton Falls, it was past one o'clock by the time DZ arrived there, and Volmer was finishing his lunch when DZ slid into his booth and introduced herself.

A retired grain merchant as well as a still-practicing farrier, Volmer was taut and sinewy with shrewd blue eyes and a lick of snowy hair poking out from under his tipped-back, red hunting cap. He wasn't surprised by the arrival of someone from the law to ask questions. He had a home satellite dish in his yard, he told DZ, and was up-to-date on all "the goings-on with that Guest killer-guy." He'd figured covering the bases might bring the police sooner or later to Stoner's hometown.

Answering DZ's questions, Volmer explained that shoeing the plow horses had often taken him out to the Stoner farm. When he first visited the place, it was a happy environment, with a bunch of active kids helping at chores, raising their own animals to bring to the 4-H competitions, and fighting noisy, make-believe wars with wooden swords over barnyard battlements. Then overnight it seemed to change, to become as he put it, "a place that had its own dark clouds sittin' right over it." The change had not been due solely to the accidental death of Stoner's younger sister, but to a sickness that had struck "one of the older boys." The old man didn't know the nature of the illness, only that it forced the boy to give up school and stay confined to the house; coming along with the girl's death, it cast a pall over all the family. The other kids seemed even afraid to talk about it. Then the father had died suddenly, and Mrs. Stoner had declined and passed away. Under DZ's gentle probing, Volmer confirmed that the mother's death was hastened by chronic drinking.

"Not many folks here remember or care that Barry Stoner came from this town," Volmer said. "He's never been back, so it could be he's just too high and mighty now to remember his roots. But I'd say there was just too much heartbreak tied up with it, he had to put it far behind him. One way or another that's what sent all those other four Stoner kids away for good."

Volmer had finally given her the directions to travel back roads and find the farm.

As she looked now across the hay field, DZ reflected that it was probably the same desire to distance himself from heartbreak that had caused Stoner to idealize the memory of his home, having the mural painted without the silo that had caused his younger sister's death. But the sight of this towering cylinder spurred DZ to leave her car and walk up the dirt track toward the farm buildings. A girl had died there; she had the detective's urge to take a closer look.

She was halfway to the silo when a man in jeans and a khaki workshirt came out of the farmhouse and ambled toward her at an easy pace. He was about forty.

"Hi, there!" he called. "Somethin' I can do for ya?" He had the unfussy look of an outdoorsman, tanned, hair shaggy.

"I'm told this used to be the Stoner place. . . ."

"Long time ago." His expression turned wary. DZ supposed he pegged her as a curiosity seeker, attracted by Stoner's notoriety. After she showed her credentials, he was cooperative. He gave his name as Dave Haskins and said he lived here with his wife and two kids. Then he asked DZ what connection the farm could possibly have to what she was working on. "Must be a good thirty years since the Stoners left. I don't get it—I mean, a New York cop coming *here*. Whattaya expect to find?"

"I had to be in Indiana, anyway, close enough. I thought it was worth a look."

"Okay. C'mon inside." Haskins started for the house.

"The house isn't what interests me. I wanted to see where the girl died."

Haskins regarded her blankly. "What girl—where?"

"Stoner had a sister who died in that silo when she was twelve."

"Shoot, never heard a thing about it. How'd it happen?"

"Evidently an accident. She fell."

Haskins was silent, staring at the cylinder of shiny, dark blue metal with a conical tin roof. DZ could imagine the effect on a man with children suddenly learning a child had fallen victim to an element of his property. It gave an ominous air to something that had been innocent.

Without another word, Haskins motioned DZ to follow. When they got to the silo he pointed out features of the structure, and explained the ways in which it was possible for someone to perish there accidentally. Used for storage of animal feed or harvested grain, the eighty-foot tall cylinder had entry points all along its height—accessed via a stairway in the connecting barn—through which additional silage could be added or a farmer could look in to check his supply. The grain bed was not solid, so a fall through one of these openings might not cause fatal injuries by impact, Haskins said. The greater danger was smothering since the air inside was thick with grain dust, and the panicky effort a child would make to climb out could cause the grain to cave in around her like loose sand, burying her alive.

They had moved into the passage between the barn and the silo. As DZ craned her neck back to look up the long, open, metal stairway, the farmer studied her. "It *was* an accident . . . ?" he said at last.

She thought of the clippings from a local newspaper that mentioned another girl of about the same age who'd died similarly on a farm in the area. But she'd raised enough ghosts for one day for the nice farmer. "It happens," she said.

They left the silo. "Fortunately, it's rare," he said. "Farm kids know the dangers. Mine certainly do." He seemed to have gotten over his anxiety about the past death.

She thanked him, and declined his invitation to stay for coffee and a look at the house, explaining she had to get to Cedar Rapids to catch a plane. She didn't add that there was something else she had to do in town, a need that only occurred to her when she was wondering if Laurel Stoner's death had really been an accident.

THE OFFICE OF THE *DALTON FALLS JOURNAL* WAS ON THE upper floor of a two-story brick building on Main Street, which also housed the town's only bank. When she climbed the wooden steps and pushed open the glass-paneled door marked with the name of the newspaper in flaking gold letters, DZ half expected tinkly bells to jangle, and to be received by a crew of withered old men in green eyeshades. But the door opened soundlessly and she entered a long, open space lit with modern ceiling fixtures. Half a dozen desks were spaced around a pearly gray carpet, and computer terminals were on four of the desks, but no one was working at them. The only occupied desk was near the entrance, where a woman sat at an electric typewriter. She was in her thirties, with blond hair waved in a style DZ associated with shampoo commercials of thirty years ago. The woman looked up from her typing.

"Good afternoon," DZ said, "I'm—"

"I know who you are." The woman tapped the button of an intercom. "Guess what, Charlie? That lady cop just walked in."

Small towns. Of course, someone from the diner must have run here to report on her activities: she was news.

A door opened at the rear of the long space, and a lanky, silver-haired man emerged. He made a circling gesture with one arm. "C'mon back, Miz Hayes!"

"Charlie Foster," murmured the receptionist, "the owner."

Nearing the door, DZ saw he was actually quite young, late thirties or early forties. Dressed in dark slacks and a white shirt overlaid with cheery yellow-and-red suspenders, but for the prematurely gray hair he would've made a passable stand-in for Jimmy Stewart in one of his idealistic crusader movie roles. Foster extended a hand and she shook it. "Glad you came by," he said. "Matter of fact, I've got both my reporters out trying to track you down."

"I'm not here to sit for an interview, Mr. Foster. I was hoping you could give me some information."

"Happy to oblige if I can." He led her into the office, waved her to a chair, and invited her to call him Charlie.

The *Journal*'s modernization had stopped at his threshold, DZ saw. An ancient partners' desk and wall cabinets were mounded with yellowing papers. He sat down at the desk and shoved the papers aside to look at her.

"It's about something that happened almost thirty-five years ago," she said.

"I think we already answered a request to fax articles from that period to the police in New York?"

"Yes, for bio material on Barry Stoner; but I'd like to focus now on his sister's death—and a second, quite similar death around the same time. Could you pull everything from your files that bears on either of those things?"

He shot a disheartened glance at the papers banked high against the walls. "My late dad's filing system. He founded the *Journal,* and all those stories were on his watch. I've managed to computerize some of the backlog by subject and date, not nearly all. No problem pulling the stuff we sent originally, because you made a general request for biographical data on Stoner, and we can reference by date among back issues to the time he moved away. But if you want *everything* that touches on a subject like those girls' deaths, it takes going through stacks of back issues. The *Journal*'s only a weekly, but we put out forty pages. Over time it adds up."

"I'd still like you to try and find the stuff. It doesn't have to be overnight."

"Okay, do my best. How does this tie in with your case?"

"I doubt there is a link. But . . ." She shrugged. "Just a cop's itch that needs to be scratched." To encourage his help, she added, "If you do send me anything useful, I'll try to return the favor, tip you to how things are developing. This is a hot story now, maybe you'd like a scoop."

He smiled. "I don't know, Detective. This isn't exactly our kind of story. Paper like mine, we try to print stuff that's important to the people in our community. If they want to read about blood and thunder from far away . . . well, better they drive over to Hobbsville and pick up one of those scandal sheets at the supermarket."

DZ raised her eyebrows in appreciation as well as surprise. "Never thought I'd hear anyone in the media turn down a world-class hot story."

"What you call 'the media,' Detective Hayes, is made up of scaremongers who have a hunger for stories that make people want to run to the doors and lock 'em. I'm a newspaperman, and I want to print stuff that'll help folks think about whatever it takes to make their lives better—so they can leave their doors unlocked."

"You keep yours unlocked?" DZ asked.

"Since the day they were put there." He smiled again. "Pardon me while I step down off my soapbox."

He had the same winning ingenuousness of vintage Stewart, too; she would've liked to know him better.

As if he read her thoughts: "You planning to be in town a day or two? I could show you around. There's better places to eat than The Blue Ribbon." He lowered his voice conspiratorially. "Though don't you dare tell anyone I said so."

She laughed. "That's a sweet invitation, Charlie, but I have to get back to New York." She expressed regret that she had to catch an evening flight in Cedar Rapids, and he walked her up to the entrance.

"Funny how life works," he said idly. "You turning up on my doorstep to ask about Barry Stoner. . . ."

"How's that funny, Charlie?"

"Well, it was my dad who gave Barry his start."

"Oh?" DZ stopped.

"Barry had a paper route in town to make a few bucks. In his teens, he started hanging around here, askin' to be a reporter. There wasn't a thing for him to do—Pop did it all himself in those days, reporting, even typesetting. But he knew the Stoners needed money, so he got Barry a job sweeping up and whatnot over at the little radio station in the county seat. That was the beginning."

"Then you must have known Barry yourself. . . ."

"Not hardly. I was just seven or eight when he was around here. He was already up to making a pretty big name before Dad told me how he'd played his part." Charlie Foster laughed lightly. "Dad liked to tease me that he should've kept Barry, trained *him* to run the paper, and sent me off to become the big TV star."

DZ appraised the editor. He wasn't just attractive; he struck her as the kind of decent, humorous, content, and appealing man she never got to meet anymore—if she ever had. "I don't know, Charlie," she said. "I'd say you got the better deal."

"Oh yeah," he said sincerely. "I know I did, too." They were at the door, near the receptionist's desk. Foster opened it. "Well, don't forget us, Detective. If there's any part of this story that truly relates to the town, I won't mind getting that kind of news ahead of the pack."

"I'll remember." Then one more notion came to her, something that had nagged at her since talking to the local realtor and Chet Volmer. The first had mentioned the sale of the Stoner farm being undertaken by bank executors on behalf of the surviving five children—i.e., not counting the girl who'd died. Then Volmer had spoken of "the other four kids" who'd gone away after the loss of their sister . . .

and the mysterious illness of one brother. Total of six children.

Yet DZ believed she was accurate in recalling from Stoner's publicity releases that he spoke always of being "born into a family of five kids." What did it mean if Stoner had fiddled the numbers to write one of his siblings out of existence?

"Charlie, it'll mean more work for you, but I'd like to ask another favor. . . ." If he couldn't find the statistic reliably documented in his old issues—through birth announcements, perhaps—then she would appreciate if he could put one of his reporters onto checking birth certificates or church baptismal records, anyplace a true count of the Stoner children might appear. "It might mean a story for you," she concluded, "though I'd expect you to hold back until I give permission to print."

"Fair enough." They shook hands. "You expect to be out this way again?"

"I'll let you know if I am."

Emerging onto the street, DZ paused to register the easy flow of things on a sunny Saturday. A man loaded bags of animal feed into a pickup truck. Two women talked in front of a stationery store. DZ glanced up again at the second-floor windows with DALTON FALLS JOURNAL stenciled across. If she did sign off on the job when this was over could she ever be satisfied in a place like this—hitched up with a sweet, decent, Jimmy Stewart look-alike? There had been a touch of chemistry with Charlie Foster, she felt.

She caught herself. *C'mon, girl!* Forget this nostalgia for the simple homespun childhood she'd never had, costarring in some real-life remake of *It's a Wonderful Life*.

She shouldn't be surprised, either, that Stoner had written this place out of his life. You didn't have to be running away from something to want to leave a dull, sleepy little backwater like Dalton Falls.

CHAPTER
23

*O*N THE EVENING of DZ's first day back in the city, a fax of several pages came to the Task Force. It had been another long, frustrating day, and she was eager to get home to a cold beer, and a hot bath. Clark had asked half an hour ago if she'd wanted a ride home, but she'd told him to go while she finished writing the daily report. The other duty detectives were on supper break. The squad was minimal; with all the manpower the FBI had thrown onto the case since the Indiana killing, Leacock felt able to cut back the Task Force by two-thirds, so no one else was around to collect the fax.

Above the message on the first page, DZ saw the letterhead of the *Dalton Falls Journal:*

> To: Detective Lieutenant DZ Hayes
>   New York Police
>
> Dear Detective Hayes,
>   Following are items I've found relating to your questions about the Stoner family. It was a great pleasure to meet you. (Your visit is still the favorite topic over at The Blue Ribbon.)
>
> Charles Foster

Handwritten at the bottom was another line. *If you're out this way again, I'd enjoy seeing you—Charlie*

Sweet guy. Seems he'd also felt a bit of the same inexplicable tug she had. Nuts, though. Jimmy Stewart did not end up with . . . who would she be? . . . Angie Dickinson?

As she was about to continue reading, a burst of laughter echoed up the elevator shaft, men returning from dinner. DZ made a snap decision to keep the fax to herself. Even if Charlie had sent the stuff here, her curiosity about Stoner and the trip she'd taken to Dalton Falls could be classified as extracurricular, not police business. She tucked the pages into her shoulder bag.

A trio of detectives emerged from the elevator. "Knocking off?" asked one when they saw DZ.

"Yeah. What's keeping you here?"

"Still running that list we got from Ohio BOP."

She had suggested going through the Bureau of Prison's roster to see who had been locked in Marion at the same time as Portreck, comparing MOs of crimes that had put them there, seeking any who had shown an aptitude for electronics. A mountain of work with a marginal chance of a hit. But that was detective work, after all, shoveling through a mountain of shit on the search for a grain of gold.

THE DEEP PURPLE OF SPRING TWILIGHT WAS COLORING THE loft's huge windows when she arrived home. Through the gloom, she spotted the winking red light of the answering machine on the kitchen counter. She tapped a wall switch to turn on the overhead tracks and went to the machine. The digital counter showed twenty-three calls—interest was tapering off. When she'd returned last night from her Midwest trip, the machine had shown ninety-nine calls— no more only because the LED display had just two digits. All but four had been from newspaper or television reporters, and producers or researchers for television tabloids and talk shows—Stoner's and others. Their calls to her home pissed her off. Like many cops, DZ kept her number unlisted to avoid harassment by suspects under investigation or cons she'd sent up who might leave prison nursing a wish for revenge. Didn't stop the newshounds, though.

She took a beer from the refrigerator, and drank as she listened to the messages. More reporters and TV producers. DZ skipped to the end of each until she was listening to none other than Barbara Walters pitching a free lunch at Le Cirque 2000 "or anyplace else you'd like." She sounded nice, DZ thought, like a favorite aunt. Too bad—lunch with Barbara would've been a hoot.

Then a call from Vicky Parsons to propose taking in some theatre next weekend. They had been rookies together, but Vick had quit the force after a year, gone back to school for a teaching degree, and now headed the English Department at a high school in New Jersey and coached girl's basketball. Lucky Vick.

More fucking reporters. And finally—evidently not long before she'd walked in—"DZ, it's Barry. Call me. Home now, office in the morning." *Click.*

She noted the assumption of familiarity. Also a different tone in his voice, not that star timbre but a hint of . . . vulnerability, as though in need of someone to talk to.

Could it be just personal? Or did he still look upon her as simply a "get"?

She took salsa from the fridge, tortilla chips from a cabinet, and munched while she eyed the phone. Leave it till morning, she decided. She was dog tired, reflexes dull, apt to make a wrong move. And nothing he'd said made it sound urgent. She went to run a hot tub.

Emerging from the bath, she remembered the fax and retrieved it from her bag. She switched on the kitchen radio —always set to a station that played a straight run of standards—and sat down to read. The five pages following the cover letter were birth certificates arranged in chronologi-

cal order for children born to Sarah and Raymond Stoner
between 1946 and 1957—the first born being a boy named
Daniel, and five years later Laurel, the sister who had died.
Two more boys and a girl had been born over the following six years—Beryl, Gareth and Nancy—two years between each.

Damn. She should have remembered to look at the file
and check the names of the Stoner siblings who'd been
contacted by the force—three of them. She'd spoken to
one herself, Gareth; but Gable had made the other contacts. She went to the phone by the kitchen counter and
tried Clark at home. No answer. She pictured him having
supper alone in Burger King, reading a Harlequin—the
only man she'd ever known who avidly devoured the
quickie romances.

She went back to the couch and continued reading. The
next pages were clippings from the *Dalton Falls Journal*.
The first was three columns beneath the headline WAR
HERO WEDS MISS SARAH CLARK. On the top margin of the
clip was the date of the issue, March 12, 1946. A photo was
included, a young man in a marine uniform standing beside a slender, pretty, blond woman. The text was the sort
of prideful report that must have been printed in ten thousand small-town papers back then. Dalton Falls was happy
to make a fuss over twenty-eight-year-old Raymond
Stoner, "originally from Pennsylvania," who was marrying
one of its native daughters. He was described as a hero, not
based on action under fire, but for being among the first
marines taken prisoner in the invasion of Guam, and thereafter spending a year in a Japanese POW camp. The newspaper continued:

> Since his return to Dalton Falls, Raymond has re-
> covered his health completely, and he looks forward
> to farming the Maple Hill property that Miss Clark in-
> herited from her father. Sarah has given up her job

with Hal Kenney's insurance agency to work with her husband, but will continue teaching Sunday school.

DZ mulled over the article. She was left with a sense of the story being incomplete. Was it the picture that gave the hint? It couldn't have been taken at the time the couple was married since Raymond Stoner was wearing his marine uniform, though the text said he'd been discharged—long enough previously that he'd recovered from time in a POW camp. So why not a wedding picture? The report also said Raymond was "returning" to town, though originally from another place, but what had first brought him there? Minor omissions, perhaps, just part of the patchwork that made up the lives of small-town people anywhere.

Next came smaller cuttings from the newspaper. A birth announcement on a page datelined December 28, 1946 read: "Mr. and Mrs. Raymond Stoner of Maple Hill Farm are pleased to be parents of a boy, born at home Monday. Mother and child are doing well." No name for the boy was given, but by comparing records she identified him as Daniel, the first.

DZ counted off the months on her fingers. The baby had come just nine after the marriage. Just fast work maybe—though the odds were the mother had been pregnant when she wed, which would account for a discreet cermony, no photographs. By having the baby at home, particularly in winter, the young woman could have stayed out of sight, announced the birth weeks after it occurred. Fifty years ago the ruse could have made a difference in the way the couple and their child were regarded in a rural community.

The next clipping was another birth notice: "The Raymond Stoners announce the birth of their third child Friday evening at County Hospital, a daughter not named at press time." The clip was undated, but on the page to which it had been taped for fax transmission someone had noted "6/23/51."

The next announcement for another boy, Beryl, appeared only as one of several names in a column headed BIRTHS. No further clippings related to births were included, but a handwritten note had been inserted: "All I could find, C.F."

Next came half a dozen clips bearing on the death of twelve-year-old Laurel Stoner—including a story about the accident, and several items about an inquest that had ended in a finding of accidental death. There were two brief items related to the similar incident that had occurred a year earlier in a neighboring town, a girl named Trudy Willingham, who had died at her family farm. Clipped to the second item reporting her funeral was another handwritten jot from Charlie: "Not local girl, less coverage." DZ read each clip and saw nothing to suggest more than coincidence.

Next, a brief obituary of Raymond Stoner who had "succumbed suddenly while at work on his farm."

The last of the pieces from the *Dalton Falls Journal* was an obit for Stoner's mother. The few lines described Sarah Stoner as "our beloved former Sunday school teacher," said that she had been "sadly ill" in recent years, then added one insight by mentioning that she was "the granddaughter of Jonas Clark, a charter settler of our town." A hint of prominence that might explain some extra chagrin about the circumstances surrounding her marriage.

Having worked her way through everything, DZ sat back and tried recalling exactly her conversation with Chet Volmer. Decades had passed since he'd done horseshoeing at the Stoner farm, but his recollections hadn't seemed at all murky. He'd talked about an older boy who'd been ill *before* the girl's death—yes, "one of the older boys," he'd said—plus four more kids and the girl. A total of *six*.

The records said otherwise, though. Five birth certificates. DZ picked up the fax sheets again, and went through them again, searching for the proof of a lie.

This time it jumped right out at her, so blatant she was

amazed she'd missed it earlier. "The Raymond Stoners announce the birth of their *third* child Friday evening at County Hospital, a daughter not named at press time." The third child. But the date handwritten next to the clipping was 1951, same as the birth certificate that was chronologically *second* among those she'd received from Foster. Which seemed to indicate a birth certificate was missing, the one for the second child. *One of the older boys . . .*

DZ pulled the fax cover letter with the address and phone number of the *Dalton Falls Journal,* then went to the phone. As the connection went through, she glanced at the kitchen clock showing 9:20.

After two rings a man answered, sounding a bit preoccupied. "Foster."

Yeah, just as she'd pictured it, working late on some crusading editorial. "Charlie, it's DZ Hayes."

"Hey, DZ." His voice perked up. "Get the stuff I sent?"

"I did, thanks. I've just been looking it over, and something doesn't add up. I'm glad you're still at the paper, so I can—"

"I'm not at the office, I'm home."

"But I dialed—"

"It rings here when the office closes. Got no round-the-clock newsroom, but I still want the story if someone's barn burns down in the middle of the night."

"Well, I'm glad I got you." But she was more subdued now. His mention of home conjured possibilities for Charlie Foster left unconsidered. "It's late, though—sorry if I'm disturbing your family." It sounded so damn obvious once it was out, but she couldn't stifle her curiosity.

"Nobody here to disturb but me and Bonnie," he answered, "and I'm very glad to hear from you."

Bonnie. *Sure.* Guys like Charlie didn't hang around untaken. Stupid to feel let down—hell, she'd spent five minutes with the man!—yet she did. She raced ahead. "I just had a couple of questions about those faxes."

"Whatever I can tell you . . ."

"The birth certificates, were they hard to get?"

"Easy as pie. Sent a reporter to County Hall to ask Ben Littlefield for a set—Ben's the county manager."

"So records like that—births, deaths, marriages . . . they're all easy to access?"

"Nothing to it. Pull 'em out of a file cabinet. New stuff's going straight into a computer, but those old records don't take much space. Fifty years ago we didn't have but four thousand folks in the whole county."

So, DZ thought, a room watched over by a clerk who must be on friendly terms with many of the locals. No trouble to walk in and lift something from a file. No problem if Barry Stoner had wanted to revise his family history.

"Why'd you ask, DZ?" Charlie Foster asked. "What'd you mean—'something didn't add up'?"

When she'd first sought his help, DZ hadn't actually described her conversation with Volmer, the doubts it raised. If she explained now, could she count on him to help probe the mystery? If there was a secret worth guarding in that town, could Charlie be one of the sentries?

"Just something about the birth dates," she replied. "I wondered if they could have been tampered with."

"Why would anybody do that?"

She thought of a good lie: Stoner was in show business, it helped sometimes to knock a few years off your age—*c'mon, you had to trust somebody!* "Charlie, I'll level with you. It's not really birth dates that may have been tampered with. . . ."

As she imparted the whole truth of her suspicion, he interjected only an occasional word of surprise or doubt. "Golly . . . I can't imagine . . . gosh . . ."

She was nearly done with the explanation when a dog began barking in the background. "Hush, Bonnie!" Charlie said. "I'll get to you in a minute." Then he apologized to DZ for the interruption: "I haven't fed her yet."

A *dog*! Yes, Charlie *would* have one, a devoted pooch he'd take along for walks on country roads. DZ felt more buoyant as she summed up. "I know my idea sounds far-fetched, but how else would you explain that birth announcement from your own paper? Says it was the Stoner's third child."

He chuckled. "Could be Dad just gettin' his facts wrong. He did that a fair amount. But I'll talk to Chet again and—"

"Other people, too, Charlie. There's got to be other people around who remember the Stoners."

"That's going back forty years, DZ, can't be too many left. But I'll see what turns up."

"Thanks."

"No bother. I'm glad to be . . . your deputy. I just wish you were right here to pin on my star."

She laughed. Because taking it as a joke seemed best. She liked Charlie Foster; but encouraging him to develop a personal interest in her, she decided, wouldn't be fair. "I'm pretty tied up here, Charlie," she said. "I doubt I'll be out there for a good long while. And by the way, they don't give out stars anymore."

"Oh, I'd settle for one from your eyes."

It was getting heavy. Her mouth had gone dry. "Thank you, Charlie," she said quickly, flustered. "Let me know what turns up."

"Soon as I have anything. Good night, DZ. Sleep tight."

Fat chance. She fought an impulse as soon as she'd put down the phone to call right back, ask him what he was wearing, what he'd eaten for dinner, what kind of dog Bonnie was. She found her eyes misting then. *Dear God.* How nice it would be to investigate a good man's heart, not the dark soul of a killer's.

Fuck it! Forget it! She'd never be giving in to this stupid schoolgirl crap if she wasn't totally worn out.

Desperate to push Charlie Foster from her thoughts, she wondered if she ought to call Stoner after all, confront him with her suspicions. His reaction might tell her whether she'd tapped into something significant or not.

No. Better wait, build the file, look for proof.

Yet even if she was right, that the existence of one of his brothers had been erased, it wasn't yet certain that Stoner himself had done it. Why would he?

God only knew.

God only knew, for that matter, how it might even be connected to all the other inexplicable and evil things for which Barry Stoner was a lightning rod.

CHAPTER
24

ON WEDNESDAY NIGHT, at twenty minutes after eleven, Ned Pettick returned to his midtown apartment from the weekly two hours of tennis doubles he squeezed into his schedule. Pettick shucked off his sweat-sodden clothes as he walked around the apartment, getting himself a diet soda, then stopped at his telephone answering machine to see if anything had come in from the News Department—they called if any big stories were breaking.

The machine had a couple of messages—another divorced pal setting up a poker game, his daughter-in-law inviting him for Sunday lunch—then he heard a vaguely familiar man's voice, though he couldn't place it right away. "Hi, Ned. Sorry you're out, but there's no real need for us to talk. I wanted you to know first what a fine job you've been doing of reporting the story, giving it the coverage it deserves. . . ."

The recognition kicked in. Pettick turned up the volume on the machine. Far as he knew, this was the first word from the Mystery Guest since Monday's murder; Pettick was more excited than frightened by being chosen for the contact.

"Loving news as you do, you should be glad to hear I'm going to make some more of it tomorrow. I'll be back to duke it out with my favorite talk show host—providing you do your part. But then you always do as you're told, don't you? So listen carefully, and follow these instructions. . . ."

Pettick stood transfixed before the machine, listening to the killer as he methodically listed what he'd need, how it should be set up. He was carrying through, all the way, the murdering prick: he'd killed, yet it wouldn't stop him from coming back. And not by satellite this time—probably because he guessed they'd expect that and activate special measures to trace him.

The message finished with a jaunty "So long, see you tomorrow." There was nothing else on the tape.

Even those last words rang a bell for Pettick. *So long, see you tomorrow.* If he remembered rightly that had been the sign-off for one of the first network anchormen, John Cameron Swayze, back in the '50s and '60s. The Mystery Guest certainly knew his TV history.

And how to make news. Pettick's heart was beating hard with the excitement of realizing he was first on the next beat of the story—a story that was only going to continue and get bigger.

As he reached out to the answering machine to replay the message and make sure he got his instructions right, still standing naked before the machine, Pettick suddenly became aware he had an erection.

And why not? News, more than anything else, was what really turned him on.

CHAPTER
25

*E*NTERING THROUGH THE audience section of the studio, DZ was confronted with the sight of a small crowd standing around drinking their morning coffee. Along with the technicians setting up the special equipment for today's show, workers from nearby studios had heard the scuttle-butt and drifted in to kibitz.

"Listen up, everyone!" she shouted. She waited until there was absolute silence. "For any of you who don't know, I'm Detective Lieutenant Hayes. The only other thing you need to know is if you belong here. If not, you've got thirty seconds to get your ass out. After which anybody without cause will be arrested, charged with impeding a murder investigation—or maybe held as a suspect."

For a few shocked moments everyone gazed back, then they filed toward the exits. Soon only five people re-mained on stage, Candelli and three men and a woman, who were arranging computer components on a large table at the center.

The only others present were DZ and the two men who had followed her down the aisle—Gable, and a slender young Japanese dressed in chinos, a blue button-down shirt, and white running shoes. However, he broke the preppie mold by letting his thick black hair grow very long and be gathered into a samurai-style topknot, and slit-lens sunglasses more suited to warding off snow blindness on an Alpine glacier than for casual indoor wear. Traversing the open area where four cameras stood on moveable dollies, DZ and her companions joined Candelli.

"Where's Stoner?" she asked, surprised he wasn't as curious as everyone else about developments.

"I filled him in this morning," Candelli said. "He'll be here in time for the show."

DZ was annoyed. Marilyn DeJesus had suggested ways Stoner might goad the M.G. into exposing more of himself, and DZ needed time to prep Stoner with certain questions. Turning to the computer setup, she said, "Is that everything?"

Candelli nodded.

"Ko . . ." DZ called to the samurai preppie, who was observing the technicians unspool a thick length of cable and hook it up to the computer. He returned to DZ's side. "Joe, this is Kobo Tashahiro. The FBI suggested I bring him in." As long as she took Chafee's recommendations, he was content to let DZ oversee aspects of the case involving Stoner's show.

"I've read about you." Candelli said welcomingly.

Nineteen months ago Tashahiro had played a central role in the capture of Daniel Paskin, a computer hacker who had become the country's most wanted cyberthief by using phone lines to loot government and corporate computer systems of everything from credit card numbers to secret Pentagon codes. Paskin had evaded capture for years, and his arrest had been used by both *TIME* and *Newsweek* as a launching point for stories on the rise in computer crime. Ko Tashahiro's role had earned him the covers of both magazines, and though only twenty-two, he had since parlayed the publicity into founding a very successful firm that designed corporate computer security.

The young man shook Candelli's hand and took off his strange sunglasses to bare glittering black eyes. "The equipment here is what you were asked to provide?" he said to the producer.

"Exactly," Candelli replied. "Mr. Pettick played me the phone message, and this is what the M.G. specified. A regular desktop PC with the fastest processor available, and a large-screen monitor. He wanted it networked to the mainframe, the one GBS uses for all its corporate operations. The monitor was to be positioned center stage, facing the cameras, power left on during the show."

"Evidently," DZ said, "the Guest intends to use an Internet hookup to broadcast his voice and image."

"Precisely," Tashahiro agreed. "With this computer linked to telephone lines he will be able to call in and activate it whenever he chooses. Videocam interface will permit him to send his image. He wants a link to the mainframe because that will have a fiber-optic line to the transmission system over which digital information can be transmitted to form images as smoothly as if broadcast on a television frequency."

"But making contact here *will* depend on phone lines," DZ affirmed. "So he'll have to stay on those lines for as long as he wants to be on the air, and during that time we hope you'll—"

Tashahiro's stopped her, his hand rising like a semaphore. "Lieutenant, the man who arranged this method of communication surely wants absolute security from detection. From what I've seen here, my involvement is likely to be futile."

"You're telling us we won't be able to trace him?" Gable said.

"Understand this," Tashahiro replied. "When someone steps into a phone booth, and is connected in the ordinary way, the location of that phone can be traced in a minute.

But phone companies route calls through switching equipment—computer controlled. A person with sufficient expertise can use a computer to connect directly to these switchers, and generate instructions that subvert a trace."

"Subvert it how?" DZ asked.

"Every phone number is connected in phone company files to an address. The essence of an effective trace is that when the phone number is established, you have the address. But if you connect to the switching equipment and scramble routing tables, phone numbers will not correctly match addresses. Your caller might be in a hotel lobby, but when the number is traced—"

"I remember now," Candelli broke in. "That was the big problem with catching Paskin. The FBI would trace his calls, dispatch a team right away—and they'd end up busting in on some little old lady in a retirement community."

Tashahiro smiled thinly. "Another time it was a bordello in San Francisco's Chinatown—while Danny was actually calling from a YMCA in Sacramento."

Gable turned to DZ. "Gotta be a group. Two or three people involved, maybe, and one of 'em's the computer whiz."

"I see no reason to assume," Tashahiro remarked, "that a murderer cannot also posses the required expertise."

That coincided with DZ's conviction that it was all the work of one man.

Central to everything the M.G. had done was the expression of one gigantic ego.

"Ko," she said, "if phone company switching equipment will be involved, can't we make it more secure? Detect changes as they happen?"

"Your man apparently likes to keep moving around the country. His next call is as likely to come from a hotel in Las Vegas as from a phone booth around the corner. I wouldn't know how to guard against all the variables—so many points along the electronic highway where tampering can occur."

"You're telling us," Candelli said, "that if we let the bastard on the air again, he can talk as long as he wants and we won't get any nearer to him?"

Tashahiro slipped the sunglasses back on to mask his eyes as he nodded.

Candelli shook his head and wandered off to the table to watch bleakly as the technicians connected the computer.

"Do whatever you can to find a chink in the armor," DZ told Tashahiro. "Rig a computer to run in tandem with the one on stage, get the same signals." To Gable, DZ explained, "Ko will monitor a terminal backstage. There's a chance he can pick up something useful directly off the computer."

"A *small* chance," Tashahiro reminded her.

"I understand, Ko. But get onto it."

With a polite bow, Tashahiro left to organize his own equipment.

"Got to be a group," Gable repeated. "Just look at how stuff is happening thousands of miles apart."

"Days have passed between what happens in one place and the next," DZ noted. "The distances could be covered easily in that time. In fact, tracing that trail on the map may be what finally enables us to pick him out."

A loud voice came from the rear. "Okay, what's he got for us this time?"

She turned to see Skip Corcoran heading for a look at the computer onstage. "Good to see you're on the job, Lieutenant," he said as he passed her.

"He loves this, doesn't he?" Gable muttered, eyeing Corcoran with distaste.

"It's all showbiz," DZ said tartly as she watched Corcoran join Candelli and start questioning him. Quickly the producer appeared agitated, gesticulating to wave off Corcoran before he went backstage.

"Clark, give Chafee a call," DZ said. "Thank him for suggesting Tashahiro, and see if he's got anything new on cross-checking the travel facilities." Gable nodded and headed backstage, where he was sure to find a phone.

DZ joined Corcoran at the computer setup.

"Internet," he said. "Sure is touching all the bases."

"Safe at every one."

"Is it definite he'll call today?" Corcoran asked. "Joe got awful touchy when I asked for details."

"Well, Mr. Corcoran, for some of us this whole thing was disturbing from the start. We can't all deal with it as if it's just one more corporate asset."

He gave her a steely once-over. "Listen, Lieutenant, I didn't invent this new routine for committing murder. You might also consider that if I am a coldhearted, manipulative prick, it gives me perceptions about this killer that are sharper than yours. I might even have better ideas for stopping him."

"Such as . . . ?"

"How about offering a reward? Say . . . five million. Or ten if he kills again—a million for every dollar he'd have gotten on *What's My Line?* . . ."

She eyed him carefully for a full ten seconds. "You're serious . . . ?"

"Absolutely. We'd announce it on Stoner's show today."

"You really think it would work to wave a fortune at a guy who only collects if he goes to jail for murder."

"Listen," Corcoran said, "the bum he shotgunned—can you tell me that piece of shit didn't deserve to die? If he surrenders, he could plea-bargain for manslaughter, be out of jail in a few years with the rest of his life to spend the money."

DZ studied his executive's eyes. Their cool ocean-blue color had no calming effect; sea monsters swam in those waters. "You don't get it, do you? This guy hates television. Hates the way it's used, the power it has, and probably the people who control it. God knows why he feels it so deeply, but part of his motive seems to be to put a new slant on the medium—mock it, shock it, even wake people to what he hates about it by using it." A sound escaped her lips, an amputated laugh. "You talk about knowing his mind. But you're just his organ grinder monkey, Corcoran. He'd expect you to pull a bullshit stunt like this reward, publicity-seeking PT Barnum crap. And he'd just turn it back against you."

The network head regarded DZ disdainfully. "What gives you such cocksure insight? I heard about the analysis your psychologists did. This guy is smart, and sane— and there are hints he's a businessman. He'll have his price."

DZ shook her head slowly back and forth. At last she said, "Ever wonder why he was wearing that sailor suit the first day he came on?"

"He told us—a disguise, good as any."

"No, Corcoran, no. It was his joke on *you*. Because he's just a plain sailor—one of the crew. But you . . . you're 'the skipper.'" She walked off the stage, looking for Gable.

Gazing after her, Corcoran's expression kept darkening as he worked it out.

CHAPTER
26

*P*LAIN OPENING AGAIN; no logo, no snappy music. The silence of the empty studio against a view of the stage. The computer equipment was at the center on two brushed aluminum pedestals, one for the monitor, the second for the keyboard—at a height that made it easy to use without sitting. Stoner came on dressed in a dark blue suit. In a subdued tone, he said:

"If you've been watching my program, you know we've become embroiled in a horrifying situation. It has now cost one life, and everything possible is being done to find those responsible. Part of that effort is to keep open our line of communication to the man who says he is the killer, and hope this helps end his reign of terror. We've been alerted that he intends to appear again today. I caution listeners that what he says may be upsetting, and urge parents to keep children from watching."

He went on to explain why the computer was there, and the way it was expected to be used during the hour.

Leaning against a wall of the control booth, wearing a hands-free headset that enabled her to communicate with Tashahiro, DZ reflected that the solemn tone Stoner was using had a more genuine ring than the first time he'd prefaced the M.G.'s appearance. Though perhaps he simply had the ability to dial his sincerity up a notch at will. Except for his opening speech, she'd had no opportunity to gauge his true state of mind. He'd arrived in the studio minutes before airtime. She'd only had time to pass him the sheet of notes with questions DeJesus had suggested for the M.G.

Other than the director, the engineers at the control console, Lori Swann and one other production assistant to field phone calls, no one else was in the booth today. Gable was at Tashahiro's side. Chafee was monitoring the show in Washington, summoned for a meeting at FBI headquarters about extra measures to deal with the situation. As for Corcoran, DZ had intended to bar him from the booth, but it wasn't necessary; he was watching in his office.

Stoner ended his preamble by mentioning that the phone lines would be open to receive calls. Then he introduced a panel of seven people—social critics and technology experts (to explain the Internet)—hastily assembled as filler while waiting for the M.G.'s contact.

But for an audience promised an interview with the devil, nothing else would do. As the minutes passed, it only got became more irritating to listen to Stoner and the panel, as if the pregame chatter of football announcers went on and on without the game ever being played. Calls from viewers expressed dismay, even anger, at not seeing the Mystery Guest.

As the first half hour ended, an MIT professor from the university's famed Media Lab was suggesting the influence of technology had helped to create a kind of cyberman, who could commit murder with the same emotionless calculation as a computer. "The killer may even use one to make foolproof plans," the expert said. "He's not making mistakes. And he seems to regard what he's doing as a kind of game; computers can play chess and beat most humans every time. . . ."

In the booth, a cry suddenly went up from Lori: "He's *here*!"

She was looking transfixed at the computer monitor on the stage. Until a moment ago, the large screen had been dark, in standby mode. Now it was glowing, no picture yet, but radiating light.

DZ turned on her headset. "Ko—this it?"

Tashahiro's voice came through her earphones. "Yes, the computer is being accessed from outside."

Stoner hadn't noticed. As he moderated the discussion, he was positioned with the monitor behind him. The director spoke into his headset, giving Stoner instructions through a tiny earpiece. "Barry—the monitor."

Stoner swung around, which made the panel members also look and fall silent. "I guess this is what we've been waiting for," Stoner said grimly.

A word filled the screen, black letters on a white field:
ENTER

DZ spoke into the headset. "Ko, what's that about?"

"Stoner's got to hit Enter on the keyboard," Tashahiro told DZ, and the director passed it along. Stoner moved to the keyboard and struck the key. At once a line of letters, numbers and other keyboard characters came onto the screen, preceded by an instruction to type them in.

"I guess this is a password," Stoner said over his shoulder to the camera as he tapped at the keys.

"One more layer of security," Tashahiro told DZ through the intercom. "A trace is practically impossible."

The last three characters of the password were dollar signs, $$$. As Stoner typed them, the monitor filled with a moving image in black and white, another old clip from *What's My Line?* DZ realized. The MC, John Daly, sat at a rostrum wearing a tuxedo. His voice came through the speakers of the computer monitor, hearty, jovial: "Will our Mystery Guest sign in, please."

The old kinescope cut to a close-up of a hand picking

up a piece of chalk and scripting a signature on a black-board.

J...o...h... n   W...a...y...

Wayne—DZ finished the signature in her mind. But before the whole name was written, the image of the sign in was replaced by a view of the same featureless chamber that had been the setting for the killer's first appearance. As before, he sat in a chair, but the clean, sailor's uniform had been replaced by the winter outfit of an infantryman who might have just climbed out of a battlefield foxhole. Dirty flak jacket, mud-caked boots, and a dented brown helmet, it's visor shadowing a face darkened more by a growth of stubble and smears of grime.

DZ tried again to discern some element of the man Marilyn DeJesus had speculated must be notably handsome; but all she saw was a grizzled, war-weary veteran. Why a soldier this time? Maybe Gable was right: Some maniacal paramilitary group was responsible. Wasn't John Wayne a hero of the far right?

Stoner began. "Well, what should I say—welcome? You're not exactly welcome here."

DZ frowned. *Easy—don't chase him away.*

The soldier laughed. "C'mon, Barry, would you rather keep talking to that bunch of blowhards you've got there? You'd much rather hear the stuff I tell you."

"Depends on what it is."

"As promised. Today we get to the nitty-gritty, the play-by-play. I'll tell you what it was like to kill—"

Stoner had begun bobbing nervously on the soles of his feet, practically jumping out of his skin. He couldn't maintain the pose of the cool talk show host for another second. "Damn it, what do we have to do to end this?"

"Hey, hey," the soldier said in the gentling tone of an adult pacifying a child's tantrum. "We won't get anywhere if you go crazy on me."

The ironic thrust of the words stymied Stoner. He cast a

frustrated look toward the cameras. DZ was astonished to see Stoner at a loss, the Mystery Guest taking control.

"How're we doing down there?" she asked Tashahiro through her intercom. A trace was initiated the moment the connection had been made.

"All I can tell so far is that the call is being switched through long-distance lines," Tashahiro replied.

Stoner was fighting to regain his composure. He turned again to the monitor. "Okay, one question at a time. Tell me about your costume. Why the switch from Popeye to G.I. Joe."

The soldier waggled his head, a quiet laugh. "Let's say . . . it's a tribute to the men and women of our armed forces."

"Two-zero-two area code." Tashahiro's voice in her ear. *Washington?*

"Did you fight in a war?" Stoner was asking.

If only he'd admit it, there could be a war record—

"I'm fighting one now, Barry."

"You against the world, huh?" Stoner was back in stride. This was the old cocky sarcasm with which he'd confronted thousands of villains over the years.

"No, I'm not alone in this. I've got quite a few people in my army—and more joining up all the time."

Stoner squinted cannily at the image on the monitor. "Care to tell us who they are—all these recruits of yours?"

The director called for a tight close-up, and a split screen to broadcast the soldier's face alongside a close-up of Stoner. But the face was obscure, and masked by shadow and the dirt and seemingly real unshaven stubble.

"They're all the people who don't want me to stop." The Mystery Guest tilted his head back so his eyes were suddenly lit as they stared into the camera, eyes of a pale blue-gray that stood out all the more starkly from the surrounding carbon black. "All of you out there," he said, staring mesmerically out at the vast never land into which his image was being sent.

"No! You're wrong about that!" Stoner said. "We don't share your sickness."

The soldier tucked his chin down combatively, and his face receded again into shadow. "*I'm* sick? Why? Because I thought it was a good idea to get rid of a piece of human filth who trafficked in smut, and went free after the torture and murder of two little boys? Let me tell you, it felt *good* to kill him. He deserved it. C'mon folks, are you with me on this or not?" He held out his hands, appealing to the unseen masses. "Blowing that bastard's head off—well, you might say it was . . . a no-brainer." He laughed at his own joke.

Stoner said harshly, "That's funny to you, huh?"

DZ whispered urgently into her headset. "Any progress, Ko?"

"I'm into the Washington switchers," Tashahiro said.

"You bet," the soldier said, laughter tailing off. "It's a joke—what we call justice—and I felt proud to pull this one off, settle accounts with this child killer. Want to know Mr. Portreck's last words?"

Stoner's mouth curled with a show of distaste: "Tell us."

" 'You're not going to kill me, are you?' " Another dry little laugh. "That's what he said, sitting there in his pajamas and shaking all over. I told him to settle back, watch TV and not worry about a thing. You know what was on? *Leave It to Beaver.*" He laughed again.

"And then you shot him in cold blood. . . ."

"Roger. And he died watching innocent little boys having their innocent fun—the kind of kids he liked to kidnap and torture."

"C'mon, Ko, c'mon," DZ urged. "He may cut it any second—"

"I'm *trying*! But it's shielded. . . ."

Before she could ask what he meant, DZ's attention was drawn back to the broadcast.

". . . the right to appoint yourself judge and jury?" Stoner was saying. "Sure, some people who deserve pun-

ishment slip through the cracks, the system's not perfect.
But if we all decided to pick out anyone who, in our private opinion, deserved to die, and then did the job ourselves—"

"This world would be a better place." The soldier leaned
back so the light caught his eyes again as he stared into the
camera. In a parody of an infomercial TV pitchman, he
said. "Let us know what *you* think folks. Our lines are
open, operators standing by . . ."

"Oh shit," Lori Swann said. She knew what what was
coming now. A second later it *did*. The telephones in front
of her all lit up.

Stoner could imagine what the reaction had been to the
killer's invitation. "You think you can turn this whole
country into a lynch mob?" he demanded. "Okay, you murdered a piece of garbage . . . and, you know, if you gave
yourself up tomorrow, there are those who'd say you
should be given a break. . . ."

"I'm not giving up anything," the M.G. said flatly.
"Catch me if you can. Until then I'll go on about my business."

Jesus, DZ thought, her eyes rolling heavenward. Give us
something. "C'mon, Ko," she pleaded.

"Can't break the code," he shot back—angry at his own
failure.

DZ could hear Lori and another production assistant answering call after call: "Yessir, thank you for your opinion,
sir. . . . Yes, madam, your views are appreciated . . . ." All
evidently expressing support for the killer.

Seeking a hook to pry out useful information, Stoner
said, "Speaking of business, just what *is* yours? How do
you make ends meet?"

A smile showed through the grime. "What's my line,
you mean? Sorry, Barry. Gotta figure it out for yourself."

Stoner glanced down at his side—looking at the notes
with lines of questioning DZ had pressed into his hand before the show. "You won't tell us one thing about yourself?

Maybe just this: how'd you come up with this whole idea? Why must you do it this way?"

The soldier took a breath and said wearily, "I'm a child of the television age, I guess, like you."

"Don't lump me in with you." Stoner declared furiously. "I'm no murderer."

"But you don't mind protecting one, do you?"

Stoner glared at the monitor, and leaned forward as if trying to see through the glass window. Then the question roared out of him, all remnant of cool detachment torn away. "What the *hell* do you mean by that?"

DZ was amazed to see how deeply and painfully the M.G.'s words had reached inside Stoner. Even the way he was standing now—slightly bent at the middle as he peered into the monitor—looked as if he'd been physically impaled.

"Just that we're more alike than you'd ever admit. But you know that, Barry. It's why you *had* to be the one."

Stoner edged back from the monitor, his head cocked as if trying to get a new perspective through the electronic window, to see beyond the shadows.

"Well, folks, I guess that just about wraps it up for today," the M.G. said, once more using a jaunty tone. "Any last words for me, Barry?"

Stoner said nothing.

"He froze up, for chrissakes!" the director exclaimed. "He's like a fuckin' amateur out there. . . ."

"Ko!" DZ pleaded again. "You don't have much longer."

At last Stoner found his voice. "Who *are* you?"

The man on the monitor ignored him and looked into the eye of his own lens. "Too soon to tell. Because then the show would be over. And I know you're all going to be thrilled with my next victim."

"Who . . . ?" Stoner said softly. Perhaps begging again for the M.G.'s identity.

But the soldier's mind was on his prey. "One of the

enemy," he replied. "And don't you worry, Barry, I'll be back to talk about it afterward. Meanwhile, everybody, keep those calls and letters coming. It gets lonely out here on the battlefield." He put a hand up to the helmet and snapped a salute.

The screen went black.

"Transmission's cut," the director called out. Into his intercom, he said, "Take a little time to react, Barry. Walk the stage, we'll do a pan. Let it sink in, that's okay. . . ."

"Anything?" DZ said into her mike. "Ko, you must have *something*. . . ."

"Sorry, DZ. I couldn't break the shield."

"What does that—?" She broke off, distracted again by what was happening on the stage. Up to this moment, Stoner had ignored the director's instruction to move. Hands at his sides, clenched into fists, he was clearly fighting a battle for self-control. Now, in a sudden blur of motion, he grabbed up the column of pedestal on which the keyboard was resting, and swung it into the monitor, shattering the screen in a spray of glass, sparks flying from its electronic innards. Then Stoner threw down the pedestal and walked off the stage into the wings.

In dumb disbelief, the whole control booth crew watched their star go berserk. Candelli rushed off in pursuit. In a moment the booth came back to life. "Barry! Get back on stage!" the director screamed into the mike connected to Stoner's hidden earpiece. "We're on the air! What the fuck are you doing? Barry?"

DZ grabbed up her bag and started for the door. The director barked at his engineers. "Roll tape—cue to where Stoner types in the password!" He picked up a phone. "Got something ready there?" he said to whoever answered. As she left, DZ heard the director tell his engineers that the newsroom had said they'd be ready with a bulletin in sixty seconds. Down the steps from the control booth, she ran across the studio floor and backstage to where Tashahiro had set up his own computer rig. He was still at his keyboard, typing furiously.

"What did you mean about a 'shield'?" DZ asked him.

Tashahiro stopped tapping at the keys. "We got a Washington area code for the call's origin. The next step was to go to the area switcher, which kicked me over to a phone number. That's when I hit an electronic firewall—impenetrable computer security. It's probably 'cause the routing tables were reconfigured—the M.G. just made it *seem* it came from there—"

"From where, Ko?" DZ demanded urgently. "For chrissakes *where*?"

"The place *all* soldiers work for, DZ. That call looks like it came from the Pentagon."

CHAPTER
27

JOHN IS COMMON slang for a trick, a hooker's customer. In that context, 'John Way' could refer to doing something that takes sexual advantage of a woman."

"Which gets us what?" DZ pressed Marilyn DeJesus. She had brought the taped broadcast straight back to the office for analysis. She would have preferred to talk first with Stoner, but after walking off the program, he had vanished. DZ had half her squad trying to track him down. Now, with Gable and the police psychologist, she was running the videotape for the fourth time, studying the M.G.'s every word, brainstorming for meanings in everything the killer did. Suggesting John Wayne's name—but not using it whole—must have some significance.

"He chose his first victim—a sex offender—after giving us the Peter Lorre hint," DeJesus observed. "Maybe he's telling us he'll go after another pornographer . . . or a pimp. Maybe he identifies with the people they victimize."

"Because—what?" said Gable. "He saw his beloved mother forced to turn tricks?"

"In fact, an unhealthy, sexualized relationship between

child and mother is an element we've seen before in forming the psyche of serial murderers."

"This guy's not serial yet," Gable said. "Only one on the scorecard."

"But he's on the record as wanting to do many more," DeJesus countered.

Even so, DZ thought, explanations of other cases were too pat to explain this guy.

The psychologist continued her speculations. "The M.G. also states the person he plans to kill is 'one of the enemy'—and says it while dressed as a soldier. And the way he scrambled the phone—tying into the Pentagon—fits into playing a military role."

"So his next victim might be someone with whom we're at war?" Gable said.

DZ advanced the idea. "A foreign terrorist, or a dictator in another country? Maybe a place that traffics in children." If distances between victims didn't matter, the M.G. might take his terror campaign international.

They continued through the tape to the point where Stoner's agitation with the M.G. began to escalate. *"I'm no murderer,"* Stoner said to the M.G., and back came the reply, *"But you don't mind protecting one, do you?"* They watched as Stoner violently smashed the monitor screen and hurried offstage.

DZ stopped the VCR. "What do you make of Stoner's behavior, Marilyn?"

The psychologist thought. "Attacking the TV set is his way of assaulting the killer. A calculated display, perhaps—playing to his audience."

"It didn't seem calculated to me. Remember, a good part of his audience sympathizes with the killer. They *approved* of the murder—thousands called in to say so."

"He blew up when he was accused of protecting a murderer," Gable pointed out. "What do you make of that?"

The psychologist tapped her chin thoughtfully. "The killer might have been referring to himself—protected in the sense he feels television programmers don't want him to be caught, he's been so good for business."

"But suppose Stoner is truly shielding someone else," DZ said, "and the Mystery Guest knows it. That would explain Stoner being thrown off-balance. Even why he disappeared——to avoid answering questions about it."

The psychologist simply gave a puzzled shake of her head.

They had covered everything——and it was still all guesswork. DZ told DeJesus she could go, then sent Gable back to his own desk to run another check on Stoner, call his various homes, see if he'd surfaced anywhere.

Alone, she ran the tape back once more over Stoner's explosion. It left her even more convinced the outburst had been spontaneous; he had been genuinely thrown by the M.G.'s accusation.

Gable returned to inform DZ that a doorman at Stoner's Fifth Avenue apartment building had seen him arrive by taxi not long after leaving GBS, remain briefly at his apartment, then leave the building again on foot.

At a little after nine, DZ took a last phone call at her desk before heading home: Candelli. When she told him Stoner was still missing, the producer said, "The way he cracked, Lieutenant, I've been worried he might have gone out and . . . done something to hurt himself."

"You talking about suicide?"

"He had to be very upset to walk off the show and vanish. And the past few days he's been saying things I'd never heard before—like about quitting the show."

"Really?" From what DZ had seen of Stoner, he hardly acted like a man at the end of his rope. "Joe, I'm sure he'll turn up in good shape. He never struck me as anything like suicidal."

"Me neither. But I was remembering what happened with his father." He paused. "Look, no one's supposed to know this—Barry's been careful to keep it out of the bios—but his father killed himself."

DZ thought back to the report of the death in the *Dalton Falls Journal*—simple and straightforward. "Are you sure?"

"There's nothing about it anywhere, I know. Barry kept the lid on. In all the years, he mentioned it only once to me—and more or less by accident. We'd done a program about teen suicides. A mother who'd lost her kid was telling how it happened, that he'd shot himself playing Russian roulette with a school friend, and Barry started to cry—on the air. Plenty of times he's gone misty, but this was different—tears streaming down his cheeks. It was great TV. Later, when I asked him about it, he tossed it off, said it wasn't the kid or the mother he was really crying for—just that hearing how the kid had put a bullet in his head made him think about his dad."

"So he *told* you his father shot himself."

"Not in so many words. But I *think* that's what he meant."

DZ again reassured Candelli that Stoner didn't seem the type, and the producer sounded better by the time he hung up. But she knew the true weight of the revelation. Children of suicides were ten thousand percent more likely to take the same way out. The Hemingway syndrome.

She got home at a little after 10 P.M. and went straight to the kitchen. She opened the drawer where she had left the clippings faxed by Charlie Foster, and flipped to the photocopy of Raymond Stoner's brief obituary. *". . . succumbed suddenly while at work on his farm,"* she read, then put the clippings back in the drawer, and stood thinking while she had a beer. It could be another small town euphemism for an unpleasant fact that everybody knew, but found it nicer not to set in black and white.

DZ glanced at the kitchen phone. Charlie might know the facts—or could find them out. And she realized it was nice to have an excuse to talk to him again.

Before she could pick up the phone, it rang. With all the press bugging her these days, she usually waited for the machine to intercept; coworkers had learned always to use her beeper number and she'd call back. But she had an intuition: some miraculous telepathy was at work. She snatched up the phone eagerly. "Hello!"

"DZ, sorry to bother you now—"

The familiar voice. "Oh Charlie! No bother. I was just thinking—"

"It's Barry," he said curtly.

A stunned second, then she was pissed. All the more for being embarrassed. "Where the hell have you been?"

"I want to know first if you'll meet me here. I need to talk."

He did have that ragged at-the-end-of-my-rope sound. "Tell me where."

SHE DROVE NORTH ON THE PARKWAY FOR TWO HOURS, THEN exited to a winding country road. At last she rounded a bend and saw the destination he'd described: a one-story cabin with faded yellow paint, the name "Ferris" on a mailbox in front. A gray compact with rental plates was in the drive. DZ glanced at the dash clock as she pulled in. 12:51. What would he make of her willingness to come at this hour? A male cop could do it and still be just a cop. She'd worn a basic, tan pants suit to play down her appeal, but being conscious of the need was as bad as ignoring it.

As she crossed a patch of grass to the house, he emerged onto the porch. By the light through the open door, she saw he was dressed in jeans and a dark blue pullover, a pair of reading glasses plowed up into his thick brown hair. As she climbed three rickety steps to the porch, he said a simple, "Thanks," and she accepted it with a diffident bob of her head.

They entered directly into a big open room with a varnished pine-board floor dominated by a large fireplace with a hearth of rough-hewn stone. The furniture was a hodgepodge, tasteful without being fussy. She recognized

a Stickley armchair and an early American hutch only because it was the kind of stuff she often saw for sale at killer
prices in Tribeca storefronts. The room was lit by several
table lamps and warmed by the glow of a dying fire. On
the arm of the Stickley chair, a book was turned turtle—a
new bestseller by an ex–White House insider. Stoner
hadn't been pacing the floor and tearing his hair out as he
waited for her, but calmly reading.

"Who's Ferris?" she asked.

"Man I bought this place from."

But he'd kept the name on the mailbox. "For a hide-
away . . ."

"Walk out the back, cross a field, and you're in my horse
pastures." Stoner waved to the hutch at one side of the
room, where bottles of liquor were clustered. "Can I offer
you something?"

"No. You wanted to talk; I came to listen." She sat on a
settee facing the armchair.

He went to the fireplace and dropped another log onto
the embers, then took his book to the hutch and slid it onto
a shelf. Delaying, she thought. Whatever he wanted to tell
her wasn't easy for him. "Candelli was worried," she said.
"He thought you might have gone off to kill yourself."

"Hell, why? Sure, this thing has me in a twist. But how
could Joe think—?"

"Because of your father."

His green eyes narrowed. In the glint of lamplight, they
gave the impression of a pair of glacial lakes glimpsed
through a tiny clearing. The silence and stillness held for a
moment. Then he came back to the chair and sat down.

"Not the best place to begin," he said, "but, yeah, it's
part of the story. Got up from breakfast one morning, said
he was going out to plow a back field. We ate at day-
break—a farming family, you know—but I was up to
muck the cows, so I saw him walking to his tractor carrying his shotgun."

He was seeing it now, DZ realized.

"I ran over and asked him what the gun was for, and he said a bunch of damn crows was eatin' up the grain. Then he climbed up onto the tractor and rode away. We didn't think to look for him again until supper time, and Ma sent Nonee—Nancy, my youngest sister—to see where he . . ." He went silent.

"So she found the body," DZ said gently. "Must've been terrible for her."

Stoner leaned back, eyes on the ceiling, as if he couldn't face DZ while describing it. "Until she got up close she thought he was dozing. He was still propped up in the tractor seat; he'd bent over to put the barrel in his mouth."

"Awful," DZ said quietly. "And how is that 'part of the story'?"

He pulled himself up and looked at her steadily for a second. Then he bolted from the chair to the hutch and opened the door of a lower cabinet. He pulled out a couple of crystal lowball glasses and set them on an open shelf where the bottles were. Raising a bottle, he said, "Very good brandy. Join me?"

If she merely held the glass it would set a mood, smooth the flow. "A little."

He put a little in one glass, a lot in the other, gave her the first and sat down again. He sipped, and began: "A big family, I guess there's always a chance one of the kids will be—how'd we say it back there?—not right in the head. In our family the odds were even better 'cause of Pa. I never heard what he was like before the war, but the way he came out of it you could see he'd been . . . well, changed doesn't cover it. Where I'm from, one more quiet farmer passes easily in a crowd. But Pa . . . he was totally bottled up. He'd been captured by the Japanese right after he was sent to fight in the Pacific, and had some horrendous experience in the POW camp. I don't know what exactly— he never talked about it. Kept it all inside. And it affected us kids. It was the first thing that made me want to get inside people, made me yearn to know what was going on in there." He tapped his head. "My brother, though—one of my older brothers, Lyle—it did something different to him."

Stoner took another sip of his brandy, and DZ took her first. It went down smoothly, hints of fruit beyond the warm burn on her tongue.

"He was a funny guy, Lyle—ha-ha funny . . . and funny-strange. A show-off, too. He'd stick a pitchfork upright in a mound of pig shit so those sharp spikes'd be poking straight up in the air, then he'd high jump over it. A goofball—but smart, too. Soon as he read Shakespeare in high school he had it memorized. Used to walk around the barnyard spouting Hamlet." Stoner smiled at the memory. "I wanted to be like him."

He paused, longer. DZ took another sip from her glass.

"Something happened to one of my sisters," he said at last.

"I know. She died in a silo."

He didn't remark on her knowledge; evidently he'd guessed she might explore his past. "At first Ly denied he'd been anywhere near when it happened," Stoner resumed. "I was there the first couple of times it came up, and he denied it. But Pa found out different. As bottled up as he was mostly, when he blew it was ten on the Richter. So one day the rest of us kids were told we couldn't go in the barn for a while. Nonee peeked in anyway, and told the rest of us she saw Ly chained to a roof post. Meanwhile, we could hear a whole lot of hammerin' coming from an old icehouse way out in the woods by a pond. A few mornings later, that icehouse . . ." Stoner winced at a memory and pulled off a big slug of his drink. "It had a lock on the door, and if you went anywhere near you'd hear a pounding sound, or a voice calling. Pa warned us not to go near it, though. And because we knew what was in there, we were so damn scared, we obeyed. Never even swam in that pond anymore. Only Pa went, every morning and night, bringing the food Ma fixed."

He'd been talking with his eyes down, but now they came up again to meet DZ's. They seemed to beg her to save him from spelling it out himself.

"He locked your brother away," she said, "for murdering your sister."

Stoner sprang up again. "Ly was fourteen!" The words came in a stricken cry. "Fourteen, for god's sake . . ." Suddenly he flung the tumbler in his hand against the rock facing of the fireplace. All across the floor shards of glass lay picking up the firelight, like bits of hellfire that had rained down into the room.

"It wasn't just about your sister, though," DZ said. "There was another girl who died the same way. . . ."

She could see only his back, still she knew she'd gotten it right. The way he set his shoulders, arched his neck back, like a man preparing to have sentence passed.

He started to pace around the shadowy edges of the room. "Her family was from another town, but Ly knew her. Pa just couldn't conceive of any other way to handle it. He knew Ly had to be shut away. But . . . imagine how it would've been for all of us if he'd just turned in his own son as a murderer . . . ." Stoner's voice sank. He went to the hutch, grabbed up the brandy, and chugged some straight from the bottle.

"People must have noticed when Lyle dropped out of sight," DZ said.

"I don't know. The local folks were so involved with giving us sympathy about Laurel. My folks spread it around that Ly had taken it hard and was sick, and curiosity about him dwindled away."

She remembered Chet Volmer describing the atmosphere of doom on the Stoner farm. "How long did it go on," DZ said, "keeping your brother like that?"

"Three years."

"Jesus," she whispered.

"I suppose it's hard to understand, but we—my brothers and sisters—we just lived with it. I don't mean it didn't affect us. With me, it made me glad to be away from the farm. That's what led to my working jobs like the radio station."

"And after the three years?"

"Pa realized it couldn't go on. That's when the state was called in."

"Your brother was turned over to—"

"Sent to the state hospital for the criminally insane, over at Widmer Lake. 'Wonderland' as it was known locally. All us kids knew was one morning the icehouse door was wide open. Ly had been taken away in the middle of the night."

"God," DZ said in a pitying whisper. Forty years ago a provincial prison asylum would have been a snakepit. Being committed to such a place at the age of seventeen was unthinkable. "If your brother was treated as a criminal, then your father must have told the authorities—"

He interrupted again. "I got hold of the hospital file only years later. I learned then what Pa told the doctors—him *and* Ma, 'cause she must have gone along with it. They said Lyle had tried to kill them both and also that, with Ma he'd . . . oh Christ, use your imagination. They said whatever it took to put him away, but without owning up to the truth." Stoner stopped circling and brought the bottle up to his mouth.

DZ let him finish a long swallow before saying, "Could you put that away now?"

He shot her a glance, but went to the hutch and set down the bottle. "Four days after we saw the icehouse was open, my father took his last tractor ride. Looking back now, I think I knew as soon as I saw him carrying his gun that morning, he wasn't going out to shoot crows. We all should've known. *Did* know, maybe. But we'd gotten so goddamned used to pretending every day was just another day down on the farm." He moved back to the fire and gazed disconsolately into the dying embers.

DZ rose from the settee and went to stand at the other end of the mantle from Stoner. She wanted to offer comfort in the form of a touch on the shoulder, an embrace. But the most she felt comfortable giving him was mere proximity.

"So this is why you rewrote the family history. Five kids—not six."

He glanced at her, and smiled thinly, acknowledging her detective work. "A time came when I knew I had a shot at becoming a star—and I decided my own crap had to be buried first. So I took a trip back to Dalton Falls, dropped in here and there—polite visits to the county clerk, the school principal. Told them I wanted to go into files, get copies of my own stuff. They left me to do it on my own."

"There had to be at least a few people who remembered your brother."

"We lived ten miles out of town. I assumed there'd be enough confusion about who was who so that any stranger who ever came asking questions about me—general questions, anyway—wouldn't learn about Lyle. I pretty much cut myself off from Dalton Falls, too, so it wouldn't be a place anyone looked first for background. The only reason you went is 'cause this maniac turned up."

DZ watched him, his eyes cast down into the fireplace, his face gently bathed by the low flicker of flame. She could see the muscles of his jaw working, the mouth still drawn taut. Making his confession hadn't done much to ease his soul.

"So you think the killer could be someone you know?" she asked finally. "If the Mystery Guest knows about your brother—if that's what he meant by saying you were protecting a murderer—he could be someone from a relatively small circle."

Stoner spun away, and answered in an angry growl. "Or he could be someone who just did some very thorough research before starting out on this . . . this crazy crusade. Learning about this could be the whole *reason* he picked my talk show instead of one of the others. It doesn't have to mean I know him."

Possibly, DZ thought. But also possible was that whoever had tossed the secret back at Stoner was someone who'd stumbled onto it without the research. A witness to the tragedy. A relative of someone from his hometown, maybe. Or—

This idea lit up her dark ruminations like a lightning bolt. Wonderland! A whole loony bin full of people who'd been judged criminally insane. Easy enough for any one of them to learn about Lyle Stoner—straight from the horse's mouth.

"Tell me about Lyle," she said. "What happened after he was sent to the asylum?"

"What happened, as far as I know, is that he stayed there for the next eight years."

" 'As far as you know?' " DZ repeated.

"I could never face going there. None of us could."

"But didn't you say you'd been to the hospital?"

"What I said was I saw the hospital file. But not while he was there."

"So after eight years Lyle got out. Where did he go?"

"I have no idea."

"You never saw him, talked to him? Even after he was released?" It was on the border of forgivable that Stoner had never visited Lyle Stoner in confinement, hadn't been able to confront the reality of his adolescent brother locked in a madhouse. But this callousness was worse, not to have cared—to have tried to share some of his good fortune— even after his brother had done his time.

Stoner stared bleakly at DZ. "I told you he got out," he said. "I never said they let him out."

Only then DZ understood that this was the main truth, the crucial fact he had realized she must wait no longer than tonight to hear.

CHAPTER
28

AT 7:19 A.M. on Friday, Detective Antonio Saldina of the San Diego Police received a call at home telling him to report to the scene of a double homicide in the city's upscale Cliffridge section. At the scene, Saldina was joined by his partner, Jerry Munk. After a look at the two victims—an elderly man and his grandson, a freshman at Stanford—Saldina hurried to the house next door, where the shocked girl who had discovered the crime was being tended to by neighbors. A student at San Diego's Scripps Institute of Oceanography named Andrea Walters, she had been the girlfriend of the younger victim in high school and was to meet him for an early breakfast at his house before he returned to his college. When no one answered the doorbell, she had looked through the windows of the house until she spied the scene that caused her to run next door and phone the police.

After taking the girl's statement and arranging for her to be driven back to her dormitory in a patrol car, Saldina moved on to questioning other residents of the area about the two victims. The older man, who owned the Cliffridge house, was known familiarly in the neighborhood as Joe

Farben. The retired owner of three stores that sold photo-graphic supplies, his actual name was Johannes Fayrbahn, and he was a native of Switzerland. Fayrbahn had lived in Cliffridge for at least thirty years, the last twelve as a wid-ower. After his wife's death he had shared his home with his divorced son and a grandson. The son—who had Americanized the family name to Farben—had remarried and left for a job elsewhere two years ago, but the grand-son had elected to remain with his grandfather until com-pleting high school.

After the interviews that provided this background, Sal-dina went back to the crime scene for a closer examination. Entering the house through the front door, he encountered the first body, sprawled faceup, eyes open, feet toward the entrance, on the slate-tiled floor of a wide foyer. *Scott Far-ben: male, white, Caucasian, nineteen years old*, Saldina mentally catalogued the corpse as the M.E. circled it, doing his prelim. The body was clad in jeans and a blue Oxford shirt stained on the chest with an enormous nebula of dried blood radiating out from a stab wound. Dried blood was also pooled around the head.

A pathologist who noticed Saldina watching supplied an analysis without being asked. "Skull was crushed by a massive blow from the rear. Death would have occurred within an hour, but the killers wanted to make sure. Victim was rolled onto his back, and knifed once in the heart."

Saldina noted the use of the word "killers." Whoever had clubbed down the young man would have presumably continued the bludgeoning if a cohort hadn't applied the knife. It was practically unknown for a single killer to switch weapons in the middle of committing a murder.

Saldina's partner, Jerry Munk, a stubby man with blow-dried, light brown hair, came into the foyer from a door to-ward the rear that led to a den. On his previous inspection, Saldina had seen the body of Joe Fayrbahn in there, dressed in his pajamas and robe, seated in a leather club chair facing the TV.

"Robbery gone wrong," Munk said. "The old guy must've been alone in the house. There's a B and E, he's rousted from bed, marched downstairs and quizzed about where he keeps the goodies. One guy holds a gun on him while another goes off to look for the stuff. Then the kid shows. Perps hear the car pull into the drive, and when the kid walks in they clobber him. At that point they decide it's best to scratch the witnesses."

"Hangs that way only if there were three," Saldina said. "Someone to watch Joe while the other two take out the kid." He offered an alternative scenario: the old man had been shot *before* his grandson walked in. But if he'd been shot first, and the kid's arrival an unexpected accident, then the killing had probably been an execution. Which conformed with the gangland style of the killing, the victim's brains blown out by a shotgun. Yet for a respectable widower who had lived quietly in his community for so long to be executed also struck an off note.

"See if you can find a safe around," Saldina told Munk. "Check if any valuables seems to be missing—jewelry, art. This doesn't strike me as a random B and E."

The other detective started his survey and Saldina went back to the den. A couple of handlers from the M.E.'s staff were there, spreading a black, plastic body bag on a gurney. "Okay to take him?" one asked.

Saldina nodded.

With the body gone, Saldina stood at the center of the room, turning slowly to take it in. A comfortable den, a place to read, watch TV. The chair in which the victim had died was positioned a few feet in front of a wall of bookshelves directly facing a large, carved, wooden armoire that had been adapted to serve as a cabinet for a television and VCR. A handsome piece of furniture, Saldina thought, perhaps an antique from the victim's native Switzerland. But most interesting to the detective was the collection of framed photographs crowded together atop the armoire. In

a homicide like this—if it were an execution—family photographs provided a useful inventory of potential suspects.

Saldina went to inspect the pictures. Posed portraits,
candids of people in groups. It was fairly easy to guess
who was who—the deceased wife, the son who had gone
away after remarrying. Saldina pushed aside frames in the
front ranks to look at pictures they were blocking. The
photo shop with its owner and his employees, and just behind that—

Suddenly it was plain that all the half-baked speculating
so far meant nothing. Hidden until now on a rear corner of
the top of the armoire, was a rectangular black placard
with a bold white number at it's center:

1 0

From what Saldina had seen in the news, it was similar
to the one that had been left at the scene of a murder of the
first Mystery Guest murder. Though there were differences—the number on the card, for one.

And this time the placard left by the killer had been
placed in a frame—an extremely nice one, for that matter,
tortoise shell with solid gold brackets at the corners.

CHAPTER
29

*T*HE AROMA OF coffee came first. Then the feel of smooth sheets up and down her nakedness. DZ opened her eyes. Stoner stood nearby in the gloom, a mug of coffee in his hand. He put it on the bedside table. "It's after ten. I let you sleep, but—"

"Hell!" DZ jerked up onto one elbow. "I should've been at my desk hours ago." She recoiled as he pulled the curtains and sunlight struck her eyes.

"I have to get back to the city, too," he said. "I've called Candelli, told him I'll make today's broadcast." He started for the door.

"Hey!" she called. "You tell him I'm here?"

He looked back and shook his head. " 'Course not."

For few moments after he left she lay staring at the ceiling, letting the memory play in her mind—gently, without any self-judgment. Okay, she'd comforted him—no, they'd comforted each other—with a wildly abandoned mind-numbing fuck. Did she have to beat herself up about it? He'd been in pain and she felt for him and—

And she was a cop clinging with her fingernails to a

remnant of responsibility for the big case she'd waited years to catch. So it was stupid. Criminally stupid.

Gulping coffee as she went, DZ ran to the bathroom along the hall. Under the hard spray of the old-fashioned tub-shower, she couldn't avoid thinking about the potential backlash of what had happened with Stoner. No real harm done as long as no one found out. She could explain arriving late this morning by saying she had an appointment at the dentist for a cleaning, whatever.

As she toweled off, she thought back over all that he'd told her. His brother's escape from an institution for the criminally insane was far from the end of the story. What followed were all the failed efforts to find and recommit him. Not surprisingly, in view of the treatment he had received at the hands of his family, Lyle Stoner had made no attempt to contact any of them. He'd simply disappeared.

In the twenty-odd years since his escape, his family had given up thinking about him. Until the M.G.'s remark about Stoner's protecting a murderer, it had never crossed Stoner's mind that his brother might be the killer. The file from Wonderland, Stoner had told DZ, had noted suicidal longings Lyle expressed during his incarceration. It was assumed he had carried out his wish once he was free—stripped himself of any clues to identity and jumped in a lake, or stepped in front of a freight train; the mangled bodies of derelicts were regularly found on the rails of the Midwest.

Yet, even if Lyle Stoner had survived, it was beyond belief he could have since become the man who spoke and functioned as well as the M.G.

DZ had covered that with Stoner last night: "We suspect the guy we're looking for has spent time in the corporate culture, could be an executive now. Do you imagine your brother escaped from a nuthouse . . . and carved out that kind of niche?"

Stoner resisted the argument. "I told you he was very

smart. And there's a question about whether he ever belonged in that asylum."

"You think he wasn't seriously disturbed?"

"Was he guilty of murdering those girls? Ly never had his day in court. My father was his judge, jury, and jailer."

"Wait a second—you saying he was *innocent*?"

"No, DZ. I'm answering your question about whether it's conceivable he could have clung to his sanity, worked his way up in the world. If he's a killer now, I'd have to believe he was a killer then. But that doesn't mean it *showed*. I told you: he was the brother I idolized. You know how he got out of the loony bin? A nurse there fell in love with him, and he talked her into letting him go. He was only twenty-five, and he was funny, smart, good-looking. If I think of him putting those qualities to good use—yeah, he might have gone far."

And twenty-four years was time enough to do it, DZ mused. "Does the man you've seen bear any resemblance to Lyle?"

The question had to be asked, though his answer was predictable. Add up the time since the escape, time in the institution, and the cruelest period of the young boy being kept like an animal in a shed, it came to a total of thirty-five years since Stoner had seen his fourteen-year-old brother. Even if the Mystery Guest didn't disguise himself, identifying him as Lyle would be quite a feat.

By the time their talk had wound up, DZ was back to companionably sipping brandy with him, a couple of fresh logs on the fire, the mood sympathetic and reflective. She told him the whole story would have to be passed along to the FBI, but promised every effort would be made to keep it confidential.

"It's bound to leak," Stoner said, resigned. "How many agents are working on this case, how many cops all around the country? Somebody'll pass it to the *Enquirer*, if not the *Times*."

"And you'd lose some fans," she remarked.

"In my line of work?" He laughed. "They'll understand for the first time why I think it's more than entertainment."

"If the M.G. *is* your brother, will they like that?"

"As long as they like *him*. You know, my call-ins indicate support for what he's done. But if that changes, who knows? My show—the whole talk thing—may be finished. Seems to me people everywhere are getting . . . talked out."

"What would you do without your show?" she had asked.

Give more time to horse breeding, he'd said, develop television shows of other kinds. And it wasn't too late to start a family if the right woman came along.

The morning after she could barely remember at what point the late night confessional mood had generated deeper desires and made caution give way to surrender; she remembered only that at a moment when she was saying that she ought to be leaving for the city, and he was telling her she could spend the night in the cottage while he went back to the farm, they had taken a step closer and then the pull had been too much. Right there, in a frenzy of shared need, they had stripped each other and begun a bout of unrestrained carnal sex as consuming as any DZ had ever known. Clinging, devouring, penetrating, even past the point of exhaustion. Not for the sake of romance, simply surrendering to a hunger for the relief to be found in pure sensation.

Now, after putting herself together as well as possible in yesterday's clothes, she lingered in front of the mirror, brushing her hair, endlessly delaying the moment she'd have to face him again. When she went out, he was reading a newspaper at the table in the bare unstylish kitchen—the antithesis of the one in his modish duplex.

"I made toast." He nodded to a counter.

"I have to go. It's not good I was out of touch."

They were silent a moment, then he rose. "DZ, I hope you don't think—" He stopped, realizing that whatever she thought wouldn't be changed by anything he could say. "I guess I don't know if I owe you an apology or not."

"I never said no."

"I am sure about one thing, it helped a lot."

"The talking or the fucking?" she said, deliberately crude—to make the break sharper.

"Both," he said evenly.

The waves of attraction began to pulse again. DZ turned away.

He followed her out to the car. "Think it'll make a difference?" he asked as she got behind the wheel.

"About Lyle? Maybe. Hard to imagine it could be him." She switched on the ignition. "But everything else you told me is pretty hard to imagine, too."

He leaned back from the car as she started to back out of the drive, and watched another second as if considering whether to come after her and say something more. Then he walked away into the house.

As soon as she was back on the road, she reached for the cell phone and punched in the numbers.

"DZ!" Gable roared as soon as he heard her. "Where the hell you been? I've been trying to call you. Our boy's been busy again, California this time. . . ."

By reflex, she pushed down on the accelerator as she listened to the details, racing back to work.

"Chafee been trying to find me, too?" she asked when Gable finished.

"You better believe it. So where you been?"

It would probably come out. "Stoner called me last night, and I went to meet him—upstate."

"Oh, DZ," he moaned.

This much she could hide, maybe. "It's not what you think, Clark. I came . . . to hear his confession."

"His *what*?"

"I'll explain when I see you," she said. "Right now, I should get on to Chafee."

"He's flying out to San Diego from D.C., government

plane. Would've stopped off in New York for you . . . if you'd been reachable."

"Do me a favor, Clark, see if you can raise him for me. Tell him I can be back in the city in two hours."

If she kept her foot to the floor, there was a chance she could still catch that plane ride.

CHAPTER
30

ABOARD THE GOVERNMENT-FLEET 737, DZ saw many of the seats were occupied by a contingent from Washington: FBI agents, a couple of high-profile journalists—a *Times* man, a network television reporter, probably reps for a media pool—and a sprinkling of anonymous VIPs who might have hitched along out of sheer morbid curiosity. Apparently it was because so many people had to be gathered that she'd had a three-hour grace period to get to the airport before the plane's New York stopover.

Chafee had saved her a window seat beside him and caught her as she came aboard. He was in his shirtsleeves, and looked wiped.

"Quite a junket," she said, buckling in. "I'm lucky to get a place."

"And don't forget it," he replied, staking his claim to a future favor. He pointed to a front section shielded by curtains. "The A.G.'s up there, and Tauresco, not to mention some biggies whose interest in this I can't begin to figure out."

The pilot had begun a roaring engine test that rattled the

plane. Chafee raised his voice over it. "Gable mentioned you got something important from Stoner. . . ."

"Tell you after takeoff?" The atmosphere was still fairly rowdy in the crowded plane, and she wanted his full attention. But no sooner was the plane out of its climb and banking West than an agent came and told Chafee he was wanted up front.

He unbuckled and stood. "Sorry."

"Ken, the thing from Stoner is something you should hear. It adds a new slant to the case."

He retrieved his jacket from the overhead. "The A.G. awaits. That's first." He brushed a hand over his marine-style crew cut as if to make sure every hair was standing at attention.

Too much to tell to give it in a sound bite, she decided. "Any chance I could sit in with you, let everyone hear?"

"I'll ask." He hurried up the aisle.

She hadn't been summoned by the time they were over the Great Plains, a vast patchwork of greens and yellows visible six miles below. Had Chafee asked for her to be included? Either way, it meant she was out of the loop, the case having started in her jurisdiction no longer had any weight. It was a national issue, in need of federal authority to pull together events taking place thousands of miles apart. And her Task Force had failed to come up with a single lead.

Until now—the stuff about Lyle Stoner could be a break. But since they'd locked her out of the club she took revenge by holding it back. What the hell, while they were high in the air nothing big was going to break.

Drained from her debauch with Stoner and the race to the plane, DZ tried to nap. But her mind was still buzzing with Stoner's revelations. At last she went to the rear of the plane where she'd seen a couple of air phones when she boarded.

Luckily, DeJesus was at her desk, and she'd heard about the latest killing. "Marilyn, I'm flying out to the crime scene," DZ told her. "and I'd like your opinion on a couple of points. You spoke about the killer's rage being directed at television. Is it possible that the anger is actually aimed at Stoner himself?"

"My initial reaction is almost certainly not," the psychologist replied. "Stoner's not really a victim, after all; its been a boon for him. The killer's using him, but I sense a kind of . . . respect, an appreciation that Stoner isn't so quick to condemn him as others might be. You might say the Mystery Guest regards him as . . . a partner in crime."

Partner. Funny the psychologist should hit on that word with its affinity to "brother." Yet DZ had posed the question assuming there would have to be rage against his family felt by the boy who'd been locked away and abandoned by them—circumstantial evidence the killer *could* be Lyle.

"Next one's harder," DZ said. "Imagine the sort of man we're dealing with as he would have been when he was a boy. Given the fact he's become this diabolical character who sees murder as a game, and wants to involve everyone in playing it with him, is it conceivable murder is something he could have done long before now, even back when he was young?"

"How old are we talking about?"

"Fourteen. Even thirteen."

"Wow. A hell of a thing to potshot guesses at. Why do you ask?"

"I'm afraid I have to hold that back. Would you take a crack at it, anyway?"

A long silence, a lot of thinking. DZ looked out a window by the phone. Amazingly she could discern the detail of a combine cutting a swath through a field of wheat far below. *Amber waves of grain,* she thought, *America the beautiful.*

"Best guess?" DeJesus said finally. "No. The complexity of this crime suggests the killer planned it for a very long time. The rage behind it might have been brewing since childhood, but it took till now to find its outlet. The

Mystery Guest conceivably regards what he's doing now as his life's work, a crowning achievement."

"Does that have to mean he never killed anyone until now?"

"Look, there's little doubt he was massively troubled as a kid. But the degree of control he exercises indicates he learned early how to internalize his feelings, keep them concealed. You've heard him. Look at how he commits murder, then sounds so normal, even cheerful. Still—is it possible his rage led to acts of violence in childhood? Sure, we see murderers now as young as seven. But you know as well as I do they're caught a hundred percent of the time at that age—because they kill someone they know and their involvement is obvious, or they don't have the sophistication to conceal the crime. Once caught, if not treated successfully, such a personality disintegrates further. It seems impossible to me that any young murderer could have turned into a man who's as self-possessed and capable as the Mystery Guest. This man has clearly managed to make a life that required functioning normally up to this point. Plus, he has a conscience—which is why he's choosing victims who can be judged objectively as deserving to die."

"So you feel fairly certain—"

"I can't assure you the victims we know about are the only ones. But any other murders would be fairly recent."

"Great, Marilyn. You've helped." DZ asked her to tell Gable she'd check in with him later, and said good-bye.

When she returned to her place, Chafee was there, leaning back, eyes closed. He looked even more tired than he had before.

He heard her sit. "So what have you got?" he asked without opening his eyes.

"Takes awhile. You going to doze off on me . . . ?"

"Try not."

Soon after she began to unfold the story of Lyle Stoner, the FBI agent opened his eyes and fixed them on her in horrified fascination. He interrupted only when she came to recounting that Lyle was committed to a state mental institution nicknamed Wonderland: "So the kid was seventeen then, and he'd already spent three years locked up like an animal in a shed? Jesus, it's his old man who should've been shot."

"Was, in fact . . . by his own hand. Killed himself with a shotgun not long after he sent his son away."

"Holy shit," Chafee murmured. "Go on."

"Lyle Stoner spent eight years in the bin then escaped. No one ever saw him again—at least no one who *knew* him."

"So Stoner's own brother could be our boy," Chafee said when she was done. "Why didn't you tell me this before?"

"You got shanghaied. Anyway, it may not really explain anything—except maybe why Stoner became who he is."

"How do you figure?"

DZ ran through the conversation she'd had with Marilyn DeJesus. "I understand everything I've told you has to go into the hopper," she said then. "But I hope you'll help me keep my promise to Stoner not to—"

"He doesn't want to see it in print tomorrow, okay. But if we could circulate a picture of his brother . . ." DZ frowned, and he added. "What your shrink gives us is only guesswork. Whatever her textbooks say, murderers come in all sizes and styles. We have to follow up."

"I'll ask Stoner if he has a picture," DZ agreed. "But it may only add to the confusion. Put out a picture of a fourteen-year-old, you'll get fifty thousand tips, everybody telling you it's some sad-assed middle-aged loner living down the block."

"Nevertheless. . . ." Chafee leaned forward in his seat as if to go and bring his superiors up to date. But he hesitated, then eased back into the seat. "I did ask about bringing you into the meeting, DZ. I'm sorry you were closed out."

She gave him a resigned nod.

He looked again as if he might leave, but didn't. "I think you deserve to be in the picture, though. Keep giving me whatever you get, I'll do likewise."

"Appreciate it, Ken." Though he wasn't just being nice, she knew; he was acknowledging she might be the one to come up with the big break.

He lowered his voice. "Some big guns are flying with us whose presence seems odd. One's a four-star army general."

"Ties to the killer dressing as a soldier."

"That's not the half of it. There's another guy on board from the CIA."

"You've gotta be kidding." The whole thing was getting too wild, almost as if everybody felt they *had* to get in on the action, the biggest game in town.

"See if you think it's funny when I'm done. Turns out that Johannes Fayrbahn was no Swiss gentleman who just owned camera stores. He was another Nazi SOB who made the right contacts with our side after they'd lost in '45. Before that his interest in photographic supplies was as head of a group that kept a pictorial record of genetic experiments being done on the inmates at Dachau. One set of tests determined genetic damage done by certain chemical agents, things our own side has explored for use in chemical warfare. You don't ever want to hear details of those experiments, but Johannes saw it all, looking through his camera lens. After the war, he offered to provide useful information to our side—including the film— in return for having his war service overlooked."

"Who gave him a Swiss passport?"

"The official version is he got it for himself before coming here in '51. But if his story was in our files, they were obviously tracking him all along."

"So this is what the M.G. meant when he said his next victim was the enemy. It's why he wore the uniform, too. And," she added, "executing a Nazi who made himself at home in sunny California is bound to win more members for his fan club."

"The lucky thing—if you can put it that way—is that he killed the grandson, too. Scott Farben was an all-American—literally, champion swimmer up at Stanford. Olympic possibility. Throws a different light on the whole thing."

"For some people," DZ admitted. "Though it was an accident, of course. The killer went there to do the Nazi, and the kid walked in at the wrong time."

Chafee stared at DZ. "Now *you're* talking as if you believe he's a good guy."

"I'm not joining the fan club. But I'm starting to know what he's about."

Chafee reclined his seat again and DZ turned to gaze contemplatively out the window. Below, the plains had given way to mountain peaks capped with snow, glistening in the sun. What a vast, beautiful country it was—as long as you could look at it from this high up. How wonderful it must have been to live in that time when it was being discovered, a time of stalwart pioneers and craggy-faced cowboys as exemplified by—DZ turned abruptly to Chafee. "Ken—you speak any German?"

"*Ein bistle.* Did my own army tour with NATO in Frankfurt."

"Johannes. Isn't that like 'John' in English?"

His eyelids lifted to look at her. "Yeah."

"What can you make out of Fayrbahn?"

"*Bahn* . . . that's path, or road. And there's another word, sort of similar to the name—*fahrbahn*—which means roadway."

DZ nodded. "See what the M.G. did this time?" Chafee shook his head. "Gave us the name of his victim in advance," she explained. "John. Way."

CHAPTER
31

WITH THE I.D. tag Chafee gave her to wear, DZ was allowed to poke around the crime scene on her own. Crime scene tape was strung to form lanes where walking was permitted, and the house had already been vacuumed for evidence; still she worried that vital evidence might be compromised because so many people were tramping around—the OJ problem. A stray fiber or something rubbed off a shoe could be anywhere, you could never be sure you'd gotten it all.

No keeping out a senator, though, or the A.G. and her staff, or that tweed-jacketed guy who looked like a college English professor but DZ was positive must be the CIA back-roomer.

In the entrance hall, DZ looked at the outline of a body drawn on a beige marble floor in red marker, feet toward the door, patches of crusted blood from a stab wound to the heart and a crushed skull. Curious—bludgeoned *and* stabbed. So was this the M.G.'s work—or was she wrong to believe he worked alone? Why use a gun on one victim, then two more weapons on the other?

She was mulling it over when she noticed Senator Francis Tauresco emerging from the den beyond the foyer. The senator looked slightly green. Seeing DZ, he crossed the hall to her. "You're from New York, the one in charge. . . ."

She didn't feel in charge of anything anymore. "I was the first detective on the case, Senator. . . ."

"You know we can't let this thing go on, Miss—"

"Detective. No, sir, we can't; I do realize that." *Nice to have such smart men running the government.*

He nodded, and thrust out his hand as if collecting votes in his next campaign. "I intend to make sure we throw everything we've got into getting this job done." He walked outside.

If even the CIA was here, she thought, what was left to throw into it? She went to see what had made the senator green.

Unlike the squalid place where the child pornographer had been killed, this den was the retreat of a tasteful, affluent man; thickly carpeted, walls lined with built-in wooden bookshelves, a late-model, large-screen television set into a massive antique armoire. Yet similarities in the two murder scenes were also apparent. The victim had been shot while seated in a chair facing the television, and with a heavy-gauge weapon that had blasted his skull to pieces. The chair was positioned with its back a few feet in front of the book-lined shelves that were spattered with a wide swath of dried blood and gore. Chafee and some of the New York agents were studying the walls. DZ noted the piece of white cardboard propped on top of the armoire, leaning against one of the framed family pictures. Printed in ink across it were the words "Note Found Here."

She went over to Chafee. "Where's the calling card?"

"The original already went back to our lab. I can show you photographs." He turned to an agent and asked for the pictures to be brought to him.

DZ looked at the TV set. "Did you check—"

"Yeah. Time of death was around three A.M. TV was still on when the cops came in—tuned to a cable station showing a rerun of an old sitcom called *Hogan's Heroes.* Remember it?"

"American POWs during the Second World War . . . ?"

"Yeah—in the *stalag* with their jailers. *Funny* Nazis."

The agent was back with a bunch of black-and-white blowups. He gave them to Chafee, who passed them to DZ.

The top shot showed the black placard with it's white "10." Following were close-ups of the frame's tortoise-shell edging, the dusted whorls of a couple of fingerprints found on the frame, and of the inscription that had been written in white on a corner of the placard: "Kindest Regards, the Mystery Guest." DZ flipped back to study the shot of the fingerprints, one on each edge of the frame. Thumbs.

"Seems the old man was given this to hold by the killer," DZ said, "while he was alive."

"So . . . ?" Chafee gave her a where-is-this-leading squint.

So what? DZ was quiet, working to conjure the mood at the time of the crime. Three o'clock in the morning, the M.G. thinks he has the time and ease to talk with his victim—maybe justify himself, that was important to him. Then she factored in what she remembered of the scene at the last killing—the time that had been taken to cover his tracks, right down to digging a bullet out of the wall.

Suddenly it all made sense, how and why it could have been done by only one man. She moved in front of the bloody chair. "So the killer gives the Nazi the calling card to hold and they talk. He wants Fayrbahn to know why he's going to die. Then the M.G. takes the frame away, and walks over here"—she went to the TV—"puts it on top. Has to do it before he shoots or it would get messed up." She turned and went back to stand in front of the chair. "Time for the kill. One shot's plenty with the cannon he uses. Maybe it wakes the neighbors, but it's only one sound—could be a backfire. Now he starts to clean up, taking his time because he always does, very methodical. Wants to be sure nothing's left to help us.

"But the kid shows up, unexpected!" Chafee offered.

"Check. It's a weekend, he's come down from college, maybe to see his old girlfriend, and he arrives late." Staying in the killer's shoes, DZ went to the door of the den. "The M.G. hears the car pull into the drive." She moved into the corridor, along to the entrance hall, and crossed quickly to the front door, placing herself as if to hide behind it when it opens. "The house is dark, the kid suspects nothing. The killer waits here and he's holding the one thing he came in with—the shotgun. But he can't shoot again. Here at the front, the shot will be louder, and a second will arouse suspicion. But the gun is all he's got to bring the kid down. . . ."

Chafee reached over and pulled open the front door. "So when the kid walks in, the M.G. clubs him. . . ."

"He's unconscious, but the M.G. can't leave it unfinished, so he gets a knife from the kitchen. After the kill, he's here by the door—maybe freaked 'cause things didn't go the way he likes." She turned to the still-open door. "Out he goes."

Through the doorway, she could see Tauresco at the fringe of the lawn, holding forth for all the media people who'd been kept behind the cordon. She shut the door and turned to Chafee.

"It works," he said

"Look in the kitchen," DZ advised. "Could be a cutlery set with a knife missing."

"Locals might've already done an inventory. I'll ask." Chafee hurried away to the interior of the house.

Alone, she tried to stay with the stream of logic she'd conceived. Something didn't quite fit. Would the M.G. leave right after the second murder? As methodical as he was, he would be all the more rattled by the unplanned act, an accident. With him, everything was premeditated so he'd want to put this behind him quickly. But why would he even have to kill the college boy? He was supposed to be hunting baddies, evening the score—

"Detective Hayes!"

DZ turned. Two men were coming down the stairs from the second floor.

"Anthony Saldina," said the one who'd called to her, as his partner went off to another part of the house. "I recognized you from some of the stuff that's been on the evening news."

She appraised him for a second. Handsome, Latino coloring, black hair and eyes, dressed in a nicely pressed tan sport jacket and dark brown slacks. West Coast detectives seemed to be a different breed from the Eastern herd, who were usually rumpled, pocket flaps half in and half out from always reaching for a cigarette, coffee or pizza stains on a lapel, stress hovering around them as palpably as an electric charge. "I would've gone looking for you if you hadn't found me, Detective Saldina—"

"Tony."

She smiled. "Fine. And I'm—"

"I know: DZ."

"Tony, I think this was done by one man." She ran through her theory of the crime for him. "See any holes in it?"

Saldina thought. "It gets shaky for me when it comes to doing the second one. The man the killer came for is already dead, the kid is coming in the front way, ready to tiptoe up to bed thinking granddad's asleep. So why didn't the murderer just slip out the back? That's how he came in. We've found force-marks on the backdoor locks—clean work but you can see tampering. So if he didn't want to do the other job, he could've avoided it easy, gone out the way he came."

A sensible reservation, DZ thought, particularly since she clung to the belief that the M.G. depended on his vigilante rationale to kill, and the young man was an innocent.

Then it hit. "Unless he needed to finish what he'd started," she murmured to herself."

"Finish what?"

But DZ didn't hear; she was already heading for the den. She turned into the room with Saldina on her heels. It had emptied of the FBI crews except for two men who looked like lab specialists. One was taking detailed photographs of the several hundred fingerprints that had shown up by dusting all the surfaces; the other was using a scalpel to scrape away bits of brain tissue from the spines of books lined up on shelves behind the chair, and putting his harvest into plastic bags.

"What are you looking for?" Saldina asked as DZ scanned the room.

"The reason. He killed the kid because what he was doing here was interrupted, and he had to come back to finish it."

It came through as suddenly as if a blindfold had been stripped off. She walked over to crouch down by the chair, adjusting her sight lines. Saldina moved up beside her, observing curiously.

She straightened up. "You find a lead slug about so big?" She formed her fingers into an O the size of a gum ball. "It's what he shoots."

Saldina shook his head. "Must've lodged in the skull, you'll get it in the autopsy."

"Last time it went clean through." She raised her eyes to look at the blood-spattered books. A section roughly five feet across was sprayed with the stains of blood and flesh. It was from this area the lab technician was still gathering samples.

"Would you mind moving aside?" DZ said to the tech.

He obliged. Now she could see the whole area. With the colored spines of the books for background, the wide area of spattered blood, dried to a blackish brown, resembled a grisly art abstract.

But the composition jarred her eyes, almost as if she was

looking at the area through a lens with an optical flaw. "Do me a favor," she said to the technician, and waved her hand over a group of the volumes at the center of the stained section. "Take these off the shelf."

"Things have to be left as they are, ma'am." The tag clipped to his shirt identified him as FBI.

"Look, I can get Agent Chafee if I have to. . . ."

The technician looked around to make sure his violation wouldn't be witnessed, then pulled a pair of latex gloves from his pocket and put them on. He started pulling the books DZ had indicated off the shelf, and had removed eight or nine when the hole in the wall behind them became visible. He paused.

"Clear everything from in front," DZ insisted.

He removed another dozen books and they could see the complete opening, roughly the size of melon. The backing of the shelves was plywood, and was broken away around the hole, leaving jagged, splintered edges.

"This is why he killed the kid, why he didn't leave after doing the old man," DZ said. "He wanted to take the slug with him, and needed time to work."

Saldina took a penlight from a pocket to aim it into the hole. Through the opening, DZ could see interior wood studding for the walls, loosely packed insulation, a section of electric cable. "He went digging," Saldina said, "but he didn't get it."

"How can you tell?"

"Look, he obviously went to some trouble on the chance we wouldn't catch on. Took out the books that got torn up by the slug—must've carried those away with him—and put others in their place, even splashed blood on them so they'd seem to fit. If not for you, we might never have moved the books. But why bother to hide the hole unless he didn't want us to find it? And why care if we found it, unless the evidence is still in there?"

DZ charged out of the den in search of Chafee. She

found him in the kitchen, but before she could boast of her discovery, he was congratulating her on something else.

"You were right about the knife," he said. "There's one missing from a set in the kitchen—the expensive kind, you know, German steel."

"That's not all. . . ." she said, and told him the ballistic evidence was probably still in the wall.

"Well, what are we waiting for?" Chafee shouted. "Let's start ripping this fucking place apart!"

The wall was opened and the interior structure searched and examined. It was discovered that the slug had penetrated the circumference of a large pipe in a plumbing stack within the wall serving the kitchen on the opposite side. The hole was only on one side, however: the slug had evidently run out of steam and dropped down inside the pipe.

A plumbing crew was brought in. The pipe was discovered to lead to the sewers. Special vacuum hoses were run, and the sewer lines were reamed. The police and FBI kept their fingers crossed that the evidence hadn't been washed away. The search went on for hours. DZ let the VIP flight back East leave without her.

It was approaching midnight when an FBI agent came up to her and handed her a cell phone.

Gable: "The M.G. checked in five minutes ago."

She looked at her wristwatch—still set to Eastern time. 2:49, predawn hours. "Who got the call?"

"Mister Edward Corcoran—at his weekend place. Seems our guy needed a quick executive decision: he's demanding airtime on Monday. Told Corcoran he wants to apologize."

DZ understood at once: for killing the boy. But if he got airtime, he could also use it to announce plans to kill again. "What was Corcoran's answer?"

"Dunno. He called the Task Force, the night-duty man called me. But the phone company was able to tell us the M.G.'s call came from the Denver area. Got a number, too—for a camera store, closed at the time the call was made."

No surprise, the M.G. had screwed with the lines again. But the area code was probably correct. Another geographical leap, but Denver was close enough to San Diego that he could've taken a bus, driven a car, if he didn't want to fly.

"Keep hitting the travel angle, Clark. Look at all flights and buses into Denver from California. Car rentals, too. Match passenger names against the records we've already got from—"

"DZ, I've already told our night guy at the Task Force to call the FBI. They're handling all that."

Right, she wasn't running it anymore. Time that sunk in. "All right, Clark. But before you go back to sleep, call Corcoran. I want to know his plans for the M.G."

She added that she'd be back at the Task Force tomorrow.

After the call, she found Chafee in the kitchen helping himself to pizza and coffee brought in for the troops. He'd already heard about the call to Corcoran.

"We can't let him back on the air," DZ said.

"You got another way to crack the case before Monday?" Chafee said.

"The travel pattern may be the key," she said. "The amount of territory the M.G. covers is practically unique with a serial killer. It's proof he's got money, maybe has work that keeps him on the road. So hit that angle hard. Check passenger manifests for every flight in or out of Denver in the past day—even if it didn't come from San Diego."

An agent bustled up to them, sweaty and red faced from running. He thrust a polythene bag into Chafee's hands. "This came out of the muck."

Inside they saw a sizable hunk of dull, silvery metal, misshapen from colliding with whatever it met in its flight.

"Looks to me like the head of a bullet, not just a slug," DZ remarked "See? It's sort of cone-shaped."

"Banging around in the wall probably gave it that shape. I doubt it's a bullet. You'd be talking about a cartridge that could knock over an elephant. Why use that for a close-up head shot? At that range even a twenty-two can be fatal."

"But not always," DZ observed. This guy makes sure his victims never survive."

Like with everything else he did: no room for error.

NO ROOM FOR ERROR.

Lying awake in airport motel, all she could think of was all her own errors. Even the choice of work that had led her to this place seemed, tonight, to have been a mistake. She'd never gotten what she'd wanted out of it, and she'd stayed with this case, expecting her choice might be redeemed by solving The Big One . . . and now even this chance had been wrested away. All the evidence from this murder scene had been seized by the FBI, anything that might yield a connection to the killer to be analyzed by their people. Chafee had said he'd pass along all the reports, but she could count on maintaining the liaison only as long as she had something to give in return. And what did she have to trade? What was she likely to get?

Stoner's brother—that was the one angle she could still explore on her own. She'd written off its significance after talking to Marilyn DeJesus. But suppose Marilyn was wrong? Impossible, everyone thought, that Lyle Stoner could have prospered after his escape, remade himself into a man with the external and inner resources to manage everything the Mystery Guest had achieved.

Except this killer had already done a thing or two they'd once thought he couldn't. . . .

DZ stared upward into the darkness for another minute, listening to the roar of jets taking off near the motel. At last she switched on the bedside lamp and picked up the phone.

It was too soon to be going home.

CHAPTER
32

*F*ROM THE WINDOW of the bus she saw him standing by a vintage Buick ragtop in the parking lot of the agricultural supply store—the local bus stop. The afternoon sun shone on his face, the hair that fell across his forehead not shading his eyes so he had to squint, etching lines in his cheeks to go with the creases that formed a parenthesis around his friendly smile. The top of the shiny blue convertible was down and a floppy-eared, brown-and-white spaniel was in the backseat.

When she'd called to say the case was bringing her back he'd offered to meet the commuter flight at Davenport, but she declined. Having him drive all that way would have loaded it with too much significance. Now she realized it made no difference; meeting here felt no less charged. The feelings surprised her by their force.

"Upon my word, Detective," he said, giving her his hand to help her down from the bus, "did you come back to pin my star on in person?"

She smiled. "I'm afraid I didn't bring any stars with me."

He looked straight in her eyes another second. "Oh, I wouldn't say that."

She realized suddenly her cheeks were burning. Hell, had she ever blushed before? She glanced quickly to where the driver was setting luggage on the sidewalk. "I'll get my bag," she said, glad for an excuse to step away and compose herself. She had bought a small valise in the airport at San Diego, stocked it with basic things. She wished now she'd taken the time to choose at least one special dress.

"That's Bonnie back there," Charlie told DZ as he put her valise into the backseat with the spaniel. "You like dogs?" He opened the passenger door for her.

"Never got to know the animal kind, but she looks easy to like."

Charlie slipped behind the wheel. "He. He was a gift, and he came with the name Prince Charlie. Too close for comfort, so it became Bonnie Prince Charlie, then Bonnie for short." He started the engine. "I got you a room at the Falls Inn. Costs more than the motel, but I thought you'd like it better."

"Sounds fine. The department'll pay for this, anyway. . . ."

He nodded, then turned to her. "DZ, I hope you won't take it amiss, but I can't see a reason to spend the money when I've got plenty of room at my house. I understand, though, if you feel it's not proper to—"

"No . . . I'd like to see your home, Charlie." She'd never had another man worry whether she'd take it "amiss" or think it wasn't "proper." Jimmy Stewart words.

The ride provided an opportunity to see more of the town than on her first visit. A residential section of streets lined with huge ancient trees and ample houses behind wide lawns, more than one tall-steepled white church that looked like every girl's dream of the place to walk down the aisle, and a high school with a notice board out front that read BASEBALL AT HOME SAT'Y VS. MURRAYVILLE. GO

FALCONS!!! How did murderers get born in such clean and decent places?

They went beyond streets closely lined with homes, then he turned onto a road that climbed a gentle hill. At the crest stood a wood Victorian, white with dark green trim. A porch ran across the front and a turret rose from one corner. The driveway up to the house was shaded by towering oaks and elms and bordered by roses and azaleas. She guessed the property had been passed down to him—the sort of place the publisher of a town newspaper would have built sixty or seventy years ago.

"It's lovely, Charlie," she said as the car pulled up in front of the house.

"I was born in that corner room." He pointed to the turret.

Good intuition, Detective Hayes.

Inside she was relieved to see that it didn't have the fusty feeling the Victorian exterior led her to expect. Light flooded in through large windows. The walls had been painted pale pastel, wood floors stripped to a natural color. A large central entrance hall was hung with large abstract paintings, swaths of bright colors that DZ thought remarkably effective. She paused before one, about to comment, but Charlie raced up the stairs carrying her bag. "Let me show you your room," he said.

"Mine's there," he said on the landing, indicating a door farthest to the right. Then he went to the farthest room on the left. It, too, was refreshingly bright and done as if with a decorator's touch, the spread on a four-poster of a floral fabric matching the upholstery on a chair at a dressing table. It struck DZ now that he'd once lived here with a woman—the one who'd done the decorating, and given him a dog named Prince Charlie.

He pointed out that there was a bath adjoining the room. "When you're ready, I'll take you wherever you need to go."

After showering, she put on the tan skirt and plain white

blouse bought in the airport shop, and went down. She heard dishes clattering from the rear, and followed the sound to the kitchen. It was large, with modern appliances and lighting, but many original fittings had been left and refinished, glass-front cabinets, a big porcelain double-sink where he was doing dishes. By a bay window, a breakfast nook had been built in. The window looked out on a patio surrounded by a lush flower garden.

Seeing her, he shut off the water.

"You live very nicely, Charlie," she said.

"Thanks." He smiled tautly, and paused in a way that made her think he was weighing a decision, something he had to tell her he thought she might not want to hear. She headed it off.

"Let me tell you why I came back." She slid into the breakfast nook.

He looked relieved. "Like some coffee while we sit? Made some fresh . . ."

She said she would, and he brought an old metal percolator from the stove and cups and milk and sugar to the table. The way he moved around the kitchen, reaching for things almost as a blind man might, no need to see his target, told her that even if there had been a woman once, he'd been alone for a long time.

Over coffee, she repeated all that Stoner had told her about his youth in Dalton Falls, and the brother whose existence he had wanted to blot out.

At first Charlie couldn't square it with his lifetime experience of the quiet, uncomplicated place in which he lived. But he couldn't cling to disbelief for long; he understood there was no gain for Barry Stoner in concocting such a story.

"So you think what was done to that boy," he asked finally, "hooks up to what's happening now?"

"The man we've seen on television indicated he knows about this buried secret. That, and the fact that he chose Stoner's show for his outlet, are the only links. But it's enough to make it worth tracing what became of Lyle Stoner, if I can. This is where he was formed, where his motives came from—the best place to pick up his trail."

"You know I'll help any way I can. Where do we start?"

"Scene of the crime," she said at once.

"Where the girl died."

"No, I've seen that already," she said. "I meant the crime against *him*."

CHAPTER
33

*T*HEY WERE RECEIVED this time by the wife of the farm's owner. Her husband was out plowing, she said. A plain woman in a faded, flowered dress, she asked Charlie and DZ into the house for iced tea, but DZ didn't want to get mired in chitchat.

"Never knew there'd been any trouble like that out here," the woman said, eyeing the silo as they all stood at the kitchen door. Her husband had told her about the girl's death. "I get a funny feeling now when I look over there."

"Accidents happen," Charlie consoled her. "And it was a long time ago."

"My husband got the impression it wasn't any accident. I mean, this lady being police, that says something right there." She turned to DZ. "And now you're back."

"To see something else, though. Your icehouse."

"Icehouse?" The woman returned a blank look.

"One of the outbuildings," Charlie said. "The shed used to store ice back in—"

"I know what an icehouse is, Mr. Foster. But there's none on our property."

DZ and Charlie exchanged a glance.

"Mind if we take a walk around?" Charlie asked.

"Suit yourself. Stop back if you want a cool drink when you're done."

"Stoner said it was back in the woods somewhere," DZ remarked as they walked away.

"Even so," Charlie said, "Farmers know every inch of their property and what's on it. There have been several owners since the Stoners. If the building no longer served a purpose, it may have been torn down for the lumber."

"Or maybe it never existed," DZ said. "Perhaps Barry Stoner had a reason to make up that story."

Charlie halted and looked at her. "That's stretching things mighty far—"

"Charlie, if you tried to imagine this whole case before it happened that would've been a stretch."

"Let's start back there." He pointed to a forested area a hundred yards away.

They walked into the forest. Thick boughs overhead kept sunlight from penetrating, cooling the air, but the trees were far enough apart that they could see a fair distance ahead. At ground level there was nothing but the forest floor of decayed leaves, spotted with mushrooms and fern and Indian Pipe.

They'd walked a few hundred yards when DZ caught the sparkle of reflected sunlight. "There's water up there. Stoner mentioned a pond. . . ."

"Icehouses were always near water. In winter, they'd cut the ice in blocks, then store it in sawdust."

They arrived at a small pond. Once it could have been a source for clean ice, but over the years several trees had toppled into the water and decayed, and the leaves of many autumns had blown in and rotted. In the warm air, the pond smelled fetid, as if whatever evil had been kept near had been absorbed into it. DZ stood at the edge and scanned the perimeter. To the left, there were fewer large trees, the existing growth younger and lower. She pointed it out to Charlie. "Could have been a building there," she said.

"Or it's where those trees once stood." He pointed to the rotting trunks in the pond.

They circled the shore toward the clearing. "Why do you think they fell down?" DZ said

"Trunks look charred. They were probably hit by lightning."

Yes, she saw it now. Several trees around the edge of the clearing were also reduced to blackened spindles. Moving to the center of the open area, DZ pushed her feet through the layer of leaf mold and dirt, searching for signs of a foundation. Almost at once she saw a flat piece of charred wood. She lifted it from the ground. It could have been a piece of siding. Continuing around the area, she found other fragments of blackened planking pressed into the ground. Soon she had unearthed more than enough siding to be sure a sizable wooden shed had once occupied the site.

Charlie had been watching her. "Fire took it all," he said.

She imagined what it must have been like when the walls had stood, the hurt and hopelessness and craziness of the boy trapped within them, a boy afflicted by a sick mind even before this cruelty. "Charlie, remember what you told me about the reason you had a phone line at home tied to the newspaper office?" He shook his head, puzzled by the connection. "You said you didn't want to miss the story if a barn burned down in the middle of the night."

"Figure of speech. I meant I didn't want to miss anything worth reporting."

"But a barn burning—that really is what people care about around here. . . ."

Now he understood. "I suppose there would've been something in the paper if this place burned. Would it help you to see the story?"

"I'd sure like to know," she said, "if it was an act of God—or something else."

· · ·

They got to the newspaper office past closing time. It was quiet and empty.

"Nice thing about running a weekly," Charlie said. "Never have to work late to get out an early-bird edition."

So you'd be home for dinner, she thought, then smiled to herself at the way she was letting herself get carried away with this domestic fantasy.

He glanced at her. "What are you grinning at?"

"Just . . . how different it is from the big city."

He led her to his private office at the rear, and waved to the stacks of yellowed newsprint piled around the edges of the room. "You remember the filing system."

She'd done some figuring while they were in the car. At fourteen Lyle Stoner had been sentenced by his father to three years in his solitary hell, then there were eight years in the institution, escape at the age of twenty-five. She had to go on the assumption that if he'd been involved in burning the icehouse, it wouldn't have happened too long after he stole his freedom. Twenty-four or twenty-five years ago should cover it.

"Where are the *Journals* from 1974 and '75?" she asked.

Charlie went over to an oak table by a window that was heaped with cartons stuffed with bundles of newsprint. He picked among the cartons and carried one to his desk. "All of '74," he said. He took a handful of the papers from one end of the box and spread them out. "They're packed chronologically, first week to last."

DZ picked up the first January issue and started to look through it, then something pricked at her memory—something about Lyle's escape. Barry had said a nurse had helped after falling in love with Lyle; it was connected to that, she felt, an image of passion . . . of heat. *One summer night*—that was it. Barry said his brother had escaped in summertime. DZ reached into the box, and found the issues for June, July, August, and September. She pulled them out, and spread them in front of her. "What do you think, Charlie," she said, "would it have been front-page news?"

"A fire in a small outbuilding? Not unless there was more to the story, suspicious circumstances, arson."

That was what she'd assumed. She gave the front page a hard look, but also checked the first few inside pages, which also carried news.

In ten minutes she'd given the four months of issues a pretty thorough once-over. Maybe she ought to look at the rest of the year's. . . . No. The way she had it figured, Lyle wouldn't have waited that long. "Let me see '75," she said.

He brought her the second box, and she dug out the June–September issues.

It was on the front page of the *Dalton Falls Journal* for the week of August 2, 1975. A small item, but made eye-catching by the box of heavy black lines around it:

> D.F. Volunteer Brigade responded
> early this A.M. to a fire on the Maple
> Hill property owned by Lawrence
> Weston, formerly the farm of R. Stoner.
> Details not available at press time.

"Why is this in a box?" She showed Charlie the paper.

"Probably slugged in last minute after the paper was put to bed," he replied, and read through the item. "Yup, says right here the volunteers were called out in the early morning of press day. For sure it got more play the next edition." He reached past DZ to extract the next paper from the box. He unfolded it to read the front page.

Indicative of its news value in a quiet community like Dalton Falls, the headline was set in type much larger than any DZ had seen used in the paper previously:

> BURNED BODY FOUND
> IN SUSPICIOUS FIRE

Directly beneath the headline were photographs of a number of men standing around smoldering earth, and a covered stretcher being loaded into an ambulance in front of a barn. DZ raced through the story reporting the brigade chief's opinion that the speed with which the burned structure had been consumed indicated the use of gasoline. The local police chief was also quoted as saying that the body had been burned beyond recognition. Fortunately, the chief added, it couldn't have been anyone local, since there was no report of anyone missing in the week since the fire.

As she set the paper aside, DZ felt simultaneously pleased at the positive resolution of her hunch, and deflated by what she had learned.

Charlie saw her dismay. "What's the matter?"

"I've lost my prime suspect. The arsonist was almost certainly Lyle." She spelled it out. The suicidal longings he had expressed while he was institutionalized, the rage formed while he was locked away by his father—fury layered over a personality so diseased it had probably incited him to kill two girls when only a boy. And why commit arson on an icehouse? "Lyle wanted his freedom only to destroy the place that had been his personal hell. That was his deliverance."

Charlie looked around at the walls of his office—and past them. "Just breaks my heart," he said, "to discover all that sickness and misery was right here."

"It can be anywhere, Charlie. Some folks—like you— are just too good to see it."

Abruptly, he said, "C'mon, let's get out of here. Been a long day. Bet you'd appreciate a nice, home-cooked meal."

"You cook, too?"

"Have to. I like meeting the guys down at The Blue Ribbon, but down there chewing the fat is something you can almost take literally."

"Oh, Charlie," she moaned half seriously. "If your cooking is any good, I think you're in real trouble."

He was smiling as he turned out the light.

CHAPTER
34

*H*E WOULDN'T LET her help, so she sat in the kitchen nook, the spaniel curled up near her feet, and watched him prepare a couple of different recipes that involved cutting and chopping onions and peppers and tomatoes and sectioning a chicken, and mixing egg and cornmeal and some dark amber liquid he poured from an unmarked bottle. They talked, simple Q and A about how they spent their spare time, movies and books they'd liked. Finally she asked about the food.

"The recipes are Mexican," he said, "with a few twists of my own."

"Where'd you learn that?"

"I lived in Mexico for a couple of years after college. Dropping out, as they called it then. Fifteen bucks a month, and you owned the world."

More surprises. He looked like such a straight arrow; hard to imagine he'd ever bummed around.

He seemed to have read her thoughts. "Back then I had different plans. Traveling the world, writing great tales of adventure."

"What changed your plans?"

"I just realized I belonged here." He transferred the cut vegetables into an oiled pan. Watching him, she detected no sign of regret, yet in some ineffable way the atmosphere had grown heavier, tinged with sadness. She waited—as she might wait for the rain when a sky darkened. "Before," he said at last, "you complimented me on the house. But—you might have guessed—I'm not the one who made it so nice." He glanced at her now, and she nodded. "The painting in the hall—good, isn't it?"

"I thought so," she said.

He went back to watching the food cook, and she saw a series of expressions flit across his face as he raced along a gallery of memories. "My wife did it," he said. "We were married only four years, but I knew Ellie my whole life. Her dad owned the five-and-dime here in town. We went all through school together, then off to Iowa State. At graduation, I asked her to marry me and she turned me down. She had a desire to paint." He shook his head. "No—not just a desire. A passion. She headed up to the Art Institute in Chicago . . . and I went to Mexico. I sat around in dingy cantinas, writing the first lines of a novel. . . ." He laughed lightly. "More like fifty different novels. I thought if I could be some kind of artist, too, we might still have a future. But I never got too far past those first lines." He'd stopped looking into the pan, was just resting his spoon on the edge of the stove while he stared at the simmering past. "Two years . . . then Dad got sick and asked me to take over the paper. If I'd gotten a little farther with my own ideas . . ." He shrugged. "It wasn't in me. Lucky, I know now, the right thing for me was to be here. Ellie gave herself longer, six years. She was good, but she'd had a terribly unhappy love affair with some Chicago intellectual heavyweight—married, older. I looked better to her then, so we got hitched. And . . ." He breathed deeply, letting it go. "And we were happy. Very happy." He glanced at DZ then as if needing permission to continue. She showed her readiness with a little smile. "Dad was gone by then, my mom was frail and I was taking care of her, so we moved in here. Ellie made the house what you see. Turned the attic into a studio—still a load of her stuff up there. I haven't . . ." He broke off again, and resumed stirring the spoon, but absently, as though he just needed to keep his hands busy. "She had one early-term miscarriage. And my mom died. Then one afternoon the year after that, Ellie complained of a terrible headache, and she lay down for a nap. . . ." He lifted his shoulders helplessly. "Brain thing, a weak vessel. Jesus. Just . . . the cards, y'know? She was thirty-one. Pregnant again, though I didn't know till the autopsy. I guess she didn't either. Twelve years ago."

DZ had seen a hundred dead bodies without feeling a shadow of the pain she felt now. "Oh, Charlie," she moaned in sympathy. "How awful."

"Yeah. It was. Truly. Just . . . just . . . gosh . . ." His voice died. She would have liked to embrace him, but she could tell he wouldn't have been alone inside her arms.

He shook his head, then lifted the pan from a burner and drained off some excess liquid into the sink as if he were pouring the tears off his soul. Then he put it back onto the stove and lowered the flame. He was back in the routine, taking comfort from it. "For the next I-don't-know-how-long I was numb. It's easier, though, in a place like this because people really do care. They give support, but they don't push into your life if you want to be alone." He chuckled. "Up to a point. Then *they* decide it's time for you to snap out of it. After that it never ends. Invitations to Sunday lunch, reminders not to miss the church supper, a thousand schemes for getting you together with somebody to help you forget. They were all sweet women, too, perfectly nice . . . but they didn't help." He turned off the burners, but stood looking down into the pans, as if making sure everything was truly done the way he wanted. Then he let go of the spoon and crammed his hands in his pockets like a shy schoolboy and faced her. "Then one day somebody walks in from nowhere, and god-knows-why but right there you know there could be a second chance. . . ."

He came toward her, and she was already trembling but the emotional wave got stronger the nearer he came. She couldn't move or speak, could only wait for him to reach her. He didn't pull her up into his arms, though, didn't demand the passionate climax to his confession. He sat down at the table and put out a hand, and without a thought she gave him hers.

"Forgive me if I'm rushing things, DZ," he said, "but the way things are happening—you turning up here for a day or two, then going back to chase a crazy murderer—if I didn't say this now, I don't know when—"

"It's okay, Charlie, I don't mind."

"Well. So. Whattaya think? Is there a chance . . . ?"

She wanted to believe . . . but she had to be honest. "I don't know. We're such different people, from such different worlds—"

"Yeah, that's what brought us together, isn't it? Your big-city job brought you to my small-town newspaper. But I'm not alone in feeling there's a chance we could cross the gap, am I?"

She smiled back at him. "No, Charlie," she said, barely able to raise her voice above a whisper, "you're not alone."

He rested his gaze on her a bit longer, making her feel beautiful without needing a single word. Then he rose quickly. "Okay, so let's eat. I've got one hell of an appetite."

SEVERAL TIMES IN THE MIDDLE OF THE MEAL IT STRUCK HER that never before had she been with any man without some part of her being held back, in reserve against disappointment, against being taken too seriously or not seriously enough . . . against being deserted like her

mother. But with Charlie there was none of the fencing
and anxiety that seemed inevitable on the urban scene
when you'd known a man too little or too long. Had she
ever talked so freely about herself, the job and its problems, to other men? Yet he never pressed beyond where
she wanted to go. Over a second bottle of wine, he shared
his own thoughts, more of his history, and he made her
laugh like a sailor with tales of the town and its characters, not mean-spirited gossip but simply the result of a
keen eye he turned on his own world.

On top of it all, he cooked like a dream. After the spicy
Mexican chicken and a vegetable tamale, he pulled a con-
tainer from the freezer and spooned out a delicious apri-
cot ice cream dotted with chunks of the fruit, and spiked
with raspberry liqueur. Also homemade, he said, while
apologizing it was a few weeks old.

After a few spoonfuls, she said, "The truth now, Charlie: this is left over from the last time you had some babe
at your table you wanted to knock off her feet."

He laughed. "Made for the church committee that met
here to ask my help raising funds for a new roof. Not a
babe in the bunch."

She had a couple more tastes of ice cream while neither of them spoke. Now she began to feel the stirring of
despair that she wasn't able to give herself to him completely right now. Coming so soon after her romp with
Stoner, sleeping with Charlie would feel cheap, and she
wanted it to mean so much more. She wanted to feel . . .
virginal, as if she had saved herself for him. And, too,
even before she could explore if they had more of a future than one night, there was the case.

Finally she said, "I have to leave very early tomorrow.
It would have been so much better if I could assume that
Lyle Stoner was still alive, that he might be the killer.
Then maybe I could feel I'd done my bit, leave the catch-
ing to others and stay here longer. But it's not that way,
Charlie, so I have to go back."

He sat forward. "Why, DZ? The way you talked before, it sounded like you'd be happy to give it up, and you've told me your boss wouldn't care if you sign off. So why stay with something so discouraging and dangerous?"

She had to rummage in her mind for an answer. "It's about finishing things, I guess. Corny as it sounds, about duty. You should be able to understand, Charlie. It's part of what we call values, the stuff we like to think is still at the core of places like this town. Doing the things that are hard in order to earn the things that are good. Getting at the truth. At the heart of it, Charlie, you know what I feel it comes down to?" She reached out to him, both hands grabbing for his like a trapeze artist counting on the perfectly timed catch to keep her in the air. "You," she said, smiling though her eyes had filled. "I know we'll have the best chance of being good together if . . . if I can just feel I've earned the right to. . . ." She glanced around her. "To all this." Her eyes came back to him. "To you."

"Hey," he said, his way of accepting the terms, "I'm only human."

She felt a burst of panic, then, that it could go on and on, and whatever magic had flared with Charlie, it could die. Suppose the case lasted another few months, a year, suppose the M.G. was never caught. They'd never gotten the Green River Killer, or Jack the Ripper for that matter. Still, she couldn't let go of her commitment to stay with what she'd started. She could only resolve all the more to make it end soon.

But right now all she wanted to do was get off the subject. "I'll help clean up."

He washed, she dried.

"How much have you figured so far?" he asked. "About who he might be, his reasons."

"Not much," she admitted. She told him about the scant bits of evidence they had, and the psychological profile: an achiever of technological sophistication who killed with cold brutality, ranged the whole country, used a weapon that could kill an elephant, had such rage at the medium of television that part of his purpose was to shame it, corrupt it.

"So that's the motive for his method," Charlie said. "What goes into choosing his victims?"

"They're people who've escaped justice. He sees himself as a good guy, setting things right."

Charlie circled a scouring pad over the bottom of a pan. "You say he travels far and wide to kill. But why *those* people, DZ?"

"I told you. Because they're—"

"Criminals, yes. But you can look anywhere and find people who've bent the law or escaped it, even gotten away with murder. If he was simply hell-bent on exacting justice, he wouldn't have to travel so far between one victim and the next."

She stopped drying to listen. He was on to something, maybe, a perspective that had been ignored by all the clever analysis. But playing devil's advocate, she said, "Maybe the traveling is job related, he looks for a victim wherever he happens to be."

Charlie rinsed the pan. "I don't think so. It must have taken some extra effort to track this ex-Nazi. There may be a couple of dozen in the U.S., but they're not that easy to find—and less likely to be living in a town you just happen to be passing through on a sales trip or whatever."

She went along with it now. "So if he picked a pederast and one of Hitler's alums . . . you think he had a specific beef with each of them."

"Not necessarily the particular person. But with that *type* of criminal."

She mulled it as she finished the rest of the things in the rack. If the M.G. was targeting his justice against specific evils, it should be added to the profile. When and if they had a suspect, it might indicate whether he was a good match.

The cleanup was done. The kitchen clock showed it

was almost ten o'clock. DZ thought it was worth cueing Chafee into this new notion about the killings, and she had a Washington phone number that could be used to reach him at all hours. She asked for a phone, and Charlie led her into his home office, a small, neat, book-lined room with a computer, fax, and copier arrayed on a built-in desk. He turned on a desk lamp and left. She called first to confirm her plane reservations for tomorrow, then dialed the Washington number. The connection came through quickly.

"Agent Chafee." The words slightly muddled, as if he had a mouthful of food.

"It's DZ. Where are you?"

"On my cell in some crummy coffee shop in New York. What's up?"

She led off by reporting her discoveries about Lyle Stoner, ruling him out as a suspect. Then she brought up the idea Charlie had suggested.

"If you're saying the killer may have known both the Nazi and the porn dealer," Chafee replied, "it doesn't wash. We've tried to find anyplace in their lives where the lines cross, and it's not there."

"Knowing them isn't the point, Ken. It's simply trying to figure out why these men were chosen. If he picked a child molester and an SS grad, what does it tell us about *him*?"

"Maybe nothing—but, sure, I'll tell our profilers to look at it. I just wish he'd just leave us more solid stuff to work with, like the bullet and the frame."

"Frame—the one the M.G. used for his calling card? You get a lead off that?"

"You saw it—tortoise shell, with gold brackets at the corners. One of the brackets is stamped with the word 'Cartier.' I brought it to their New York store today, and they told me that frame design hasn't been sold since the 1930s—and only in the Paris store. The price then would have been close to three hundred bucks. Now, they say, it's become a collector's item; could be worth up to ten thou."

"So maybe it belonged to Farben. Could even be Nazi loot."

"No way. There's glass in the frame, and our lab found a residue of ink and paper filament that was left on the inside of the glass, the part in contact with the M.G.'s card. From the amount, they concluded the card had to be in there a day or two—which means the killer brought that frame in with him."

"Pretty generous, leaving a ten-thousand-dollar gew-gaw as if it was a crackerjack prize."

"He couldn't have known the value. Which gives us a couple of new lines of inquiry. It's worth enough so that if it was stolen, it might be on a police record somewhere. Our killer may also have a record for burglary on file."

New lines of inquiry that would involve thousands of man-hours of poring through records across the country. But DZ wondered now if the lines of inquiry weren't so many and complicated that they were becoming a net in which they were tangled up, confusing themselves more than finding the way to a solution. Perhaps that was even part of the M.G.'s game—the reason he'd *deliberately* left this solid clue.

But of course the lines had to be followed wherever they led. She finished the call by telling Chafee she was returning to New York tomorrow to be at Stoner's broadcast.

With the frame on her mind as she turned from the phone, her eye stopped on the rectangular shapes she saw propped on shelves in the dim recesses of Charlie's office. She went over to look at the framed pictures. A man in shirtsleeves in front of other men stiffly posed behind desks in a place DZ recognized as the same long room still occupied by the *Dalton Falls Journal*—Charlie's father with his staff, no doubt. An elderly woman in a broad-brimmed garden hat. DZ laughed softly at one of a younger Charlie in shorts, with a scruffy beard, standing with a group of Mexican guys outside a cantina.

And then, against the background of a lakefront, there was a young, extremely pretty blond woman in camping clothes, holding an ax raised to chop firewood as she looked up, laughing as the camera surprised her. The look, the moment, told it all. Charlie and his wife had been deeply in love, had compiled a history of enjoying certain pleasures that were still alien to DZ. She imagined herself camping with Charlie, doing it to please him . . . being so conscious of trying to fill *her* shoes.

Hold on, girl, getting ahead of yourself again. She left without looking at any more pictures.

She found him seated in the kitchen nook, a book spread open in front of him, his hand resting on the handle of a ceramic mug. "What are you reading?"

"A book about the Lewis and Clark expedition. Came out last year. Fascinating."

Another vision: folded into a comfortable chair across a room from him, reading all the books she'd never had time for. *Enough, damn it!* "I'd better get to bed," she said. "I'll need to be up early to catch my flight."

He stood. "I'll drive you to Davenport."

"Great."

There was a silence. She took a step toward him, wanting to be kissed, just that.

He hesitated, gestured to the mug. "Like to take some warm milk up to bed?"

She shook her head, and then all at once she lost it, all of her shaking so the sudden tears began spilling down her face. He caught it as she spun away, looking for an excuse to beat a fast retreat, but before she could his arms were around her.

"What is it, DZ, what's wrong?"

She leaned against him, sobbing. "Warm milk, for chrissakes! Damn it, Charlie, it's just *you* all over! You make me feel like . . . like I'm back in a safe, cozy world where there's nothing to be afraid of. Like I'm a kid, right inside some version of Winnie the Pooh."

"And that's bad?"

"I can't *afford* it, that's all." She pushed back from him, swiping the tears off her face as roughly as if she were slapping herself. Glaring at him, she went on, "It fools you into thinking everything will work out fine in the end all by itself. And that dulls the reflexes when you may need them the most. In my work, you've got to expect the worst—of people, fate, whatever. Then maybe you're ready for it when it comes. Because it will. You know damn well it *will*!"

His arms dropped from around her, and he studied her sadly. She thought he was reappraising, seeing the impossibility of crossing the gap. But he leaned closer again, put his fingers under her chin as lightly as if he were sifting rainwater to retrieve a feather, and lifted her face. Then he kissed her, as long and tenderly and fully and lovingly as she had ever been—ever would be— kissed in all her life. As if she were all tenderness herself, not the least bit tough.

"I'll be here," he said when he pulled back, "whenever you can afford it. Good night, DZ."

It was too soon for the only words that filled her. She lay her palm against his cheek, then turned and went upstairs.

She was on the landing when she heard his footsteps cross the wood floor downstairs to the front door. Looking down through the stairwell, she saw him turn the bolt to lock it, then walk back to the kitchen. The extra protection wasn't for himself, she knew, only for her.

Fool, she renounced herself as she got ready for bed. *Poor pathetic stupid fool.* She ought to stay, throw over a job on which her participation was no longer wanted, so they could go on canoe trips, read together on quiet evenings beside a fire.

But she couldn't leave it undone.

Still reproving herself bitterly, she lay in the dark and recalled his kiss, one fleeting, perfect moment in her mean world; a memory that finally soothed her into sleep as gently as a mug of warm milk.

CHAPTER
35

*S*HE HIT THE office at noon, straight from the airport. Gable, at his desk, on the phone, saw her arrive. She dropped her luggage, paused to look past him at the rows of empty desks, then walked through to her office. Standing, she riffled through the stack of message slips by her phone. The commissioner's office alone accounted for eight, six of them yesterday, all marked urgent. She hadn't made any effort to inform him she'd be taking a Sunday to make a detour while she traveled back from California, and she realized now he must have been enraged to find her unavailable. There were also two from Stoner.

Gable entered. She looked up. "Where the hell is everybody?"

"One team's at Stoner's studio, advance surveillance for today's broadcast; four men mopping up the last names from the ticket mailings that seem worth a face-to-face; two guys visiting companies that make satellite transmitters to see if they'll coordinate on getting us lists of dealers and customers; I'm working the travel angle."

"And the rest?" she asked. Even after Leacock had

halved the Task Force there had been more than thirty detectives left.

"You see a newspaper today, DZ? The commissioner sent out a press release last night saying our role in the investigation has been downgraded. We're moving out of here to go back downtown by the end of the week."

"That prick! One fucking day I follow my nose, and that's all it takes!"

"That's not why, DZ. Look at the way it shapes up. Stuff happening all over the map. None of the action's here except for the broadcasts. It's federal all the way. We'll do backup, like other local agencies involved."

"So what has he left me? A dozen men?"

"Eight—with you."

"What about DeJesus? I need her."

"She's gone back to routine counseling."

For this she had clung to her duty, DZ thought ruefully, the glory of leading a charge. Only they'd shot the horse out from under her. And she knew it wouldn't have been done to a man. Not *this* way.

She slumped into her chair and stared at her desk for a few seconds. Then she looked up, resolved. Fuck Leacock! She'd be the one to break it! Her and her seven men. Her alone if it came down to it. "Travel stuff getting us anywhere?" she asked.

Gable shook his head. "He must have a fistful of false IDs. FBI has passenger manifestos from all flights that would've gone within a few hundred miles of either murder within forty-eight hours either side. They've looked for cross-matches a dozen different ways; names, cash users, card numbers, guys traveling with just carry-ons who show on any two flights that match the M.G.'s movements. Nothing's come up."

DZ looked back at the littered papers on her desk. What next?

Gable took the seat across from her. "He'll be on Stoner's show today, DZ." He snatched a look at his wristwatch. "About three hours from now. We'll have another crack at him then. Always a chance he'll let something slip."

A chance in a million, she thought, but didn't say it. Her mind was running along a different track. "You heard about the picture frame?"

"Yeah," Gable said. "Strange. More games, I guess. The guy he killed had a photo supply store; probably sold picture frames, too. Something to do with that. . . ."

No, never that simple, DZ thought, not with the M.G. Yet maybe connected somehow to the man he'd killed. "I need DeJesus. Got her new number handy?"

Gable went to get it. DZ sat at her desk and finished checking the message slips. Now she saw one from Corcoran's office at GBS—"requests protection" it said. Only one. He must have arranged it with downtown when she couldn't be found.

Gable returned with the phone number. DZ dialed, and the psychologist's voice mail answered. "I'm busy at the moment and unable to take your call. . . ."

With a patient, DZ guessed, a cop confused or depressed by the unstoppable drift away from normality. Like herself. She left a message.

"I'm going home, clean up, then to the studio," she told Gable after the call.

"I'll drive you," he said.

"No. We need someone here if the commissioner calls. I don't want him to think we're out of business completely. See you at the show."

The show, she thought as she walked out. How could they still call it that?

THROUGH THE DOOR OF THE LOFT, SHE STOPPED. IT LOOKED so different suddenly. Not the welcoming space she had carved out for herself in the middle of the brutal city, where she did a brutal job, but a place where she had isolated herself, a walled refuge.

"What have you done to me, Charlie?" she said softly. Setting her valise down by the door, she looked toward the answering machine. Had he called? She wasn't ready to hear it yet. She took a hot shower to wash off the grit of travel, put on a *ghi,* then she went back to the answering machine.

The commissioner's office had called a few times, and reporters looking for her reaction to the Task Force being tanked. Then one from Stoner asking her to call when she got back from California. The time-date feature told her they'd all come yesterday.

This morning's started with Stoner: he expected her at the broadcast, but hoped they'd have a chance to talk first. It was obvious he thought there was personal business as a result of falling into bed together. For herself, she wished now it had never happened. She couldn't avoid talking to him—she had to tell him what she'd learned about Lyle—but preferred to wait until she saw him on the job.

The ring of an incoming call automatically interrupted the machine. DZ picked up the portable on the coffee table.

DeJesus. She started by commiserating over the "Sunday night massacre."

"Never mind, Marilyn," DZ said. "I'm still on the job, and I've got a new puzzle for you. . . ." She told the psychologist about the picture frame left at the latest murder scene. "What's he telling us, Marilyn?" DZ asked then. "Everything's been meant to tell us *something.*"

A sigh came through the phone. "DZ, I know it's frustrating to have so little to work with, but you expect too much. I can't interpret each little move he makes. The killer may have framed his card to give it extra importance, a bit of grandiosity breaking out. Or the significance may be related to the man he killed. I can't begin to guess."

DZ was unapologetic. "You agree it's an unusual thing to do, leave such a valuable—"

The psychologist broke in. "Look, this man enjoys taunting his pursuers. He knows whatever he does will be analyzed and pored over by us. Playing this game—and doing it in an arena that makes tens of millions of people an audience for murder—is no less important to him than the killing. From now on, he could keep piling on one odd little detail after another, but you can't be sure when you'll get one that really helps. All you can really count on is that sooner or later you will."

"If only I could be sure of that."

"That I can promise," DeJesus said. "From a psychological standpoint, you know the rock-bottom importance of every clue? It's a signal that this guy *wants* to be caught. He'll go on daring you to do it, and the longer you take, the more daring he'll get, the more he'll test how far he can go . . . until he tips too far. Because," the psychologist added, "he wants to be caught."

"How do you arrive at that?"

"He's dared you from the beginning to catch him—I mean, confessing to murder *publicly*—doesn't that suggest he'll push the envelope until he goes too far? For whatever the reason, sooner or later he must want to be caught. We're already seeing signs of a guilty conscience. Don't the ads say he'll be on Stoner to apologize?"

That froze DZ. "Ads? What are you talking about?"

"You haven't seen them? GBS is running promos every half hour for the—"

"Jesus," DZ hissed with disgust. "I'll get back to you later." She banged down the phone, then glanced at the kitchen clock. Seeing it was only a few minutes before one, she went to the television and tuned to Stoner's network. The climactic scene of a soap opera was playing out. DZ grabbed the remote, muted the sound, and went back to finish the phone messages while keeping an eye on the screen.

Stoner again; call him at the office.

The building agent to inform her a neighbor had seen a

rat in the building, and he wanted to schedule an extermi-
nator. It made her smile: rats . . . such a small problem.

And finally the words so instantly warm and welcome:
"Hi, DZ. It's a lovely day here in my part of the world, and
I'm wondering how things are going for you? Did you—"

But suddenly she
   "—have a good—"
  realized it wasn't
    "—trip back?"
     Charlie.

She approached the answering machine slowly while
the voice continued in an amiable tone. "I just called to say
I'm sorry. I've been keeping up on the news, and I see
you're getting bumped off my case. Doesn't seem fair. You
were there at the start, you know me best. . . ."

Her body, still damp from the shower, turned icy cold.
She pulled the *ghi* tighter around her, but feeling the thin-
ness of the material made her more aware of her nakedness
beneath it. She had the illusion of standing stripped in front
of *him*.

"I wish you were there so we could chat. But if you'd
like to talk to me, maybe you'll call me back at 478-6637.
So long till then, DZ. Have a nice day."

Disconnect. The time-date stamp said the message had
come today at 11:45.

With the same furious reflex that would make her grab
for her gun, she snatched up the phone and punched in the
numbers. 4-7-8-6-6-3-7.

A recorded operator came on to say the number was not
in service.

Had she dialed correctly? DZ rewound the message
tape, listened again to the number, then dialed it again.

Not in service.

Of course the M.G. might not want to make actual contact, but he had the ability to play a more elaborate joke—
have her call routed back to the commissioner's office, for
example. Not his style to supply a nonfunctioning number.

She ought to know him better than anyone, he'd said.

She glanced down at the telephone keypad, looked at the letters on the numbered buttons. Now she had it! 4786637 also spelled out 4STONER. *The show's toll-free number for call-ins!* It had to be preceded by the toll-free 800.

She picked up the phone again.

The hearty voice of a woman answered: "Thank you for calling the *Stoner* show. Our operators will be here to take your calls from one hour before showtime. Please try again at that time. Barry appreciates your interest and wishes he could answer all your questions. Thank you." A recording.

So there it was: she could talk to him on the show. Today.

In a rush to dress and get to Stoner's studio, she whirled from the kitchen—and froze in her tracks. He was only paces away, staring at her, in his sailor disguise—

No. Merely his image on the screen. But the fear had barred the reality for just a heartbeat. She grabbed the remote and unmuted the sound. The picture had changed to show the M.G., now as the soldier. An announcer spoke over it in a stagey baritone: ". . . most wanted man in America, back again to provide another look into the very soul of evil. He says he's sorry. But is he? It's an hour of television you won't want to miss."

Stoner came on in close-up: "Today at four. Be there." That part of the promo she'd seen in the past, a standard plug for other shows spliced onto this one. Even so, she blamed Stoner for exploiting the morbid interest attached to the murderer.

Dressing hurriedly, she kept pondering what she should say if she were actually able to speak to the killer. She realized then she'd want a record of the conversation, so she put a tape into the VCR and set it to record the program.

And now, imagining herself in the spotlight with the M.G., it struck her that she was in no position to criticize any of those who had him call the tune. He had told her he wanted to speak to her, and here she was, eager to seize the

opportunity because she believed what DeJesus had said—
that sooner or later he would give away the clue that would
trap him.

You know me best. Yes. And because she did, because he
might give that clue sooner to her than anyone else, she
was more than ready to join the circus.

Take a flying leap right into the center ring.

CHAPTER
36

ALERTED BY INTERCOM, Stoner was waiting at his office door. As she approached, his arms came up to receive her in an embrace. She raised her hands to fend him off.

"Oh?" he said. "Is that how it is?"

"That's how. I'm here on business."

After she had crossed the threshold, he said, "No explanation? Not even a—"

"I made a big mistake. Let's leave it at that."

He shook his head as though he'd been doused with ice water. "New York's finest—they sure are tough."

She hesitated on the brink of telling him it had been a nice interlude, but she wanted more and now there was someone else to supply it. But sharing with him what was so important to her felt too much like being one of the whimpering wounded who crowded onto his stage to confess before the world. "I think I know what happened to Lyle," she said.

He gave her a look, then pushed the office door shut.

She told him about her trip to Dalton Falls, and what she'd concluded from finding the burned icehouse, the old newspaper files. She never mentioned Charlie.

Listening, he stood by a window facing west. At the end, he said, "So my brother died twenty-five years ago."

"There's no proof, no body to match against dental records or DNA. But it makes sense. That's where he went to burn the bad memories away, himself with it." After a pause, she said, "You had no idea at all?"

He whirled on her. "If I had, why would I have told you—" He stopped. "Oh. You think I let you suspect a dead man to make it harder to track the real killer."

"I don't know what to think. I have to cover the bases."

His eyes flashed. "DZ, I wouldn't pay to have people killed no matter how much my stock goes up."

"Except if you get more magazine covers and it revives your dying talk show and makes you the hottest thing on TV, you won't exactly *mind*." She advanced on him. "And you don't mind running ads to tell the world not to miss today's show."

His glare cooled. "That's Corcoran."

"Then rein him in! It's *your* program. For godsake, Barry, this is an attack against the whole foundation of law. You can't just keep saying 'that's showbiz!' "

He gave a defeated nod, moved to drop down on the sofa. "I'll keep him off today's show, if you want. Say the word, I'll never let him on again."

"No—as long as he keeps coming to us, it's better than losing touch. But I'd like it if you'd do it with a minimum of bells and whistles." She walked nearer to him. "And put me on, too." He looked up sharply, intrigued. "No, not to be interviewed by you," she explained. "One-on-one with him."

Stoner leaked a smile. "And you're the one who says it's not showbiz! The cop grills the bad guy right on the air. . . ."

"It's not exactly my idea." She told him about the message the M.G. had left on her answering machine.

"He wants you to call in," Stoner said. "Not the same as going on camera."

"He'll be happier if he can see me. He must watch the show while he's on it."

Stoner rose and paced again. "Your department goes along with this? I thought there were policies about—"

"Fuck their policies! I'm not asking permission."

He raised his eyebrows. "You know how it'll look to them. Your authority gets whittled down, next thing you're—"

"So I'm grandstanding. Barry, listen, my psychologist says he has to keep playing it closer and closer to the edge, that he wants to tip himself over. Making contact with me fits that. I know him best. Maybe I can push buttons others can't."

Stoner walked in a shrinking circle, stopping at last to face her. "It's a setup. You're giving him a chance to laugh right in your face, and that'll finish you. Some pictures people get off that little screen get burned in here forever." He tapped his skull. "What this'll put into people's minds is the showdown between you and the bad guy. The next murders will go down as the ones *you* failed to stop."

"What can I lose? They're cutting me out of the case, anyway."

"And me?" he asked. "What part do I play?"

"None. You just stand back and give me room."

Stoner hesitated another few seconds. "Corcoran's going to be thrilled," he said. "You were always his number one 'get.'"

THE M.G. HAD SAID NOTHING IN ADVANCE ABOUT HOW HE'D appear this time. The FBI had called back Ko Tashahiro to set up his super-fast Internet connection, and a monitor had been placed onstage. The boys in the Sat-Center were also standing by. There were also a couple of SWAT teams on the scene, police and FBI having reconsidered the possibility the M.G. might show up in person with a hostage.

Chafee was in the studio today, and DZ caught him before the broadcast to let him know what she planned. He warned her against it, but agreed there was a very good chance she could shake loose something more than if Stoner did the talking.

"What did your lab get from that bullet?" she asked him.

"Not much. Going through the wall, then banging around the plumbing stack, left it badly deformed. But with the firepower to kill and keep going, it had to come from a big shell—in the neighborhood of seventy-five millimeter."

"Seventy-five! That's military ordinance."

Chafee nodded. "Bullets like that get fired out of anti-aircraft batteries."

They puzzled over it silently. Did it prove the M.G. had a military connection? In any case, the distinctiveness of the bullet explained why he hadn't wanted to leave it behind at the crime scenes. Yet to kill a human using the same projectile that could cripple an airplane or penetrate the armor of a tank was the most extreme application of overkill. How could you call it anything but crazy, whether or not the killer could distinguish between right and wrong?

CHAPTER
37

AT THE TOP of the hour, a written declaration was posted on the screen:

This edition of the Stoner program is a special presentation of GBS News.

Since being called before the Senate committee, Corcoran had felt it wise to shore up the network's right to claim freedom of the press anytime the Mystery Guest appeared.

Following the announcement, Stoner came onstage wearing his office clothes. No formal suit today, not even the sports jacket. This was reality, the plain format informed viewers. Indeed, nothing had been prepared as filler until the M.G. appeared. Stoner had told Candelli that, until the M.G. showed up, he'd stand out there by himself—just talk about feelings the case had aroused, review the long career that had led to this bizarre event, give his views of American society.

"Do the old Jack Paar thing," Candelli summed up approvingly. "Bleed in front of them."

Arriving before the cameras, Stoner spent a few moments looking around at the studio—rows of empty seats, no audience today—as if it was an alien place he'd never seen before. At last, gazing reflectively at the stage with only brief glances at the camera, he spoke:

"I've been doing this a long time, and I never thought the day would come when I'd feel maybe it's wrong to be out here at all. That digging too deeply into human nature, into what makes us all what we are—at least doing it this way, as a public spectacle—isn't healthy. I always thought it would be a good thing, a help to those among us who are troubled to know they're not alone. But it seems to work the other way, too. It can release a kind of virus that spreads infection, brings on a sickness in those who . . . who have low resistance." His gaze came around finally to meet the camera's steady eye. "But it's here and we can't help looking, can we? The way we slow down when we pass a car crash. Rather than speed past, turn our eyes away, we want to see the worst details, brains spilling out, smashed lives. I suppose we think going through that ritual may somehow protect us from becoming victims ourselves. . . ." He dropped his gaze, momentarily lost in his own thoughts.

Watching from backstage, DZ could tell it wasn't a pose. His diatribe was too unfocussed to be the product of any careful, advance thought; the rambling words were completely spontaneous.

Lifting his eyes, he resumed. "Anyway . . . nothing to do now but go on with it. Keep the line open to the man who's carrying the virus, and hope we'll get him off the streets before too many more of us are infected." He moved closer to the camera, peered into the lens as if looking through a gate. "Plenty of us are already, though. Oh yeah, I'm like you. There's three dead so far, but have we had enough? We're scared, but still curious to see how long he can keep it going. . . ."

Abruptly, Stoner brought up his hands, and reached

out. "So c'mon, wherever you are, come out, come out. The faithful are here assembled, waiting for the answers." He turned to the onstage monitor and waited, as if he expected his taunt to produce instant results. The screen continued flickering with blank luminosity. Stoner faced front again, gave a look of exaggerated helplessness to the camera. "Think he's not coming? Gonna disappoint us? Maybe some of you ought to call in, let him know how much you were looking forward—"

Dead stop. A glance toward the control booth. This was it, DZ knew at once.

Back again, good as his word.

The screen behind Stoner filled with a black-and-white picture, a kinescope of the old game show again, the MC in his tuxedo saying with gusto, "Will the Mystery Guest sign in, please!"

DZ looked to Ko Tashahiro at his nearby listening post. "You tracking this?"

"It's not coming over the phone lines," he told her.

Satellite again. Where was he this time?

On the stage monitor, the sound of applause and laughter broke out to accompany the close-up of a blackboard, a hand picking up a piece of chalk. Rapidly it scrawled the name "Chico" . . . then put the chalk down. Another hand took the chalk, and drew a quick, skillful, little line drawing of a harp. Then a third hand drew a cartoon mustache with protruding cigar.

The Marx brothers.

So what was the message this time? Merely a thumb in the eye of his trackers, telling them he could go on writing a plot as zanily anarchic as in any screwball comedy?

The picture on the monitor changed to show him calmly seated in his monochromatic chamber. Again he was in uniform—a baseball player, but his clothes of a style that went back to the earliest days of the game. Knickers with socks pulled calf-high, a shirt with longer sleeves, a squarish cap. And his facial disguise was also in keeping with the period, a fulsome handlebar mustache and puffy, muttonchops. He sat erect, his arms rigidly folded, exactly as DZ had seen baseball players of that era posed in photographs.

He was having fun with this, she saw, enjoying the mockery it made of a manhunt.

She had made Stoner promise before the show there would be no advance mention of her coming on. Once the M.G. appeared, Stoner would simply yield the stage. Quicker the better, element of surprise. But Stoner lingered now in front of the monitor.

"Afternoon, Mr. Stoner," came the voice from the ballplayer. Even the greeting had an echo of more genial days.

Stoner drew a breath, and what emerged then was a soft hiss not meant to be heard on the air: "You sick fuck." Then he turned to the side, to where DZ stood off-camera, beckoned to her impatiently, and walked off.

The ballplayer unfolded his arms, suspicious of what he had seen on his own television. But as DZ came on camera, he relaxed. "Well, this is a most pleasant surprise," he said heartily. "I hardly dared hope you'd accept my invitation with such alacrity, Detective Hayes." Old-fashioned language, too.

She went right at him. "Why the baseball stuff?"

A smile tilted his handlebar. "Where's your set-side manner, Lieutenant? No 'welcome to the show'?"

"I'm not here to play your games."

"But you *are* playing, Lieutenant."

Great. Already she had egg on her face in front of millions. But she kept on track. "Explain the baseball thing."

"I like playing dress-up. And I need to, don't I?"

Everything meant something. "There's more to it," she insisted.

"Okay. It's a tribute to our national sport. From one sportsman to another."

She knew what that meant. *His* sport was murder—perhaps the *new* national sport. "And your hint about the next victim—the Marx brothers—what does that mean? C'mon! If you're going to make a sport of it, you've got to play fair."

"I have no wish to be fair. Any more than my victims were fair to the people they killed."

DZ paused. Fencing with him, exchanging repartee, was still playing his game. She turned from the monitor and strolled the stage, taking her time as she would in a police interview room. He said nothing either, showing his own disdain for the demands of the medium.

DZ turned again to the image in the box. "We've got a psychological profile based on everything you've said and done so far. The analysis says you're a very angry man. In a murderous rage . . ."

"Congratulations. Good figuring."

"But not just mad at your victims. The shrinks say it's all this"—she gestured to the monitor, the studio—"television itself that makes your blood boil. What's your reaction to that?"

"Interesting theory," he said. "But it's crap. I love TV. Mad at it? Hell, I'm mad *about* it. Why shouldn't I be? It made me what I am today."

"Made you? How? Made you a murderer?"

He didn't answer, and for the first time DZ had a sense she was leading him, not the other way around. He'd let something slip. Now he rubbed his hands over the knickers of his old-fashioned baseball uniform. The hand movement reminded DZ that there was a switch somewhere around the chair or under it that he had used before to break his transmission. Anxious to keep him engaged, she changed tack quickly. "Why the game show stuff?"

"When is it anything but a game? A rough game, a life

and death game, but still a game. Or we could call it a sport."

"A sport!" DZ spat the word back. "Is it sporting to brutally bludgeon a defenseless, innocent young man, then stab him when he's already unconscious?" She mimed the plunge of a blade, banging a fist against her chest, hoping that making the crime more vivid might inspire some shame in the watchers.

The ballplayer looked away to the side, as though unable for a moment even to meet the camera's gaze.

Whatever the effect of her outburst, DZ reminded herself, she mustn't shut him down. Give him the leeway to say whatever he wanted in the hope he'd let something useful slip.

He brought his eyes front again. "That's one reason I'm here," he said. "I wanted to say to everyone I'm truly sorry about the boy. It's not what I planned."

"Right," DZ said. "That was the come-on for today— you want to apologize." She whirled to the cameras, speaking to all the spectators. "And that's all it takes to get him off the hook! To keep you out there watching this God-awful game."

"Of course it is, Detective Hayes." The cheerful tone was back in his voice. "They've gathered around the ol' boob tube to watch killers get chased, watch 'em get surrounded and hauled in, watch 'em on trial. This is just the best show yet."

DZ stared at the man inside the box, overcome with the futility of being caught in this situation. It was like being in a dream, too surreal to be able to find her bearings. And that was the problem for the viewers, too. The man performing for them—costumed, giving out hints like any game show host—was no more real and dangerous to them than the made-up villains they saw on the cop shows.

It was wrong to be out here, she felt suddenly. She'd hoped today she could break him open somehow, the

way you could when you went one-on-one with a suspect at a precinct. But within the four walls of the real
thing, you could make the suspect sweat. Here the perp
was safely out of reach.

She had an urge to simply walk off. But that would be
surrender. What could she do to save face, shake him,
persuade their audience he wasn't untouchable?

Stay with standard technique. Keep the interview
going. Wear him down. "You left us a very interesting
clue last time," she said. "Did you know that picture
frame was worth maybe ten thousand dollars?" She
watched his reaction closely.

He didn't flinch. "If money was ever a consideration,
Detective, I'd never have started this—and you and I
would never have met."

"I haven't met you," she observed. "Only seen you
from a distance."

He smiled at the distinction, then leaned forward, his
face moving into his camera eye. "Would you like me to
come closer?"

It sent a chill through DZ. He meant it literally, a hint
he might stalk her—make her one of his victims. Just the
kind of dare that fit with the rest of his scheme,

But there was nothing better to do than encourage it.
And doing so, she realized, gave her just the kind of exit
line she'd been hoping for.

"Like it? No." She moved up and looked square into
the eyes of the image in the box. "But I can't wait for it.
Come as close as you want. Come and get me where I
work or where I live. Come day or night. Just come if
you dare, you sonofabitch. Because you won't get away
if you do!"

Where DZ was standing now she obscured the monitor from the cameras, so up in the control booth they had
switched the Guest's picture to broadcast direct from the
satellite. On a split screen, alongside DZ's expression of
iron resolve, he was seen smirking.

"Good try, Lieutenant," he said. "And I may take you up on it someday. But first I've got other fish to fry."

Other victims, he meant. And she'd achieved nothing that provided the least edge for saving them. It burst out of her. "Give it up now for godssake, and we can still make a deal!"

"A deal," he echoed. "I've been waiting for you to mention that. Because I've got a deal for *you*." He slipped a hand inside his shirt and pulled out a couple of yellowish strips, as if cut from a manila card. He shifted one to his other hand, held them both out upright, as if holding two candles. "Interested?" he said.

He had set up a choice for her, she understood, like drawing straws. "I told you," she said, "no games."

"But this is a *deal*. And it's a lifesaver. . . ."

She took a step backward, caught between caution and curiosity, the need to save face and the need to know.

"One of these has a mark on it," he continued, "one doesn't. Point to the one you want, and if it's the one with the mark . . . well, too bad, tomorrow I'll kill someone."

She shook her head, disgust as much as denial.

Louder, he said, "You don't want to take *my* deal? The right choice would save *two* lives!"

"You said one—just *one*!"

"Oh . . . that's for the one with the mark. Choose the one without"—his voice sank to a sinuous purr—"I'll kill three."

For one more horrified second she stood rooted to the stage, desperate for words to arouse his humanity. But her mind was a blank. She was aware only of the same impulse that had driven Stoner to his display of fury and frustration. If she'd had a gun, she might have emptied it into the television monitor. Instead she ran headlong from the stage.

Left alone on camera, the ballplayer spoke to his audience as coolly as any talk show host. "Well, that's a shame. Now it's fielder's choice. And since there's no one left on the show to talk to, I might as well take my leave." He tipped his cap like a ballplayer acknowledging the cheers after a home run. A moment later his transmission went black.

CHAPTER
38

"Y̶OU'RE SUSPENDED. EFFECTIVE immediately."

The call summoning DZ to Leacock's office had come to the studio just ninety seconds after her appearance on the show ended. When she left the GBS tower, his car and driver were already at the curb to bring her directly to Police Plaza.

His order of suspension was the climax of a fifteen-minute rebuke that omitted nothing—the arrogance of ignoring department rules and regulations, the damage done by her hunger for personal publicity to public confidence in the department, and the incompetence demonstrated by her conduct of an investigation that had produced zero results. For good measure he snidely threw in the grapevine talk that she'd compromised her authority by "fraternizing naked" with a principal in the case.

The first dep, who remained at one side barely concealing a smug look of redemption, now came forward, his palm extended. DZ took the gun and badge from her shoulder bag, but held them back. A brilliant speech of indignant self-defense started to form, then gave way to the basic instinct for self-preservation.

"Sir, there's a chance he'll come after me now. He knows where I live."

"Are you asking for protection?" Leacock said.

"I'm asking to keep my gun."

"You know how it works, Lieutenant," the first dep said. "Not while you're on suspension."

"A departmental hearing will be scheduled to decide your future status," Leacock said. "Until then protective surveillance will be available to you if necessary."

Like if she heard a window break, a footstep in the hallway. She was trained, after all, she ought to know how to take care of herself. But without a gun?

The first dep's hand was still out. She turned over the gun and badge.

When she left, Gable was in the corridor. He'd heard about her hasty departure from the studio and had followed. "How'd it go?" he asked.

She studied him. How and where had Leacock picked up the knowledge of her tryst with Stoner? "Suspension," she said.

"That sucks. What you did was the best play we had." Gable looked angrily toward the door of the commissioner's suite. "It was *his* call to let him on in the first place. If you're shitcanned, then I'm—"

She grabbed him as he started moving toward the door. "Leave it, Clark. I should've known better than to put myself out there. It was dumb."

"Not if you'd gotten something."

"If. All I got, probably, is three more people killed."

He stopped straining and she let go. "C'mon, I'll drive you home."

Of course, there were other ways the commissioner could have picked up the gossip—Stoner himself boasting to someone too loudly; or one of the other detectives listening in on her radio call to Gable the morning after. Still, DZ felt cautious. "I think I'd rather be alone."

He let her walk away.

As soon as she entered the loft, she went to check the phone machine. She couldn't help hoping that Charlie had called, even if she'd tried to chase him off.

With the suspension hanging over her, she wondered if it made any sense not to go straight back to him.

Looking at the bright number indicating eight calls since she'd last listened to the machine, it struck her suddenly that the ones she'd heard earlier had been automatically erased, including the M.G.'s—a serious goof, she realized now.

She started listening to the new messages. A couple of reporters wanting comment on Leacock's news conference. A guy she couldn't remember meeting wanting to take her to dinner. She hit Fast-forward repeatedly. Then . . . what she'd hoped for:

"Hi, it's me. Hope you had a good trip home. I miss you already, and Bonnie's lookin' kinda mopey, too. DZ, I'm worrying about you, so please take care of yourself. I'll try you again later because you might have trouble reaching me at home for the next day or two. I've got to go up to the state capital to speak to a few people. But I'll call from there. I . . . uh . . . well, just please be careful. So long . . . dear, Detective."

Thank God for a touch of normality. Sounded like he hadn't even watched the Stoner program. It lifted her mood, an affirmation of hope for something better to come. She skipped through the last messages—another few from the press.

Would the M.G. call again? Or come after her? Or was it enough that maybe he'd killed her career? The shrewd bastard. No surprise if he was a success at something besides murder.

Her mind went back to their face-off. There had been only the tiniest crack in his facade when she started probing his feelings about television, a moment when she thought he might run away. Her memory played back the moment: *It made me what I am today.* . . . At the time she'd thought he was crowing about the notoriety obtained by twisting the medium to his purposes. But the phrase also connoted the attainments of a long career. What other shadings of identity might have slipped past her in the heat of their exchange?

DZ swooped up the remote controller on a table by the sofa. She turned on the VCR and the large-screen television set, rewound the hour of tape that had recorded the Stoner program, and sat down to watch. As she saw herself on television, she grimaced self-sconsciously. God, was that what she looked like?

She ran it through to the point where the M.G. had cut his transmission. He hadn't really given her a thing. Did he really want to be caught?

She ran the tape through again, watching his body language, pushing herself to speculate on the impulses and meanings behind each word and movement. The tenth time through she began to feel she was putting herself into a stupor, as mindless as she felt when channel-surfing, reflexively clicking through sixty or seventy channels on cable without really caring what the hell was on. But it was all that was left of her contact with the case. Turning it off represented surrendering completely.

Once more. It came to that point where she'd asked him his feelings about television—the moment where she felt she'd rattled him for the first time.

I love TV. Mad at it? Hell, I'm mad about it. Why shouldn't I be? It made me what I am today.

She stopped right there.

. . . made me what I am . . .

She'd asked him what he meant, and he hadn't answered. Aware, maybe that he'd gone too far, given something away. . . . She ran the tape back just far enough to play the last phrase again.

made me what I am

Boasting about it. So suppose you lifted the concept of

achievement up a notch or two. Suppose he was a big success, really big. . . .

Rich.

It had never occurred to anyone he might be on that level. Not that the rich didn't commit murder: crimes of passion, crimes of insanity, thrill killings, paid assassinations, carefully plotted or careless, amateurish slayings to remove an inconvenient wife or business partner. There were plenty of those in the files committed by people with tons of money in the bank—even banks that they owned.

But you just didn't think of very rich men deciding to trade their lives of luxury and privilege to take up a solitary campaign of common terror. That was for losers, down-and-outers. The failure to consider this sooner was a mirror of the same attitude that made it hard for juries to convict the rich and successful, to believe they could be guilty.

DZ turned the tape on again, ran it backward and forward.

. . . a sportsman . . .

Once she started thinking of him as wealthy, there were new interpretations for everything. A new slant on his disdain for the popular amusement of the masses. A new perception of the ease with which he could fund the expense of moving around so much, and obtain the expensive equipment he'd required.

And his itinerary! The thing she'd been harping on as a key for identifying him. Suddenly she had a new take on that, too. An idea that had the potential to provide the name of the killer within hours. If she was right—and if she could access all the records necessary for proving it . . .

DZ jumped up. Along one interior wall of the living area in her loft there were floor-to-ceiling bookshelves with all the volumes she owned. She went to the shelves and scanned an area of reference books, unable to remember for sure if she still had what she needed. Yes, there!—an atlas, probably acquired when she was in high school. She pulled the atlas off the shelf, brought it to the kitchen's galley counter, and opened it to a section devoted to the United States. She found two facing pages with a map that embraced the area of the Mississippi Valley, including the state of Indiana. After locating the town of Goshen, she took the message notepad by the phone and made a list of all the large and medium-size cities within a radius of no more two hundred miles, an amount she considered a comfortable driving distance.

Chicago
South Bend
Fort Wayne
Indianapolis
Terre Haute

She turned to the Western states and repeated the process with San Diego.

Los Angeles
Santa Barbara
San Bernadino
Palm Springs (small, but it would have the facilities)

The lists might get longer, but this was enough to get started. She took a beer from the refrigerator, downed a swig, then picked up the phone.

SHE ARRIVED AT THE STONER PRODUCTION SUITE IN JEANS, a tan safari jacket thrown over a tee, and sneakers on her feet. It was past nine, and, as she'd hoped, the place was deserted.

After a couple of hours on the phone pursuing her theory, she'd called Stoner at his Fifth Avenue apartment to ask for his help. Despite the way she'd cut him dead earlier, he was gracious: "You want to use my office? Sure. But why?"

"I need a fax machine, and a fast computer. I don't have them at home." She'd told him then about her suspension to explain why she couldn't use department facilities without having the results taken out of her hands.

He was waiting for her in his corner office. "What's this about?" he asked.

She hesitated, uncertain of whether to trust him. Yet she believed he'd had enough, wanted now to end the madness and would do nothing to jeopardize a good result. Taking a chair by the couch, she pulled out the penciled lists she'd been making until she realized how much faster it would go if the information could be faxed to her. He sat down across from her and she passed the sheaf of papers to him.

He glanced at her jottings. "What are these?"

"Airplane registration numbers. I've called every airport within two hundred miles of the murder sites capable of handling jet traffic. The FAA requires every plane in transit to file a flight plan, so airports have records of which planes took off or landed on any given date. If I find one that was in the vicinity of both murders on the dates they occurred—even within a day of the killings, it could point to the killer."

Stoner looked puzzled. "I thought you covered this already."

She'd left out the most important fact, she realized—so self-evident to her now that she assumed it went without saying.

"The commercial airlines, yes. But now I'm looking for a *private* jet, maybe owned under a corporate title. It would be his. My guess is he even flies it himself."

"The Mystery Guest? DZ those planes cost—"

"I know. Ten million—and up."

He stared her. "So let me get this straight, you've decided this homicidal nutcase is—what?—one of the Forbes 400?"

She returned a leaden gaze. "You think he *can't* be?"

"I don't believe anyone is that greedy."

"Barry, it's not about stock price. It's about the obsession of an unusual man."

"Even so, damn hard to imagine. . . ."

"Yeah, isn't it? The real world gets harder to imagine every day." She grabbed back her lists. "I got on the phone this evening and started taking dictation from flight controllers and tower supervisors in all these airports. After I spoke to a couple of them I wrote down these numbers, I got around to O'Hare in Chicago. Guess how many private jets flew in there on the day of the Goshen murder alone. More than a hundred. Just thinking of them all gave me writer's cramp, so I asked if they'd fax the registrations for that day, and the days before and after. They'll do it as soon as I tell them a fax number, and I'll have all the other airports do the same."

"We've got half a dozen fax machines in the office."

"Great, it'll go even faster. Once all the registrations are scanned into a computer, I'll be able to tell if any one of those planes was within striking distance of *both* murders."

"And the owner of that plane would be your man?"

"That's the theory."

"Well, we've got the computers, too," Stoner said. "But I don't know which buttons to push."

"Ko is on his way here. Give me the phone numbers for your fax machines, I'll make my calls, start the info coming."

He pointed to the fax on a cabinet to the side of his desk, and told her to start with that one, then left to gather the other fax numbers.

By the time Tashahiro arrived, DZ had faxes from a score of airports listing registration numbers of all private and corporate jets that had been on their runways at any time during the specified three-day periods, and more answers were coming in. More airports than she'd originally estimated were able to handle jet traffic.

Ko went to work analyzing the data. He didn't need to use Stoner's office computers; the laptop he brought along was more powerful than any of the available desktops, equipped with its own scanner to input lists without his having to type them. In ten minutes the computer whiz stepped into the doorway of Stoner's office and beckoned to her. She ended her call to a tower supervisor at the Pasadena airport and joined him. He pointed to his laptop screen where a series of numbers and letters were highlighted:

N2HB95   N1GA47   N00AG1   N7SA14

"So far these are the ones that appear on any two lists you've given me."

"Four planes . . ." she said, faintly surprised.

"Statistically not unlikely. Two of the airports covered are major hubs, Chicago and Los Angeles. There's a high probability more than one heavy hitter would have legitimate business in both places at the times you've specified."

"Print that out for me, Ko," she said.

He connected his laptop to an office printer and brought DZ the printout. Looking again at the plane registrations, she noted they were somewhat similar. "Do you know what the letters and numbers mean?"

"I'm not sure, but I believe all planes registered in the U.S. start with N."

More faxes came in over the next hour, and were scanned into Ko's computer, but the list remained unchanged. Just four planes had been within a two hundred-mile radius of both crimes within a three-day bracket of the dates they were committed.

The next task was to find out to whom the planes belonged.

"Is there a way to do that right now?" she asked Ko.

"By modem, I could go directly into the FAA computers where that information would be stored—their firewalls are nowhere near as secure as the Pentagon's. But unauthorized penetration of any government computer is a major crime, DZ. You must obtain that information through regular channels."

She nodded understandingly. "You've been a tremendous help, Ko. Thanks."

Tashahiro put on the strange sunglasses he wore day and night, except when at a computer, and began disassembling his equipment.

DZ knew she could give what she had to Chafee, let the FBI run with it. But would he bring her along? He would know by now she no longer had any official status. And it wouldn't satisfy her if she couldn't have what belonged to her; it had been her case at the start, she deserved to be there at the end. She spoke up suddenly: "Ko, hang on. These registrations may be the first solid lead to the killer. We know he's got as many as three people on his hit list. If he's true to form it could happen within a day. Saving a few hours right now might save those lives."

"The FBI should be able to access the information and follow up quickly." He continued packing.

"Help me, Ko," she pleaded. "By the time I pitch my theory to the Bureau and they call in an FAA computer operator, hours will be lost. . . ."

He turned to her. The slit lenses of his glasses made it impossible to read any reaction in his eyes. At last he said, "Recently a cracker who penetrated government computers was given four years in federal prison. If you use whatever information I obtain, the responsibility will be entirely yours. I will deny any part in it."

"Understood," she said.

Tashahiro set up his equipment again. Stoner had been in his office fiddling with paperwork, but he drifted out to watch silently with DZ as Ko tapped hectically at his keyboard, trying one phone number after another on his modem, going through a trial-and-error process of various passwords. From the speed with which he executed the process, it was obvious he had a sizable amount of classified computer codes already stored in his computer's memory. Whatever Tashahiro's avowed concern for the law, on his own he evidently gamboled through the cyber meadows of government secrets at will.

Soon he handed her a printout specifying not only registered owners attached to the four numbers, but the home airports, make and model of the airplanes, and, for those which were always flown by the same crew, the name and address of the regular pilots. DZ folded the papers away in the pocket of her safari jacket.

"I've done all I can," Ko said, hastily returning his equipment to an attache case. "If you're asked where you got this information—"

"You won't ever be mentioned."

He was gone in a minute.

"So," Stoner said, glancing toward the pocket where DZ had buttoned away the list, "you don't trust me with all the information." He moved closer. "And I thought you didn't mind giving me . . . the bare facts."

She raised her hands like a traffic cop. "Halt or I'll shoot," she said quietly.

He eased back. "What changed, DZ? Do I ever get to know?"

She looked away. Did he have a *right* to know?

"It may surprise you to learn this," he went on, "but I didn't think what happened between us was meaningless."

She whipped her eyes around to meet his. "So what did it mean, Stoner? A chance to see what it's like to fuck a cop? What can anything be for you now except one more addition to your scrapbook of human behavior. After running your endless lineup of sad, screwed-up, miserable people for so long, I don't think you can see any of us now except as 'material' for the show."

" 'Us?' " he echoed in surprise. "I never thought of you as among the sad, screwed-up, and miserable."

"Well, I am. *Was,* anyway, when I fell into bed with you. But I'm quitting the club—as soon as I can put this behind me. Cleaning up this one outbreak of sickness in the world will earn me my ticket out." She headed for the door.

When she was almost through it, he called, "Good luck, DZ. I mean it. Call me if I can help."

She waved without looking back.

CHAPTER
39

A T HOME, SHE laid out the pages of FAA data Ko had obtained. She noted first that ownership of all four planes was registered to businesses:

Hutchings & Berends, Houston, Texas
Genesis Artists Agency, Los Angeles, California
The Keytron Corporation, Framingham, Massachusetts
Stellar Airways, Inc., Chicago, Illinois

Comparing the list with the registration numbers, she realized that some of the letters seemed to represent the initials of the plane's owner. For the first plane, the designation began N2HB—for Hutching & Berends; the second started N1GA, the last N7SA. However, the plane belonging to the Keytron Corporation should have been N00KC if the pattern held; instead the initials were AG.

She started her calls with the Los Angeles firm. Not much past seven o'clock on the West Coast. There was a chance she'd find a couple of go-getters working late.

A man's voice answered: "Genesis."

She did a standard intro, including her rank with the

NYPD, and got no further before the man broke in: "I know who you are, DZ. Saw you on TV this afternoon. The whole office watched. We've already got guys tracking this for the film rights."

And who would do her part? she wondered. Would she end up a star, or only a bit player? "I need some questions answered about your company plane," she said.

"Our plane? What's that got to do with what you're working on?"

"Please," she said firmly, "if you can't give me information about it, get me someone who can."

He put her on hold, one of those annoying systems where the wait time was used to advertise—in this case, a new action film, no doubt starring or directed by one of the agency's clients. In half a minute, another man came on. He identified himself as Greg Barsky, a partner in the agency. When DZ told him what she wanted, he supplied quick, clear answers.

The agency owned a Learjet, which was used not only by Barsky and the other partners, but as a courtesy to transport important clients on their roster. Naming a fairly popular movie actress, he explained that the plane had flown her to Chicago on the date coincident with the Goshen killing for publicity appearances in connection with her new movie. It remained there a second day, then flew the star to New York for a nighttime appearance on the Letterman show, before returning to California. As for being at the Palm Springs airport on the date of the San Diego murders, Barsky said, it had flown him and a studio executive there for a round of golf.

"Anyone on the first flight also on the second?" DZ said.

"No. Except maybe the pilot, and even that's not certain."

"Why not?"

"We don't employ one pilot. We have a contract with a firm that maintains our plane and some others. The deal includes hangaring, maintenance, and crew from a regular pool. Three or four different guys fly for us."

DZ made a note. The pilots would be worth checking if she didn't find a more promising suspect among the bigger fish. "Can you supply names of people who'd confirm your answers?"

"Sure. I don't like having my important clients disturbed, but if it's necessary I'll cooperate any way I can."

She judged him to be sincerely unruffled by her request. "I'll get back to you if I need to check further. Thanks for your help."

"Before you go," he put in quickly, "I might as well ask if you've ever given any thought to working in television . . . ?"

"What do you mean?"

"Well, DZ, watching you with Stoner, I thought you generated sensational heat on camera. And it occurred to me that my agency could pitch you to front a kind of *America's Most Wanted* thing. There's a big appetite now for true crime, and don't forget some of the people tied up with the OJ thing parlayed it into talk shows and—"

She didn't hear the rest as laughter rose out of her and drowned out the words.

Wouldn't this be the ultimate success for the M.G., if he succeeded in turning her from his pursuer into just one more pitchman for his notion that violence and murder was nothing more than another product for the endless hours of airtime to be filled.

His voice finally cut through as she trailed off to giggles. "So—does the laughter mean you're happy about the idea?" the agent asked. "Or that you just think it's stupid?"

"No, Mr. Barsky," she replied. "It's something worse than stupid."

"What's that?"

"Dangerous," she said, and hung up.

• • •

THE NEXT COMPANY ON THE LIST WASN'T UNKNOWN TO HER; Hutching and Berends was one of those huge, nationwide accounting firms that did high-level corporate work. Houston was the headquarters.

No answer there, switchboard closed. Referring again to Ko's printout, DZ saw that permanent hangar facilities for each plane were also recorded, including phone numbers. The man who took her next call identified himself as a maintenance supervisor for many corporate aircraft based at Houston International. When DZ explained her needs, he consulted a log book that confirmed that the jet she'd specified had been on flights to both Chicago and Los Angeles on dates coinciding with the murders. Though unable to tell from the log who the passengers were, he supplied a home phone number in Houston for an employee named Stevenson who oversaw use of the plane at the accounting firm.

Before letting him go, DZ got him to translate the meaning of letters and digits in the registration number.

"We call it the tail number, actually, 'cause that's where it's displayed—or the N number, because they all start with N. What comes next depends on what we put in for. 2HB means it's the second plane in the company's fleet, and the 95 at the end means that's the year the plane was bought."

"So you specify your own number?"

"As long as there's none like it, the FAA doesn't mind."

She'd interrupted Mr. Stevenson's dinner, but he answered her questions pleasantly. As the outside auditor for a number of oil companies, he said, his firm had sent a team of accountants to Chicago on one occasion, and Los Angeles on another, to spot-check sales records of large gasoline retailers in those areas.

"These checks are standard. There's a lot of fiddling in retail gasoline sales. Add up the pennies that don't get accurately reported, and oil companies can easily lose fifty, sixty million dollars."

"Any of your accountants made both flights?" she asked.

"Nope. The team that regularly checks West Coast retailers is different from the one that tracks the Midwest."

"I may want to double-check your information. Any objection to giving me the names of all the men on those teams?"

"None at all. But they're all fine people, Lieutenant—"

She was in a hurry to move on to the next call. "If I want their names, Mr. Stevenson, I'll get back to you. For now, please keep this call strictly confidential."

"Can't tell my superiors?"

"*No*body at the firm, please. Your word on that. . . ."

He agreed, and she hung up.

Next, the Keytron Corporation. When there was no answer, DZ tried two numbers at the home airports of the company's jet, one listed as being at Boston's Logan Airport, the second at the airport in Hyannis, Massachusetts.

Again, no answer.

She was dialing the number for the last company when the intercom buzzer sounded, someone at the street door. She put down the phone and headed for the intercom by the elevator. But halfway there, she stopped short.

Could be anyone, of course. Friend dropping in unexpectedly, the landlord wanting to put down the rat poison. Still, she went back to the kitchen, and picked out a knife with a long blade before continuing to the intercom.

"It's Clark," the answer came from the voicebox.

DZ held back a sigh. He'd never done this before, come uninvited. It was awkward for both of them. "What is it, Clark?"

"I couldn't stop worrying about you."

"I'm fine."

"Can I come upstairs? I've got something for you."

Too harsh to send him away. She pressed the button that opened the street latch, and set the knife down on a nearby lamp table. The whine of the big elevator's motor rose up the shaft. Suddenly it popped into her mind: a killer who played with different identities ... not hard to know Gable's name if he knew hers ... easy as well to approximate a voice through the low-fi speaker of an old intercom system.

The noise in the shaft told her the elevator was nearing her floor. She darted back to the lamp table and grabbed for the knife—so hastily that her hand knocked it to the floor and sent it skittering under the corner of a chair. The elevator stopped. She dropped to her knees, groped under the chair, and felt the knife handle as the elevator's big doors parted horizontally. Her hand closed on the knife and she swung around, coming up, blade extended in front of her like a jungle commando as he emerged—

Seeing her, he lurched backward. "Holy shit, DZ! What the hell—!"

Her hands dropped to her sides as she exhaled with relief. "Well ... the way he plays different roles ..."

Gable relaxed. "Okay, I get it. Not a bad idea to be prepared."

She put the knife aside. Aware suddenly that her tongue felt like she'd been licking sand, she went to the refrigerator. "Want a beer?" she asked.

"No, thanks, I won't be staying."

She took one for herself and turned back to him.

His hand was just coming out of his pocket with a pistol in it, and she freaked again for a second, going rigid.

He saw it. "Jesus, you are wound tight." He turned the gun around, offering it to her by the grip. "I thought you could use this."

She didn't reach to accept his offering. For him, she knew, it was a gift of love, which only made the distance she kept seem crueler.

"Go ahead, take it," he urged. "It's my spare—a Glock semi, twelve-shot clip. I don't want you out on the street buying a shitty piece that jams up in the crunch."

At last she extended her hand. "Thanks, Clark. I'll pay you."

"Just give it back when you don't need it." He looked at her longingly another second.

She thought of giving him a kiss. But a kiss for a gun was a rotten exchange.

"Well, that's all I came for," he said. He started for the elevator.

"Clark—"

He stopped.

"You wouldn't have told Leacock there was something between me and Stoner, would you?"

"No, DZ. But he might've got it from one of the other guys on the squad after you spent that night upstate."

His wounded look brought her full around to knowing she ought to trust him at least as much as she'd already trusted Stoner and Ko. "C'mere, I want to show you something."

She sat him down with the FAA printout, and explained it's possible importance. "I've been following up," she said. "The first two on the list seem clean. I was just going to try another."

"Can I stay and listen?"

DZ was glad he'd asked. If he was willing to help down the line she could wait to bring in Chafee.

She called the fourth company, and a woman answered. She explained that Stellar Airways of Chicago owned several small jets, which were leased on variable terms of anywhere from a day to a year by corporations and individuals. Her records showed that, on the day before the Goshen murder, the plane DZ inquired about had done a hop from Chicago to Fort Wayne, Indiana, and stayed overnight before returning. At the time of the next killings, the plane had flown from Chicago to Pasadena and back the next day. Again, though, the two flights had carried different passengers: in the first case, executives with an advertising firm; in the second, a wealthy individual who owned a horse in a race at Santa Anita. The crews had also been different.

"Sounds legit," DZ said to Gable after the call.

"You've still got one more." He grabbed a look at the list. "Keytron Corp."

"Nobody at the phones."

"It'll keep till morning. This is a long shot, anyway, DZ. It wouldn't hurt, either, if you got a little rest."

She nodded wearily and walked with him to the elevator. "Clark, until I say the word, I don't want anyone downtown—"

"I won't say a thing. I'd love to see you break this alone and shove it up Leacock's ass. But don't go too far out on a limb by yourself, DZ. You can always call me for backup."

"I'll count on it."

When he was gone, she went back to the portable phone, and again tried all the numbers related to the third plane, let each ring ten or twelve times before giving up. Clark was right. It was a long shot, anyway. What she needed right now more than anything was to unwind.

CHAPTER
40

*F*ROM THE MOMENT DZ woke she could practically hear the countdown ticking in her head. Three more people marked for death (his *marks*—the Marx brothers).

She started the morning by calling the research department of a stock brokerage, and asked the analyst who answered if he could supply information about the products and personnel of the Keytron Corporation. He checked Standard & Poor's bluebook and other business references, then told her he didn't see the company listed at all.

"You're telling me it doesn't exist?"

"No, it's just not in my sources. A privately owned company, without publicly traded stock, wouldn't be something we track."

He advised her to contact the authorities in the state where the corporation was chartered. "I believe the state attorney general's office would be able to help."

Keytron's home base was given as Framingham, Massachusetts. An assistant in the office of the Massachusetts attorney general told DZ that the corporation was privately held. "The sole owner of record is a man named Alex Granton," DZ was told.

That explained the corporate jet's tail number, DZ thought. N00AG1.

As for any other information about the company—it's products and revenues—the assistant was loathe to give out more without written requests and authorization.

By now it was mid-morning. When she called the company offices and asked for Mr. Granton, the switchboard put her through to a woman.

"He won't be in today," the woman said when DZ asked for Granton.

"Are you his secretary?"

"Yes. And *your* name . . . ?" the secretary countered frostily.

There might be some mileage, DZ thought in playing the role of mystery woman. "I'm just a friend. I was worried about him, frankly. Can you tell me if he's flying his plane?"

"He is, yes," the secretary answered, sounding more wary.

DZ's pulse began to race. She'd crafted her inquiry on the premise that the M.G. could be a flyer himself—flying his plane, not flying *on* it—giving him total control over his movements, the ability to operate in maximum secrecy. The secretary's reply seemed to confirm the premise

"Could you tell me where he's gone?" DZ asked.

"Look, if you'd like to leave your name," the secretary said stiffly, "I'll tell Mr. Granton when he calls in for his messages." A loyal employee, not ready to disclose her boss's whereabouts to an anonymous woman.

But DZ opted to stay with anonymity. The chances that Mr. Granton was the M.G. were slight—even if he did know how to fly a plane—but *if* he was, let him be the one who was puzzled for a change. She disconnected without another word.

She pondered her next step for a minute. Then she called downtown and fortunately got Gable at his desk. She went straight to business.

"Clark, I need to know the destination of a plane on my list. It could've taken off yesterday or earlier today, probably from Logan Airport in Boston—or maybe Hyannis. FAA requires every plane that size to file a flight plan, so the information will be on record. I'd go after it myself, but you'll get it much quicker through the department." She read off the jet's N number, and told him the make and type was listed as a Gulfstream V.

Gable said he'd go right to work on it. "You sound pretty juiced," he added before hanging up. "Is this the one?"

"No good reason to think so yet. But I have a research project of my own that may improve the picture."

LORI SWANN SLIPPED INTO THE BOOTH OF THE COFFEE SHOP down the street from the GBS tower, where DZ had been nursing a cup of coffee. "What's this about, Lieutenant—calling me down from the office, asking me not to tell a soul? I heard you were taken off the case."

"Yeah, right—for making a public spectacle of myself on your program," DZ admitted. "But that doesn't mean I care any less about catching this killer." She tried for a more relaxed footing. "Can I buy you something?"

"I've had breakfast," Lori said flatly. "Tell me what you want." She was clearly uncertain about being here.

"Your network news division must have computer links to many databases. I'd guess you use them a lot, preparing files on topics and people that Stoner deals with on the show. I'd like you to go to the database and check something for me."

"Check what?"

DZ had kept one hand over a page from her notepad,

prepared before Lori arrived. Now she pushed the slip of paper across the table.

Lori picked it up and looked at the name DZ had written. "Alex Granton?" she said. "Who's he?"

"That's what I hope to learn that from the database."

"Why are you int—" Lori stopped. Instantly her cool executive manner fled. "It's *him,* isn't it? This is the one. You think he's—"

"It isn't very likely, but there's a chance."

Lori laid the paper on the table and regarded it as though it were radioactive. "I don't want to be involved. This creep has already called my producer. If that's him, and if I'm one of the people who *knows*—"

"Hey! Calm down. I'm not asking you to steal atomic secrets. It's research, something you do all the time."

Lori stared at DZ. There was panic in her eyes. "Can you be sure he's not watching me? Jesus, why ask *me* to do this?"

"Because you're my best shot at getting some important information fast without bringing anyone else into it."

Lori studied DZ curiously. "Why wouldn't you?"

"Because the more people who know, the bigger the chance of blowing the case. If we were in position to swoop right down, guaranteed to grab the right person, I wouldn't have to tread so carefully. But this killer has given us almost no evidence, not a thing that guarantees he can be tied to these crimes."

"Fifty million people have *seen* him," Lori protested.

"In disguise. We have no fingerprints, no handwriting samples, no blood or hair that belongs to him, no telltale fibers, no tire tracks or footprints, and only the crudest ballistic evidence. If we don't proceed carefully, he could easily remain free—even if we find the guilty man."

Half true. And half self-serving. The FBI could move as carefully as she would alone. Yet equally true was that too many bloodhounds massing around one hot lead could confuse or even obliterate a trail as often as clarify it. Witness OJ's case. Witness that tiny beauty queen somewhere over the Rockies.

Lori slid out of the booth. "If Research has anything, I should be able to access it quickly. If I'm not back in . . . half an hour, then it means I couldn't find anything."

Or, DZ thought watching her go, it might mean the panic had won.

TWENTY MINUTES LATER LORI RETURNED. IN ONE HAND SHE gripped a manila mailing envelope. She dropped it onto the table without sitting down. "That's everything I could get. Now, remember, Lieutenant, leave me out of it."

Gone again—in twenty seconds.

From the envelope, DZ extracted a thick packet of papers. Even for a cop it could be disconcerting to see how much of a person's life it was now possible to mine from the vast interconnected web of public and private information sources.

Fanning through the pages, DZ registered that the top sheets were the basic documents gathered from such sources as census records, motor vehicle bureaus, hospital files, and city clerks—birth and marriage certificates, college transcripts. Then came lots of reproduced stories from newspapers, small and large, and magazines—the *Times, Washington Post, Wall Street Journal, Newsweek, Fortune, Forbes,* as well as a newspaper from Albuquerque, New Mexico—many going back thirty, forty years. These were followed by articles from scientific and technical journals, transcriptions of interviews conducted by U.S. occupation forces in Germany after the Second World War, and a collection of papers with the heading of the U.S. patent office.

Quite a collection. Especially for a man who had managed to keep his name from becoming a household word.

DZ called over the waitress and ordered a turkey sandwich and another coffee—and, what the hell, an order of fries. Making sense of the life of Mr. Alex Granton looked like it would easily take her all the way through lunch.

CHAPTER
41

KNOWING SHE HAD to steer clear of the squad, Gable met her by a loading dock on a street of warehouses a block from the old Varick Street headquarters. He pulled a piece of paper from inside his jacket and held it out. "Came through just ten minutes ago."

DZ took the fax and scanned it—the copy of a flight plan obtained from a tower supervisor at Hyannis Airport, dated yesterday. She found the line where the plane's destination was given. "That's where it happens next," she said, pointing out the line to Gable.

"Jackson, Mississippi?"

"Within a one- or two-hundred mile radius, anyway. He likes to put some distance between where he flies and where he kills. He'll drive the last stretch."

"We hit a wall when we tried matching up car rentals."

"He doesn't rent," DZ guessed. "He buys a car off a second-hand lot so he doesn't get asked too many questions, and they provide temporary plates. Then he ditches it when he's done."

"After using it once? DZ, cars aren't running shoes."

"No difference to this guy. Four grand for a car? That's

probably a fifth of what it costs each time he rolls out his jet."

Gable eyed her intently. "You're convinced, aren't you?"

She held up the envelope Lori had given her. "I wasn't till I read more about him. Let me put you in the picture," she said, and turned to walk toward the river.

Gable ambled beside her as she summarized the material in the envelope received from Lori Swann.

Alex Meyer Granton was the possessor of a fortune currently estimated at between five and six billion dollars. The greater part had been earned in the past decade by taking large, early positions in the stocks of companies formed around leading-edge technologies. Computers, cellular telephone providers, genetic engineering, and other biomedical developments, Internet affiliates—Granton had the ability to recognize the potential value of all of these at an early point, and buy in on the ground floor. Operating out of a small office along Route 128 outside of Boston—the East Coast hub for techno development akin to California's Silicon Valley—Granton remained unknown to the general public. In the world of high finance, however, he was recognized as a financial wizard who regularly turned stakes of several million dollars into holdings worth fifty times as much.

"He's evidently got an eye for seeing where society is headed," DZ said, "the mechanics of progress, what makes a society tick. His father had talent, too—which is where the first money came from: he was a German-born inventor named Hermann Grundton." She gave it the guttural German pronunciation.

DZ continued with the father's story, gleaned from post-WWII U.S. Occupation Force transcripts. In Berlin in the 1930s, Hermann Grundton had been an electrical engineer involved with researching commercial development of electronic components with the potential to make radio transmission and reception more powerful and efficient.

As Hitler's regime began gearing up for war, Grundton became engaged in government work to refine electronics intended for military use—sonar for underwater submarine tracking, guidance systems for rockets Hitler hoped to use against his enemies, and indeed managed to employ by the end of the war.

Opposed to the Nazis, Grundton attempted to resign from these projects, but was blackmailed into continuing when a young Jewish woman he planned to marry was sent to the Dachau concentration camp with the rest of her family in 1939. Given reassurances it would earn their release, Grundton continued his work. Later, the reassurances were adjusted to the mere promise that, while others perished in the camps, his fiancée would be kept alive.

"After four years of that," DZ said, "Grundton cracked, and refused to continue unless reunited with the girl. At that point he was sent off to Dachau himself; once inside the camp, he learned that the girl had been gassed years before along with her family."

By now she and Gable had crossed the West Side Highway to the promenade running along the Hudson River. From this part of lower Manhattan, they could see the reaching fingers of factory smokestacks on the opposite shore. They fell silent, reminded of the chimneys that had carried away the ghosts of millions of families half a century ago.

DZ and Gable headed downtown. Ahead, a view of the gleaming towers of a new section of the financial district spurred her to the next part of the story.

"Grundton survived Dachau, probably because Hitler's gang thought someday—after they won the war—he might be put back to work. When his record was examined by U.S. deNazification teams, the value of his expertise was instantly recognized. He was allowed to emigrate to the States, and became employed in a government facility in New Mexico developing electronic-based weapons systems. While he was there, he got married."

Some circumstances of the marriage were important in evaluating whether his offspring could have grown up to be an obsessed killer, DZ told Gable, and spelled out details she had drawn from a story printed later in an Albuquerque newspaper.

"When he married in 1949, Grundton was over fifty and his bride was eighteen, a Native American girl from a destitute tribe called the Haulapai. They met while she was working as a waitress in a roadhouse that had a reputation for providing other forms of relaxation besides alcohol. For an immigrant in that part of the country—one who was badly bent by his war experiences—maybe it was the only way to connect. For the girl it was a way to move up. Four years after they married, the Grundtons had a baby—that's Alex."

By then, DZ went on, Hermann Grundton had rebelled once more against weapons work. On his own, he was developing electronic components that could be used to replace the function of the bulky vacuum tubes used in radio reception and in early television sets. He got patents on his inventions, and refined them further.

"The technical data is Greek to me," DZ said. "But I know he secured dozens of patents for elements that were adopted by manufacturers. By the late fifties, with TV moving into every home, Hermann's royalties added up to millions."

"The stake his son ran into billions . . . ?"

DZ nodded.

"So where's the tie to the M.G.?" Gable asked. "He's supposed to hate television. It made this Granton guy rich."

"'Made me what I am today' is how the M.G. put it," DZ reminded Gable. "Let me tell you the rest of the story. Living through the death camps has been known to leave survivors pretty damaged. Mr. Grundton became reclusive and paranoid. He holed up in a big house, that had television sets and cameras all over the place, a surveillance system that monitored the grounds around his house against intruders. Which brings us to some events that made the New Mexico papers in the summer of '62. Despite being closely watched by her husband's surveillance system, his wife took to sneaking out of the house when her husband wasn't around, and going back to the roadhouse where she'd been a working girl. She'd pick up some young stud and do it for free. One afternoon, it went bad. She took a ride into the desert with three cowboys and, according to news reports, they raped her for two hours, a session that only ended when she got hold of a gun belonging to one of them and took a wild shot. Nobody was hit, but the men retaliated by beating the girl so badly she died on the spot. The men buried her there to cover it, but somebody who'd seen them pick her up at the roadhouse gave their names to the police. At the trial the men pled self-defense." DZ paused, wrestling with her own fury. "They were acquitted."

"Shit," Gable interjected. "How—?"

"Since she'd been a prostitute years earlier—the rape wasn't even an issue. And she was just an Indian, no matter how much money her husband had. Remember, this is back in the sixties. Grundton made an effort to forget; he moved with his son to a house in Albuquerque. Then one Sunday night he barricaded himself in the house and started taking potshots at anyone passing by. Nobody was hurt, he just wanted to scare people away—as if he thought the SS were breaking in again. But before the police could get into the house, he put the gun to his head and killed himself."

DZ recounted a few more details from the old newspaper stories. When the police entered the house after Grundton's suicide, they found seven-year-old Alex unharmed, transfixed in front of a television set though it was past midnight. It appeared he'd sat there through the whole siege, hadn't even looked at this father's body. The boy told the police that all his life his mother and father had left him in front of the screen for hours at a time while they

went out of the house. "Oh yes," DZ added, "one more little detail. It was a Sunday night when this happened. Sunday—you remember what would have been on that night
in 1962 about the time Daddy went berserk?"

Gable didn't even have to think about it. "*What's My
Line?*"

"That's almost all of it," DZ concluded. "Not a lot is
known about how Alex was raised thereafter. He's always
refused to do interviews. *The Wall Street Journal* did a
sketch four years ago that used the stuff about his father's
inventions, though all they said about the father's death
was that he'd been a suicide. Some new info they threw in,
however, was that after Alex was orphaned, his guardian
was an uncle, a brother of his mother's who looked after
young Alex until he took control of money his father had
left in trust and went off to college in the East. While Alex
was in college, the uncle was sent to prison, where he was
murdered by a fellow inmate."

DZ stopped walking, and leaned back against the promenade railing to look at Gable. "That's all of it."

"So the father went nuts," he said after a moment. "You
think that's a fair basis for accusing this guy?"

"C'mon, Clark, that's not the half of it! Just take the fact
that he picked Stoner to deal with. He said Stoner should
relate to him because he'd protected a murderer in the past.
But what might bind them even closer is that Stoner's father also committed suicide."

"That wasn't generally known. . . ."

"The M.G. found out even bigger secrets that Stoner had
buried. Assuming he's someone with a ton of money, he
could pay an army of private investigators to dig into
Stoner's past. Whatever I found out with my detective
work, others could."

Gable nodded. "Okay. What else?"

"Choice of victims. We've speculated they each represent a type he has his own reasons to hate. Granton's father

was warped by the Nazis, which led to the events that destroyed his own childhood."

"That accounts for the guy killed in San Diego. What about Indiana, the pervert—"

"I can only guess," DZ admitted. "But maybe the uncle he went to live with molested him; that would explain why the uncle went to prison later, and was killed there; child molesters often get taken out by other inmates. Whatever happened to Granton, he was without the protection of any parents from a young age. He'd identify with other defenseless kids, perhaps feel rage toward anyone who preyed on them. It's not uncommon, either, for serial murderers to come from mothers who've been promiscuous, usually prostitutes."

"And the hatred of television?" Gable tossed up for analysis.

"He was stuck in front of it instead of having the real affection of a mother or father. He could easily think of it more as the source of all that he lost rather than gained."

Gable mulled it for a minute. "Jesus, DZ, talk about circumstantial! The stuff fits, but as far as getting us anywhere close to nailing the guy, it's worth shit."

"It gives us a suspect, though, someone to watch."

Gable straightened suddenly. "Then we should be on him right now. Let's get on the horn to Chafee, put out an APB to police in Mississippi, get that plane under surveillance. . . ."

"Think about it, Clark," DZ said, not a hint of racing to get started. "This guy's a *billion*aire—and you said yourself there's no reasonable cause. I go back and forth myself, thinking I'm talking myself into it because I want so badly to break it. Do we dare put out an advisory to arrest on sight, put hundreds of people on alert?"

"If it kept three more people from getting killed . . ." Gable said.

DZ looked across the river again. "I doubt that's doable, anyway. Granton's plane flew off yesterday. If I have the right man, his next three victims were already dead last night."

"You want to bet on that with their lives? How you gonna feel if they die tomorrow?" DZ kept looking across the river, thinking about it. Gable pulled her around to face him. "Is keeping the bust for yourself all you really care about?"

"No! But I don't want to lose this guy because we jump the gun. Once he knows we're onto him, we better be able to prove our case, or he'll never pay for any of it."

Gable shook his head. "We *can't* do nothing!" He turned back toward HQ and started walking.

She ran around to block him. "I'll stay on him."

He bulled past her and walked faster as if to escape her. "You think you can tackle this alone? All right, you've had a rough deal, but is getting the glory all that counts?"

"Wait, damn it!" She scurried alongside. "It's not about me. I'm just so sure that if we come down on him now, it'll win us nothing. Clark, there's not a shred of evidence."

"If you're right, we can prove he was near the murders—"

"Within a couple of hundred miles, within twenty-four hours. Not worth much. No weapon, no witness, no fingerprints or DNA ties. He'd never be prosecuted, you know it. If he still feels safe, there's a shot at catching him with his guard down, at my getting close enough alone to find—"

"Alone? Alone you're not going to stop him, DZ. Bring in the troops, if nothing else we'll end his goddamn game, stop him from killing anyone else."

"Until you have to *stop* watching him," she said. "For how long would they keep surveillance on Granton? With this guy, Clark, bear one thing in mind even if you forget everything else: the interest his money earns in a year, just the *interest,* is more than the *whole budget* of a department like ours. Maybe even more than the Bureau's. If he can outspend us, don't you think he can outlast us?"

Gable stopped. They were near the corner onto Varick Street. "And what that adds up to, probably, is that your hunch is plain nuts. Guys who've got the world on a string don't have to pull a trigger to feel good. They may kill for love, or revenge, or . . . or just because they go berserk. But not just to feel good. Which is one more reason I might as well throw it to Chafee and let him decide what to do with it." He plowed past her.

By the time she followed him around the corner, he was already entering the building.

She made it into the elevator with him, but rode up silently, still trying to think of other arguments that might hold him back. Maybe he was right, though. She was letting her hunger for redemption interfere with plain, good judgment. If Granton was a reasonable suspect, the sensible procedure was to interview him and place him under surveillance.

Except that he was *swimming* in an ocean of money. Which was going to make him hard to watch and too slippery to hold.

As soon as they stepped out of the elevator, DZ knew something big had happened. She could see it in faces that swung around to greet her and Gable.

"It went down!" Ray Culver called to them. "Three this time, all at once."

"Where and when?" DZ shouted back.

"Some little dinkhole town in Mississippi, of all places. Last night sometime. Found the bodies an hour ago."

Gable shot a look at her, then strode to his desk, pushed some paper around until he found a phone number he'd scribbled earlier, and dialed it.

DZ thought she knew where he was calling, knew it was useless, but she stood silently while he talked briefly on the phone, then hung up. He looked as if he was about to speak to her across the open expanse of the squad room, but he hesitated, walked over, and pulled her aside. Softly he said, "His plane left Jackson airport this morning a little after five A.M."

She waited. She'd made the case for the way to play it; it had only gotten stronger now.

"I'll sit on it," he said after a minute, "for now."

"Thanks." She started to go.

"You're sure?" he said quickly. "Alone . . . ?"

"It's just the best way," she said, moving toward the elevator. "I'm no hero."

CHAPTER
42

IT HAD HAPPENED at the Tall Pines Motel outside Waggs-ville, Mississippi, seventy miles from the state capital. Three men, lined up front to back facing the television set in a seedy motel room, killed by a single shot that blasted through their skulls as if they were no more than three co-conuts in a row.

Police were told by wives of two of the victims that their husbands had gone to the motel to meet a man named Wyatt Smylin. Claiming to be a producer for the television magazine program, *Top Story,* Smylin had called with an offer of ten thousand dollars to each of the three men in re-turn for telling whatever they knew about activities of a small, white-supremacist group in their corner of the state, The Brotherhood of Aryan Purity.

The three dead men, Lester Dillman, his younger brother Orville, and their uncle Randy Quort, had been re-leased just thirty-nine days earlier from the state prison, where they had served fifteen months for aggravated as-sault. The charge stemmed from the use of a baseball bat, passed among the three men, to bludgeon to death a nineteen-year-old named Clinton Parkhurst on the athletic field of the Waggsville high school. The defendants claimed that following a baseball game played between the local high school team and one from a neighboring town on which Parkhurst was a star outfielder, they and two young women in their company had encountered the young man and he had made lewd remarks to the women; when they sought an apology, he had attacked them with the bat, which they had wrested away to defend themselves.

At the trial, the only witness willing to testify for the prosecution was another player on Parkhurst's team. Questioned about the motive for the violence, he stated it was obvious: like himself, Parkhurst was black, and he had hit the two home runs that kept the all-white team of opponents from advancing to the state finals. Parkhurst had made no lewd remarks to anyone, had threatened no one with a bat.

Unfortunately, the prosecution's case was damaged by a mix-up of several baseball bats in the police property room, so that the one used as a murder weapon could not be entered into evidence. Another setback was the judge's ruling that membership of the three defendants in a shadowy, white-supremacist cult was inadmissible as hearsay.

The same judge passed the sentence of three years, with parole after fifteen months. The three men had served not a day more than the minimum.

Police and FBI agents called to the Tall Pines Motel noted some differences in the modus operandi between these murders and those previously attributed to the Mystery Guest. No calling card was left propped on the TV; instead, a number 15 was written with a white substance—determined to be typewriter correction fluid—on a mirror. Also, the discovery of the bodies was not left to happenstance. Police in Waggsville and the FBI field office in Jackson had both received telephone calls from a man who said he was "the baseball player you've seen on TV" and that he had just made "a triple play" at the Tall Pines Motel.

The number to which the calls were later traced was a telephone in the house of Matthew Bellaver—the presiding judge of the county court who had levied the sentence of fifteen months on the three victims for their crime.

THE PATTERN WAS CLEAR TO DZ NOW: BEFORE HE TOOK another life—or would it be *four* next time?—he'd want to be on the show, drop a hint about the next victims, keep the game going. She had time.

She read again through all the material on Granton and made notes to herself. There was nothing absolutely conclusive, yet it all fit perfectly: Granton flew his own plane, which had been within a hundred miles of each of the murder scenes within twenty-four hours of the crime. He had the money and know-how to support a scheme requiring elaborate equipment. His biography indicated motive to strike against the particular victims chosen—a child abuser, a Nazi war criminal, a group of murdering bigots.

Reviewing the details made DZ even more sharply aware of how cool and intelligent this killer was—and how warped. All the while he took lives, he remained playful. Even the name he had used when luring his latest victims to the motel—Wyatt Smylin—was simply a twist on the name of the old game show which had played a part in all his television appearances.

But if Alex Granton was the Mystery Guest, confirming his guilt remained a problem. It was strangely true with a number of other serial killers—most famously Ted Bundy—that even after law enforcement had exposed their suspicions through surveillance, even arrest, they had been unsuccessful in making charges stick, or stopping the killings. These murderers were a special breed, so separated from feelings of guilt that they operated in a bubble where the usual rules of detection and intervention didn't apply.

Into the evening, DZ continued to pore over her notes, looking for new insights. Finally, she felt that to expose the guilt of Alex Granton there was nothing but to act as any cop would—interview him and see how he stood up to it. And her best shot at getting a glimpse behind the mask was to dare him to show it when he was least at risk—to go up against him one-on-one. No witnesses. No protection.

Would he turn on her? The profile of this killer was a man fearless of detection, always the one to call the tune and force reaction from others. DZ didn't think he'd feel threatened, or have accomplices who'd act against her. He worked alone; she believed it now as she had from the start.

It was past nine o'clock when she halted her concentrated study. She threw together a salad—lettuce that had been wilting in her refrigerator from the last time she'd done some real food shopping two weeks ago. Sitting at her kitchen counter, she nibbled at the greens and thought how nice it would be to have someone for whom to buy fresh food and make good meals. She grabbed up the phone to call Charlie. They'd been missing each other the past couple of days, speaking to answering machines, but this time she got him at the newspaper.

"I was praying it'd be you," he said.

"Praying? That's serious stuff."

"You blame me for worrying if I can't reach you?"

"You're not so easy to find yourself."

"I told you I'd be away," he said, a bit defensive.

She smiled. "Hey, is this our first quarrel?"

He laughed. "If it is, I wish we could kiss and make up."

She wanted to be there, too, but she was silent. The impulse when she'd called was to tell him about the threshold on which she stood, ask his blessing so she could come to him soon if all went well. But now she realized that telling him would only crank up his anxiety. He wouldn't understand the chances she had to take; he'd only want to reason her out of it.

"How's everything going?" he tossed into the silence. Perhaps he sensed she was holding something back.

If she shared nothing, then her belief in him was meaningless. "I've been suspended from duty."

"Sonofagun! Why?"

"My boss didn't like the way I came across on TV."

"When—what do you mean?"

It turned out he didn't even know about her appearance on *Stoner*. He'd been running around the offices of the Iowa State government, he explained, researching *his* big story on a cut in subsidies for county roadwork around Dalton Falls. Preoccupied with the concerns of his small town weekly, he hadn't picked up any larger daily papers, either, had missed all reports having anything to do with the Mystery Guest.

"Well . . . it must feel bad to be thrown off the case," he said after hearing about her televised exchange with the killer, and the latest killings. "Awful, too, that you were put in that position—made to feel responsible for what happened to those three men. But of course you aren't, DZ. That crazy killer is the only one responsible."

"I wish I could believe that, Charlie. But I think we're all to blame. It's like . . . human cannonballs, or guys who dive from eighty-foot-towers into a wet sponge. Nobody would take those chances if there wasn't a crowd to applaud."

"That's pretty cynical, sweetheart. I haven't heard any applause."

"You haven't been listening, Charlie—any more than you've been watching." In the pause she heard the echo of her accusing tone. "Sorry, I shouldn't blame you for ignoring this. There's nothing wrong with keeping the ugliness out of your life. It's what I long to do myself as soon as this is over."

"It can be over now, DZ. You're off the case, so come to me. Let's *begin*!"

She squeezed the phone tightly, wishing the passion would travel to him somehow. Knowing it couldn't, she had to release what she felt, even if it went against all the rules she'd lived by—in a profession where you moved carefully until you had collected the evidence. "Mister Foster," she said, "I love you, and I can't wait to be with you."

"Praise the Lord."

"But after I've done my duty."

"But you just told me you're off the—"

"Duty to myself, Charlie. That's the way it's got to be. Please understand. Good night, my love. I'll call again soon." She hung up before he could put in another bid.

If he was right for her, she thought, he'd leave it there instead of calling back to press her. He would—as she'd begged him—understand. To have a future, it had to start when this part of the past was over and done with. Complete.

She stayed by the phone until she'd finished a beer. It didn't ring again.

CHAPTER
43

SHE GOT AN early start, picking up the six-year-old Nissan ZX she'd bought used from another detective and kept in an open lot by the Hudson. The June day was clear and sunny, good driving weather, and by mid-morning she was crossing the Bourne Bridge to the lower end of Cape Cod.

Before leaving New York, she'd phoned the tower at Hyannis Airport, the listed home base for Granton's plane, and ascertained it was there in its hangar since returning from a flight yesterday morning. Three hours into her trip, she had stopped on the New England Thruway to fill with gas and make a phone call to Keytron, Inc., where the secretary said that Mr. Granton was not expected in all day.

From the profile of the billionaire she'd found in *Forbes* magazine, DZ had learned that while Granton had apartments in New York and London, a house in Aspen, and a recently purchased ten-thousand-acre ranch in the Patagonian region of Argentina, his principal home was an oceanside compound in the mid-Cape town of Chatham. Since his plane was at its base, and he wasn't at work, DZ proceeded on the assumption she'd find him there.

Nearing Hyannis, signs on the main road indicated a turnoff for the airport. On the spur of the moment, she decided to have a look at the plane.

The airport was the only one on the Cape large enough to handle jet traffic, upgraded back in the days when John F. Kennedy's home in Hyannis had served as a summer White House. DZ left her car in a short-term lot, and went to a ticket desk in the terminal to ask where private aircraft hangars could be found. She was advised to check at the terminal manager's office. But DZ didn't want to go through channels and have to identify herself. It occurred to her that the plain, dark blue suit and white blouse she'd worn today looked conveniently enough like the uniform of a stewardess that she might move freely as long as she seemed to know where she was going. Continuing through the terminal, she peered through doors until she saw a corridor leading to the open field through a baggage-loading bay.

On the field, she hailed a man passing in a small tractor-like vehicle and asked where private aircraft were parked. He squinted at her. "I know you from somewhere," he said.

"I fly in and out of here all the time."

It diverted him from making the connection, and he waved toward a far end of the field. "Most of 'em are down that way."

With the summer season near, more than two dozen private jets were parked there, a few the size of commercial aircraft. In a hangar facing the line of parked planes, DZ saw a couple of men in overalls doing maintenance on a small jet. She walked into the hangar. "Either of you guys know which of those planes belongs to a man named Granton?"

One man pulled a cloth from his back pocket and wiped oil off his hands. "That's it right there." He shot his eyes to one end of the line.

Turning, she took in the details. It was the largest of the jets, and with a distinctively decorated fuselage, gleaming sky blue over all with a long silver stripe that ran along the side, then climbed the tail where the line curled into the outline of a giant, old-fashioned key. It looked like a lot of plane for one man to handle alone.

The mechanic kept his eyes on her. "You gonna be flying on it? We haven't gotten word to get it ready."

"No. I mean . . . not today." She groped for a story that might get her aboard. "I heard he might be hiring a cabin crew, and I thought it could be a nice gig. Think I could get onto it? Y'know, for a look around, to get an idea of the setup. . . ."

"If you find someone to give you a boarding ramp. There's stairs built in, but you need a remote to make 'em come down."

Maybe she could arrange it later. "What's the range on those?"

"Like to know what kinda trips you'll be going on?" The mechanic chuckled, and she gave him a conspiratorial nod. "Bring your bikini, sweetheart. Could be all the way to Hawaii from here. That's a Gulfstream V—it'll do sixty-five hundred miles without a refuel."

More than enough to cover the distances from here to any of the M.G.'s crimes, and back without refueling. "You know anyone who's flown with Granton? I'd like to be sure I'm in safe hands."

The mechanic scowled. Was he growing suspicious? "I can tell you myself he's a crackerjack, as good as any pilot going."

"I'd still like to meet his copilot."

The mechanic gave a little shrug, an indication that there was no way he could help fulfill this desire.

"He'd need one to operate the plane, wouldn't he?"

"To meet FAA regs, yeah. Plane that size isn't supposed to take off with one man."

"But technically, could he handle it alone?"

The mechanic gave her a long, cool look; he had clearly decided there could be something besides a job behind her questions. Yet professional pride impelled him to display his knowledge. Turning to admire the plane he said, "Honey, that's more than forty million bucks worth of flying machine out there. It's got an FMS on the flight deck that'll leave even one pilot twiddling his thumbs once you feed in the right data."

"FMS," she echoed questioningly.

"Flight management system. Totally computerized. Thing can fly itself, no exaggeration." The mechanic didn't wait for another question. His expression had cooled a few more degrees. "Sorry, miss, I ought to be getting back to work. That's about as much as I can tell you."

She gave the mechanic a nice thank-you, and walked out onto the field. She wondered briefly if it would be possible to enlist some airport worker in actually getting her onto the plane, then abandoned the idea. Any evidence aboard would have its value in court fatally compromised by an illegal search. On top of which she ought to leave room for the possibility she was wildly off-base. Looking at the plane, an ultimate toy for a rich man, she began to doubt her reasoning all over again. Would a man like Alex Granton jeopardize a life filled with pleasure and privilege to satisfy a bestial craving for blood?

THE TOWN OF CHATHAM SAT AT THE BENT ELBOW OF THE Cape, which jutted out from the Massachusetts coast like the flexed arm of a muscle builder showing off his biceps. In spring a fog formed by the collision of chill air coming in off the Atlantic with warmer air over the land often hovered over the town. In July and August the sun would quickly burn off the morning fog, but today it lingered. The blanket of fog intensified DZ's uneasy feeling of picking her way blindly into perilous territory.

While she knew Granton owned a large beach property, she had no exact address or location. In town, she pulled into a gas station and asked directions to the Granton property.

"Sorry, ma'am," said the young pump jockey. "Can't help there."

But she wondered if he knew, and wasn't willing to share the information. Granton might be a customer who tipped well all over town to preserve his privacy.

DZ tried next at the post office, a small brick building on the town's Main Street, where a spindly, gray-haired woman was the lone clerk. DZ waited until the woman served a couple of people already in line, then stepped up and identified herself as a police detective. "I need to know how to find the home of Alex Granton," she told the clerk.

The woman narrowed her eyes. "Let's see your credentials."

Even if her badge hadn't been lifted, DZ knew it would be a violation to use official ID while she was on suspension. "I . . . don't have anything with me," she answered lamely.

The clerk tucked her chin in smugly. "Hah! Reporter are ya? We get lots like you snooping for stuff on Mr. Granton."

DZ shook her head. "I *am* a police detective."

"And I'm a federal employee who can't go round giving out personal information to any Jack or Jill. No proof gets you no help."

Proof. The importance of that was something DZ could appreciate. She went back onto the Main Street of Chatham, looked up and down the row of storefronts. Then, almost directly across the street, she saw the solution to her problem. She crossed over and entered the florist shop. A girl with a long, blond ponytail was there alone.

"Could you do a nice arrangement to deliver in the next hour?" DZ asked her.

"Probably. Our delivery man is out at the moment, but he'll be back soon."

The girl asked how much DZ wanted to spend, and DZ said the arrangement was for someone special. Would fifty dollars be enough for something nice?

The girl said it would be fine, and listed a variety of flowers she could include.

"To whom will it be going?" she asked after DZ had paid.

"Mr. Alex Granton. Do you know where he lives?"

The look in the girl's eyes turned cautious as she nodded. No question that over the years hordes of unwanted people had tried prying into Alex Granton's life.

"Good," DZ said. "Just deliver it as soon as you can."

The girl's expression relaxed again when DZ didn't ask for an address. "We'll do our best." DZ started to leave, but the girl called out. "Wait!" DZ spun around. "Didn't you want to include a card?"

"Oh yes, of course. . . ."

Once she thought of something to write, the card struck DZ as the perfect touch.

SHE SAT IN HER CAR FOR A MORE THAN AN HOUR BEFORE THE shop's delivery man carried a large cellophane-covered basket of flowers from the shop to the delivery van and drove away. She tailed at a distance as it left the town, following a road that wound along a stretch of oceanfront, then veered inland to travel past stands of pine stunted by wind and sandy soil, and intermittent growths of wild beach plum and sea grape. After several miles, the van pulled up at the roadside and the driver got out. As DZ continued driving past, she saw him speaking into an intercom set into a brick pillar beside a pair of high, metal gates, their aspect softened by the fact that they were also impressive artwork, sculptural friezes of human figures covering a surface of burnished bronze. Tastefully set back into the trees, heavy chain-link fencing extended away on either side of the gate. She drove on past a curve, then pulled over.

For fifteen minutes she sat listening to classical music on the radio, then she drove back slowly to where the van had stopped. The radio music ended, and an announcer came on to say it was time for the midday news. A news reader began, *"Police in a small Mississippi town are still trying to—"*

She switched off the radio, and glanced at the closed gates. Was he in there? What she had written on the card might frighten him . . . or intrigue him—or mean absolutely nothing at all if he were innocent.

She left the car, went to the intercom, and pressed the button. A man's voice answered simply: "Residence."

"I'd like to see Mr. Granton."

"Your name?"

She held it back. "I just sent him some flowers. I thought he might like to thank me in person."

"Wait there, please."

A few minutes went by. DZ scanned the concealed fencework, guessing a sophisticated security setup would include video cameras. He might be watching her.

A voice broke into her thoughts: "Mr. Granton will see you."

Slowly the solid metal gates swung open. She got back into the car and drove through. A white gravel drive wound for a few hundred yards through a field of tall dune grass that screened what lay beyond, then opened abruptly onto a vista of lush lawn surrounding a spectacular, modern house set by a curved strand of beach forming an idyllic private bay. Off to one side of the house was a tennis court, beyond that a building DZ assumed must be stables since a couple of horses were grazing in a fenced pasture beyond. To the other side of the house she saw the flags of at least three golf holes fluttering at the end of lush, mown fairways. Out on the water, tethered to moorings, were a sailing yacht and a sleek Cigarette boat, chrome pipes shooting across the afterdeck from its supercharged engines.

DZ stopped the car in a circular parking area fronting the house. Standing around at careless angles were a black Mercedes convertible, a dusty, battered pickup truck, and a Humvee, the battlefield vehicle that in its expensive civilian form was the jeep of celebrities. She got out of her car and stood gawking at the house, an amazing stack of levels cantilevered to form glassed-in corners and terraces that hovered in midair. The man who lived in such a house seemed to like balancing acts.

Looking across the rest of the property, she noticed people engaged in various tasks. On the green of a golf hole four hundred yards away, a man dipped his hand into a bag then flung it outwards, scattering seed; another man was by the stables, stacking bales of hay; a third hacked at shrubbery on a far edge of the pasture. None close at hand, yet the men made her feel more secure. Alex Granton might be evil, but DZ strongly doubted his secret was shared with anyone who worked for him, and he'd be loathe to expose it by acting against her where it might be witnessed.

She started for the house, then realized she'd left her bag on the car seat—Gable's gun inside. She went back to get it.

As she searched for a button to press by the entrance— large double doors of teak marked by Chinese symbols— one door was opened by an attractive young man with dark, reddish skin and shiny black shoulder-length hair. He wore jeans and a white shirt with colorful beadwork at the collar.

"Come in, please," he said.

She stepped over the threshold. "Mr. Granton?"

The young man gave her an amused smile. "No, I'm his assistant." He put out his hand and she shook it. "Ted Standingbear," he introduced himself.

"Unusual name."

"Not where I come from," he replied a bit stiffly.

A Native American. DZ remembered that Granton's mother had also been Native American, and had suffered a common fate of young women in oppressed minorities, drifting into prostitution. Giving this young man a good job bespoke a sense of a wealthy man's social obligation. Strange it hadn't been in her consciousness until now, but a corner of her own background was marked by the same bloodlines from her father's side. She almost never thought about that part of her heritage; she identified with her mother, with the milieu that had formed her after being deserted by her father. Staring into the face of the young man in the doorway, she wondered if there was the smallest chance that Alex Granton could have known her own past as well as Stoner's . . . could have somehow contrived—

Standingbear broke into her reverie. "Follow me, please."

Within the house, broad open spaces gathered in light from everywhere—an atrium above a curving ramp that took the place of a staircase, wide portals that looked into rooms and terraces facing the sunlit ocean. The light gleamed off polished marble floors, and bounced from large marble and metal sculptures. DZ recognized the art as top of the line, a Henry Moore, a Brancusi. There were other hints of rare and expensive tastes. Passing a room with black laquered walls, she saw the lush gold-and-black striped fur of a tiger hide spread across a black marble floor. She paused to stare at the hide, not only because it was beautiful, but because it stirred some buried nugget of relevance to the case. But she couldn't bring it into focus before the assistant urged her forward.

"This way," he said, guiding her out to a broad terrace facing the ocean. "If you'll wait here . . ." He disappeared through an opening in a balustrade, where a flight of stairs descended.

Moving to the balustrade, DZ looked down on an enormous patio with a swimming pool. Exotic plantings edged part of the large pool, and at one end water from multi-level tiers cascaded down in a silvery fall. She watched the assistant cross the patio and disappear under a striped umbrella amid a grouping of patio furniture. Visible on a glass-topped table was a ceramic vase holding the flower arrangement she'd had delivered. Standingbear reappeared from under the umbrella and walked into the house. A moment later another man stepped out into the sun.

Monday's child is fair of face. The lines came back as DZ looked at him.

He stood in a bathing suit, his profile to her, and she saw at once he was strikingly handsome, eyes so blue they shone like gems even at a distance, blond hair graying into a filigree of silver and gold. His tall, lean figure displayed the sculpted muscles of a man who worked at maintaining himself. He laughed suddenly, then said a few words DZ heard only indistinctly, speaking to someone still under the umbrella. Whoever it was tossed a robe to Granton, and he slipped into it, a short Japanese-style jacket of royal blue silk. As he tied the sash around his waist, DZ realized she had to be mistaken. This man—not merely handsome, she thought, but beautiful in a way, graceful in his movements, the way he held himself as he spoke—it was inconceivable he could indulge in the kind of savagery the Mystery Guest evidently craved. Would he stake this life against a search for such perverted thrills? Only an error could have brought her here. A wrong digit in the airplane registration number, a leap to the wrong conclusion—or the same one-in-a-million coincidence that sometimes put the wrong man behind bars for a crime he didn't commit.

That much was clear even before DZ saw the woman. She emerged now from under the umbrella, looping one of her slender arms around his neck and pressing her long body against his. Then she kissed him quickly on the lips, the kind of last-minute attention and playful little farewell passionate lovers might share even if a parting was only to

last minutes. She was lovely, with chestnut hair cut in a
fashionable, boyish bob, and a spectacular body clad only
in the most minimal bikini. DZ thought she recognized her
as a model often seen on the covers of fashion magazines.

Granton and the woman parted from their embrace, she
vanished again under the umbrella, and he headed across
the patio. Halfway to the balcony steps, he cast the star-
tling blue eyes upward, his gaze abruptly targeting DZ as
though he had known all along she was watching, even exactly where she was standing. He kept his eyes on her as
he reached the steps and mounted them.

Reaching her, he extended a hand in greeting. "Detective Hayes . . ."

DZ stepped back without accepting his handshake. "You
know who I am. . . ." What did that indicate? She hadn't
written her name on the card with the flowers, had purposely not identified herself to the assistant when he introduced himself.

Granton dropped his hand without apparent offense. "It
would be hard not to. Your picture's been all over the
news, especially the last couple of days."

The voice had a pleasant timbre. She compared it with
her memory as he went on. "And of course there was
this. . . ." From a pocket of the robe, he took the card she'd
sent with the flowers and held it up. She glanced at the
"message" she'd written:

20 ?

"Enough to get me through the door," she said point-
edly.

He put out his hand to take the card back, but DZ hesitated. Would it ever constitute evidence? She yielded it
rather than disrupt the flow of their exchange.

"I was intrigued," he said. "I called the florist right away
to ask who'd ordered the flowers. They told me it was a
woman, described you. When you came to the gate and I

saw you on my surveillance cameras, the card began to make sense."

"Did it? What kind of sense?"

"I've read about your case in the news, the numbers left at the killings so far—five, ten, fifteen. Seems obvious twenty would be the next in sequence. . . ."

They still hadn't moved from the top step, and he continued looking at her steadily while she searched for any sign of nerves, any shadow of guile in his eyes. She saw none. "It doesn't seem strange to you," she said finally, "I jotted that down instead of something else?"

His eyes narrowed briefly, then his face relaxed again into a smile. An instant later, his gaze shifted to look over her shoulder, which made her turn. The assistant had come onto the terrace. He stood by a door in expectant silence, as though he'd been summoned, but DZ hadn't noticed Granton give any signal.

"Can I offer you a drink?" Granton asked DZ.

Something drugged? "No, thanks."

"I'll have a lemonade, Ted," Granton told the assistant. "Bring a pitcher and a couple of glasses. My guest may change her mind." Standingbear left. "Now, where were we . . . ?" Granton said. He went to a table on the terrace and sat down.

"I was wondering why you let me in here?"

"I told you: I was intrigued." He crossed his legs, very relaxed.

"But you understood why I came. . . ."

"Did I say that?"

". . . the card . . . what I wrote. . ."

He stared at her for a long silent moment. She became aware of the sound of surf breaking on his private beach, a sound like whispers in the background. "It would seem," he said at last, "that you think I can tell you something about the case you're working on."

She walked to the table. "Can you?"

He squinted up at her. "The sun's in my eyes," he said, pointing to the chair opposite. "Won't you sit down?"

His air of cool self-containment was completely consistent with the profile of the Mystery Guest that had been assembled from all his actions so far: an iceman, a game player, generally polite and cheerful. Yet would a very powerful and wealthy man, sure of his own innocence, react any differently?

DZ took the chair. She slipped off her shoulder bag and set it on the ground close beside her.

"Thank you," he said. "Now I can see you clearly."

"Well," she said.

"Well what?"

"Can you tell me something about this case?"

He shook his head slightly, not a refusal, but a sign of bemusement. Then he shot a glance past her: Standingbear had returned. He brought a tray to the table bearing the lemonade in a crystal pitcher, two glasses, and a small silver ice bucket and tongs. Also, clipped into a little silver stand—a fancy device for delivering mail or holding a place card—was a white envelope.

"If you'll be busy here awhile, Mr. Granton, I thought you might want to review that first."

Granton unfolded a letter-size piece of paper from the envelope, scanned it, and put it away in the pocket of his robe.

"Thanks, Ted," Granton said. "We won't want to be disturbed for a while. If Jensen calls for my okay on the Forstmann deal, say I'll get back to him at the end of the day."

The assistant nodded and left, closing the two sliding glass doors.

Granton lifted the pitcher, "Change your mind?"

"All right."

He dropped ice cubes in the glasses, poured the lemonade, then picked up his own and downed half of it. "Refreshing," he declared. "Now . . . let's see, I think you wanted to know if I'm the man you're looking for—that very cunning fellow who goes on television to talk about killing people?"

"And then kills them." She eyed him squarely. "Yes. That's what I want to know. If you are . . ."

He gave her another of his equally steady looks, then leaned into the table, very close, exaggerating the sense of sharing a confidence. "And tell me, Lieutenant Hayes, what if . . ." He came to a full stop, and gave her a slow smile.

". . . what if . . . ?" she prompted, puzzled.

The attenuated sound of a wave curling and breaking along the crescent of beach below almost drowned out the voice he had lowered to a purr.

But not quite. Two words came through to complete his hypothetical phrase:

". . . I am."

It didn't seem to be inflected as a question. Or was that only, she wondered, because he had been interrupted by the waves?

CHAPTER
44

DZ STARED AT his perfectly handsome face as he sat back again and lifted his glass to take another sip of lemonade. The words played again in her mind as she tried to process them: *What if I am?* Neither admission . . . nor denial. More a riddle, in fact. Which by itself fit the profile of the killer who made everything into a game, a puzzle.

As he sat smiling at her—a smile that in any other circumstances she might have described as beguiling—she had yet another failure of belief in her senses. A new wave breaking on the beach whispered through the silence between them, and she wondered if the previous confusion of sounds hadn't distorted what she'd heard.

"What did you just say . . . ?"

"I'm sure you heard me," he said calmly.

"I *think* I heard you." He raised his eyebrows, miming inquiry, inviting her to repeat it. "You said, 'What if I am?' "

"Why do you find that strange? The question, I mean."

She couldn't stop staring. His hair had been wet when she first arrived, darkening it—he must have been swimming right before she came—but the sun had dried it, making it lighter, making everything about him seem more golden. She could see golden rings around the irises of his blue eyes. The German heritage dominant in the coloring, but in the chiseled features, the cheekbones—and the look behind the eyes—there was also the stamp of the original Americans who hunted to survive.

Still, what she saw refused to mesh with what she thought. "It suggests," she said, "that it's at least possible you're . . . a murderer."

"At least possible," he echoed mildly. "But there's no one alive who isn't capable of murder—if pushed far enough."

"Not everyone could kill six people in cold blood," she said.

"No," he said. "Not everyone."

There was a pause in which DZ tried to center her thoughts again. What was happening here? He seemed to be taunting her with the prospect that she had come to the right place, and all she could do was sit and *debate* it. Almost as if once again it was nothing more than a goddamned talk show!

But just as she had played along before in hopes he might accidentally reveal himself, she did so now. *What if I am?* She went back to the question, to deal with it. "Well, Mr. Granton, if you are the murderer I'm looking for, then I'm going to make sure you pay for your crimes."

"And how would you do that, Detective Hayes?" he asked calmly.

"By never giving up. Working until I have the proof."

"Noble. But from what I've read about your killer, he's very careful not to leave evidence."

The very way he was permitting the conversation to continue without any denials, teasing her, conformed not only to the M.G.'s habit, but fit with DeJesus's analysis that the killer wanted to be caught, would keep skirting the edges of safety until he went too far. It struck DZ suddenly that she might be able to jog him into believing he had already overplayed his hand. "I wonder," she said, "if other law officers heard this conversation, what they'd think of it. I mean here I am, suggesting you could be America's most wanted man, and your only response is to act as if it makes no difference. That could strike people as odd."

"Then I suppose it's lucky no one else will hear it."

She tensed at the reply—with its implication that he might prevent her, the first hint of threat. But she kept pushing. It meant she was getting through, worrying him.

"Can you be sure they won't? I could be wired. . . ." As she spoke her right hand dropped casually to the side of the chair and she groped for the opening in her bag in case she had to pull the gun.

He gave her an indifferent smile. "You know, Detective, a man of my means has to give a lot of thought to security. When I built this house, I had a device concealed in the entrance—one of those things normally used at airports to reveal if passengers are carrying weapons or little radio bombs. . . ." From his pocket he took out the paper his assistant had brought earlier, unfolded it, and set it in front of DZ.

It was a kind of X-ray picture. In tones of gray and black, it outlined the ghost of her own form and the shoulder bag she'd carried in. Solidly spaced around the image were all the objects made of metal—small ones like the key ring and the cartridge of the pen in her bag, even a hook on her brassiere. It revealed that there were no hidden wires or microphones taped to her body. Also evident was the skeleton of a gun in her bag.

Almost at the moment she noticed it, he leaned over to sweep the bag from the floor into his lap. Plunging his hand inside, he brought out the gun, released the clip and put it into the pocket of his robe. Then he dropped the gun back into the bag and replaced it beside her chair. "There. We're both safer now."

She tossed the paper on the table. "Funny, I don't feel safer."

"You're completely free to go." He opened his hands as if setting loose a captive bird.

"Suppose I go to the police, the FBI, the people looking for—" For *you,* she was about to say. Yet it remained difficult somehow to cross that line. Within the boundaries of hypothesis—where he felt safer—it seemed she might have a better chance of trapping him. "For the killer," she said. "They'd certainly be interested in hearing about this conversation. . . ."

He regarded her passively, then leaned forward, laying his hands on the table, fingers splayed, as he might to emphasize terms at a conference table where he was negotiating a big deal. "Tell people whatever you want, Detective Hayes. But have you thought about how I'll respond? It's possible that I'll simply ignore it. But if your actions become enough of a nuisance, I'd be forced to bring in my lawyers, launch some very expensive lawsuits. I believe that would bring your behavior into question as much as— if not more than—mine. The result would be for people to assume that you were just too desperate to make a splash after losing your job."

"There's reason enough for anyone to accept you as a serious suspect."

"Oh? Let's hear . . ."

"Things that led me to you, for a start. FAA flight plans showing that on or very close to the dates of the murders, you flew your plane to Pasadena, Chicago, and Jackson— all within easy striking distance of the crime scenes."

"Ah!" He leaned back, and tossed his arms out expansively. "Now I see where your confusion began. I have so many business interests. In California, I was looking at a possible investment. In Gary, Indiana—just down the road from Chicago—I checked on another company in which I already own a stake. And just a couple of nights ago I had a late dinner with the head of the chamber of commerce in Mississippi's capital who'd like me to use my influence to locate a new cell phone factory in Jackson. You see, I never go anywhere without making it pay."

Yes, she saw: He could dismiss the itinerary as coincidence. She groped for something else. The bullet? It had to be connected to a gun that belonged to him, a weapon he could hide forever, or even destroy.

Then she remembered the most interesting piece of evidence, the clue that seemed to signal he wanted to be caught. "The picture frame," she blurted. "That can't be explained away so easily. It's valuable, something a man of means would own. I'm sure it can be traced, connected to you."

"Undeniably," he agreed. "I've traced the history myself, and I'm glad to pass it along. My father bought that particular frame on a trip to Paris in 1936, and gave it to the girl he loved along with a picture of himself. When her Jewish family became afraid they were no longer safe in Germany—a fear about which they were sadly correct— they sent most of their valuables to cousins in England. Last year, when I was in London making other arrangements, I located the heirs and they sold me that frame. I wanted it very much for sentimental reasons." He paused before adding, "I was quite distressed when I discovered it was missing from my possessions. . . ."

"Did you report it stolen?"

"I didn't realize it was gone." He shrugged. "A drawback of having too much."

"You don't think it looks terribly suspicious? Your property at the scene of the crime—along with the proof you were never far from any of the other murders."

He nodded thoughtfully, before saying, "The way I think it would look, in fact, is that I'm being . . . framed." He took delight in using the word.

He was right. It was all too circumstantial to stand up. At the same time, the very pleasure he took in showing off the difficulty in making a case against him made it clearer than ever to DZ that Alex Granton must be the Mystery Guest.

The frustration at having him at arm's length, knowing he was guilty, yet being unable to touch him, exploded into a declaration. "It *is* you, damn it!" And without waiting for a reply, she went on. "But why? I don't get it. With all this . . ." she gestured to the luxury around her. "For god's sake, why?"

He said nothing for a few seconds, then abruptly bolted up from the chair as if to vent a restlessness he could no longer contain behind the relaxed pose. He went to the balustrade and stared at the ocean.

With his back to her, she thought for a moment about making a move—slugging him over the head with a chair. And what then? Truss him up, sneak him past the assistant, drop him with the FBI, and make him confess? She'd look even crazier when he wanted to discredit her.

She hadn't budged when he turned to face her again. "DZ, do you know how much money I have?"

The first time he'd referred to her familiarly. It triggered the memory of the voice on her answering machine. "Sources say between five and six billion," she answered.

"Way out of date. Figuring in all my assets, as of close of business last Friday, my actual net worth was seven billion, four hundred, seventy-eight million and some petty change. Nearly seven and a half *thousand* million. Since then, of course, it's even more. At a conservative rate of growth, with interest compounding, there's another couple of million every day. *Every* day," he repeated. "Or put it this way: for each and every sixty seconds we've been sitting here, I grew almost three thousand dollars richer." He paused to let it sink in.

"Yeah? So?" As if she *wasn't* impressed.

"So what do you think it's like to have that much money?"

"I can't imagine. All I know is what poor folks like to say—it can't buy happiness."

His charming smile demonstrated he wasn't the least unhappy. "I couldn't imagine either—before I had it. I used to think the point of money was only to be able to afford anything your heart desires. Cars, planes, the biggest damn yacht, a mansion here, a chateau there. And the women. But could that really be the point? Nothing more than a slogan on a T-shirt—'The one who has the most toys when he dies, wins?' " He shook his head. "You can't have all this wealth, without wondering what it's *really* for. Wondering why you have it and others don't. Or, as in my case, wondering what meaning there could be in the accidents of destiny—that if my father had died in Hitler's camps like so many others, then there would never—" He stopped suddenly, and laughed. "Well, thinking about it can drive you a little crazy—if you know what I mean. But then I realized . . ." He started to pace slowly along the edges of the terrace, head down, like a philosopher puzzling through a universal mystery. "Every year in Wyoming at one of the homes belonging to—well, I'll just say it's another immensely rich man—there's a gathering for the rest of us: movers and shakers, the richest men in the country. It's always informal, three or four days of barbecues, horseback rides, softball games. The friendly atmosphere is meant to lull all us sharks into pulling in our teeth so we can freely exchange ideas about where the world is headed, and where our money should be going." He glanced over to see if she was paying attention. Her gaze was locked right on and he continued his circuit of the terrace. "On the last evening we're together, our host always provides some special entertainment. Three years ago, he flew over thirty Afghani tribesmen—along with their horses—so they could play a particularly rough sort of polo in front of us, a game they've played for centuries. Instead of a ball, they use the bladder of a sheep. God, those devils can ride, but of course the skill is dying out now—since the Russians fought that war, and a lot of those Afghanis died fighting them. Anyway, it was thrilling to watch, particularly with the sun setting against the view of mountains that border the host's hundred thousand acres. Then, after the game, there was an outdoor feast prepared by a couple of the best chefs from France—three-star guys. But that wasn't the best touch. A group of glassblowers from Venice had also been flown in, artists—and while we had drinks before dinner, these men were crafting the very plates and wineglasses from which we'd eat and drink—each unique, small works of art for us to use and keep if we wanted. . . ." He came back to the table, stood behind a chair, facing her. "That evening, watching dying traditions, watching artisans far from where they would have ordinarily done their work, that's when I finally understood the true value of what I have, such astonishing wealth. Not that it could buy *things*—but that it could buy experiences, allow me to be a witness to anything that happened on this planet, no matter how rare or unusual." He gave a diffident shrug. "Saying it now, I suppose it seems very simple to arrive at such a realization. But when you can have anything, you have to pass through satisfying all the other appetites before you reach that understanding. Experience is the purpose of wealth, the best it can buy—any experience you want, anything at all."

"And the one you want," she said, "is to murder. . . ."

"Me?" He sat down again facing her. "I don't think you understand. I've only been speculating on why a man in my position might conceivably undertake this amazing crime you're investigating. I mean *if* he felt he had a reason, even a right to some justice he couldn't find elsewhere. But it's only guesswork. All I can do is . . . give you an opinion."

Her turn to smile. Though perhaps he wasn't just being cute, she thought; dissociating himself from the crime might be a symptom of whatever madness drove him. She remembered reading that Ted Bundy, killer of thirty or forty women, had never admitted his guilt, but while awaiting execution on death row, he had been willing discuss the crimes with which he'd been charged, and "speculate" about the motives of the man who'd committed them.

"Well, then," she said, "in your expert opinion, what happens next?"

"More of the same, I imagine. Because that's part of the experience . . . I'd guess. Seeing how far it can go."

Regarding his smug expression, she realized that "the experience" he'd designed was meant to include this very moment—where he was confronted, and could test his wits against his accuser. More, his design was intended to change the nature of *her* experience, and of all the millions of people who'd participated in his crime, if only as witnesses.

"No," she said. "It can't go on." Nor *this,* the pretense that they weren't talking about him, *his* killing. "You're going to be stopped. I can raise suspicions about you, if nothing else. And even if nobody listens, I won't give up. Sooner or later, Mr. Granton, I'll get the proof. I'm going to nail you."

The smile was back, gently held on his lips as he let a thousand dollars worth of silence go by. "Well," he said, "if you ever do, that could be the best part of all."

It stumped her for an instant. Until she thought again of the psychologist's diagnosis that this killer wanted to be caught. But DZ suddenly perceived that DeJesus had been wrong with the rest of her analysis. He didn't want it because of shame or guilt or any subconscious wish to be punished for doing wrong. If Granton was looking forward to being caught, it was because even that would be part of his precious experience.

And now one more thing in his design became clear. Stricken by a visceral repulsion that hadn't stirred before, even with his confession, she edged back in her chair. "You're sure you'll get away with it, aren't you?"

When he said nothing, she rose to her feet and moved back farther. "You think because you're rich, the rules simply won't apply—that you can go right on and even when you're caught nothing will happen to you."

"We're not talking about me," he reminded her sternly. "But I'll venture one more opinion. If they catch your Mystery Guest, and if they can ever put together a jury that isn't tainted by all the publicity, the trial should be fascinating." He laughed softly, and even gave her a puckish wink. "All covered on television, every damn channel."

The sick feeling swelled in her gut. Not a reaction to him so much as to the prospect of what he envisioned—the realization he could be right. With a "dream team" of lawyer's making a case that the victims were all scum the society was well rid of, if he presented himself in the courtroom as he did right here, he could well be acquitted.

Though first, true, he had to be indicted, a jury found. Twelve people unprejudiced by what they'd read or seen or heard about the case. Hard enough.

From below the terrace came a loud splash, someone diving into the pool. Moving a quick couple of steps, DZ could see over the balustrade where the gorgeous model was swimming a graceful lap. She wondered how much the girl knew that might be valuable.

"Beautiful, isn't she?" he said, coming over to watch, too. "Such a good person, too. We're very much in love. This morning I asked her to marry me. . . ."

It was his way of telling her that the girl knew absolutely nothing of the truth.

DZ turned to look at him once more. How astonishing that however coldly he'd schemed, however savagely he'd acted, he still felt entitled to be loved. It furnished the final insight into his motives: exposing the corruption within the society was his revenge for all the crimes and perversions and inequities that had robbed him of a mother and father and left him, when he was most vulnerable, with nothing but a little boxful of moving images from which to draw his companionship and comfort and lessons. To make him what he was today.

For a second or two, she actually felt a welling of sympathy. Then she remembered again how much every second was worth to him, and she walked away.

"Good-bye, DZ, come anytime," she heard him say pleasantly as she went through the doors from the terrace, down the stairs, past the fine art, out the front door into the sun.

Free to go.

But she went no farther than turning her car out through his gates onto the public road before DZ realized she was too shaken, her mind too inhabited by what had just transpired, to drive safely. She'd had to pull over and sit, digesting it.

The logical next step shouldn't seem so elusive. His behavior constituted a kind of confession. On or off duty, she was a *cop*! If it came down to her word against his, who was supposed to be trusted?

But that equation could work when the suspect was an ordinary citizen—not against a man like Granton. The bottom line would be the word of a discredited woman eager to recover her reputation—against that of a successful, glamorous man of immense wealth. Even if she could succeed in persuading someone to trust her, what would they do? Put surveillance in place. So if putting him under a watch was all that could be done, then why not spare herself being put on the carpet and ridiculed—and take up surveillance herself?

But not here and now. Impelled by a need to put some distance between the gravitational pull of his arrogant evil, she turned the car back onto the road at last and drove back to New York.

All the while the highway unfolded in front of her, she thought about him. haunted by the memory of his words, all that he represented. The longer she lived with it herself, the easier it was to accept that Granton practically conceived of what he was doing as reasonable. Sure, he had to be a little nuts, too. But didn't you have to go a little off the scale of normal just to acquire that kind of money, if not from having it? No, it wasn't sheer craziness that made him kill.

What was out there beyond the ribbon of road, in this country, the way of life, that made murder as irresistible to some as . . . falling in love? That produced schoolboys who killed their classmates, mothers who killed their offspring, mailmen who knocked off their coworkers. And someone like Granton. All of it practically routine by now, worked right into the schedule of talk shows and entertainment news long before he'd come along.

Whatever made it more and more part of the fabric, Granton certainly seemed to have his finger on the pulse, to know what had to come next. But then his talent—the *genius* that had made him so rich—was to know where the society was headed, where progress would lead, what people would want.

She arrived home not much more than half a day after she'd left. And now she *knew.* But Granton didn't have to be watched yet. Whether because he wanted to be caught or he didn't, he was sure to wait to see how she reacted before he took his next steps. He'd be quiet for a while, no danger to anyone—at least until his next appearance on the tube.

CHAPTER
45

*E*VENING FOUND HER sprawled in front of the big screen, swilling her fourth beer. She watched the people moving behind the glass as though they were fish swimming in a tank. The world in that box was its own kind of isolated habitat.

Since the Mississippi murders, the M.G. story was all over the air, a feeding frenzy surpassing even what had gone before. The evening news broadcasts and tabloid shows all had camera crews scavenging the town where the victims had lived, interviewing parents, wives, neighbors, fellow racists. Featured, too, was the news that NYPD Detective Lieutenant DZ Hayes had been suspended due to lack of progress in the case and her public humiliation. Over and over DZ had to watch clips of herself on Stoner's show with the Mystery Guest. Even now, watching him, she had trouble believing it was the same man she'd met earlier today.

Who is he? Who . . . ? And why . . . ? The questions were repeated over and over by anchor men and reporters, the obvious tag lines to punch up their narratives.

And she *knew*! But what to do with it?

At last she switched off the TV. She drifted to the kitchen, opened the refrigerator, and mulled whether to eat something. No appetite.

Then she paused to stare at the phone. All day she'd resisted calling Charlie, afraid that in her present state she'd lose his respect by sounding so helpless and ineffectual. What he'd liked about her, surely, was that she was so capable, bravely on the trail of a killer. He'd responded to her too quickly for it to be . . . just her. Why did people fall in love, anyway? As hard to fathom as why some people had to kill. . . .

Damn it, Alex Granton made the whole world hard to understand.

Cling at least to the simple hope she was loved, DZ told herself, that at the end of the madness a sweet, sane life would be waiting. No, she decided, she couldn't call him now. If Charlie was ready to take her, she might be overwhelmed by the temptation to throw in the towel, go to him. And damn it, she couldn't let Granton practically boast about his guilt and have it mean *nothing*! Dispirited as she was, DZ pulled a stool up to her kitchen counter, grabbed the pad she used to jot down shopping lists, and started listing anything that might constitute evidence against him.

Time and place—the flight plans proved he'd been within the vicinity of all the murders on the dates they occurred.

Picture frame—if ownership at the time of the Fayrbahn killing could be connected to him

Bullet?—potentially the most damning, if only it could be connected to a weapon in his possession

What else? Legwork might unearth the way he'd transported himself from the airports to the murder scenes—though as she'd said to Gable, he could buy used cars for cash, discard them after one use as easily as a pair of running shoes. He'd use disguises of course, as he had on television, and false names. No, he wouldn't slip up easily.

Leaving a trail was a mistake criminals made when moving quickly, acting spontaneously. But Granton had put too much planning into this. That was evident in the story he'd told her about the picture frame. He'd taken some trouble to find it and procure it—because, she guessed, he'd particularly wanted to leave it at the murder of the Nazi, as a gesture to the memory of his father. . . .

Her mind went back to the story; it seemed important, to hold some buried meaning that had passed her by when she was with him, virtually hypnotized by his audacity. She listened to it in memory: he'd talked of buying the frame in London from relatives of the Jewish woman his father had loved. But . . . something more . . .

"I located the heirs . . . when I was in London last year—"

That was it! When he'd said he was in London—the time thing! "When I was in London *last year,*" he'd said, "making other arrangements."

Yes! While he was talking freely, she hadn't pulled it out of the flow for examination. When he'd spoken of "making other arrangements" in London she'd assumed it meant arrangements unrelated to his murder plans, doing other business. But running the phrase again through her mind, she thought it could easily refer to dealing with other matters *also* involved with the killings.

What, then? Hiring someone to work with him, someone far enough outside his usual orbit that they couldn't be quickly found, used as a witness against him. . . . No. He worked alone—a matter of ego as much as security. Having his disguises made? No, that wasn't necessary. All of that could be bought off a shelf somewhere.

What else would he need to "arrange?" She thought over the crimes, everything that set them apart—

Suddenly it struck her, something a man with a plan like Granton's would go to the English to "arrange" not just because the distance would make it harder to connect him to vital evidence, but because this was a service they might provide better than anyone else—and had provided for a century. . . .

Every extra second she lived with the idea, the more right it seemed. Going back to the first murder, she saw the way it tied into his singular movements at the scene. It even clarified the association she made with the tiger skin. God, yes, it cleared up several puzzles.

If she pursued the idea, she thought, it could result in getting the kind of vital evidence that would link Alex Granton irrefutably to the murders. Enough to prosecute.

Energized by the possibility, DZ snatched up the phone. She had her own arrangements to make.

CHAPTER
46

"*H*EY," STONER SAID brightly as he opened the door, "glad you—"

"Don't be, it's not what you think." She walked past him. When she'd reached him at his apartment tonight, she knew he misunderstood her sudden eagerness to see him. But she didn't correct his impression on the phone. If he saw her quickly even for the wrong reason, it might leave him more willing to listen and believe.

Stoner noticed now she hadn't made the least effort to look sexy. She had merely thrown an old trench coat over the same set of rumpled at-home sweats she was wearing in front of the TV. Her hair, usually so neat, wasn't even brushed.

"Can I get some coffee?" DZ said. She needed a chance to collect herself.

He crossed the foyer and touched some wall switches. The twilight gloom in his large living room was chased by a soft, restful glow. "Wait here," he said, "I'll put a pot together."

She stood at the window and looked down at the sequined velvet of dusk, Central Park with its lighted pathways. She remembered the case of the raped jogger she'd worked on when she was at Sex Crimes. Never solved. She could make up for all the unsolved ones, if this—

"It's perking." He was back, standing at her shoulder.

She spun around, preempting a touch. "I know who he is."

The hour and her edginess told him she was telling him first. "From the plane thing . . . ?"

"That was the beginning. I checked flight plans, matched them against times and places of the murders." DZ moved from the window, and paused to order her thoughts: how to lay it out so it was most believable. It didn't work one way any better than another. Might as well start with the name. But first: "I need a promise from you, Barry. It stays between us. Swear you won't try to use it."

Stoner hesitated. Her demand made it seem even odder that she had come to him first. And he was reluctant to limit himself. He'd gone beyond being just a talk show host now, he was a newsmaker. Just yesterday, Corcoran had begun talking seriously about giving him a nighttime hour, a *Sixty Minutes*–type thing. *You'll come out of this thing on top of the heap,* he'd said. *Especially if it goes on awhile longer. . . .*

"Why even tell me," he asked, "if you're going to put me under a gag order."

"Because I need to buy a favor, and this is the best currency I've got."

He thought another second. "Okay. Sounds reasonable."

Not even close to a promise. But she had to trust him. "His name is Alex Granton."

Stoner's eyes narrowed thoughtfully. "Heard of him, I think. Businessman, isn't he? Very rich."

"Very is an understatement," DZ said. "A billionaire."

"Right—I've got him now. He's into media, communications." Stoner snapped his fingers, excited. "So—what?—he set it up. The stock angle, after all?"

"No. The last thing he needs is more money."

"Need is beside the point. If the filthy rich didn't always crave more, there wouldn't be billionaires."

"Barry, there's no money angle. It's exactly what it looks like on the surface. He wants to kill people and make it a kind of public statement."

Stoner paused, inhaled deeply. "A statement. I see. So you've solved the case: this billionaire is flying all over, leaving the good life and his business deals behind to devote his precious time to killing a bunch of lowlife human garbage or anyone who happens to get in his way." His tone was more than slightly mocking.

"I know how it sounds. Funny, though, when it's some poor slob who lives alone in a mountain shack with no plumbing, we have no trouble believing he'll take a screwy political position, anonymously mail bombs to all the advertising men who sell junk, or all the rocket scientists who gunk up space. So now we've got a rich man with a bloody ax to grind. The only difference is he has the wherewithal to work on a much bigger scale."

Stoner studied her. "So tell me again how you arrived at this? Based on where he's flown his plane, you decided he—"

"No, I haven't *decided*," she snapped. "I know. I went to see him and he practically admitted it to me."

"To *you*. You alone, I gather. Admitted it—just like that."

"Well, not an out-and-out confession. But he never denied it."

Stoner lifted his chin to give her an openly wry look, then turned away. "I better check on that coffee. . . ."

Seeking escape from the fantastic in the mundane. She didn't stop him, let him be alone with it for a minute. Taking off her coat, she tossed it onto the couch, then settled herself, determined to look composed and sensible when he came back. He returned carrying a tray with a single cup, a sugar bowl, and milk in a carton. He set the tray on an end table near her then sat on an ottoman and watched her intently.

"Thanks," she said. She sipped the coffee black. Quietly, she continued, "Look, I know it sounds off the wall. Why do you think I'm telling you, instead of the brass. Since the story gets me put down as a screwball, right now I'm better off telling you than any of the people I work with."

"You also mentioned trading the information for a favor."

"I want you to keep him off your show. No more Mystery Guest—no appearances, calls, nothing. End it."

He went quiet.

She knew how hard it would be for him. Whatever qualms he'd had about the way the case unfolded, at this point there was a momentum he didn't want to stop. All the more if there was any chance what she was saying could be true. Wouldn't he love to expose the man's identity on the air!

She pressed on with her appeal. "Barry, he's not done. He'll go on with this until. . . ." She broke off. It wasn't going to make her sound any more reasonable.

"Until what?"

"Until he's ready to be caught. He doesn't want to be stopped now, but down the line, he'll dribble out the crumbs so the investigation comes right back to his door."

"Why on earth—?"

"As far as I can figure, he's . . . making some kind of . . . of political or philosophical statement."

Stoner chuckled. "Just how does what he's doing add up to any kind of philosophy?"

"I don't know exactly. He sees people getting killed and murderers getting away with it. Seen it all his life. It happened to his own mother. Also, in a way to his father.

Now he's pushing it to the outermost limits, showing how rotten it is. First by knocking off people the system didn't settle with—then by showing how he'll get away with it himself. He doesn't expect to be punished—because he's rich. And he *may* be right. He won't be the first out-and-out guilty man who got acquitted simply because convicting him was too difficult politically."

Stoner rose. Face taut with concentration, he stalked his big living room the way she'd seen him pace the stage when he was looking for a zinger to shoot down some wild statement by one of the panelists on his show. All he came up with now was denial. "No, DZ," he said. "No, it's just too far out. I can't buy it." He picked up the coffee cup and saucer she'd left on a side table, and moved toward the tray.

He seemed to be ending the conversation and her frustration boiled over. Leaping up, she took a couple of quick steps and blocked his retreat. "You aren't *buying*?" she said furiously. Tossing her hands up to punctuate the question, she accidentally hit the edge of the saucer, knocking it from his grip so both cup and saucer flew against the edge of a table and shattered. She didn't apologize. "Is that because you think I'm just making this up? Or because you simply don't want to keep the deal?"

"I can't!" He moved away, avoiding her fierce glare. "Don't you realize, DZ, it's not just my call. There's too much wrapped up in this now. If a blackout was ordered by the FBI or NYPD or any official source, okay. But it hasn't been. I don't know if they're in legislative gridlock or what, but for all the huffing and puffing, they're letting it go on. Because nobody wants to shut him down. Not the network or the audience—or the cops. Like you said, it's a hostage situation. The best shot is to keep the lines open, keep talking. What the hell, the damage is done now, he's got his slot. So now we'll keep him on TV, and try to catch a clue from something he says."

"We don't need clues anymore! I've got the *answer.* I know the who and why. "Barry," she pleaded, "if you'll just stop playing his game, the killing can end."

"DZ, whatever I do on my own can't end this. The Mystery Guest—whoever he really is—is plain and simple the best 'get' there ever was. If I turn him away, there are others who'll be happy to pick up where I leave off.

"You're overlooking one possibility."

"What?"

"The very thing that made him come to you in the first place: You're the *only* one he'll talk to."

Stoner turned to her wearing a wry lopsided grin that said he knew when he was being conned.

"No, truly," she said. "You're part of his scheme. He only wants to talk to you."

"Why should he?"

"Because you're the best."

Answered with the same smile: he knew she was being facetious.

"Also—because of what he knows about your brother," she went on. "And because his father also committed suicide. Because he's always known you're the one who'd be on his wavelength, have a real appetite for it and make the right kind of dialogue. He may have helped to make you . . . but you also helped make him." What she didn't say, but also believed, was that perhaps—indeed *probably*—no one but Stoner would have been quite so hungry to let the M.G. on in the first place. Would have taken the steps that had led them to this result.

Stoner put a hand up to his face, and rubbed it like a blind man trying to take an impression through the features: was he *that* special? At last he said, "You can't be sure. If I pull the plug, you're only guessing he won't go to someone else. . . ."

"Even if I'm wrong, it won't happen right away. You

could string him along; let him think he'll bring you around, but hold him off. Do that for a few days, anyway. Please. That'll give me the time I need."

Stoner gazed at the shattered china on the rug, as if the decision was so marginal the breakage might even tip the balance.

"Sorry about that," DZ said, and stooped to collect the bits of china in her palm.

When she stood up, she found him staring at her. "For what?" he asked.

"The cup—"

"No—about needing time, you said you need time. For what?"

"To get proof against him. Something that will stick."

He eyed her shrewdly. He had evidently guessed she was already following a certain track. She'd let it slip, now she could only hope he wouldn't ask for more, make it a quid pro quo, because she wouldn't share the rest with him until it was locked up tight.

He also seemed to know her limits. "All right. I'll stall. But I can't say for how long. I'm telling you now, if it looks like he'll switch to someone else, I'll cave."

"Fair enough."

"Also . . . Corcoran may take it out of my hands."

"You don't have to let that happen. You're too big now."

"As long as I deliver what made me too big."

Nothing left to say. Mission accomplished. DZ reached for her coat. He came to her, took the coat to hold for her.

"You sure you won't stay?" he said as he stood behind her. "We could have dinner and—"

"Double sure," she interrupted, and turned to him. "But I'll take it as a compliment that you asked."

He stood with her while she waited for the elevator. "If the crunch comes," he said, "where can I reach you? You're not at your desk downtown . . ."

The elevator arrived. She almost tossed it off as she stepped in, telling him where she'd be—but that would really get him going.

"I'll be in touch," she said before the doors closed.

His words, she realized on the way down.

CHAPTER
47

*T*HE KLAXON BLARED loudly as DZ stepped forward,
freezing her in her tracks. In the next moment she registered a blur of red passing before her eyes, and a line of
faces staring at her blandly through panes of glass.

Christ, almost killed right there! DZ watched the London bus rumble away. Look *right* not left, she cautioned
herself once more on the reverse direction of English traffic before continuing carefully across the street. Reaching
the curb on the other side, she paused to consult the tourist
map before heading for the next stop on her list.

As she walked along Piccadilly, she noted one of the
old-fashioned news vendors who still dotted London side-
walks, today's come-on to buy the paper chalked on his
signboard: TV KILLER LATEST. The newsstands at Heathrow
Airport had already reminded her the story was as big
abroad as at home.

Before her visit to Stoner last night DZ had already
made her reservation for the night flight to London. Of
course, she might have followed her hunch by using the
phone, but she was convinced that working at a distance
would make it impossible to wangle the kind of answers

she was seeking out of the old British firms with whom she would have to deal. The information she wanted was the kind they were likely to regard as confidential. Getting results from a reluctant source could depend on using the same means that had worked on her regular beat—a combination of charm, guile, even perhaps a quick payoff slipped to an eager hand.

At ten this morning local time, she'd arrived here. Sleeping on the plane left her rested enough to go right to work. In a terminal locker she stowed her carry-on, containing enough clothes for two or three days. With any luck, she might be on her way back to the States without having to stay over.

Before leaving the terminal, DZ paused at the Information Desk. "I wonder," she asked the female clerk "if you could tell me where to go to buy a gun."

The clerk's welcoming smile for tourists quickly faded.

"A good one," DZ went on. "For hunting."

The young woman confessed to only the most limited knowledge of such matters, but hazarded a guess. "Try Harrods," she said. "Harrods has everything."

THE MAMMOTH DEPARTMENT STORE IN THE KNIGHTSBRIDGE section of the city did indeed have a department that sold fine guns, and the gentleman in charge of the department was very knowledgeable and helpful. Yes, it was true, he told her, the finest hunting guns were custom-made, personally fitted to their users as painstakingly as a Savile Row tailor would fit a suit. True, too, that a fine custom-made gun could take several craftsmen more than a year to complete. And, the gun salesman asserted confidently, London remained, in his words, "the undisputed best source for high-end hunting weapons."

At Harrods, DZ hadn't uncovered the particular evidence she was seeking, but the salesman had been good enough to write down the names and addresses of other

London gun makers that had been turning out these lethal treasures for discerning sportsmen over the past two centuries.

Audley House on South Audley Street was DZ's next stop. Located a short walk off Piccadilly, the redbrick building was the headquarters of James Purdey & Son, Gunmakers. The man at Harrods had said Purdey was considered "the Rolls-Royce of shotguns." Depending upon which options were ordered, and what degree of special craftsmanship applied to the design, the price for a custom-made Purdey could easily rise over a hundred thousand pounds.

In a foyer off the street, a young woman sat at a reception desk. DZ informed her that she would like to speak to someone about the purchase of a gun.

"Your name?" the receptionist asked.

"Hayes—Dorothea Hayes." Somehow in England the hated name sounded exactly right.

The receptionist picked up an intercom phone, and spoke briefly to whoever answered. A man soon emerged from a rear alcove. He was gray-haired, mustached, and dressed in a pinstripe suit and vest with a gold watch fob draped across the front in a perfect parabola. "Miss Hayes," he said, "I'm Desmond Weyland, director of Sales."

"How do you do, Mr. Weyland." For once, she didn't correct his form of address. Presenting herself as a detective might only raise obstacles.

"So. You've come to Purdey's for a gun." He guided her to the alcove where an elevator waited. "Let's go up to the gun room, shall we?"

As they glided up, Weyland made conversation. "Forgive me if I seem forward . . . but did I detect an American accent?"

"Yes. I've come from New York expressly to look into buying a gun."

"I see. It's not every day we have a woman coming to

Purdey's—on her own, that is. When they come, almost always they're with a man, and the gun is for him."

Anyplace other than this bastion of English sporting tradition, DZ might have been surprised by such pointed male chauvinism. Here she could turn the attitude to advantage. "I'm here by myself, Mr. Weyland, but you're not wrong to assume I'm shopping for a man."

The elevator stopped and they stepped onto the landing. "You do understand," he said, "all that's involved in shopping—as you put it—for a gun of first quality . . . ?"

"If you mean do I know it will be expensive, I'm aware of that. But the man in this case wouldn't settle for anything but the absolute best."

He regarded her carefully, then gestured across a hallway to doors of polished mahogany inset with large windows. Through the glass DZ could see a long room decorated in the manner of a library at an exclusive men's club, all oiled wood and leather. Unlike a library, however, the walls weren't lined with books, but with scores of guns, unbroken rows of gleaming barrels and highly polished wooden stocks standing upright in glass-fronted cabinets. In several table-high display cases placed around the room lay other guns—the more exceptional weapons, Weyland explained.

DZ was left for a bit to drift on her own surveying the weapons. Pausing by one table case, she looked in at a shotgun with engraved golden sidepanels, and gold filigree worked into the barrel. Its burled walnut stock was inset with ivory panels intricately carved to depict a tusked bull elephant charging out of the jungle toward a hunting party. A card with an inked inscription lay near the weapon:

"THE MAHARAJAH"—OVER AND UNDER 4-BORE PRODUCED FOR
H.H. THE MAHARAJAH OF LAHORE, 1872.

Weyland glided up beside her. "A museum piece," he said. "Mind you, in perfect working order."

"Is it for sale?"

"To those who can afford it."

She imagined the sort of reaction a billionaire's consort might have. "Try me."

"This weapon can be had for two hundred and eighty thousand pounds."

In the vicinity of half a million dollars. DZ worked to look unimpressed as she turned away to the other cases. "It might do. What else do you have?"

"It would help," Weyland said with exaggerated patience, "if you could give me any specifics about the particular kind of weapon you have in mind."

"I'm mainly interested in something that packs a punch," DZ said. "That might, for example, be used to kill a tiger . . . or an elephant."

"Would there be a preference for double or single barrel, side by side or over and under . . . ?"

He was testing her, DZ thought. "It depends on what the user prefers, doesn't it?"

"Quite. And if the gun's going to be suited to the user, there are individual measurements that play a part —as well as other personal preferences. For example, would the user prefer a Prince of Wales grip versus the pistol type." A smug smile flitted across his lips. "So Miss Hayes, it does seem instead of coming here alone you should have—"

"But I want this to be a surprise." She improvised. "And I assumed you'd be able to tell me the preferences. You must keep records of past sales. If you made a gun to order for this gentleman in the past year or two, you should know what kind of weapon he prefers, isn't that right?"

"Madam," he declared. "We have records going back to the day James Purdey opened for business in 1814. I could tell you the preferences of any man for whom we've made a gun in the past *hundred and fifty* years! But if you believe this gentleman has already been our customer, are you sure he'd want another of our guns?"

"He's the sort of man who doesn't mind having more than one of what he likes—collecting the things that give him pleasure." Even victims, she thought to herself. "So would you kindly check your records, and tell me what I need to know?"

"Very well. The gentleman's name . . . ?"

"Alex Granton."

The Englishman's eyes flared with recognition. Not that this proved Granton had been a customer: for a man in Weyland's position, learning the names of all the world's billionaires could be part of his regular homework. He went to a phone on a table between two of the gun cases, and hit the button to make an inter-office call.

"Francesca, would you tell me if a Mr. Alex Granton has been a customer of ours within the last . . ." He turned aside to DZ. "Would ten years cover it?"

Last year, Granton had said. She nodded.

Weyland spoke again into the phone. "Yes, ten will do. It's G-R-A-N-T-O-N, Alex. Ring me back in the gun room." He hung up. "We'll have it quickly if he's on the books. Nowadays we enter everything into the computer for quick—"

He was interrupted by a soft chirping from the phone. He went to pick it up, listened. "I see. Thank you, Francesca." He returned to DZ. "Not a jot. I rather doubted we'd ever served Mr. Granton; I would have remembered a customer of that caliber. But it's double-checked: Alex Granton has yet to be a customer of Purdeys."

For the first time DZ wondered if she'd been foolish to invest so thoroughly in following a hunch. "I know he . . . he appreciates guns," she said. "I was certain he would have bought the finest."

Weyland took her back to the elevator. Riding down, he said, "Might I suggest that if you look at the gun he has, you're apt to find the marque on it. Not only our weapons, but our ammunition is imprinted with our name, and others do the same."

Of course: another reason he had wanted to keep the shells. "I should have thought of it," she said. "Now, unfortunately, it's too late. The gun is . . . out of reach."

"Then you've set yourself quite a task to track down the origin," Weyland said. "There are excellent guns being produced by a number of makers other than Purdey."

Outside on Audley Street, she paused to look at the names of other London gun and rifle makers she had given by the man at Harrods, and referred to the tourist map of London she'd picked up at the airport. The address of another fine gunmaker, Holland & Holland, was only a few streets away. She set out in that direction, her hopes reviving; there were a lot more places to go before the hunch was played out.

At a crossing on the corner of a large square, she paused to check for traffic, saw none and stepped off the curb.

In the next instant, she felt her arm clamped in a painful grip and was yanked forcefully off-balance from behind. Fighting to recover, she stamped a spiked heel into a shoe she glimpsed to her rear, and twisted away as she heard a grunt of pain and felt the grip on her arm loosen. Even before she was fully turned, her hands came up, reflexes automatically shifting from the defense to the offense. Stupid it had never occurred to her Granton might follow—

Focusing on the figure now standing in front of her, arms raised in surrender, she saw an unknown middle-aged man dressed in a tweed jacket with leather elbow patches, and a green suede waistcoat, with a full head of possibly dyed ginger hair.

"The wrong way," the stranger stammered. "You were looking the wrong way, and there was traffic coming. I had no choice. . . ."

DZ glanced at the street, and saw a stream of cars and taxis racing around the edges of the square where there had been none moments ago. A traffic light must have changed just as she was about to cross—again looking in the wrong direction. She relaxed her combative stance. "Yes . . . I see. I'm so sorry! Are you all right?"

The man looked down at the shoe in which DZ could still see the dent made by her sharp heel. Then he shrugged and forced a nod. "I suppose . . ." It seemed to DZ that despite having saved her from a serious accident, he looked guilty, regretting he hadn't managed to do it in a gentler way.

"Thank you. That was very kind. I'm so sorry if I hurt you."

The man hesitated, then did a brisk about-face and hurried away.

"Thank you," she called out once more as he disappeared around a corner.

Before moving on she glanced about her, searching the faces of people lingering on the perimeter of the square. As the sense of threat evaporated, she felt inclined to trust again that Granton wouldn't have pursued her. That wasn't his MO. He felt secure, in control, untouchable—until he chose to be touched.

Nevertheless, she resolved to remain watchful. If there was one thing about Alex Granton that could be predicted with any certainty it was that he was absolutely unpredictable.

CHAPTER
48

*H*OLLAND & HOLLAND also occupied it's own building of several floors, and presented credentials that were no less impressive. ESTABLISHED LONDON 1835 was engraved on a brass plate by the entrance along with the royal endorsements: BY APPOINTMENT TO HRH THE DUKE OF EDINBURGH—RIFLEMAKERS and BY APPOINTMENT TO HRH THE PRINCE OF WALES, SUPPLIERS OF BESPOKE GUNS. However the firm appeared more in tune with the go-go marketing of the modern world. On the street level, DZ saw a company-owned shop displaying a variety of luxury articles that took advantage of the name and *cache* of the company while not related to guns or hunting.

Also, the salesperson summoned to assist DZ was a woman. Dressed stylishly in a dark skirt and a gray silk blouse, she was slim with pale blond hair and the creamy skin associated with the classic English rose. Her name was Abigail Forester, and she evinced none of the pseudo-aristocratic stuffiness encountered in Desmond Weyland.

As DZ was again taken by elevator to an upstairs gun room, she remarked that it was refreshing to be able to deal with a woman in a matter like buying a gun.

Abigail Forester replied that her company felt there was no great advantage in dealing with guns as gender specific, especially since the firm had become a subsidiary of the same conglomerate that owned the French fashion house of Chanel. "I'm sure I can tell you whatever you wish to know about our products," she informed DZ pleasantly.

A subsidiary of Chanel, DZ mused. How long before guns became a fashion statement? "Are you a hunter yourself?" she asked.

"Actually," she said with a laugh, "I don't enjoy blood sports at all."

"Then how did you acquire your knowledge of guns?"

"I was the silver medalist in target shooting at the Seoul Olympics in 1988."

The gun room at Holland & Holland had the same clubby atmosphere as Purdey's, but added a theatrical touch by having a pair of young men dressed in the manner of Victorian apprentices—linen aprons over business clothes—working on guns at a large workbench by a window.

"Is there anything particular I can show you?" the saleswoman asked DZ.

"I'm looking for a weapon with substantial firepower."

"Shotgun or rifle?"

"I'm not sure at this point. It should have very good penetration—perhaps even the ability to bring down an elephant."

The saleswoman turned toward the workbench. "Henry, would you come and unlock the rifles." One of the apprentices pulled a chain of keys from his pocket and moved to a cabinet. Abigail Forester went on, "In the past, the traditional favorite for killing very large game was a large-bore gun, using a shell with a dispersing charge to increase the likelihood of lethal injury. But that was in a time when the need to quickly bring down large animals such as rhino or elephant might be simply defensive as much as for sheer sport. Now, sadly, there are so few of these animals left that when they're hunted by true sportsmen, making a clean kill with a well-aimed shot to heart or brain is part of the code. Large bore shotguns aren't considered sporting anymore. I'd say the kind of weapon that would appeal to you, Miss Hayes, is a rifle."

Interesting, DZ thought, that no assumption had been made that the weapon wasn't for her own use.

By now the apprentice named Henry had opened the glass doors of the wide cabinet. Within were a score of rifles, distinguishable from shotguns by narrower barrels, the firing mechanism, and telescopic sights on many. As she looked them over, DZ noticed that the apprentice pulled the saleswoman aside for a quiet word.

Returning to DZ, Ms. Forester said, "Before going further, Miss Hayes, may I ask what amount you're prepared to spend? The cost of these rifles can be rather high."

DZ guessed the apprentice had offered his opinion that she didn't look like any of the better-paying customers. "Let's say price is no object," she replied.

"Then my recommendation would be our Royal Double Rifle. It's available in every modern caliber, but if you're going for the big animals you'd want one of the larger. We offer .577, .600, and our own .700 H&H, a special hunting caliber unique with us. With that one, you'd have to use our own special Nitro Express cartridges."

DZ recalled the theory, based on the lump of metal recovered at the Fayrbahn house, that the weapon used could even be military issue. "Show me the largest."

Abigail Forester selected a rifle from the many in the cabinet and held it laterally in both hands for DZ to examine. Its beautifully grained wood and satiny gunmetal gleamed with hand-rubbed oiling. "An example of our point-seven-double-oh," the saleswoman said. "The stock is made of the finest grade walnut, and would have a gold oval inset engraved with your initials. Standard engraving on other metal fittings is the traditional Royal scroll; the rifle number will also be inlaid in gold."

"And the price . . . ?"

"With standard specifications, eighty-nine thousand, six hundred. But that doesn't include optional extras like the telescope mount on this one, which costs another four thousand. Deluxe engraving of special patterns, game scenes, custom carving, and additional gold inlay are all extra. And if you want one of our leather gun cases for easy carrying, that's two thousand. It's not unusual," she summed up, "for the complete package to go as high as two hundred thousand."

"Pounds," DZ said, making sure, and the saleswoman returned a smiling nod.

It all sounded like exactly what Alex Granton would have wanted. At the current rate of exchange, more than a quarter of a million dollars worth of firepower.

"Perhaps I should mention, too," Ms. Forester said, "that each cartridge separately retails for seventy-five pounds."

A hundred twenty-five dollars for a single bullet, DZ reflected. Chicken feed.

Abigail Forester had continued holding the weapon out, offering it to DZ to hold. But DZ had felt an odd reluctance to lay hands on the weapon, but now at last she seized it. As soon as it was in her grasp, she swung it up to seat the stock against her shoulder as she looked through the sight. It was very heavy, but as she gripped and steadied it, finger around the trigger, she was overtaken by the unsettling sensation of correspondence with the mind of the killer. She was aware, too, although it was a violation of proper etiquette, she was aiming the gun straight at an apprentice by the window, the spot squarely between his eyes filling the telescopic sight.

Abruptly, she dropped her arms. Abigail Forester gently lifted away the valuable weapon. DZ remained staring ahead, almost as if in a trance.

"Are you all right?" the saleswoman asked, studying her with concern.

DZ came out of it convinced that she had found what she needed. She decided, too, that the best way to proceed with Abigail Forester was to drop the cover story and deal truthfully, woman-to-woman. "I'm fine, thanks." She darted a look at the apprentices, before adding softly, "Is there a place we can talk privately?"

"Certainly." The saleswoman returned the rifle to Henry and led DZ from the gun room, down a corridor into a sunny room cozily furnished with a desk, and a sitting area by a fireplace. She motioned DZ to one of two wing chairs flanking the hearth, and took the other.

"Ms. Forester," DZ began, "I'm not really here to buy a rifle."

The saleswoman smiled pleasantly. "Is that all?"

"You don't seem surprised. . . ."

Ms. Forester's smile faded. "No. I'm merely concerned about what your true purpose might be. Does it have anything to do with this terrible business involving the man our papers are calling 'The TV Killer' "?

The surprise was all on DZ's side. "Why—yes. How did you—?"

"Henry told me he recognized you from *Newsnight*—a show on our telly that goes into the nuts and bolts of the biggest news stories. He saw a bit rebroadcast from some American show. Henry says you're the detective in charge of the case."

So that was what the apprentice had whispered. Fortunately, the news of her dismissal evidently didn't carry enough international weight to get the same coverage. "Yes," DZ said. "I'm here to see if I can pin down the sort of gun the killer is using."

"Why didn't you say that at the start?"

"I though you might be less cooperative." DZ admitted.

"But surely you don't imagine this killer could be using our . . . I mean, that kind of money wouldn't be spent on a weapon by a common murderer."

"Ms. Forester, there's nothing common about this murderer."

"Detective Hayes, our most expensive guns are bespoke weapons—as I thought I'd made clear, each made to order for the buyer. The price also reflects the fact that very few are made. In the past three years, less than twenty Royal Double Seven Hundreds have been delivered—every last one sold to very rich, very reputable individuals. It's unthinkable any of them could be the man you're looking for."

"Ms. Forester, we're living in an age when the unthinkable seems to happen every day. So can I ask you to provide me with a list of the people who've purchased one of your larger caliber Royal Double Rifles anytime in the past three or four years?"

The Englishwoman held her response for a long moment, then rose, and smoothed her Chanel skirt. "Wait here," she said.

NINETY MINUTES LATER, DZ EMERGED ONTO THE STREET. When the list of buyers did indeed show the name of Alex Granton, she'd asked to see further paperwork—bills of sale, measurement sheets, anything that related to dealings between Granton and Holland & Holland. It was all on file, and Abigail Forester permitted DZ to see it. She had balked, however, at releasing the material or providing copies. During the time she'd left DZ alone in her office, the saleswoman had consulted a superior about DZ's request, and a decision had been made to cooperate in answering questions and allowing the papers to be seen, while nothing tangible would be surrendered.

"I hope you understand our position, Detective Hayes," Ms. Forester explained. "Whatever your suspicions, without our own authorities going on record, we can't be a party to abetting the defamation of one of our customers.

You see, at the end of the day, it seems quite beyond belief that you could be on the right track."

The familiar mind-set: celebrities, sports heroes, and billionaires *couldn't* be guilty of cold-blooded serial murder. Unless forced, an elite company would prefer not having its products linked to wholesale slaughter in a story that was making headlines around the world.

DZ had no choice but to accept the limitation. She settled for an assurance that the records would be kept in the firm's vault. What mattered most was that the evidence existed, a link had been established to a weapon that—once connected to the bullet that had killed one of the M.G.'s victims—would prove Alex Granton was the killer. Since the rifle fired only bullets that were made especially for the gun, even the misshapen lump of metal recovered at the Fayrbahn house could almost certainly be identified as the remnant of an H & H Nitro Express cartridge.

Laying out almost a hundred pounds of her own money (value added tax on top of the price), DZ purchased one of the special bullets to use for comparison.

On the street outside Holland & Holland, DZ looked for a cab, eager to head straight for the airport and catch a flight home. But taxis were suddenly scarce. Glancing at her wristwatch, she saw it was past one o'clock; Londoners must be traveling from offices to lunch appointments. She started to walk, then remembered that Piccadilly, a major thoroughfare where there would be more taxis, was in the other direction. She wheeled around—

—and as she did, caught sight of a figure along the sidewalk ducking into a doorway, a movement so coincident with her own about-face that she suspected instantly it was a tail caught unaware by her sudden change of direction.

She ran to the entranceway. Through a plate glass door she saw a couple of figures in a dim lobby waiting for an elevator. For a second, she wondered if she was once more jumping to the wrong conclusion, all the more on edge now that she possessed knowledge even more threatening to Granton. Then her experienced eye picked out a detail that confirmed she was imagining nothing.

The elevator came, the two waiting people started to board. DZ yanked the street door open and charged toward the elevator, reaching it just as the automatic doors were closing. Thrusting her hand into the narrowing gap, she made the doors part again.

He stared back at her, eyes wide with apprehension—the man she'd recognized by his jacket's leather elbow patches—the same ginger-haired man who had acted earlier to prevent her from landing under the wheels of oncoming traffic. Yet why hide from her now unless he was up to no good?

She went for the answers. With a lunge, she clamped one hand on his collar at the neck, the other onto his wrist. Though he overmatched her by a good eighty pounds, he put up no resistance as she hauled him out of the elevator back into the lobby. A second man in the elevator looked on in astonishment at the assault. "It's all right, we're old friends," DZ assured him as the doors slid shut. "He saved my life."

The ginger-haired man remained unresisting as DZ shoved him against a wall, yanked open his jacket to see if he was carrying and began to pat him down.

"No need for all that," he said with a crisp British accent. "I'm not armed, Miss Hayes."

"*Detective* Hayes," she said. "And who the hell are you?"

He straightened his jacket. "Graham Barnes. How do you do?"

"I suppose I should be glad you've been on my tail, Mr. Barnes. Otherwise I might have had a bad accident."

"Couldn't let that happen," he said with a small bow.

"Thanks once more. Now, why have you've been following me? Not just to save me from another bus. . . ."

"It's a job, actually." Suddenly one of his hands darted up inside his jacket. She caught it. "Only wanted to give you my card," he said. From a pocket, he withdrew his wallet, and extracted the card. At the center, printed under his name, DZ saw "Private Investigator." An address and phone number was in the upper corners; across the bottom was the motto Discreet, Dependable, Determined.

"I was a policeman, too," he said. "Retired from the London force."

DZ tucked the card into a pocket. "So how much is he paying you?" she said.

"Pardon me . . . ?"

"Alex Granton. You're working for him, aren't you?" Had to be. She'd told no one she was jumping on a plane to London, and only Granton would have reason to worry she might turn up here. He could have engaged Barnes to keep a watch on all the New York–London flights since the day he'd confessed.

A twitch of the Englishman's mouth and a nervous straightening of his tie gave DZ all the confirmation she needed, but he still tried to play it cool. "Detective, you must know the identity of my client or what I'm being paid aren't things I'm obliged to reveal—especially to a New York copper off her beat."

"I owe you one, Mr. Barnes, so let me give you some free advice: regardless of what your rights are, you should cooperate and tell me whatever I need to know. Because if Alex Granton is your client, then you're helping a murderer—in fact, America's Most Wanted."

He weighed it a second, then let out a classic Blimpish guffaw. "Oh-ho, jolly good. You've got me shaking in my boots."

"You should be, Mr. Barnes. Shielding him leaves you open to charges of complicity, and obstructing justice in a capital offense. Six murders, in fact."

His laughter died. "You're quite serious, aren't you?"

"Quite."

"Detective, I don't know by what reasoning you've deduced this man could be my client—but I'm bound to say that whoever I'm working for, I can vouchsafe that he's not the kind of world-class psychopath who's been terrorizing—"

A thought struck DZ and she broke in. "Let me throw a wild guess at you, Mr. Barnes: this isn't your first job for the same client. A while back, you helped track down a family living here in England who had in their possession a piece of property your client wanted to recover for sentimental reasons, something his German father many years earlier gave to a woman who'd died in a concentration camp. . . ."

His eyes told her she'd hit it right again and she went on, "I don't know how much detail the news reports here have included, but did they ever mention that at the home of his second victim, the killer left a valuable picture frame?"

Barnes's mouth fell open. "No. I never saw that mentioned," he said then. For another moment he gazed into DZ's face with all the experience of a one-time cop who'd heard plenty of lies and tall stories. When he spoke again the bravado was gone. "Would you mind terribly if we continued this little chat over a cup of tea?"

IN A LUNCHROOM IN MAYFAIR, OVER HIS CALMING CUP OF Earl Grey, the English P.I. gave an account of the work he'd done for Alex Granton beginning three years ago.

"Don't know why he picked me. I've done the odd job for English companies worried about embezzlement and such, so it could have been a referral. Or maybe he looked in the Yellow Pages. Anyway, he called from the States, and told me he was trying to locate an English family related to a woman named Klara Schreiber who'd died in the Nazi camps. Said finding these people was important to him, a link to his family history. Granton's name didn't mean anything to me then, but right off I guessed he must be pukka. When I told him my fee was so much per week, he offered to triple it if I took no other jobs, and to keep me on the payroll for as long as it took. Which turned out to be a fair while because the name of the relatives wasn't the same as the lady who'd died. I ended up making two trips to Deutschland. Luckily the Huns are brilliant at keeping records—even have the docs on a lot of the folks they sent up the chimneys. Eventually I learned that the maiden name of Klara's mother was Liepmann, and she had an uncle who'd emigrated here. Not so many Jews hereabouts, so I found the right Liepmann's pretty quick—in Croydon, south of here."

Once informed they had been located, Granton had flown straight over. Barnes had driven him to the Liepmann home, been present when he bought the picture frame from the family.

"Set on having it, he was. Paid five thousand quid for it without batting an eye. The family couldn't say no, I guess. Wasn't just the money; Mr. Granton spoke very emotionally about the sentimental value, because his father had spoken about how much he'd loved the young woman who'd received this gift. . . ."

After locating the frame, Barnes did other jobs for Granton. Had driven him to Holland & Holland when he was in London, later arranged for the gun and cartridges to be air-freighted to the U.S. in a bonded shipment.

"You think," Barnes asked DZ, "that's the gun he's been using for his . . . I mean, to do what he's been doing?"

"Seems so."

Barnes had been enjoying a buttered scone with his tea while he spoke. Now he pushed away the remnant. Even while he had provided DZ with information that strengthened her case, the Englishman couldn't relinquish his doubt that DZ's conclusions were correct. "Are you very sure about this, Detective Hayes? A gent like this, it doesn't seem in the least possible—"

"Mr. Barnes, surely an Englishman should have no problem believing the worst murderers can be gentlemen. Isn't there evidence Jack the Ripper was a blueblood? And you've had kings who put little princes in dungeons and cut their throats."

By the time they finished their tea, Barnes was a believer. Parting from DZ in the street, he said, "Since he engaged me to check the flights from New York, I expect Mr. Granton will be calling for a report. How would you like me to handle it? I'd be tempted to refuse further contact, but that would surely make him suspicious."

"Talk to him, Mr. Barnes, and tell him the whole truth. Tell him you saw me, that I came looking for evidence . . . and I found it."

"But if he realizes you're closing in—"

"That's the damndest part of it, Mr. Barnes: it's not unlikely he'll be pleased."

"Pleased?" Barnes echoed in disbelief.

"Quite," DZ said, leaving no doubt.

CHAPTER
49

STONER GAZED FROM his office window, considering the view before him, the city caught at that moment of a clear June evening when the setting sun turned all the glass and metal surfaces of the skyscrapers to gleaming gold. For a while he'd been king of this golden city, biggest star in the center ring. But of course he'd known it couldn't go on forever; didn't really want it to. He just hadn't realized—until the past twenty-four hours—how it was going to feel when it was over.

The realization had started when DZ told him about the evidence she was gathering against a billionaire who had designed his crime as some sort of philosophical exercise and even wanted it to end with his capture. Once Stoner thought back over the way the case had proceeded, the way it had been designed from the beginning, the more he realized it was all of a piece. If the Mystery Guest wanted people to share in his crimes as they were committed, why shouldn't he want them also to share in the sensations of being accused, caught, tried? And—he must be betting—acquitted. Morally, it was a toss-up: with one unintended exception, he was killing people who deserved to die.

Legally, his odds were better than even. Could they find twelve people who didn't know about the case, hadn't formed an opinion—and didn't have an ax to grind with pederasts and Nazis and racists?

The limits on what people would accept and permit were being stretched to new horizons these days. Give them the sensation, they'd forgive all the rest. Granton might have kept the first phase of his game going as long as no one was close on his heels, but as soon as DZ had knocked on his door, he was ready to enter the next act in his drama of public murder.

The clearer it became to Stoner, the more he hungered for the opportunity to continue the dialogue that had begun. The sensational value of talking to a disguised murderer as he was in the midst of fulfilling his darkest wishes could only be topped by conversing with the man who was willing to expose his identity, and explain his desire to face judgment rather than simply indulge in a life of luxury.

Stoner cared enough about DZ that at the time she'd sought his pledge to shut down the M.G. he'd been sincere. But now he was having second thoughts. DZ had sparked them herself when she'd called a couple of hours ago to ask if he'd heard from Granton. He'd been able to say he hadn't, which reassured her—but she was evasive when he asked her whereabouts, and Stoner sensed she was hot on the trail—on the verge, perhaps, of finding the evidence. Which meant Granton might be jailed before they could talk even one more time.

"Hey, Barry, it's past seven."

Stoner turned to see Joe Candelli entering his office. The producer had his jacket on, ready to leave for the day. His tone hinted not only at surprise that Stoner should be lingering after him, but an odd tinge of disapproval.

"I was waiting to hear from Stan Karr," Stoner said.

Karr was the entertainment lawyer who handled Stoner's contracts. This morning, after Corcoran had repeated his offer of a new prime-time magazine show,

Stoner had called the lawyer and instructed him to firm up a deal with the network chief.

"The way you're riding now," Karr had said, "I can net you eight or nine for the new spot—pure salary, exclusive of a production package if you want it. Dianne gets seven after all, and Barbara does even better." Millions per year he meant, using Sawyer and Walters as his reference points. "I'll hammer it out with Skip, maybe get back to you by the end of the day."

But of course that wasn't really the call Stoner was hanging around for—and Candelli wasn't fooled, either. "You know, don'tcha," Candelli said, "that Corcoran's really offering this new show as bait." Stoner cocked his head inquisitively. "To keep you hooked," Candelli went on, "playing this Mystery Guest thing for all it's worth."

Stoner slid into the chair behind his desk. "You've been pretty happy with the ratings, too. . . ."

"Yeah," Candelli said quietly, "I was." He shook his head. "But we've got to close it down now, Barry. It's enough. No, not enough—too much. Too damn much. We went too far when we took the first step."

Stoner examined his producer. "So," Stoner said, "she got to you, too . . . ?"

"Who?"

"DZ."

"What's she got to do with it? She's not even on the case anymore." It was plain he truly didn't know what Stoner was talking about.

To divert Candelli from probing deeper, Stoner said, "I mean, she was always against putting him on."

Candelli crammed his hands into his pants pockets and started strutting nervously around the carpet. "And she was right. I sold out, but I can't anymore. Three guys this last time. I'm starting to feel as if I pulled the trigger myself."

"C'mon, Joe. They were racists—vicious killers."

"Three wrongs don't make a right. Or six, or twelve, or however many he kills before this is done. We can't be part of this anymore." He stopped and fixed his gaze on Stoner, looking for some sign of agreement.

Stoner remained balanced at the same fulcrum of indecision on which he had wobbled all day.

Candelli came to the desk, and laid his hands on the surface as he leaned forward. "Listen, it's been eating at me while we wait for this guy to call again. And I've just reached the point that . . ." He stopped and turned away from the desk.

"You want out, Joe? Is that what you were going to say? You want to go produce some simpleminded daytime game show, or a PBS animal special?"

His back still to Stoner, Candelli said, "Aside from everything else I just don't feel safe. Being this close to the craziness—Jesus, these days when the phone rings in my home at night, I get the heebie-jeebies. He's already called me. He knows where I live. Who says one of us—all of us—won't be next? Wait till it happens to you. . . ."

Stoner rose. "Joe . . . Joe . . ." he moved to lay a hand on the other man's shoulder. "You're forgetting something. Our guest has a conscience—that's what makes it all right. He's the Lone Ranger. He wears a mask . . . but he only wants to kill *bad* guys."

Candelli spun to face Stoner again. "And we're *not*? One of the very first things we were told about him, remember, is he loathes television, has some vendetta against it. So who says he won't decide to go after the people who make and run it?"

Stoner walked back to his desk. "Okay, Joe, you want to sign off, I understand. Lori's ready to move up and produce."

Candelli glared at him. "So that's it: you're with Corcoran. Blood and ratings *über alles*!"

Only when Candelli condemned him for it did Stoner realize that he had indeed made his choice. "I can't help it, Joe. This thing's coming to a head. I've got a chance to really burrow into the mind of this guy, get him to talk about who he *really* is, why he was ready to risk so much. There's no doubt it'll be the best stuff to come out of this whole thing. Better than OJ, better than Monica. Walk away if you want, but if I did it would be—" Realizing the word that was about to form on his lips, Stoner paused for a chuckle before letting it out. "Criminal. Don't you see, my whole career is built on exploring what makes people so unusual, makes them capable of doing the best things or the worst, getting them to open up about why . . . why . . . about why. . . ."

He faltered. The memory was stuck in his mind again, blotting out everything else—

The summer day, one bright shaft of sunlight slanting down through the trees onto the door, chained and padlocked. The hell with Pa's warnings, he'd gone right up to it, leaned in so close and hard against the rough wood siding he'd gotten a big splinter in his cheek. He had to find out the truth. *Lyle? . . . Ly! Did you, Ly? Did you do it? Talk to me.* He had to know before he could do what his brother was asking—take a rock and bash that padlock until it broke, go inside and untie him. *Talk to me first, Ly. Talk to me!* And the answer had come back from the other side of the door. After that, he couldn't go against Pa. Couldn't do anything but run away, out of the woods.

From then on he talked to others, to try to understand how it was possible. . . .

The memory went out like a bulb switched off in a closet, and he was back in his office, seeing the sunlight slanting not on an old wooden shack in the forest but on the skyscrapers beyond the window. . . .

"Just . . . *why!*" Stoner concluded. "Why we do the crazy things we all do, all of us. I can't give it up, Joe! If I can have this guy on once more, it'll be the best shot at him we've had yet, the most explosive, the wildest, the absolute payoff. I know it!"

Candelli stepped backed to give Stoner a once-over. "How?"

"I can unmask him. Right on camera."

In a shocked half whisper, Candelli said: "Unmask him? You know who he is?"

"I can't go into that. I'm just saying if I have just one more get, it'll be over after that. And it'll be an hour of television that beats anything I've ever done."

"Look, if you know, why the hell aren't you—"

"DZ is getting the evidence. She swore me to secrecy while she goes after it, because the guy could get off otherwise. But if I blow his cover in front of everyone— maybe get him to admit it—then who the hell needs evidence?"

Candelli stared at Stoner another moment. "No," he said then, waving his hands at his sides like a man sinking in deep water, trying to swim away. "No, no, I don't want any part of it." He continued backward, through the office door. "I'm through here, Barry."

Stoner rushed after him. "All right, suit yourself! But don't blow it for me!"

Candelli moved into the long corridor, striding away from Stoner as he called back, "I'm through, Barry. I'll come back in a few days to clear out my office."

Stoner screamed after him. "Swear, Joe! Swear you'll let it play—!"

"Do it your way! I just want *out*!"

Stoner watched Candelli until he reached the door from the production offices into the elevator lobby. Did he have to pursue him, wring out a stronger commitment?

No, Joe was a pro. He'd never kill a show that had so much potential. Stoner turned back toward his office. Walking to his desk, he eyed the phone. Silent.

Call me, damn you. *Talk to me!*

Skittish, his pulse still racing from the collision with Candelli, he moved back to the windows. It was getting dark. The alchemy of the light was gone, the golden city reverted to lead. There would be no call now. The M.G. wouldn't expect anyone to be here.

Stoner looked at the phone again. And now he realized his choice went beyond wanting the other man to begin the conversation. He didn't need to wait. Not another minute.

CHAPTER
50

S HE LEFT THE taxi from Kennedy at a corner near her loft
building, and stopped in the corner coffee shop for a
large black to go. Busy plotting her next moves, she'd
dozed fitfully on the return flight, and felt ragged from her
lightning trip abroad. But she couldn't see how she could
take any time to lay her head down. Not yet.

Through the door of her loft, she beelined for the phone.
The kitchen clock showed only a couple of minutes past
seven, a good time to find Stoner at his apartment. Before
anything else, she had to know if things were still in a
holding pattern.

His voice mail answered after four rings. She hung up
without speaking, and went to get her notebook from the
shoulder bag. He'd given her a second number that would
ring through.

She gave it twenty times before accepting he wasn't
there.

At the country house, his housekeeper answered
drowsily, annoyed at the early call. Mr. Stoner? No, he'd
be in the city—he had his show to do.

His unavailability bugged DZ. Gable might know what was happening.

Still home, he picked up on the second ring, wide awake.

"Hi," she said.

"DZ? Jesus, where the you been?"

"Doing detective stuff. Clark, anything new in the past twenty-four hours?"

"Not that I've heard, but I'm in Siberia, too. Where were you yesterday? I was worried."

Only now she glanced at the answering machine, ignored in her haste to reach Stoner. The counter showed twelve calls. "I'm in a hurry to nail this down, so I'll make it quick. I've tied Granton to the weapon, and the frame he left at the Fayrbahn house."

"That's enough for an arrest!"

"No, he'll be ready. Gotta get my ducks in a row first, make this ironclad."

"DZ, this isn't just rousting some street punk. You can't go it alone."

"Hey, I turned up more than the whole goddamn FBI? You in my corner or not?"

Quietly: "Always."

If she needed him, he said, he'd be downtown on an eight-to-four. She hung up, went to the messages on the machine.

A magazine writer doing follow-up on her fall from grace. An aid in the first dep's office to schedule her disciplinary hearing. Mixed in were two calls from Gable, and Charlie's—four of them, the pitch of concern escalating to anxiety then sinking to dejection at his failure to connect. In the fourth call last night he rambled for a few minutes, spoke of being so worried he was thinking of coming East to be with her.

"I tried you at work, too, and they said you're not coming in while you're on suspension . . . so I'm mixed up about why I haven't heard anything. The Association of

Newspaper Editors is meeting in Washington next week, so I thought I'd come early and . . . well, hell, DZ, I don't want to lose you. . . ."

Jesus, how consumed she'd been by chasing the evidence that she could leave him suffering in doubt. If she couldn't love him better than that . . . She halted the tape with one message still unplayed and snatched up the phone.

His own machine answered. She glanced at the clock as she heard his own recorded voice. Not yet seven-thirty. He might even be on his way here. And not because of that editors' conference; she knew that was only a face-saver. *Oh God.* A sweet gesture, but she didn't want him anywhere near while she was getting this wrapped up,

Now she remembered to play the last unheard message. Stoner! 3:28 A.M., according to the time stamp. He sounded very cool and controlled. "DZ—sorry you're not there. I wanted to put you in the picture. Call Lori if you need to reach me."

What the hell? At that hour? Was Stoner sleeping with her? DZ fished out the notebook where she'd listed home numbers of all the principals.

No answer at Lori's either. Where the hell was everybody?

Candelli might know.

He picked up the phone at his beach house. He'd been asleep—also a promising sign, no emergency keeping him awake.

"I couldn't get Stoner or Lori at home," DZ told him. "I was starting to wonder if you'd all been taken hostage."

"I don't know where Stoner is," Candelli said. "But Lori could be at the office."

The kitchen clock showed 7:16. "This early?"

"She'll have lots to do. I quit last night, DZ. Lori's producer now—and she may have a whale of a show to put on."

"What do you mean, Joe?" DZ had a bad feeling about what might have led to the shake-up.

"Stoner's putting him on again, and I couldn't go along with it. Oh, Christ! So he heard from the—"

"Maybe. But he wouldn't have to wait for a call. Told me he knows who it is."

"He gave you the name?"

"No, he wouldn't. But for a payoff, I think he's planning to—"

Shit! The sonofabitch. No need to hear the rest. DZ banged the phone down furiously. If Stoner was going to use what she'd told him, his other plans weren't hard to figure. What she had to find out fast was how far he'd already gone down the road to fulfilling them.

THE PRODUCTION SUITE SEEMED DESERTED. DZ WENT PAST the unoccupied reception desk to the maze of cubicles. "Lori . . . ?" she called down the corridor beyond.

The young woman emerged from the door to the office that had been Candelli's. Her short, pale blond hair stood out in unkempt spikes, as though she'd just gotten out of bed. DZ hurried toward her.

"What's up, Lieutenant?" Lori asked anxiously.

"That's what I came to ask you. What've you been doing here?"

"Barry's flying down to Mississippi. He asked me to come in early and line up a camera team—"

"How long have you been here?"

"Came in at four. I had to locate the guys, arrange their transportation. . . ."

A clearer picture was forming. If Lori was here at four, sometime earlier Stoner must have connected with Granton. She guessed Granton had agreed to meet with Stoner for today's show—on location. "So Barry told you he's going to Mississippi?" DZ said. "That's where he'll broadcast from today . . . ?"

Lori nodded shakily, her composure slipping from being battered with DZ's questions.

"Did he tell you Candelli quit? That you were taking over as producer?"

"No. . . ."

"Now let me tell you why he didn't mention your instant promotion: because then you'd have wanted to know why Joe quit. And if you knew, maybe you wouldn't want to fill in. Because I think the show your boss is *really* setting up is with the killer. Only this time there's a switch: Barry initiated it—he made the call."

Lori began to put it together. ". . . to that man," she murmured, her hands pushing into the blond spikes. "The one you asked me to research. . . ."

"That's right. Now, give me the rest of it," DZ commanded. "You said you arranged transportation for a camera team. What did Barry tell you to do—exactly?"

Lori clapped a hand to her forehead, and moaned guiltily. "Oh God, those guys—I didn't know what I was getting them into—"

"C'mon, Lori: how did you line it up?"

"I called the guys—a cameraman and a sound guy, sent a separate car for each to bring them to the airport."

"Which airport? At what time?" DZ had to restrain herself from seizing the young woman to shake it all loose.

"LaGuardia. Cars picked them up at 5:15."

"Did you book a flight for them, too?"

"No. I asked Barry if I should, but he . . ."

DZ saw the girl speaking, but the words were lost, reception jammed by all the thoughts screaming through her mind. Breaking away to the desk, she pulled her notebook from her shoulder bag and flipped through it to find a number she'd marked down a few days ago.

Lori looked on in silent bafflement as DZ got on the phone, made her connection, and hammered out another series of very specific questions that included times, a plane's N number, mention of a flight plan. Only after DZ hissed out a curse, and then slowly lowered the phone receiver back into its cradle did Lori speak: "Who was that?"

"Hyannis tower," DZ replied. "Granton's plane took off from there at four-thirty this morning. Destination on his flight plan was New York, LaGuardia. Figure flying time from the Cape, he probably landed there between five-thirty and six."

"So you think—"

"No, damn it, I *know.* Stoner and the camera crew are up in the air with him now."

She couldn't handle it solo anymore: Stoner was flying off to God-only-knew-where with the killer. Tracing the plane quickly required federal help, coordinating the hunt on a national scale, and perhaps calling on the military.

She located Ken Chafee right away at home in bed, and briefed the New York bureau chief on all she knew—including that she'd tracked down sufficient evidence for an indictment against Alex Granton. Then she offered her vision of Stoner's plans:

"Today's program will be the big finale: he'll expose Granton on the air as the Mystery Guest."

"Then he's putting his life on the line. Who knows how Granton will react?"

"He doesn't see the risk. He thinks his Mystery Guest only kills bad guys."

"Even if he's right," Chafee observed, "He could find himself in the middle of *somebody's* death. He can't control what's going to happen."

"I know," DZ agreed. "We'd better find them before four o'clock this afternoon!"

Showtime.

GABLE RACED OVER TO GBS TO COLLECT DZ AND DRIVE HER to LaGuardia.

They hit the control tower first, and had been there ten minutes when Chafee arrived trailing a clutch of agents.

While Gable went on taking a statement from the tower supervisor, Chafee pulled her aside. "What do we know?"

She read off her notes. "Granton's plane landed here shortly after six A.M. It remained on the ground a quarter of an hour, engines running. A gate employee saw four people arrive and go aboard."

"Stoner and who else?" Chafee asked.

DZ flipped to another page where she'd noted names obtained from Lori. "Ted Lowenstein, a soundman, and Steve Palmer, camera operator. No make on the fourth guy yet. I'll go from here to the boarding gate and see what else I can get."

Chafee turned to one of his agents and told him to get hold of phone company logs for Stoner's and Granton's calls.

DZ continued. "After they went aboard, the plane took off again at 6:18. Traffic control tracked it across the northeastern sector on a westward course."

Chafee glanced at one of several clock faces surrounding them. "Been in the air ninety minutes. What'd you get on present position?" Chafee looked at the men monitoring a bank of radar screens and monitoring devices.

"Nothing yet."

"Well, let's check it!" He stepped toward them.

"I did, Ken. They've *got* nothing! The plane just dropped off the screen."

Chafee spun back to her. "What do you mean—it crashed?"

"I'd guess Granton's plane is equipped somehow to confuse the radar."

"He flies a fucking stealth bomber?"

Gable joined them. "It's not that hard to slip the system," he said. "Turn off his transponder, put out a signal that mixes it up with other traffic. The guy's an electronics whiz, after all."

Leacock came sailing into the tower's windowed enclosure along with the first dep and a few uniforms. Chafee had warned DZ earlier he'd have to keep the commissioner advised: the airport was city territory. DZ knew the manpower she saw was only a fraction of the numbers fanning out over the airport.

Leacock pounced on her angrily. "Hayes! What the hell business do you have here? You're officially off—"

Chafee stopped him. "She had the news first, Commissioner, and called me in. Which is just one reason she belongs on the case as much as anyone else. If you won't order her back on duty, then I'll swear her into the Bureau on the spot."

DZ looked at the FBI man in open amazement. Field enlistment in the Bureau probably wasn't a real option, but if she was going to wind up with any credit for a capture, the commissioner didn't want the department missing out on a chunk of the glory. "Lieutenant," he said grimly, "you are hereby reinstated."

"With command of the Task Force, sir?"

He almost laughed. "Why not?"

She knew it barely existed anymore; yet having command status gave her the latitude to operate without seeking permission for every move.

"How do you want to work?" DZ said to Chafee.

"The Bureau will stay on trying to track the plane interstate. The rest is bloodhound stuff, see what we can turn up that indicates where Granton's headed. I'll put agents on that, too, but follow your nose, DZ. Just keep me in the picture so we don't cover the same ground." He gave her the phone number for his cell, and asked for hers. She'd left department issue in her desk, so she gave him Gable's.

Leacock was still there, glowering. Being diplomatic, DZ asked, "Procedure sound okay to you, Commissioner?"

"I don't give a rat's ass how you do it, Hayes. Just get some results this time." He turned to the first dep. "Let's get back to the city. It's still early enough for a press conference to make the midday news." They marched out.

● ● ●

THE MARINE TERMINAL OF LAGUARDIA HAD BEEN BUILT when transatlantic flights to what was then New York's only major airport were "Clippers" that took off and landed on the water. Set apart from the larger terminals that handled commercial flights, its runways now handled corporate traffic. DZ and Gable went there to interview the gate attendant who had seen four passengers board Granton's jet. A chunky woman in her mid-thirties, the attendant had recognized Stoner, and her description of two other two men, both lugging equipment boxes, indicated they must be the camera team. DZ asked for a description of the fourth man.

"Tall, nice-looking." the attendant said sparingly.

"Fat . . . thin . . . old . . . young?" DZ prodded.

"In good shape. Forties or fifties, maybe. I couldn't tell how old too well. He had on a baseball cap. Casual clothes, too. Slacks, leather jacket."

What any man might throw on when dressing in the middle of the night.

"Did you overhear any conversation between him and Mr. Stoner," Gable asked the attendant. "Maybe pick up a name . . . ?"

"No, Mr. Stoner and the other two were already aboard when the last man came. He jogged through the terminal pretty fast, it's lucky I could tell you as much as I did. He wasn't the one who got off again, either. . . ."

"Someone got off?" DZ said excitedly.

"One of the two men who arrived with Mr. Stoner. He came in from the plane carrying a little package, and went around that way." She pointed past a corner to a section of the terminal away from the gates. "He didn't have the package when he went back out to the plane. There's some lockers over there. . . ."

They called airport security. A man arrived within a few minutes with the master key and began opening the bank of several dozen coin-operated lockers, working in sequence according to the number stenciled on each locker.

Impatient, DZ pointed to one on a hunch. "Do that one next."

The security guard did as she asked. Curious, Gable walked over to reach into the metal chamber himself as soon as the door was unlocked. His hand emerged holding a rectangular package wrapped in plain brown paper. Written in ball point on the paper, as if hastily, were the words "Final Lesson." Another video, evidently.

"How'd you know where it was?" Gable said.

"My mind has started to work like his." The number on the locker she'd chosen was 20.

The nearest VCR was behind the bar in a lounge at the main terminal. Chafee came down from the tower to meet them, and his agents ordered all the people in the lounge to pick up their drinks and finish them in the public waiting area. Then they watched the video.

Straight into *What's My Line?* again, the panel of two men and two women with their blindfolds on, the dapper emcee in his tuxedo cheerfully issuing his familiar invitation: "Enter Mystery Guest, and sign in, please." The camera focused on the blackboard, a hand picking up a piece of chalk. The audience was heard wildly applauding and laughing. The hand scrawled on the blackboard.

Milton

The tape went black.

"That's it?" Chafee said, dismayed. "Worth shit as usual."

"Never," DZ said. "Not if we can figure it out."

"What the hell can you get from that?"

"*Paradise Lost,*" she said, the first thing that came to mind. Chafee and Gable looked at her blankly. She reached back for the college stuff. "John Milton, 17th century poet-philosopher—wrote *Paradise Lost*. That's Granton's message: we've fucked up the country, taken paradise, and lost it by ignoring justice."

"Who the hell is he to preach about justice?" Chafee said scornfully. "The country made him rich, he pays it back by murdering its citizens."

"His mother and father both ended up dead because their rights were ignored."

Gable suddenly swung his hand down on the flat of the bar with an explosive thwack that made the others jump. "*Berle!*" He shouted. "Milton . . . Berle! Didn't you hear the laughs? Berle the *comedian*! Don't you remember? Uncle Miltie. Number one star on TV when I was a kid— hell, the *only* star in those days."

No, they didn't remember: Gable was older than both DZ and Chafee by twenty years. If this went back to when he was a kid, it must be fifty years ago, the infancy of the new medium.

"How would Berle tie into this?" Chafee said.

"Every Tuesday, eight P.M.—for that hour he was on, everything stopped." Gable was drifting in recollection, but they let him, hoping for a meaning. "You'd hear the same sound coming from every house on the block with a TV. I mean, he was *it*. . . ." He chuckled. "Corniest slap-stick, blacked-out teeth, pies in the face. But you didn't care, because that was the beginning, seeing it right in your home. It was all new."

DZ kept waiting for an insight to stir. But the flow was broken by an agent who rushed up to Chafee bringing a fax.

Chafee scanned it. "Phone log from Stoner's apartment. Shows half a dozen calls to a Massachusetts number last night. . . ."

"Granton," DZ said.

"First few didn't last more than twenty seconds. Then, after midnight, there's one that goes half an hour, and an-other ten minutes later that lasts four minutes."

Easy profile: Granton hadn't been home early, but

Stoner kept trying until he got through. They made plans—Granton made his demands—and Stoner called back later with a quick okay.

Chafee handed the log to her. "Recognize these numbers?" He pointed to three in the same time frame as the Granton calls.

DZ knew two of them. Lori Swann at 1:52—telling her to go to the office and round up a camera crew. And her own number at 3:28—Stoner's apology. In between, and right before the last four-minute call to Granton was the third number. She couldn't identify it . . . but the area code was 203. Connecticut.

"Corcoran," she said. "He's the fourth passenger."

"Why would he get on that plane?" Chafee said.

"Because Granton *told* Stoner to get him—made it a condition. Corcoran represents the television establishment, the guys who set the standards."

"But the danger . . . the chances of the whole thing exploding," Gable said. "Why take the risk?"

"Because Stoner—" *Convinced him,* she was going to say, repeating her assertion that Stoner felt there was no risk. But the answer, she realized suddenly, was simpler. "Didn't tell him," she finished in an incredulous half whisper. For all her awareness of Stoner's ambition, she was stunned by how far he'd gone now to achieve his ends. "He didn't tell any of the people he brought along what it was really about. Stoner's the only one who knows they're flying with the killer. The only one who *will* know—until he's into his show. . . ."

"That incredible prick," Chafee muttered.

For another moment no one spoke. Granton's desire to include Corcoran was ominous.

Then Gable ruptured the silence. "Mister Television! Berle—that's what they used to call him! Because he was the only TV star at the time."

"Oh Jesus," Chafee hissed.

Because there was little doubt left about the way it

added up. It came back to Granton's loathing for the medium. His final victim would be the latter-day personification of the very thing he had both hated and used all his life. The force responsible for, as he'd said, making him and breaking him—Corcoran, a bad guy indeed to his way of thinking. In the twisted recess of his conscience, Granton might even feel Corcoran was the worst of the bad guys—for allowing him to succeed in his own scheme, for letting him become, in his own way and his own time, the new Mister Television.

CHAPTER
51

*I*T WAS ALMOST ten o'clock when a Justice Department jet flew in to collect the FBI contingent, DZ, and Gable. Military cooperation had been obtained an hour before, but even with the application of satellite cameras and an Air Force radar-tracking plane, Granton's flight path hadn't been detected.

"You know him best," Chafee said to DZ. "Where do you think he's headed?"

"Best guess? Back to where he was made." The traumatic beginnings of the killer's life had occurred in the West, she reminded her listeners, in New Mexico. And wasn't it from somewhere in that part of the country he'd made his first satellite transmission?

They had no better ideas.

Airborne, they remained in constant contact with air-control stations en route, and with military trackers as they came on-line. Two training jets from the Air National Guard were sent up—one each from bases in Tennessee and Texas—to roam in hopes of a visual sighting. Though even if Granton were on a course toward New Mexico, he could be thousands of feet above or below the searching aircraft, lost in cloud cover. Air traffic control said Granton's Gulfstream V jet was rated to fly at up to 52,000 feet. When land-based military trackers picked up a few stray aircraft within the search zone, they checked out as small private planes that had drifted off course and had filed incorrect flight plans. After two fruitless hours, the National Guard fliers were sent back to base.

"The search has to be widened," DZ told Chafee. "We need more planes."

"The Air Force won't scramble for a deal like this," Chafee said. "For all we know, Granton may already be back on the ground."

"At least, he can't kill anyone if he's busy flying that plane," Gable said.

"Ever hear of an autopilot?" Chafee said. "Those people could be dead already."

"No," DZ insisted. "He's safe until he's back on TV. Then he'll go for the big climax. He wants his audience to witness where their bloodthirst leads." DZ looked at her watch. "It's past one now, Stoner goes on at four. There's three hours before Granton sets down so Stoner can start broadcasting. Then it's anybody's guess how long we've got before things fall apart."

"But if Stoner broadcasts live," Gable said, "we don't have as much time as you think, DZ. Four P.M. in New York is two hours earlier in New Mexico.

Grimly Chafee said, "Then we're too far behind. It's too late to stop him."

DZ kept cool. "Not if we keep him off the air. Granton won't do anything without an audience."

"He's got hostages," Chafee argued. "He can threaten to start the killing unless the show goes on."

"We'll do what we do in any hostage situation. Stall and hope he caves." DZ kept to herself that from all she knew of Granton, he wasn't a man to lose a test of will.

Chafee hurried to the cockpit to radio the A.G. and make a plea for emergency orders to be issued for an all-out air search. When he came back, he could only report that his request was going up through channels. "Our pilot says we're still three hours out of Albuquerque. If you're wrong, DZ, if Granton's going anywhere beside the South-west, keeping our course will put us too far away from wherever he lands. . . ."

"Keep flying west," she said firmly. "He's going back to where it began."

If she was going to be the hostage negotiator, DZ knew, it could be handled at a distance—but not nearly so effec-tively as if she was on the scene, where Granton might even agree to meet with her. But whatever instincts might help her then, DZ felt she had to trust them now as well.

A stream of radio messages about search plans kept passing back and forth. At last a number of planes already scheduled for training flights from southwestern bases were ordered into the air to try for visual sightings of the maverick aircraft.

Thirty minutes later, the pilot's voice came over the cabin intercom. "Air Force has a sighting."

Chafee ran to the cockpit, DZ and Gable on his heels.

"Coordinates for the sighting puts him over Oklahoma on a path toward central New Mexico," the pilot said.

Chafee tipped a nod to DZ as he accepted the copilot's miked headset and began a one-on-one with the flier of an Air Force jet trainer who'd spotted the plane, and was trail-ing it. He started by making him read off the tail number. The pilot toggled a switch so the replies could be heard in the cockpit.

"How close are you now?" Chafee asked the Air Force pilot after confirming the number was Granton's Gulf-stream.

"A hundred feet off the starboard wing."

"Can you see into the cabin?"

"Not completely, just faces at the windows."

"How many?"

"Three on this side. I did a flyby on the other wing before and saw a fourth man."

"They give any indication of trouble, signal for help?"

"Negative. These three look asleep."

"Listen, Air Force," Chafee said. "Those passengers may not know it, but they're in big trouble. You've got to force that plane down."

"I know, sir. I've tried to make radio contact and relay that demand, but no dice. Flying his wing, I've also made eye contact with the pilot, and gave universal hand signals to land. He gave me a universal signal, too, sir—the kind that says he won't obey. I need another couple of planes with me before he can be forced down."

"Okay," Chafee snapped, "I'll get someone to order—"

"My wing commander has already sent up two more planes. They'll rendezvous in nine minutes."

Their own pilot altered course to intersect with Granton's jet at a point computed by the Air Force.

The radio buzzed with communications from Air Force wing commanders, the A.G.'s office, and Albuquerque Police, which had ordered a SWAT team to stand by at the local airport. As soon as cell phones were connected to area providers, Chafee started calls to Bureau field offices within the area they were flying over.

DZ stayed in the cockpit monitoring the radio. At any moment she expected the peace aboard Granton's jet to shatter. His passengers wouldn't continue quietly dozing when more Air Force planes appeared in the sky next to them, and began maneuvering to force him back to earth.

FOR THE FIRST LEG OF THE FLIGHT ABOARD ALEX GRANTON'S luxurious private jet, his passengers had thoroughly enjoyed the trip. The two men on the camera crew couldn't imagine a better gig; at Granton's invitation they helped themselves to the food and drink amply stocked in a galley aft of the main cabin outfitted as a luxurious living room and visited him in the cockpit to see his state-of-the-art avionics. Then they napped, catching up on sleep stolen by their predawn call from Lori Swann.

Meanwhile, Stoner's pleasure derived from imagining the drama he'd create when one of America's richest men had to respond to the accusation of multiple murder in front of millions of people—millions already primed to be sympathetic. That should make it easy for Granton to publicly admit his guilt. The supposition that Granton actually *wanted* to be caught had been confirmed when Stoner had phoned the billionaire, said he knew Granton was the prime suspect, and offered to put him on television to refute the charge. Granton had instantly accepted, his only conditions being that the show should be done from a place he selected, and that Corcoran accompany them.

Stoner felt only minor qualms at the guile he'd used to fulfill those conditions. The others were all in the same business, they'd understand his priorities, forgive him when it was over.

Corcoran was certainly no less thrilled to be included on the flight than the cameramen. He expressed no doubts about Stoner's explanation for summoning him to the airport: for his new "magazine" program Stoner wanted to profile Alex Granton and the elusive billionaire had agreed to be interviewed after a business meeting for which he was flying to the southwest. Stoner was going with him, and Granton had asked for Corcoran to come along.

"Why does he want me?" Corcoran had asked.

"I think he wants to discuss buying the network. . . ." Given the buyout talk that had been circulating on Wall Street and the billionaire's other investments in communications, Corcoran had no trouble believing it.

That seemed to satisfy Corcoran. He'd shaken hands with Granton when he boarded the plane, and while the billionaire went off to pilot the craft, Corcoran stretched out in one of the comfortable lounge chairs and caught up on his own interrupted sleep.

Then the fighter trainer had appeared flying alongside. Only Stoner wasn't dozing at the time. He rushed up to the cockpit. "What's going on?" he asked Granton.

"That's an Air Force trainer out there," Granton answered coolly. "He's here, I suppose, because somebody doesn't like the show we've planned; they want to force me down and arrest me."

Stoner knew at once what that meant: DZ had guessed what was happening and called out the cavalry.

"It doesn't matter through, Barry," Granton said, looking up from the controls and smiling. " I'm still delighted to do a final guest shot on your show . . . if that's what *you* want."

Stoner gazed back at him soberly. "That's what I want."

"Then keep the boys back there in their seats," Granton said. "I'll handle the rest."

ON THE GOVERNMENT JET, CONFIRMATION WAS RECEIVED that three Air Force planes were now shadowing Granton, and had begun the perilous maneuver to try forcing him down—a fighter on each wing, a third forward and above, descending gradually so Granton must cede altitude or collide with the plane over his nose. Then messages started coming over an open frequency from the three Air Force pilots reporting that Granton had descended several thousand feet. However he continued to ignore attempts at radio contact so it was impossible to be sure if he would submit to the landing point chosen by his escort—Cannon Air Force Base in New Mexico just across the Texas border.

During the maneuver, Chafee inquired if the passengers aboard the Gulfstream were still visible at the windows?

"Affirmative, sir," an Air Force pilot replied. "They're awake now."

"Any signals yet for help . . . ?

"Nothing like that. They're at the windows, but they just seem curious about what we're doing up here."

Stoner must still be withholding the truth, DZ thought. For all those men knew this military escort was . . . some sort of perk for a billionaire who'd made an extra large donation to the president's campaign.

Suddenly the calm voices of the three Air Force pilots erupted in a flurry of shouts and warnings:

"Whoa! What the—!" "Shit! Swing wide, Alpha one!" "Wingman, *fall back*!"

"What's happening?" Chafee shouted into his mike.

"He did a fast dive and roll. Came out of it okay, though."

"Lost control?" DZ said. Was there fighting in Granton's cockpit?

"Evasive action," came the answer. "Not easy in that plane, but this guy's very good. He's clear now, headed away from where we were trying to take him."

Another fighter pilot chimed in. "Better lay back."

So Granton wasn't going to submit. He might sooner cause a crash, and no one wanted to take the chance.

ABOARD THE GULFSTREAM, THE CALM RUPTURED WHEN THE plane went into a sudden steep dive, and banked sharply. The sound of the engines powered up to a whining roar, and the plane vibrated alarmingly. Like any passengers jolted by the unexpected during a flight, the cameramen were terrified.

Corcoran, his yachtsman's nerves conditioned by wild storms at sea, was less scared than angry. "What does this fucking cowboy think he's doing?" he railed at Stoner. He rose out of his seat, preparing to invade the cockpit.

Stoner held him back. "Leave him alone, Skip. If we were on a boat, you wouldn't want amateurs getting in the way."

The plane had leveled off now. Through a window

Stoner could see the Air Force jets banking away to trail at a safer distance. Granton's will wasn't going to be challenged. Not here, high in the sky.

Corcoran's eyes stayed on the Air Force jets. "What the fuck are they doing out there, anyway?"

"Maybe Granton asked for an escort. We've got a planeload of bigshots."

Corcoran gave Stoner a long look. Before another question could be asked, Stoner said, "Listen, he promised me an exclusive. Isn't that what counts?" Corcoran kept eyeing him. "Trust me, Skip," Stoner tacked on, "You'll love what it does for the network."

Finally Corcoran sank back into his seat. "I'd better."

The camera crew took their cue from the network chief. Jumpy as they were, they didn't ask any questions.

AS THE PATH OF THEIR PURSUIT PASSED OVER TEXAS, THE training jets exceeded their squadron boundaries and ran low on fuel, and their places were taken by other planes sent from Air Forces bases in Arizona and California. Eventually, there were five fully armed fighters hovering around the Gulfstream.

As it neared two o'clock, DZ wondered if Granton might explode once he had to accept that his plan was thwarted. Stoner, too, was a wild card: when he knew he'd missed his regular broadcast time, he'd have to start questioning his ability to control other events, realize the risks.

The voice of an Air Force flier emerged suddenly from the cockpit radio: "He's descending!" Granton's glide path, the flier said, would take him into Arizona for a probable landing at Tucson, three hundred miles beyond Albuquerque.

In another twenty minutes Granton and his escort were entering airspace near the Arizona city. From the hectic transmissions of the fliers with local air control, and radio traffic between Chafee and FBI units already preparing to move into position with police around Tucson's airport, it was certain a huge media circus would surround Granton's plane once it landed. Even now, it was beginning: the Air Force pilots reported a slew of helicopters crisscrossing the sky over the airport.

"Fucking news choppers are right in the glide path," one flier complained. "They'll get us all killed."

Angry transmissions to local air controllers resulted in the news helicopters being ordered to move far from the descending jets.

Suddenly, the steady drone of air control exchanges was interrupted by another shout: "He's going in!"

Additional transmissions clarified that Granton was in a steep angle of descent, though still a controlled glide, apparently intent on a quick landing.

The government's copilot pulled out a map. "If he lands now, there's only one place it could be." He glanced at DZ. "Sort of a weird place—might mean extra problems for you folks. "

"Why—where's he headed?" she said.

"Davis-Monthan Air Force Base."

"What's weird about it?"

"You'll see soon enough."

Surprising her once more with the breadth of his random knowledge, Gable said, "I've heard of Davis-Monthan. They call it the airplane graveyard."

WHEN THEY SAW THE SKIES AROUND THE GULFSTREAM growing more crowded, the two cameramen started hurling panicky remarks at Stoner. *Something's fucked up . . . what the hell's happening . . . this guy Granton's flying crazy. . . .*

"Enjoy the show, guys," Corcoran said, his outward confidence engendering relief. "Looks like we're coming in for a smooth landing. . . ."

As soon as the cameramen were distracted by what was

happening outside the windows, Corcoran moved to a seat beside Stoner. "Cut the shit now, Barry," he said in seething half-whisper, "What's this really about?"

They'd be landing soon, the truth would have to come out. "He's giving up," Stoner said.

"Giving up?"

"The M.G.," Stoner said. "To me—on the show."

Corcoran returned an uncomprehending stare. Then slowly his eyes began to dance, and his hand clutched Stoner's arm in an excited grip. "Sonofabitch," he declared happily, "you did it! Made the biggest get of all!"

It never occurred to Corcoran to ask again why he'd been brought along. It was going to be a moment of historic drama, a big payoff for the network: he simply assumed he belonged there.

CHAPTER
52

AS THEY CIRCLED before landing, DZ could see thousands upon thousands of planes, both military and commercial aircraft spread out over a vast flat plain, parked in long rows with just enough room between each one to taxi in or out of place.

"Why do they get sent to the airplane graveyard?" DZ asked the government pilot.

Many reasons, he said. Some were obsolete, no longer trustworthy but valuable as a source of parts. Many of the commercial craft belonged to bankrupt airlines. There were military bombers and fighters made redundant by the end of the Cold War, or the need of Washington's politicians to fill the pork barrel—keep plants in home states producing new planes that were no longer required.

Though DZ had never heard of Davis-Monthan, there was nothing secret about it's existence. In fact it was one of Arizona's busiest tourist sites. The public wasn't permitted to roam freely on the base, but regular bus tours left from a visitors center and traveled through the ocean of parked planes, making stops for customers to take photographs.

Today, though, at shortly after two o'clock the tours had been abruptly suspended.

BY THE TIME DZ WAS OVERHEAD, GRANTON'S JET HAD BEEN on the ground forty minutes. Monitoring the situation by radio, DZ had heard each move Granton made from the time he signaled his clear intention to land at the Air Force base by flying over it in steadily descending circles. A main runway had been cleared for him, but Air Force vehicles were moved onto the runway at intervals to block the plane's path and bring it to a halt. Once he was down, however, Granton had successfully played a game of "chicken," taxiing along the sprawling web of runways, forcing the blocking vehicles to be pulled back, one after another, rather than cause an explosive collision.

Granton finally pulled his jet into an open slot in a section occupied by scores of huge B-52 bombers, ghosts of the air armada that had once rained bombs endlessly on Southeast Asia.

Then the standoff began. Cars from local and state police joined Air Force armored vehicles in surrounding Granton's plane, filling every space under the wings of adjacent B-52s. Loudspeakers were set up through which the authorities broadcast appeals for Granton to surrender, while efforts continued to elicit a response from him over the radio.

For half an hour his plane sat in the desert sun. There was no sign at all of what was happening aboard, no faces at any window. Given the risks to his passengers—now officially reclassified as hostages—it was agreed there should be no immediate attempt to attack or board the plane. But a squad of the Army's Delta Force commandoes, specially trained to deal with airplane hijack situations, was summoned from a base in California and were now en route. Meanwhile, technicians from both the Air Force and FBI assembled an arsenal of high-tech antiterrorist devices—ultra-sensitive heat and sounds sensors and X-ray cameras—that, when attached to the fuselage of Granton's plane, would make it possible to track what was happening within.

As the Justice Department was on its landing approach, Chafee was on the radio with the Air Force brigadier general in charge of the base urging him to allow Police Lieutenant DZ Hayes to take the lead in hostage negotiations.

The Air Force brigadier had not instantly embraced the idea; he preferred to handle hostage negotiations himself. "It's no easy thing to talk this guy out. We need someone strong in this situation."

An FBI officer from the FBI's field station in Tucson was monitoring the conversation, too, and chimed in. "I saw Hayes dealing with this guy on TV," he said, "and he ran rings around her. If that happens here, it'll be a slaughter."

Chafee continued to stand up for DZ. "Nobody can deal with him as well as Hayes," he insisted. "She can get inside his head. She knows the way his mind works."

Finally, the base commander yielded, though he reserved the right to step in and issue new orders if he saw the situation deteriorating.

"Okay, let the lady carry the ball," the man from the local FBI said. "But if she drops it, Chafee, it'll be your ass, not mine."

EVEN BEFORE LANDING, DZ LAUNCHED HER OWN ATTEMPT to make radio contact with Granton. She began by steadily, gently urging Granton to respond:

"Mr. Granton, this is DZ Hayes. You can see your situation is hopeless now. Let's end this without anyone else getting hurt. . . . Alex, I know you're listening. Face it, there's nothing to be gained by going on with this. . . ."

But was he listening? Did he care what pleas were made in the name of saving bloodshed? The receiver remained silent. Finally, to goad a reply, DZ took the risk of inflaming him. "Check the clock, Alex. Showtime came and went. There's no point to it, anymore. You hear me? The show's over."

At last his voice came back. "Wrong, DZ. The show goes on. There's just a new schedule."

Okay! At least she'd made contact. "Alex, the people you've got there, they're not like the others you . . . you settled with. Let them go, and you've still—"

"Where are you, DZ?" he broke in, though with that same amiable tone that had become so familiar. "I'm at my window, and all I can see are men with guns."

The rule in hostage negotiation was to keep the exchange relaxed. So she answered his question. "I'm not there yet, Alex. But I'm on my way."

"Fine. So let's talk when you get here." He cut the contact.

DZ left the cockpit. No sense staying by the radio, she knew. As in everything else that had happened right from the beginning, he'd follow through exactly the way he said.

THE COMMAND POST WAS SET UP IN THE SHADOW OF THE massive wing of the B-52 alongside Granton's jet. Air Force field radios, satellite dishes, high-sensitivity listening devices and monitor screens were brought out from base offices and stacked on metal desks and counters. Air Force technicians vigilantly monitored screens and phone lines as they became active, maintaining contact with various elements of the operation—the director of the FBI, the Delta Force contingent flying in from the West, even the White House, which had asked to be kept advised. Some monitor screens displayed views of Granton's jet from different quadrants; others were tuned to television channels showing the news coverage, including shots from news helicopters flying over and camera crews camped at the guarded entrance to the base.

As soon as Chafee, DZ, and Gable climbed out of the Air Force Humvee that brought them to the command post from their landing point, they were met by the local FBI field man. He reported that all was quiet.

"We get a look inside?" Chafee asked.

The agent shook his head. "Not yet. Nobody's gone near the aircraft to plant the sensors. We don't want to provoke a shot."

Sensible procedure, DZ thought, though she was sure Granton wouldn't start an exchange of gunfire with anyone outside the plane.

"You ready?" Chafee said to DZ.

She nodded, and the other agent led her over to one of the radio consoles. A technician who was seated in front of it vacated his chair, and gave her his headset.

DZ sat down, and swiveled the mike over her mouth. "Okay, Alex, I've arrived at the party. Can you see me now?"

The voice that burst from the receiver wasn't Granton's—not cool and controlled, but breathless, pleading. "DZ, listen! Do what he wants, and everything will work out. You understand? Don't try anything else. . . ."

"Barry?" DZ demanded,

"Yeah."

"Where's Granton?"

"Right here," Stoner answered. "But he wants me to do the talking."

Successful hostage negotiations rarely went through third parties. "I want *him*!"

There was a moment's pause. "He says no. Listen, DZ, he's got a gun—a couple of them—but no one's been hurt. No one will be, he says—if we all do what he wants."

"And what is that, Barry?" she asked.

"To go on the air. With me, same as usual."

She asked the question, even though she knew the answer "And if we won't let him?"

"Corcoran's here—"

"I know that."

"If we don't go along, he'll kill Corcoran."

Granton needed someone's life in the balance, DZ understood; it couldn't be Stoner or the cameramen, not if he wanted the show to go on. In the pause, Chafee leaned in close to whisper in her ear, "Just keep him talking." He pointed to a group of men scuttling across the runway in a wide arc to approach the Gulfstream from the tail. Some had loops of wire over their shoulders that trailed back to monitors at the command center. They were going to place the sensors.

Stoner spoke again, his voice edgy, begging an answer. "He means it, DZ. You've got to let him do the show. Once more, then he'll give himself up."

Sure, turning himself over in the end had always been part of his design. But it wouldn't stop him from killing once more. That wasn't knowledge she could share with Stoner, however.

Still, she had to drag it out, play for time. "Let me hear it straight from Granton," DZ insisted. "I've got to be sure he'll keep his word."

"Alex says no. You've got the terms. . . ."

"Give me Corcoran, then, so I can hear how he feels about it." Maybe she could think of a way to signal him he was the one most in danger.

"You don't need Corcoran. You know it's a go for him. It was *always* a go." DZ capped the microphone with her palm and tossed a questioning look at Chafee. How did they spin this out? Chafee glanced over at the Gulfstream, the men spaced out along the underside of the jet placing the magnetic sound and heat sensors.

"Tell him they'll go on the air at the top of the next hour," he said to DZ.

It was twenty minutes past two o'clock now—4:20

Eastern. Delaying forty more minutes allowed time for information from the sensors to be analyzed, and by then the Delta Force commandoes would be here, the plane could be stormed.

She uncovered the mike. "All right, Barry. Granton can do the show on the hour."

There was a momentary silence, Stoner apparently relaying the deal.

Stoner came back. "Five minutes. We go on in five minutes or—"

"Hey," DZ broke in, improvising, "it takes time to get the network in line, do the hookups. You all know that."

"DZ, we've got TV on board. We can see every network is covering the stand-off right this minute, including GBS. They'll grab a live feed from the plane the second it's available—and it's fully equipped to transmit. Just plug us in."

Of course! Granton must have done all his transmissions from the plane. DZ glanced again to Chafee, but this time she couldn't catch his eye: his attention was riveted on a group of monitors now aglow with images from the sensors. By reading emanations of body heat inside the plane, the sensors sketched the movements of people aboard in vivid shades of color—red for the hottest points, blue for the coolest. Inanimate objects came across as neutral gray. The pictures clearly showed that the five wavering human shapes were all seated, one facing the other four.

"DZ," Stoner pleaded, "No stalling. Granton's giving you five minutes. Or he starts killing."

"Bullshit!" Gable exploded suddenly.

DZ threw a hand over the mike and whirled to glare at him. If Granton had overheard that, the confrontational heat could wreck their negotiation.

"Well, look!" Gable gestured to sensor images on a monitor. "Look at what's happening in there." He stabbed a finger at a monitor screen. "Look carefully."

DZ rose from her chair to take a closer look. She studied the five multicolored figures a second. One of them had his arm crooked, a hand beside his head holding a dull gray rodlike shape—Stoner, obviously, holding the telephone. The other four, including one facing the others, sat with their hands in their laps or propping up their chins. *Not one seemed to be holding a gun.*

"They're just playing along!" Chafee said. "There's no threat at all to these guys. Corcoran and Stoner want this big finale as much as the M.G."

And Granton didn't need a gun to make the other two guys cooperate, DZ thought. He had a better form of persuasion—a few billion of them, in fact.

"That doesn't mean they're not in danger," she said. "Granton'll make all kinds of promises, but if he wants to kill Corcoran in the end, he'll do it."

"All right then," Chafee relented, "so then let him have his way. He can do the show then turn himself in."

"You don't get it!" DZ erupted. "What he's really angling for is to commit the last murder on the air."

"Corcoran," Gable said. "Mr. Television."

Chafee glanced for a few seconds to the image of the men sitting passively in the plane. He turned to DZ, and hesitated, biting his lip. "Your call," he said finally. "I've advertised you as the one with the answers."

She had only one idea that might change the odds a little. "My call . . . ?" she said, wanting it doubly confirmed. Chafee nodded. DZ called sharply into her microphone: "Stoner!"

"Here!"

"Granton, you listen, too! You can do your show. But here's *my* condition: I'm part of it. You let me in there with you."

Gable grabbed her "No—"

"You can't," Chaffee said. "You'll be right in the line of fire! His . . . and ours."

"You said it was my call," she reminded them.

A voice came through the speaker, not Stoner's this time. "I'd love to have you be *my* guest this time, DZ."

Granton. She wasn't surprised he'd gone for it. Being able to play out his scheme right in front of her would make the climax even more of a victory.

And, of course, better television.

CHAPTER
53

*T*HE LIFT-TRUCK PLATFORM was raised to the side door of the plane. DZ stood alone at the center of it, arms at her sides, wearing only blouse and skirt—showing clearly that she was unarmed—all exactly as Granton had dictated.

The platform reached the height of the rear door on the Gulfstream jet, and it opened, just a crack, enough for her to slip through. The truck backed away quickly. Everything was being done in a rush, hewing to the five-minute deadline Granton had demanded.

She expected to be received at the door by Granton, but it was another man who stood just inside, about fifty with a florid complexion and hair already gone white. One of the camera crew. "Who are you?" she asked.

"Steve Palmer. I'm handling the camera."

She gave him a quick once-over. His life might be in the hands of a multiple killer, but there wasn't a drop of sweat, not a sign of the shakes. Nor was anybody holding a gun on him to make sure he didn't take a leap for freedom as soon as he was by the door.

He started leading her quickly to the rear of the plane,

but she clapped a hand on his shoulder and held him back. "How much?" she said.

He stopped and looked at her, but didn't reply.

"Listen," DZ went on, "it doesn't matter how much he pays you. You help him willingly, and whatever goes down today you'll be charged as an accessory."

That opened him up. "Three million," he said. "Three million bucks—just to hold a camera on him for an hour. Same for my sound guy. Pulled out bank checks and filled in our names."

Like a good Boy Scout, DZ thought, Granton was fully prepared.

The cameraman shook his head in wonder. "In twenty years we couldn't put away that much. You think it isn't worth the risk? He's got the gun, I'm just holding a camera. . . ."

So for six million dollars Granton had turned two ordinary, law-abiding guys into his loyal sidekicks. The way he'd turned millions into fans in exchange for a few thrills. "You're not worried he'd kill you rather than let you cash the check?" she asked.

"Why should he? That kind of dough is shit to him."

True. What did the payment really set Granton back? Three days worth of interest on his billions, four days at most?

"And he swore to us he'll give himself up after the show," Palmer added. "There's something about this guy, you know you can believe him."

She had to go along with that, too. He always did exactly what he said: in its own screwed-up way, it was a code of honor. What he hadn't told his hostages, though, was his other plans, *before* he gave himself up—what he planned to do during his last time on the air. But DZ didn't give the game away. It was important to keep things calm.

They continued back to the plane's tail compartment, a cabin with gray walls—the studio from which the M.G.

had done all his broadcasts. Four gray club chairs were spaced out in a line, occupied as Granton had commanded—himself at the left-most end, Stoner to his right, then Corcoran. The chair beside Corcoran was vacant, at the opposite end of the lineup from Granton.

No hokey M.G. costume today. He was dressed casually in dark slacks and a pale blue jersey covered with a loose, dark blue cardigan concealing the compact automatic wedged under his belt; he looked no more threatening than any movie star on a talk show to publicize his latest film. The H&H .700 was propped upright against the side of his chair, the line of its dark barrel almost lost in shadow, but within his easy reach.

DZ noted the transmitting equipment in the compartment. Outside, she had seen the parabolic satellite dish rising hydraulically from the upper fuselage. The walls of this rear compartment were inset with a dozen monitors positioned for Granton to watch easily. One was tuned to receive Stoner's program, the others were showing the hostage standoff as it was being telecast right now by every other major network, conventional and cable. Press were being kept off the base, but long-range lenses caught views of the plane shimmering in the heat waves coming off the tarmac, surrounded by military armored vehicles, police cars, SWAT teams, and squads of armed soldiers.

"Take a seat, DZ," Granton said amiably, waving her to the empty chair. "We'll be on the air any second."

She obeyed without protest. She knew what had to be accomplished, had even formed the idea of how it might be done, but the moment hadn't come yet to make her move. It wouldn't work unless she had an audience—the same one that Granton thought he owned.

The camera- and soundman went about their jobs as calmly and efficiently as if they were safely at work in a network studio, neither showing any sign of nerves. In preparation for the broadcast, the soundman's headset was connected to a phone line through which he was in contact with an engineer and a director at GBS's Sat-Center in New York. Their signal that the feed was about to get patched into the network came through now, and the sound man relayed the message.

"Ten seconds to air. . . ."

DZ looked along the row at the others—Corcoran . . . Stoner . . . Granton. Corcoran simply looked pleased, knowing that GBS probably had nineteen out of every twenty people who were watching TV at this moment tuned to his station (and those who weren't tuned in were probably all under seven years old). Stoner caught DZ watching him and returned a tiny shrug that mimed "it's all in the game."

And Granton smiled at her, that goddamned charming smile, all the more evil because you couldn't detect anything in it but plain, unalloyed pleasantness.

The soundman had raised a fist, and he lifted the fingers on that hand one at a time as he ticked off the final seconds. "Five . . . four . . . three . . . two . . . one. . . ." His hand swung down like a starter's flag sending a slew of race cars hurtling down the track.

For the opening, Stoner had instructed the cameraman to pan quickly around the plane cabin, settle on him, then pan with him wherever he went. As the camera came around to him, Stoner rose from his chair and went to look out one of the plane windows. The cameraman widened the angle to take in Stoner's view—the siege as seen by the besieged.

"If you're being held hostage in an airplane by the most wanted man in the world," Stoner began, "that's what you see when you look out your window." A glance toward his audience. "Echoes of Waco. If your captor doesn't blow you away, your rescuers might." His level tone emphasized his own heroic lack of terror.

Stoner moved back to the row of chairs, camera panning with him to take in the others seated there, DZ and the two men. He rested his gaze on Granton a second, but said nothing about him. DZ guessed Stoner must have outlined his plans for the show to Granton before she came aboard, and Granton had given his okay.

"Before anything else," Stoner continued, "let me explain how this situation developed. You probably recognize Lieutenant Hayes sitting here; she was the lead investigator in the Mystery Guest killings until she dared to come on my program—and got fired off the case. Well, Lieutenant Hayes didn't give up after that. On her own, she found evidence pointing to the identity of the man we've been hunting for, and brought the information to me." Stoner stepped back to give the camera a clear line to the nearest chair. "And here's the man. His name is Alex Granton. An entrepreneur, a financier, one of the wealthiest men in the country, though you may never have heard of him until now. When I called Mr. Granton and told him the lieutenant's suspicions, an amazing thing happened. He denied nothing. He asked instead for this chance to come on my program . . . and talk to all of you." Stoner looked squarely into the camera. "But his idea for this appearance was a little different than the way it turned out. He'd hoped to bring me back to where he grew up; he thought it would help to explain where his feeling, his *need* to do what he's done was born. He believes that you—all of you out there—would like to know the reasons. Because a lot of crazy things have been happening in this country lately, strange outbreaks of violence, even from the kids, and maybe it would help to understand how these things happen. . . ." Stoner resumed his own chair. "Unfortunately, we didn't get to go where he wanted. As you see, our flight was . . . diverted." Stoner turned and laid a friendly hand on Corcoran's arm. "Mr. Granton's one other request was for this gentleman to accompany us. This is Edward Corcoran, head of the network that broadcasts my show. . . ."

It went on in that tone. Stoner on his talk show, covering a subject that might be bigger news than he'd ever covered before, more immediate than anything else he'd ever talked about—right in the middle of happening, rather than something that had happened last week, or yesterday—but all still talked about in a "business as usual" tone that would have seemed surreal except this was not so different than what his audience was used to by now. Not much more surreal than hearing ordinary people discuss their most private business.

And at last, after introducing Corcoran, Stoner began his chat with Alex Granton, conducting the kind of interview he'd done thousands of times on his show—with celebrities, and political hopefuls, and people elevated to momentary national attention by a news story. Stoner didn't go for a hard-driving expose that condemned Granton for his crimes, but a gentle probing of a man's complicated mind, the kind of concerned exploration of motives that Stoner would have done if this were his own brother, resurrected for one more chance to understand . . . and forgive. Granton was encouraged to go back through his earliest childhood memories and their effect on him, to talk about the brutalities inflicted upon his father under a Nazi dictatorship, the injustices that racism in America had visited upon his Native American mother—culminating in her brutal murder.

DZ looked on. Her aim was to keep the situation calm and wait for her moment. Listening as Stoner sympathetically questioned why and how a man of such wealth and success would undertake such a strangely conceived campaign of terror, she could almost forget the Mystery Guest's murders had been committed in cold blood, not self-defense.

From exploring Granton's past, Stoner shifted into discussing the immediate present. By now the reasons behind the killer's choice of victims was clear, but Stoner explored with him such peculiar specifics as the connection that had been made to the old game show, *What's My Line?*

"At the very time my father went berserk," Granton answered, "that happened to be the show I was watching. I was very young, but that stuck in my mind. And people like a puzzle, don't they? I guess . . . I used it to help keep them involved."

Whether Stoner meant to or not, everything he asked seemed to humanize Granton more, make it harder to see him as an enemy of society, more easily as its victim. Several times DZ had an urge to intrude into this all-too-normal exchange of chat, to remind Stoner and his audience that he was talking to a man guilty of multiple *murders*! But she suppressed the urge and sat quietly. Her guiding principle remained the same: let the time spin out, don't rock the boat if it looks like it might drift safely into harbor. It was beginning to seem possible that after Granton had been able to tell his side—have his day in the court of public opinion—he might even give himself up quietly.

But then things took an ominous turn. DZ saw it happening as soon as Granton ended his one-on-one with Stoner and addressed Corcoran:

"Of course none of what I've done would have been possible," Granton said as if simply saying thanks on Oscar night, "if I didn't have the help and support of Mr. Corcoran. I had to wonder myself sometimes why he was so generous with the time he gave me." Granton focused on the television executive. "Tell me, Skip—they call you Skip, don't they—why did you do it? I mean, after the first time or two when it was up to Barry, it was your call. Why did you let me go on?"

"You know why," Corcoran answered. "Because it's news."

Granton nodded and turned to the camera. "You see, folks?" he said to the unseen millions on the other side of the lens. "That's how rotten it's all become. It doesn't matter how obscenely anyone behaves, they'll put it on, right here in front of you. And do you look at the news because you care what's going on in the world? Or just to get a charge? You know the answer—sure, you all do. As long as you're not bored by what you see, it doesn't matter anymore what's put in front of you. There's no limit anymore. Whatever it is, they'll show it, and you'll lap it up. Right? There's no . . . no more. . . ." He fumbled a moment, then looked away from the camera. "In the end, you see, that's why everything falls apart."

He stopped and looked away, as if listening to an inner voice, or reliving the moments long ago when he had been transformed from an innocent child to a soul twisted into extracting his own idea of justice from all who had deprived him of that innocence, that simple happiness. For just this moment the hard glitter of his arrogance and certainty was absent, and DZ believed she could see instead some vulnerability. The magic shield of his incredibly massive wealth had been set aside; he was simply a man in need of direction, balanced on the edge, perhaps ready to topple with only the slightest push.

Her time had come. Time to bring out the only weapon he'd let her keep. Time to do her own talking.

"So you think they're with you, Alex . . . ?" she waved toward the camera, the keyhole to the world. "Because you gave them what they want, you think the people out there are on your side, ready to go where you go, let you kill whoever you want?"

He came back from his thoughts. He looked at her, and gave her the smile.

"They're watching, DZ. They're all out there watching. They don't have to be any more with me than that."

More or less what she'd guess he would say. And it gave her the opening she was trolling for. "Right," she said. "If they didn't watch, there'd be no point, would there? None of it would have happened, if you'd never had an audience. . . ." She glanced at Stoner. "If he hadn't been willing to give you your guest shot." Then at Corcoran. "Or maybe you'd have stopped sooner, if Mr. Corcoran hadn't been so eager to play it to the hilt. . . ."

"If. Maybe." Corcoran echoed. "The thing is, DZ, they were. I always knew they would be. "

"Sure," she said. "The way you know just how it plays out from here, the way you know what *they* want. . . ." Her arm swept toward the camera, the unseen sea of humanity beyond the lens.

He studied her silently for two or three seconds, knowing she was angling for something and trying to puzzle it out. Then she saw the glimmer of comprehension in his eyes, and almost at once he reached quickly over his shoulder to grab the barrel of the rifle leaning against his chair and pull the weapon across his body into his lap. Flipping it around, pointed it at Stoner. Everyone froze.

"Wait, Alex!" DZ shouted by reflex, her careful plan derailed for the moment.

"Wait for what, Lieutenant?"

"Until you can be sure they're with you," she said.

He hesitated another second.

"I'm already sure," he said then and quickly extended his arms, moving the gun toward Stoner.

DZ's muscles contracted as she calculated how far she'd need to leap to grab the gun—or throw herself against it and deflect the angle of fire. It seemed he wasn't going to give her the chance to talk, only to act.

Then she saw that Granton had one hand on the stock of the rifle, and the other placed slightly ahead of the trigger guard. His finger wasn't on the trigger.

"Take it!" Granton commanded, holding the gun within Stoner's reach.

Stoner gazed back uncertainly.

"Go ahead!" Corcoran urged. "He's giving up."

Stoner glanced to DZ. It took her a moment to decide how to respond. Granton was still dangerous, but she saw that his finger remained off the trigger of the rifle and gave an approving nod. Stoner took hold of the weapon.

Granton said mildly, "Don't be afraid, Barry, it's not loaded. This one is, though." With another deft move he swept the pistol from under his sweater, and pointed it to his right. Because of the way the chairs were arranged, his aim targeted not only Stoner but, with a fractional adjustment, Corcoran and DZ. "So just do what I tell you. Please."

DZ shot a glance at Palmer, the cameraman, then the monitors. She could see Palmer was following it all, the network was still carrying the picture. The millions were still watching. "Why'd you give him the rifle?" she asked Granton.

"Mr. Stoner wants to know all about my crimes—that's his job. So I thought he'd like to feel what it's like to hold the murder weapon."

Reminded of the lives it had taken, Stoner gave a deliberately revolted glance at the expensive gun in his hands. But he stayed with his job. "It's quite a weapon," he said. "I'd say it was beautiful—if I didn't know the horrible things you'd done with it."

"I used it to exact justice," Granton said. "Is that so terrible? Now, Barry, you're always so interested in the experiences of your guests, try lifting that gun, see what it feels like to aim it at a living target."

Stoner hesitated, confused.

"Go on," Granton said. "Aim it here." He tapped his chest. "At me."

"You said it's not loaded."

"It's not. Aim it at me and pull the trigger. See what it's like."

Stoner checked DZ with a glance again. She didn't know what to advise. Was Granton going to commit suicide by proxy on the air—turn Stoner into a murderer?

Anything was possible. But all right, let it play. A better end than many she could imagine, perhaps more certain than the one she'd planned.

In the absence of any direction from DZ, Stoner lifted the rifle slowly, fitted the stock to his shoulder, and pointed the barrel at Granton.

DZ was aware of the instrument on the cameraman's shoulders no longer holding so steady, the picture that was being transmitted jiggling. It only added to the reality, the tension.

"Pull the trigger!" Granton commanded impatiently.

Stoner hesitated.

"Pull it." Granton said very quietly but deliberately, lifting the pistol he held slightly.

Stoner squeezed his finger on the trigger.

There was a muted click as the firing mechanism fell on an empty chamber.

Stoner lowered the rifle, drained.

DZ saw Corcoran looking both pleased and relieved. Great stuff, he was probably thinking. "Alex, for god's sake," DZ burst out. "No more!"

"Shut up!" he barked at her. Shocking because they were the first words he'd ever spoken so viciously. The hand that wasn't holding the pistol slipped into a pocket of his cardigan, and he pulled out a gleaming brass cylinder about twice the length of a lipstick tube tipped with a silver point. "Catch," he said, tossing the bullet at Stoner.

One hand still gripping the rifle, Stoner made a reflex catch with the other.

"Load it," Granton said.

DZ saw where it was going now. "Barry! Don't!."

"Load it, Barry," Granton repeated. "Right now! Or I'll kill you."

Stoner gave DZ, a wild, helpless glance.

Last chance to play her card, DZ thought. She stood up suddenly. Her quick move caused Granton to swivel the gun toward her, and DZ held her breath, afraid he might shoot before he realized she wasn't going for him, had stood only to distract him.

"Let's test it," she said. "If you're so sure they're with you, you shouldn't mind. Or are you afraid, Alex?"

He knew what she meant, as he'd understood before when she'd asked him to wait. He paused another second, then smiled. "Okay, DZ," he said. "That's your big play? You're on."

She looked straight at the camera, and waited until she could see that from the monitor that the cameraman was holding steady again, and the audience was hers alone. "You heard him," DZ declared. "He believes you're all in it with him, says he wouldn't do it if you weren't there to watch it, cheer him on. And as long as you are, I'd have to agree: you don't have to be here . . . you don't have to be within two thousand miles of here . . . you're all in on the act, part of it, accessories. No fingerprints, but you're helping to pull the trigger. Because that's what he believes," she glanced to Granton, "and so far he's been right. But you can change it now. In a moment, with one quick decision, a flip of the switch. Just turn it off. Turn *him* off!" DZ glared into the camera, perceiving in a way she never had before that looking into that glass she was looking into the eyes of millions, deep into their eyes, into their minds, not only collectively, but one-by-one. "For god's sake, just do it. Switch it off and do anything but watch this murderer. Vacuum the house, go back to your desks, go to the park and play with your kids. Just turn off the damn picture, and you'll be helping to end this craziness."

She took a breath as if to add something. But there was nothing more to be said.

And all that came back from her audience, of course, was—could be—silence.

It was broken by Granton. "Nice sermon, DZ. But what the hell were you hoping for? How would we ever know if even one in a thousand paid any attention to you? There's no call-in here, no way to see out that far—only in."

What had she hoped? That she could simply make him believe she'd gotten through to his audience, changed their minds?

"So," he went on, "where was I? Oh yes . . ." He turned back to Stoner.

During DZ's appeal, Stoner hadn't moved. He still held the bullet in one hand, the rifle in the other.

"I want you to be able to explain it all to your audience, Barry," Granton said, "to know what it's like. So aim the gun again—no, not at me, at *him*." He nodded at Corcoran.

"What the—?" Corcoran exclaimed.

But Granton cut him off. "Aim and then load, Barry. And pull the trigger."

DZ was calculating feverishly. Could she jump fast and far enough to wrest the pistol from Granton?

Stoner hadn't moved.

"I'll count to five, Barry. If you haven't done what I've asked, then I'll kill you." He gestured to the camera, the audience. "They're waiting, and they've got to see someone die." He flashed a grin at Corcoran. "Good for the ratings, right Skip?"

Corcoran was sitting rigid in his chair, paralyzed with apprehenson.

"One . . ." Granton began his count, and aimed his gun at Stoner's head. "Two . . ."

Stoner lifted the rifle and aimed it at Corcoran.

"For god's sake! Barry! " Corcoran roared.

"Three . . ."

Stoner pulled the bolt, and fitted the bullet.

As he did, DZ saw a change come over Stoner. In an instant the nervous reluctance was gone, and he seemed resigned to his task. And then she realized it wasn't merely resignation, but readiness, even a reckoning with the desire to understand what made a man a murderer. He longed to take this final step toward comprehending the savage human urge that had destroyed his own family.

"Four . . ." Granton intoned.

And Stoner slipped the bullet into the chamber and threw the bolt.

Corcoran had gone from panic to defiance. "You couldn't," he said to Stoner. "You *won't*!"

But he would, DZ knew, any second. She cast her eyes

around wildly to take in every factor in the equation, preparing to move. And in the last fractional moment of her survey, her eye caught the bank of monitors.

"Look," she said quietly, afraid a loud outcry might startle Stoner into pulling the trigger.

The others turned to her, and she pointed to the monitors.

There were several showing pictures from local stations, CNN, networks other than GBS. Locked out of GBS's exclusive broadcast from within the plane, they could only cover other angles of the story.

And the one that almost all were covering now, as it unfolded, was obviously the response to DZ's appeal. Still gathering momentum, yet transpiring rapidly since it could only have begun ten minutes ago, people were shown in processions through their neighborhoods—some carrying hastily lettered placards with slogans like NO MORE and I SWITCHED OFF—and gathering on street corners, in parks. TV news reporters were interviewing them, obviously taking comments that denounced Granton. One live news report was showing a group of people on a suburban lawn heaping television sets onto a bonfire.

"There's your answer, Alex," DZ said. "They've had enough. We agreed there was no point if they wouldn't watch."

Granton stared at the monitors for a long moment. Then he looked at DZ.

"Give it up," she said. And held out her hand for his gun.

But he just smiled. "That's only a small part of my audience," he said, and began to turn back to Stoner.

Without another thought, she leapt at him. As she did, she saw Stoner start to spin around—turning his aim from Corcoran, to fire on Granton. But her move impeded his, put her in the line of fire. She tried as she hurtled ahead to dodge to the left, give him a clearer field—

The explosive report of the shot split the air. Some-

where close. Very close. She searched her senses for pain,
felt none, and in the next second the trajectory of her leap
had propelled her into Stoner, her hands forward, catching
the rifle to push it aside, as she knocked him backward
into the chair, the chair toppling so they both fell, DZ on
top. As they thumped onto the floor, DZ thought she heard
a second shot, but she wasn't sure. Rolling off Stoner, she
grabbed up the rifle and pulled her knees under her,
crouching behind the fallen chair for cover as she tried to
focus on the scene in front of her.

The first thing she saw was the TV camera, lying on the
floor nearby. The cameraman . . . ! She saw him then,
pressed against a window, but not shot. When she jumped,
he'd acted to save himself. The soundman was at his side.
The realization streaked through her mind that evidence—
the pictures—had been lost.

Then her eyes switched to Granton. He was standing in
the same place as before, but in a posture of surrender,
arms hanging at his side. His eyes weren't aimed at her,
but at the chair where Corcoran sat.

Corcoran was slumped over, dead from the two shots
Granton had fired, one into his cheek, the other above his
left eye. DZ pointed the rifle at Granton. He dropped his
gun and raised his hands in the air.

Barely a second later, the huge explosion blasted them
all off their feet, and the fuselage burst open. Sunlight
poured in along with a haze of dust and smoke. A crowd
of shadowy figures suddenly filled the space around
them.

Too late to save any lives, but not too late to make a
good show. As the smoke dissipated and she picked herself up off the floor, DZ saw that the cameraman had retrieved his camera to record the scene of Alex Granton
being cuffed by Chafee and a couple of his agents.

Granton saw her watching. Just before he was pulled
away by the soldiers, he gave her one more of his slow,
pleasant smiles. It told her in no uncertain terms that he

was content, fulfilled, exactly where he wanted to be. He had the trial to look forward to now, hours and hours and hours of time on camera, in the spotlight.

A chance to put human nature to the test all over again.

CHAPTER
54

S HE COULDN'T WAIT to leave it all behind, the reporters bugging her at all hours, paparazzi camped outside her door. She went to the office just once more, to leave the formal letter of resignation.

Until the day the phone was disconnected it never stopped ringing. Offers to be interviewed, to write a book, sell the rights to her story for a movie, a television movie. That California agent, Barsky, called: a big syndicator was developing a show called *Public Enemies* to compete with *America's Most Wanted*. They'd pay her at least ten thou a week to front it.

Let others cash in on what Granton had done. DZ wanted no part of it. She only hoped a time would come when people could look at her and see her only as a woman, their neighbor, not forever as a character in the bloody drama concocted by a monster of arrogance and wealth.

The call from the first dep was the one she minded most. Scouting for the commissioner, who wanted to tender a peace offering but knew she wouldn't listen until the path was smoothed. The idea was to give her a medal—in a public ceremony, of course, covered by all the media.

Of course, she turned it down flat. If Leacock had gotten his way, she would not forget, she would have crawled off to nowhere after she was bounced off the case—and just maybe Alex Granton would still be adding to his toll of victims. (When the FBI took his property for analysis, they found a list of forty more names on a computer—all people whose death might have been regarded as well-deserved punishment.)

But Charlie had urged her to reconsider when she happened to scornfully mention the commissioner's offer on the phone. "Why not close on a high note, DZ?" he said. "Don't nurse grudges."

"But it's bullshit, Charlie. Leacock wants to salvage a little credit, that's all, make a speech and grab time on the evening news. The pols up here are trying to talk him into a run for governor, maybe even senator." Tauresco's polls were weak; the voters hadn't forgotten how pathetic he'd looked with the M.G.

"What do you care, darling? Leave the anger behind, let's start out free and clear. Hell, don't you deserve a medal?"

And Charlie didn't say "hell" lightly, she knew.

At last she agreed; Charlie made his case that if she left nursing grudges, it would stay with her. If she took the honor, she could put the job completely behind her.

So on the very morning in early July she had first planned to fly away, DZ went down to Police Plaza and stood by the commissioner on a platform erected outside while the telegrams were read from the president and the A.G., and she tried to look suitably humble while Leacock talked about how her selfless devotion to duty had made the difference in ending what was described as "a unique reign of terror that had imperiled the very foundations of our society," and she let him pin the decoration on her lapel and read the citation.

Stoner added a few words in tribute, then she went to the microphone to dutifully mouth her own obligatory remarks, true as far as they went—how much she would miss the city, ending with a nod to Gable as the finest partner a detective could ever want, whose help had been essential to the outcome.

When it was all over, Gable was waiting with the car on a back street, a refugee from the press. She'd accepted his offer to drive her to the airport—"for old times' sake".

For most of the ride they talked only in occasional bursts, the way they always had.

"You looked good up there, kid."

"It wasn't easy."

In a while: "Pretty quiet where you're going. Won't you be bored after all the excitement?"

"No. I think I'm going to be very happy."

And finally: "What's he like?"

"He's . . ." DZ smiled as she thought of the best way to sum him up. "He's Jimmy Stewart."

Her old partner smiled. "If you couldn't have Gable," he said, "I guess that's a pretty fair second best."

At the terminal, he flipped down the visor with the police ID clipped to it to park in the forbidden zone.

"Don't come in," she said. It would be too awkward at the gate.

He nodded.

She hesitated. Would it be cruel or kind to ask the favor?

Hell, let him decide. "Clark, it's not set yet for sure, but I think the wedding will be the last weekend in August. And . . . do you think—well, you know about my father . . . so there isn't anyone . . . so I was wondering if you'd come out and . . . and give me away."

He turned quickly to his window, and for a very long time he didn't move or speak. She said nothing, waiting until he was ready.

When he looked back at her, he was as stoic and neutral as ever.

"Jesus," he said, "you haven't even left and already you're going soft."

"Yeah," she said. "About time, huh?"

CHAPTER
55

SHE WAS IN the attic when she heard Charlie calling faintly, his voice traveling up from the first floor.

She thought she might get away with pretending she hadn't heard, and kept kneeling over the tent she had spread open on the floor, rolling it up good and tight the way he'd shown her. This was going to be their second big trip, a week with a canoe on a backwoods river, and she was looking forward to it. Turned out she adored camping, being in the unspoiled middle of nowhere, away from everything.

After a minute, she heard his feet on the stairs.

"Hey, kiddo, didn't you hear me call . . . ?" She turned and saw his head poking up over the attic landing. "They just interrupted the game to announce—"

"The jury's coming in," she said. "I figured that was it." She'd guessed it would happen over the weekend. The trial had ended three days ago, and all day yesterday and the day before the jury had been sequestered. She thought they'd want to be home at least by the end of Sunday.

It was nine weeks since she'd gone to Massachusetts to

testify. Any of several states where the murders had been committed might have claimed jurisdiction—Illinois, California, Arizona, Mississippi. But the matter had been settled by holding the trial in Granton's home state. His lawyers had fought for that because none of the crimes had actually occurred there: it was neutral territory, where perhaps he'd seem more benign.

In the twenty months since his arrest there been a lot of public debate in which many people continued to express a surprising degree of sympathy with Granton, and a tremendous amount of legal maneuvering had raised questions about the value of certain evidence, the state of the defendant's mind, the degree of culpability that devolved upon the media for encouraging his acts. Even before the trial, Granton had reportedly spent sixteen million dollars on his defense. He seemed to have every top criminal lawyer in the country on his payroll, not to mention noted professors from Yale and Harvard Law who raised procedural questions that created delay, and the forensic and psychological experts who pitted their opinions against the prosecution's claims, and the specialists in jury analysis who helped pick the most sympathetic jurors. The lawyers had done a great job for Granton even before the trial started, prevailing at last in efforts to have him set free on bail. No multiple murderer had ever won that right before—but then no murderer had ever had much public support . . . or posted a bond of twenty-five million dollars. John Gotti's had been only ten.

The whole trial had been televised, and was no less a ratings winner than all the talk show appearances had been, or the interviews he'd done while he was free on bail. *Sixty Minutes, 20/20, Nightline, Larry King*—he was all over, in highest demand. The prosecution made a plea to have him barred from making public statements. The First Amendment prevailed. He was, after all, innocent until proven guilty.

The largest audiences for the trial, DZ had heard, were on the days when she testified. She was regarded as the keystone of the prosecution. She had not only been present at the one murder where there had been witnesses, but, even before the end of his crime spree, he had spoken to her, virtually confessed.

But during the eight days Granton's dream team kept her on the stand for cross-examination, they had managed to create more than a reasonable doubt as to whether her word on anything could be trusted. Why had she continued to pursue the case after her dismissal? she was asked. Why had she gone so far as to spend over a thousand dollars of her own money on a quick round-trip to England?

The intimations were subtle at first, then more direct: were her reasons strictly "professional"—or had she been obsessed with Granton, perhaps even emotionally drawn to him, her determination to see him convicted arising out of some anger at . . . well, being spurned. The absurd suggestion deserved to be laughed off. And DZ tried. Yet once the notion was planted, it took root. Women watching the trial on television thought it was entirely reasonable. Granton came across as so charming, self-possessed. If seeing was believing, it was hard to believe he could be a killer, much easier to imagine DZ might have wanted to set him up.

The most crushing blow to her value as a witness was when testimony from Stoner established that there had been—as the lawyers called it—"a sexual interlude" between him and DZ. It did seem that Lieutenant Hayes was prone to unprofessional sexual involvement.

DZ was scared silly by the revelations—scared that Charlie would rethink what had happened during the time he'd fallen in love. But of course he hadn't. He went to be at her side during the trial, and his feelings never wavered.

Still, by the time she left the witness box, it was as if *she* had been on trial, and the days of focusing on what was essentially a side issue had cast a curious haze over the central matter of Granton's guilt.

The rest of the evidence didn't hold up well, either. Ballistics experts hired by Granton's side challenged those of the FBI—who worked in a lab, the jury was reminded, that had been described in a report done by the government itself as guilty of shoddy work.

Barnes was a nearly useless witness, easily befuddled by the relentless cross-examination of sharp lawyers.

But none of that might have mattered if the act of Alex Granton murdering Edward Corcoran had actually been witnessed by one of the people present—or seen on camera. Unfortunately, at the moment the shots were fired, all had been confusion, and there were no pictures nor credible eye witness. Incredibly, the best that could be done was to infer circumstantially that Granton had done the shooting. . . .

She heard Charlie's footsteps now as he climbed up into the attic and walked to where she was on her knees, rolling the tent. The floor of the old house creaked as he knelt down just behind her. Then his arms gently encircled her. She leaned back into him, her head on his shoulder.

"So that's it," he said. "You won't watch the end."

"I can't, Charlie. I just can't. I know I won't like what I see."

He embraced her more tightly. "He won't get off, darling. The evidence was there. . . ."

"That doesn't matter. He gave them what they wanted. They can't blame him without blaming themselves."

"I don't believe that, don't want *you* to believe it. DZ,

you've got to trust the system. Trust it—or we've got nothing."

DZ turned to look at him, seeing his face, she felt such simple joy at having found him—the great good that had come from the evil. "I trust *you*, Charlie. That's all I need. You're my future."

"It's poisonous to live with cynicism, DZ. You've got to believe that good wins in the end. For his sake, too." One of his hand's moved down to caress her stomach; they'd only found out last week that she was definitely pregnant.

"Or hers," she said.

"C'mon," he said gently, still tugging at her. "Trust me. Come and see. You need to. . . ."

She hesitated another moment, then took a deep breath and stood. Yes, she needed to see justice done, a foundation for the future. She was just so afraid she would see otherwise.

He took her hand and led her to the stairs. From far below, she could hear the voice of some news anchor dramatically intoning a commentary as the special news bulletin began:

"The courtroom is settling now . . . and there's Judge Michaels taking his seat. He calls the court to order . . . the jury isn't looking at Alex Granton, but he's facing them. He still has that remarkable air of confidence he's displayed all through this trial. . . ."

At the landing she stopped, but he took her hand again. "No use hiding," he said.

They came into the living room just as the judge was asking the jury for its verdict. "Ladies and gentlemen of the jury have you reached your decision?"

The foreperson stood, a woman. "We have, Your Honor." She looked down at the piece of paper she held in a shaking hand—as if she could ever have forgotten the result of their deliberations. Yet, like the rest of the jury, she was an ordinary citizen, and the trial was being sent by television into hundreds of millions of homes, not only here but abroad. And that could make you nervous enough to go blank. She drew a breath. "We find the defendant—"

Like a small child in front of her birthday cake, DZ squeezed her eyes shut to make the wish.